AS THE TWIG IS BENT

RAYMOND GREINER

PTP

PTP Book Division
Path to Publication Group, Inc.
Arizona

PTP Book Division
Path to Publication Group, Inc.
16845 E. Avenue of the Fountains, Ste. 325
Fountain Hills, AZ 85268
www.pathtopublication.net

ISBN: 9781095794937
Library of Congress Cataloging Number
LCCN: 2019940884
Printed in the United States of America First
Edition

DEDICATION

I dedicate this novel to my two high school English teachers. Isabelle Stump and Mary Jo Stafford who inspired me from an early age to read stories and eventually become a published writer.

TABLE OF CONTENTS

CHAPTER 1

JERROD

The year was 1970. Jerrod James was born in 1955 to physician parents. His father Frank was an orthopedic surgeon and mother Judy a pediatrician. Their home was in Fairmont, Pennsylvania and Jerrod attended Fairmont High School.

Jerrod was small in stature afflicted with pigeon toes but exhibited an inquisitive mind.

Jerrod's parents are accomplished academics. This trait genetically migrated to their son. Jerrod's parents tutored him from age four. Jerrod was tested in fourth grade and advanced two grades. At age fifteen, Jerrod was a high school senior with social challenges and his physical affliction inhibited sports activities or school dances. Classmates shunned Jerrod.

Jerrod's parents played high school and college basketball and attended Jerrod's high school basketball games. Jerrod accompanied them and fantasized about being a player but this option was unavailable because of his lack of physical size and pigeon toes.

Mike Dunleavy was the best player on the basketball team and among the most popular boys in his class. Mike impressed Jerrod with his basketball skills and sat next to him in geometry class. Mike was six foot four, athletic and a good student.

Mike recognized Jerrod's agile mind from observation of his participation in geometry class. When complex problems were presented, the teacher challenged students to voluntarily solve the problem on the chalkboard. Jerrod was consistently the first to step to the chalkboard and solve the problem with ease.

"Do you attend basketball games?" Mike asked Jerrod.

"Yes, every game with my parents. I love basketball but my slight stature and foot affliction cancels opportunity as a participant. My parents played basketball in high school and college. We never miss a game," Jerrod responded.

"You may not be athletic but you're the best at solving complex geometry equations," Mike said.

"Thanks Mike, math fascinates me," Jerrod said.

It was the first time a student complimented Jerrod but teachers recognized Jerrod's academic skills.

One afternoon, as Jerrod walked home, he carried all his textbooks in two large book bags.

Mike caught up to him. "Jerrod, why are you carrying so many books?"

"Each subject needs to be reviewed," Jerrod said.

Mike frowned suspiciously. In truth, Jerrod was depressed because of anxiety from his social rejection. He was contemplating suicide and cleaned out his school locker.

Mike said, "I've something to tell you. My basketball coach asked if I knew a student who could serve as team statistician. One of the teachers presently does it but, previously, this position was assigned to a student. I told him I knew someone.

"It's an important assignment and you'd become a part of the team. What do you think?"

Jerrod couldn't believe his ears. His face beamed and a broad smile appeared. "Yes, I could do this. It'd be great fun to interact with coaches and players," Jerrod responded.

Suicidal thoughts vanished and Mike asked, "Can you ride a bicycle with your impaired feet?"

"Yes, I'm a good rider," Jerrod said.

"On weekends two teammates join me to ride nearby trails with mountain bikes. You're invited to ride with us. It's a good time and offers a break from school routine. We use these rides to condition for basketball," Mike said.

"My bike is old and not designed for what you suggest but my parents will purchase me a suitable bike to participate. I think I can keep up. I enjoy riding," Jerrod said.

Jerrod's parents were aware of his anxiety from lack of social acceptance and from their attendance at the school's basketball games they were aware of Mike's social identity status. They became equally excited about Mike's invitation for Jerrod to ride trails with Mike and his teammates. The next day they purchased Jerrod the best mountain bike they could find.

Jerrod's house was near the Allegheny Mountains and the three met on Saturday morning at nine. The teammates were Bill Jamison and Rodger Hamilton. Jerrod's parents Frank and Judy greeted the three and Judy said, "I'd enjoy having you three remain after your ride. I'll prepare a special dinner."

All three agreed and a plan was set.

"I noticed a basketball hoop and net in front of your garage," Mike said.

"Judy and I played college basketball and use the court for physical conditioning. Jerrod can't run well enough to play an active game but he's the best free throw shooter I've ever seen. Last week he made one hundred in a row. I've never accomplished such a feat," Frank said.

With raised eyebrows, the three players glanced at each other and Mike said, "Neither have we. Jerrod will be assigned as our team's statistician. Maybe he can assist us to improve our free throw percentage," Mike said.

"Shooting free throws is my only physical attachment to the game," Jerrod said, smiling.

As the four riders headed toward the mountains, Judy looked at Frank and said, "I've never seen Jerrod so happy."

"He's ignored by classmates. His impairment is a social detriment. Jerrod's friendship with Mike and his teammates offers a welcome change," Frank said.

The riders returned and Jerrod's face radiated with joy.

"Jerrod kept up all day. We never slowed down or waited for him. Good job Jerrod," Mike said.

Judy was teary eyed, as she observed her son's social acceptance. Jerrod's isolation was over.

Judy made a healthy meal of meatless stroganoff and creamy potato soup with selected spices. Judy and Frank were nutrition conscious and shared food preparation.

The next week Jerrod met with Coach Reynolds. The coach explained how game statistics are recorded. Jerrod will be assigned a seat at the end of the bench with a clipboard and proper forms to record individual player's performance data.

Coach Reynolds invited Jerrod to practice sessions and Jerrod shot free throws, astonishing players and coaches with his accuracy. He also assisted the equipment manager, organized balls and laundered uniforms and towels. The players and coaches bonded with Jerrod resulting from the serendipitous event when Mike stopped to talk with Jerrod while he was in a depressed state.

A few players had difficulty maintaining required grade average to remain on the team and Jerrod tutored them.

Mike and Jerrod spent time together and several major colleges recruited Mike, offering basketball scholarships. Jerrod's academic standing would qualify him for scholastic scholarship consideration, too. Mike and Jerrod discussed this and agreed to attend the same college and become dorm mates.

Jerrod's parents encouraged him to enter a premed program. Time commitment to become a certified physician is nine years. Four years to obtain a bachelor's degree then an additional four years of medical school plus one year internship at a selected hospital. Jerrod was ambitious to become a physician, to offer medical service to impoverished areas of the world.

Jerrod was changing classes when two bullies cornered him. One bully pushed him hard against a row of lockers. The other taunted him and said, "You think you're better than we are.

You're not as smart as you think." Jerrod pushed the bully away and the bully hit Jerrod in the face.

Mike happened by. The bully didn't know what hit him, as Mike flattened him with one punch. He grabbed the other by his shirt collar and slammed him against a support column.

Mike said, "Do you two want more attention? If not, I suggest you move along." They responded immediately to Mike's suggestion.

"Thanks Mike," Jerrod said.

"Those two are known troublemakers," Mike said.

Coach Reynolds held a meeting prior to basketball practice. He discussed the previous game, as the team was undefeated half way through the season. In addition, Coach Reynolds explained, "Fairmont will host a charitable event held at the gymnasium. We'll present a basketball free throw tournament and invite every high school in the state to select two participants to compete.

"Admission will be charged as a means to raise revenue for selected causes. They expect capacity attendance. Mike Dunleavy is our team's best foul shooter but the rules state it's not required for competitors to be on team rosters and, as we have observed, our team statistician Jerrod James is a remarkable foul shooter. I've listed him in addition to Mike to represent our school for this unique event.

"Each competitor will shoot foul shots until they miss and are eliminated. The shooter with the most scores will be the winner. It will be interesting to observe how Mike and Jerrod perform."

Mike looked at Jerrod and smiled. The message was clear. He knew Jerrod was the superior foul shooter but he would do his best.

Jerrod was surprised he was chosen and felt tense because he had no experience shooting foul shots in front of a crowd. Mike had been a player since junior high school and was comfortable performing with spectators present.

Jerrod revealed this event to his parents during dinner.

"Jerrod, your impaired feet disallow you to participate as a player but what fun it'll be to see how you perform. I'm excited," Judy said.

"We'll be cheering for you on every shot. I think you could win this competition," Frank said.

"I'm not so sure. Mike is nearly as good and many outstanding free throw shooters will be chosen to compete. I'm nervous about the competition. I've never competed in sports and I'm probably the only competitor who's never played on a team. Girl players will compete equally with boys. I've watched girls on our school's team and they're really good free throw shooters," Jerrod said.

Contest day arrived and the stands were filled. Parents, faculty, students and interested locals represented the bulk of the crowd. The gym had eight goals—three on each side and two main court goals. Competitors drew numbers for the order in which to compete. Each competitor was allowed two four minute time outs for water and to recompose. Twenty competitors were present. Jerrod and Mike were down the list and, as the competition began, they waited on the bench to be called. These shooters represent the best in the state and, of the twenty competitors; six were girls, all standout players for respective schools.

Many shooters would achieve above fifty in a row before being eliminated. Soon it was Mike and Jerrod's turn. Mike was relaxed, but Jerrod felt tense.

Two girl shooters were up at the same time as Jerrod and Mike. The shooting commenced. Jerrod took his time. As he established his rhythm, tension subsided. Jerrod approached fifty in a row and took a time out for water. Jerrod, Mike and one girl remained, continuing to build numbers. The girl's name was Sarah. She was a six foot tall senior with All State honors and attended a private high school near Pittsburg.

Mike missed his eightieth shot and walked to the bench. Jerrod and Sarah continued making shots. Jerrod's shot count was at 85 and Sarah at 90. The entire crowed began to clap in rhythm, as tension mounted. Jerrod's ninety-sixth shot rimmed out and fell to the gym floor. Sarah continued to make shots, and was at 110. She took a time out and the crowd began to chant, *"Sar...a, Sar...a, Sar...a".*

Jerrod sat next to Mike and said, "I never felt such a rush but relieved it's over. Sarah is amazing and beautiful."

"She sure is. I've heard of her through the grapevine. She's been offered scholarships from several prominent colleges and universities," Mike responded.

Sarah kept sinking shots and took a time out at shot 120. She stepped back to the foul line and sank another nine in a row. Shot 130 hit the back of the rim, bounced high and dropped to the floor. Sarah was the winner and the crowd erupted in deafening cheers standing in ovation, including Jerrod and Mike, at Sarah's accomplishment. It was a grand moment.

Sarah was presented with the winner's trophy and Jerrod was the runner up. Jerrod reached out his hand to congratulate Sarah. She stepped around his hand and gave Jerrod a big hug. The crowd cheered when Sarah hugged Jerrod.

Judy and Frank beamed with pride at their son's achievement.

CHAPTER 2

REDIRECTION

Jerrod couldn't walk down the hallway at school without students congratulating him for his shooting performance at the competition. Teachers also recognized Jerrod's accomplishment. Jerrod's social acceptance came full circle.

Judy put Jerrod's trophy on the fireplace mantel in the living room.

"Mom, you and Dad are the best parents I could ever imagine. You've guided me from my earliest memories.

"This trophy is my only sports recognition, and likely my last," Jerrod said.

"Jerrod, we love you so much and couldn't be prouder," Judy said.

The phone rang. Judy answered, "Hello. Oh, yes, he's sitting right here. I'll put him on the phone. Jerrod, it's for you."

Jerrod answered. A young woman's voice spoke, "Jerrod, this is Sarah Baker. We competed in the free throw tournament."

Jerrod nearly dropped the phone and nervously said, "Hi Sarah, what a surprise. It's the only sporting event I've ever participated in; it was so fun."

"I've been thinking about you and how amazing you performed. I'm a senior, and it looks good for me to receive a basketball scholarship to the University Of Pennsylvania.

"Our senior prom is next weekend, and the boy I hoped would ask to be my escort decided on someone else. I'm wondering if you could escort me to my senior prom," Sarah said.

Jerrod froze. He was silent and then said, "Sarah, I can't dance because of my pigeon toe impairment. I'd sure do it if I thought I could dance in a respectable fashion."

"How do you know if you can't dance? You've never tried to dance. Some dance music is slow with simple footwork. We could meet and practice. I have a car and can drive to your house if your parents agree. You need a partner. I'm a good dancer and I'll teach you. What do you think?" Sarah asked.

Jerrod said, "Give me your phone number. I'll discuss it with my parents and call you back.

"I enjoyed competing with you at the free throw competition. You were fabulous. I'm shorter than you. How do you feel about this?"

"Most of the boys in my class are shorter than me. Talk to your parents and call me. My phone number is five one four, two six five, three one six eight. I think we'd have a good time," Sarah said.

"OK, I'll call you back," Jerrod, said.

Jerrod was numb. Judy asked, "Who was the girl on the phone?"

"You won't believe this. It was Sarah Baker, the girl who won the free throw competition. She asked me to be her escort for the senior prom. I told her I couldn't dance because of my pigeon toes. She thinks I could learn and said some dance steps are easy. She has a car and wants to come to teach me to dance. Would this be alright with you and Dad?" Jerrod asked.

"Of course, this could be an opportunity for you. I'd enjoy meeting Sarah. She's quite beautiful. Call her back; I'll speak with her," Judy said.

Jerrod called Sarah and said, "Sarah, my mother Judy wants to speak with you. She's excited about me learning to dance."

Jerrod handed the phone to Judy, "Hello, Sarah? This is Judy. I'm Jerrod's mom and suggest you come early Saturday and spend the night. We have a spare room and it would allow you and Jerrod to practice dance steps. He's always felt he couldn't dance. I always thought he could, although maybe a bit less graceful, but well enough to enjoy dancing and it would be gratifying for him to learn. I'll prepare meals and help teach Jerrod."

"I'll do it, if my parents approve and I feel they will. I'll be at your house Saturday late morning. It'll be fun. I'll bring music. Do you have a stereo with a record player?" Sarah asked.

"Yes, and a collection of records," Judy said.

Judy handed the phone to Jerrod and he said, "I hope I don't disappoint you. I'll try my best."

"You'll do fine. It's not as difficult as you think. I'll see you Saturday," Sarah responded.

Jerrod gave Sarah directions before they ended their conversation. Jerrod hung up the phone and his mind was in a whirl.

Judy, Frank and Jerrod greeted Sarah as she entered the driveway. They showed her their house and the room where she will sleep. The atmosphere was joyful. Jerrod was in disbelief this was happening.

It was a memorable experience competing with Jerrod. It's nice to meet you both. I've brought dance records," Sarah said.

"I'll make tea and we'll talk." Judy said

Tea was served and Frank said, "Jerrod received physical therapy for his affliction and it improved. Dancing is considered good therapy. I feel he can learn to dance respectfully."

Sarah put on a slow tempo record to demonstrate basic steps and Jerrod duplicated her foot placement. To his surprise, he did well.

Sarah showed Jerrod dancer's position. As they moved in each other's arms, it was magical. Sarah was beautiful and it was delightful to watch this young couple gracefully move around the living room.

The music ended and Judy said, "How beautiful to watch. Thanks to Sarah, Jerrod is now a dancer. I wish parents were allowed to attend proms."

"I'm two years younger than Sara. Sarah is tall and graceful; I'm short and ungraceful. We're an untypical couple or, maybe better, we're an 'untypicouple'," Jerrod said.

They laughed and the levity added to the mood.

As Sarah predicted, Jerrod did well. He remembered how impressed he was at Sarah during the free throw competition and for her to invite him to escort her to the prom indicated she was her own person.

Judy and Frank danced and they stayed up late practicing. Judy and Frank prepared a splendid breakfast and conversation centered on Jerrod's success as a dancer.

"Jerrod's ready to dance. My classmates attended the free throw competition and they'll recognize him," Sarah said.

Jerrod's fifteen and has yet to learn to drive. Sarah will drive them to the prom.

Frank took Jerrod to rent a tuxedo and Judy purchased a corsage for Sarah. Excitement escalated as prom night neared.

Sarah was prompt and Jerrod, Frank and Judy greeted her. Jerrod was wearing his tux and Judy presented Sarah her corsage.

Judy said, "Sarah, you look ravishing. I love your dress. When you return, I'll serve tea and muffins and we'll enjoy hearing your description of this special night. It will be late and I don't want you to drive home. It's best to stay over and return home in the morning."

So, a fifteen-year-old short kid with pigeon toes is taking a tall gorgeous eighteen year-old to her senior prom. The *"untypicouple"* departed.

Sarah's high school was a private college prep school with students from affluent families. It contrasted with Jerrod's public school and the grounds were well manicured and sports fields were larger with more facilities.

Sarah parked her car and they walked to the gymnasium where the prom is to be held; the gym was decorated and a band was on a portable stage.

Sarah was greeted with compliments from classmates and they all recognized Jerrod from the basketball free throw tournament. Jerrod was a good-looking young man and girls at the dance took notice. The music started and Sara and Jerrod responded.

Proms are special events, as teen-agers dress formally and the live music creates a euphoric mood.

Sarah's grace melded with Jerrod's movements, distracting from his inward pointing toes as the two glided in a rhythmic display of youth and beauty. Jerrod's ecstasy poured out through facial expression as he looked directly into Sarah's eyes.

Between dances, partners changed. Jerrod was shy but Sarah's popularity bolstered his confidence and he asked the girl standing next to him for a dance.

Her name was Betty. She was beautiful and Jerrod's height.

"I'm a new dancer; Sarah gave me lessons. If then increase the tempo I'll be lost," Jerrod said.

"No you won't. I'll demonstrate the steps. It's the same as slow dancing but you move your feet faster," Betty said.

The band increased the tempo on their next number. Betty showed Jerrod the basic steps and he followed her and picked up the rhythm. He astonished himself as Betty flashed a smile.

"You're doing so good. I'm glad you asked me to dance," Betty said.

"I'm glad I did too," Jerrod said

After the music stopped, Sarah approached Jerrod. "Look at you. I was watching, and you were doing good with the increased tempo."

Sarah and Betty have been friends since early childhood.

"You picked a good one, Sarah, he may become as good a dancer as he is shooting a basketball," Betty said.

Everyone was having the time of their lives dancing and socializing between dances. Jerrod danced with either Sarah or

Betty for the remainder of the prom. Jerrod never felt so good in his entire life and wished the night would never end.

Sarah drove to Jerrod's house. The porch light was on and Jarrod's parents were eager to hear the prom's description.

Judy made tea. As they sat in the living room, Sarah said, "You should've seen Jerrod. He did amazingly well and danced with my friend Betty. She showed him how to dance to a faster tempo and he picked it up right away. It was a night to remember."

"I remember my senior prom like it was yesterday. You'll never forget this night," Judy said.

The next morning, Frank and Judy prepared breakfast with blueberry sourdough pancakes and pure maple syrup.

"Sarah, we're glad you asked Jerrod to the prom. This formed a social breakthrough for him," Frank said.

"Jerrod will be my friend for years to come," Sarah responded.

"Sarah, can you be my escort to my senior prom? It's two weeks away," Jerrod asked.

"Of course, I'd love to go", Sarah said.

Judy looked at Frank and smiled.

Jerrod walked Sarah to her car and Sarah said, "You can kiss me if you want."

It was like an electric shock. Jerrod never kissed a girl in his life. He kissed Sarah and she kissed him back and the two embraced in each other's arms. Young love displayed its highest bliss.

"Call me about prom time and date," Sarah said.

"I sure will. I think you are so beautiful," Jerrod said.

Jerrod's life made a sweeping turn with thoughts flying in all directions.

When Jerrod returned to school, his social confidence was at a new level as he felt energized. Books and study regimen were natural functions in Jerrod's life.

CHAPTER 3

TESLA

Jerrod's physics class enthralled him. His teacher mentioned Nicola Tesla and how Thomas Edison exploited Tesla's genius. Edison was unable to calculate conversion of direct current to alternating current, which was more efficient and less costly. He promised Tesla thirty thousand dollars if he could prove a method for this conversion. Tesla performed the challenge to Edison's great benefit then Edison refused to pay Tesla as promised. Tesla resigned from the Edison Company in frustration.

Jerrod read everything he could find on Tesla. After Tesla's disappointment with Edison, he researched the scientific theory of electrical power transmission via charged atmospheric molecules. He constructed a transmitter and sophisticated antenna to prove his theory but, without fiscal support, Tesla abandoned the project.

Jerrod read Tesla's thesis on wireless electronic transmitted energy. He was captivated by Tesla and continued to research his accomplishments. Jerrod reflected how isolated places in the world were without electrical power. His mind drifted to how remarkable it would be to use solar power to generate electricity in a central location then transmit the generated energy without necessity to install lengthy cables and wires. Many third world zones have never had electricity and may never obtain it. It's economically unfeasible to install present day methods of power production in isolated poverty-stricken areas. Industrialized countries use massive amounts of electric power and justify investment for hydroelectric dams and coal fired power production plants. Cables to deliver electricity is the costliest aspect of modern power distribution.

The main barrier for change was power providers' reluctance to install power sources to accommodate low social economic status populations, which would offer minimal return on investment.

Jerrod was inspired to construct a small-scale transmitter and seek advice from experts for his own research on how to build such a device.

Jerrod thought about Sarah and called to give the date and time for his senior prom. They would repeat the routine of Sarah's prom. They were as excited about Jerrod's prom as they were Sarah's due to Jerrod's new confidence as a dancer.

As they entered the gymnasium, they were impressed. The atmosphere was equal to Sarah's private school. Band members were music students. Jerrod's school had a restricted budget but came through with flying colors to give the seniors a lifetime memory on prom night.

"Jerrod, it's beautifully arranged, equally as nice as my prom," Sarah said.

"Yes, it is," Jerrod, responded.

Sarah and Jerrod danced the first two dances and a line formed to request Sarah to dance. Sarah looked exquisite, as she always does: tall, elegant, and wonderful on the dance floor.

Jerrod sat out for the next dance and then asked one of the girls he knew from geometry class to dance. Her name was Wilma Foster, one of the less popular girls but pretty and a good dancer.

"Wilma, I'm a beginner but Sarah's a good teacher and I attended her prom and gained confidence. I'll do my best," Jerrod said.

"I'm honored to dance with you," Wilma said.

They danced the next three dances as Sarah was a focus of male attention.

Everyone socialized between dances and Jerrod was popular because of his performance in the free throw tournament in this same gymnasium.

During the return home, Jerrod said, "Sarah, you were the most popular girl at the dance. You were the Dancing Queen."

"I enjoyed dancing with you most. We have a special bond," Sarah said.

Judy and Frank repeated their breakfast serving the next morning. Jerrod described how Sarah was the prom's centerpiece.

"I can't imagine her at any other status," Frank said.

Jerrod walked Sarah to her car. He kissed and hugged her, and said, "Sarah, I think of you all the time and I'm not sure how to proceed. You're so amazing."

"I'll call tomorrow and we'll talk it over. I chose you to escort me to the prom because you are extraordinary. We are at the starting line of our lives, and I have thoughts on this. I need to think things through until then. Love is complex but the most wonderful feature life offers. No matter what our future unveils, I'll continue to love you and cherish our time together," Sarah said.

As Sarah drove away, Jerrod felt perplexed but knew in his heart he would always love Sarah. Jerrod is fifteen and he will enter premed school in the fall

Sarah called. Jerrod answered and Sarah said, "I had the best time at our proms. The boy I hoped would ask me to the prom selected another girl, and this caused confusion. I reacted because I felt connected when we competed in the free throw tournament and this formed a unique attraction. I need to pullback for a while to sort myself out but my attraction to you remains.

"We're both facing college in fall, and we'll be separated and face adjustment to a greater degree than either of us have experienced. We'll remain connected and talk frequently. I love you and don't want to hurt you."

"You're right, we'll be separated. Mike was awarded a basketball scholarship to Duke University. I was given a full scholastic scholarship for Duke's premed program. We'll be dorm mates.

"I've never felt love's power prior to our meeting. It threw me off balance but I had such a good time, I let my emotions dominate. It's been said we never forget our first love. I know I'll never forget you; call me anytime," Jerrod said.

"I'll always remember our prom dates and we must remain close.

"I'm excited, as we confront the coming year. I know you'll eventually become a physician, but my future is dubious. I'll always love you," Sarah said.

Jerrod hung up the phone retreated to his room and sat quietly on his bed, thinking about Sarah. Oddly, his mind wandered to Tesla and how he must have faced obstacles in his life and Jerrod was, as Sarah stated, at the starting line of life.

Graduation day arrived. Jerrod was valedictorian of his class. His parents sat proudly in the family section as Jerrod was required to speak.

"Fellow graduates; I'm honored to share our special day. I've enjoyed my four years at Fairmont High School and we had the best teachers.

"A few days ago, a friend told me I'm only at the starting line of life. I never considered it in this context but it's true. Whatever path we follow from this point will differ from high school years and reveal challenges we can't imagine during today's milestone event.

"War is raging in Vietnam and some of our class may be pulled into the chaotic horror war creates. I've often wondered why humanity habitually returns to war, unable to find peaceful solutions to political, ethnic and cultural differences.

"I intend to pursue a medical degree to become a physician. My ambition is to serve human needs in impoverished areas of the world where medical treatment is less available. I'm not ambitious to chase the money wagon, as is assumed to be the common goal medical students pursue.

"I read Doctor Albert Schweitzer's book *The Reverence of Life*, which described how he and his wife established a

26

hospital in a remote region of Africa and saved countless lives treating those previously isolated from medical services. It's a compassionate story.

"Today, we'll cherish this moment and intermingle to share hopes and dreams. As a class, we'll look forward to reunions to reestablish connection and discuss accomplishments as we pursue our lives. What fun this will be.

"I'm grateful for your friendship. It's been an experience filled with wonderful memories and joyful times."

The audience stood in an ovation to Jerrod. Everyone knew and respected this extraordinary young man.

CHAPTER 4

TRANSMITTER

Frank had a workbench and assorted tools in a corner in the garage and Jerrod told his dad about his summer break ambition to construct a device similar to Tesla's electrical current transmitter but smaller and transportable. Frank responded positively and told Jerrod he would assist with material cost and contribute where he is able.

To celebrate Jerrod's graduation, Judy and Frank took Jerrod to dinner. The discussion centered on Jerrod's atmospheric electrical transmitter project.

"Tesla's idea conflicted with firmly established power distribution and his project never attained fruition. His idea was viewed as rouge and power company executives were fearful of Tesla, and attempted to block his ambition from further development. Tesla realized this and, without fiscal support, abandoned his concept. His laboratory was purchased by power companies and demolished.

"My quest is to make electric power affordable to remote regions where electrical power is unavailable funded by grants from various sources. It may seem unrealistic at this point and I'll be challenged to create a working model," Jerrod said.

Jerrod used the library to research data related to alternative electric power distribution. This speculated transmitter would require a receptor to harvest and store power to be extracted as needed.

He found the name of a scientist who pursued a similar idea but was unable to gain further knowledge of this scientist, where he lived, or if he was even alive. His name was Stephen Garrett. Jerrod spent hours studying library card files to locate scientific papers related to alternative electrical energy distribution or documents attached to Garrett's work.

As Jerrod sifted through scientific research papers written by college physics professors, he found Stephen Garrett's paper on variations of electrical distribution. Garrett taught physics at the University of Pennsylvania.

Jerrod wrote professor Garrett.

Dear Professor Garrett,

My name is Jerrod James, and I recently graduated from high school and will enter premed at Duke University in the fall.

I've studied Nicola Tesla's life and am impressed by his scientific achievements, especially his work to achieve electrical power transmission using electronically charged atmospheric molecular waves as opposed to conventional cable and wire transmission. During high school, physics and science were my favored subjects. My desire to become a physician is motivated to offer medical services to assist those living in third world countries. As I read of Tesla's life, I believe his idea has potential to allow electricity to become available where it previously has been absent and probably always will be. My ambition differs from Tesla's as mine is directed at the development of a portable device. I'm interested in obtaining information on how this type of transmitter can be designed and constructed as a prototype with the eventual installation at an appropriate test site. Fiscal support could be sought through grant proposals.

I'm requesting thoughts you may have pertaining to my pursuit of this proposal.

With sincere appreciation,

Jerrod James

A week passed, and Jerrod received a letter from Professor Garrett.

Dear Jerrod,

Your inquiry is ironic because I developed a similar unit ten years ago. I constructed a working model and demonstrated it at scientific forums and conventions. The response was overwhelming, as the device was accepted and praised among science students and teachers.

Over time I was contacted by a law firm representing several power companies who claimed interest in my development. I met with the lawyer and five board members of various American power companies. They stated how impressed they were and offered to purchase my plans and research papers indicating they would develop my idea to become more efficient and applicable for expanded use. In turn, they required me to surrender my research papers and sign documents to cease personal attachment to the concept. This sales agreement disallowed me further involvement in similar projects.

I bought their hype and sold out for one hundred thousand dollars. As it turned out, their entire presentation was a scam. They never intended to develop my transmitter. They destroyed the device and burned research data. In my entire life, I've never felt so duped.

My mind retains what was destroyed and I'm so angry, I'll assist you in any manner I'm able. They can't touch you and they never bothered to apply for a US patent. This opens a crack in the door to revitalize the project.

If we work together, what I've dedicated years of my life to has limitless applications. Your desire to utilize a small efficient unit for third world countries is admirable.

China has gained footing toward industrial development and has emerged as a world leader in electronic manufacturing. If solar powered atmospheric transmitters were constructed in China, it would isolate the concept from greed-infested American power companies. Once the device goes into production and is distributed, it will become unstoppable regardless what the nefarious moneygrubber power company directors say or do.

My phone number is eight one seven, two five four, nine one seven eight. Call or write your thoughts on this.

Sincerely,

Stephen Garrett

Garrett's letter impressed Jerrod. He read the professor's letter to his parents.

"This is a valuable connection. You must meet with Professor Garrett," Frank said.

Judy agreed and Jerrod organized his response.

Dear Professor Garrett,

Your thoughts on the atmospheric transmitter are encouraging. Tesla's intellectual scientific foresight captivated me.

I'd like to be directly involved in the prototype's construction process. My parents are supportive and we have workspace in our garage. I'm not experienced mechanically, but learn quickly.

I have until fall when I'll enter Duke University as a premed student. My time will be limited during school months and we'll maintain communication and resume active participation during semester breaks.

My parents, Frank and Judy, are physicians and instructed me to invite you to visit at your convenience. We have guest room accommodation.

We're at a beginning stage, and need to discuss thoughts and ideas. Call or write anytime. Our phone number is seven six five, three four six, two five seven four. I look forward to our meeting.

Sincerely,

Jerrod James

Professor Garrett called and Jerrod answered.

"Jerrod, this is Stephen Garret. I'm typing a descriptive outline of the portable atmospheric transmitter similar to the one I designed and built ten years ago. I'll list components required to construct a prototype. Any typical solar powered generator will serve our purpose. I have one we can use. I hesitate to purchase components for fear it would jeopardize my legal agreement with power companies and they'd sue me without hesitation. If you acquire components, I'll visit to instruct you on construction and function of the units."

"I'll arrange with my parents to obtain necessary components prior to your arrival. I'll keep you informed. I'm forever grateful for your call and look forward to our meeting. My parents said you're welcome to stay as long as needed," Jerrod said.

"You're an unusual young man and, at my stage in life, your enthusiasm rekindles ambition. I've been despondent since the power companies manipulated me.

"We'll combine efforts to activate the project. You'll receive my letter soon with details. I've listed suppliers. Call me when you've acquired the components," Garrett said.

Professor Garrett inspired Jerrod, although he would be challenged to divide academics and the transmitter's development. His ambition is to install the device at an impoverished location.

Construction of a prototype can be accomplished without interference of his academic obligations. If the project reaches the development stage, Jerrod will apply for a patent and seek a competent manufacturer. The device's marketability is unpredictable at this stage. Jerrod's primary goal remains to become a physician to assist the socially oppressed. He researched Doctors Without Boundaries, which could present an option when he finishes medical school.

As the project evolved, Jerrod continued to think of Sarah but knew they must move forward with their lives.

Jerrod's journal entry:

Our world is plagued with social separation and disparity. More humans live in abject poverty than higher modern social standards. My ambition developed as I read Albert Schweitzer's book The Reverence Of Life, which described how he and his wife discovered intangible rewards from assisting those in areas void of modern medical services.

Currently, my future is unclear but, if I'm able to deliver electrical power to isolated cultures, this accomplishment would achieve recognition and respect to allow ease of access."

Professor Garrett's letter arrived. It came in a large envelope with a photo and mechanical drawings of the unit he built and sold rights to power companies. Included were mathematical calculations to prove technical feasibility plus a list of mechanical and electrical components needed to construct the system.

Jerrod contacted suppliers suggested by Professor Garrett and his parents sent payment for the components to be shipped. A box arrived filled with electrical parts including resisters, switches, electric coils and prewired circuit boards. In addition, a large roll of heavy gauge stainless steel wire without insulation plus four separate bundles of four-foot long one-inch oak dowel rods. Two larger boxes arrived with stainless steel housings to accommodate the electric power transmitter and receptor components.

Jerrod called the professor to inform him the materials arrived to construct the transmitter. The professor said he planned to visit in two days and asked for directions, which Jerrod provided.

The professor, driving a van, arrived on schedule and was met in the driveway by Jerrod, Judy and Frank. As introductions were made, Jerrod assessed the professor was of medium height with keen features and appeared to be in his sixties.

"We're pleased to meet you, Professor Garrett. You're welcome to stay as long as needed to assist Jerrod in constructing the electrical system. We'll serve tea and scones and discuss a plan," Judy said.

"I'm delighted to meet you three and it's such a nice neighborhood," Professor Garrett said.

They sat at the kitchen table to discuss the next step.

"I have a solar generator in my van I used on my first project. We'll need this unit to activate the transmitter.

"The coil of stainless steel wire is to erect antennas for transmission and reception. The solar generator will power the transmitter and the antenna sends electrically charged molecular energy in three hundred- and sixty-degree directions, which is harvested by the receptor's antenna.

"Tesla used a large elevated complex multi-directional antenna. I developed a simpler and equally effective antenna design to be erected near the ground, elevated only a few feet and supported by hardwood stakes in a spider web configuration. Antenna erection is time consuming but, once in place, needs no maintenance and can remain for years.

"As energy is collected by the receptor wiring is necessary for it to be connected to nearby application sites. This small-scale transmitter is designed to service limited function such as a cluster of houses. It's a realistic assumption a larger capacity unit could be designed but I've never ventured this far during my initial involvement prior to exploitation by power companies.

"I'm impressed with Jerrod. He's quite exceptional for his age. When I was his age, I was a struggling high school student, never an academic achiever but fortunate enough to be accepted to college. My motivation kicked in via a particular physics professor in my college freshman year. I share Jerrod's interest in Tesla," Professor Garrett said.

"Jerrod displayed an agile mind at an early age. It's been a plus/minus condition. He was moved forward in early grades and this caused social complexities but he transcended such problems during his senior year of high school. He became socially popular and was valedictorian of his high school class," Frank said.

"I was in the lower fifty percent in my high school class and barely passed the college entrance exam. I support Jerrod's pursuit of a medical career. Our transmitter project shouldn't conflict with his plans," Professor Garrett said.

The next morning, assembly began. Stephen described the current's intertwine from the solar generator to become enhanced through a complex maze of booster components and then connected to the antenna for transmission.

The work progressed slowly as many connections were soldered and thermocouples installed at intervals to monitor temperature to activate automatic shut down if heat became excessive on components.

Jerrod was impressed by the professor's mechanical and electrical skills. Jerrod photographed and recorded notes as assembly progressed.

In less than a week, Stephen had the transmitter and receptor completed.

"The final step is to assemble the transmission and receptor antennas. Antenna dimension is dictated by distance required for molecular electronic waves to travel, similar to radio and television broadcast range.

"For test purposes, we'll construct them near each other to prove feasibility. If your parents agree, we'll place the transmission antenna on the front lawn of their home and the receptor's antenna in the backyard. For test purposes antennas will be erected small in diameter. After the test is proven, we'll disassemble the antennas and store them until an appropriate long-term test site is acquired. My original antenna design was intended to range up to ten miles from transmitter to receptor; the larger the antennas, the greater the performance range. When units are applied at a permanent site, distance separated will dictate antenna configuration," Garrett said.

Jerrod's parents agreed and Jerrod assisted Stephen by driving the oak dowels in a specified pattern and heavy gauge wire was connected to each stake. The solar generator was connected to the transmitter and, as power was applied, the receptor's gauge read one hundred and twenty volts. Jerrod was delighted. Judy and Frank shared the achievement.

"Jerrod will soon be less active because of school commitment. His next step is to locate a reliable electronic equipment manufacturer. I recommend a foreign company to separate from influence of greed-oriented American power companies. Although, he should apply for a US patent for protective purposes," Garrett said.

"You getting me to this point is miraculous and what I do from now on will be my responsibility. I'll use semester breaks to pursue options," Jerrod said.

Jerrod will turn sixteen soon after his registration to enter premed school at Duke University and has created quite a plateful for his young age.

Jerrod's parents will drive him to Duke's campus for registration and to get settled in his dorm. Mike Dunleavy will accompany them and will be Jerrod's dorm mate. Judy and Frank felt comfortable with Mike knowing he's responsible and a good student.

College campus life has little comparison to high school and Jerrod and Mike will be challenged to adjust. College classes are presented differently as professors are less connected with students and lectures are more formal.

Jerrod explained his electrical transmitter project to Mike.

"This could become monumental but will require time and effort," Mike responded.

"I know and this hinders the project's momentum. Professor Garrett encouraged me to seek a foreign manufacturer but I feel, because of my premed and medical school commitment, greater benefit can be achieved using semester breaks to locate a suitable place to install and test the system prior to production. This would create opportunity to test the worth of the concept in practical application. In addition, it'll improve the lives of those in need of electric power, Jerrod said.

"It's the best approach. You can research for possible test sites through the Red Cross and other charitable organizations," Mike said.

Jerrod and Mike begin classes in three days. Mike's basketball practice starts in a week.

Jerrod wrote Stephen a letter.

Dear Stephen,

I'm settled in the dorm at Duke University and my dorm mate is Mike Dunleavy, my best friend from high school. Mike attends on a basketball scholarship.

As I contemplate the future of our transmitter, your idea to seek a foreign manufacturer is well-founded but I feel the best method to begin would be to locate a remote settlement in need of electrical service to install our unit as a model to prove its worth over a specified test period.

I'm sixteen years old and can't visualize myself globetrotting to promote an idea to potential manufacturers from a single backyard demonstration. Additional long-term application is important to prove reliability and practicality. If we include an on-site demonstration, it will solidify feasibility as a means to attract manufacturers and enhance market potential.

As I mature, I'll become more suitable to present our unit's potential. My time will be consumed with college course study plus medical school and internship for the next nine years, although I'll dedicate effort to discover a suitable test location to install our electrical production system.

It would be a pleasure for you to assist me. I'm unsure I could install and activate the system on my own and, if we work as a team, results and rewards will be shared. During school months, I'll correspond with various sources to seek applicable advice and possibly acquire grant funding to assist installation. This would represent a valuable step forward.

During this early stage in my first semester, I will have time to formulate a plan. I'll file for a US patent using your drawings and photographs I recorded during our initial assembly and test. It's a challenge to navigate complexities to gain exposure.

Sincerely,

Jerrod

Classes began and Jerrod and Mike studied each evening. Mike is majoring in business administration.

Sarah was at the University Of Pennsylvania on a basketball scholarship. Jerrod wrote her a letter.

Dear Sarah,

I'm settled at Duke and Mike Dunleavy is my dorm mate. Classes started and evenings are devoted to study, as you are likely at a similar status.

My high school physics teacher mentioned Nicola Tesla a few times and this inspired me to learn more about Tesla's life. I became fascinated by Tesla's ambition to generate electrical energy delivered via electrically charged molecular atmospheric waves using a wireless transmission device with specialized antennas. He achieved his goal but electric power plant facilities using hydroelectric dams and coal-fired power plants were established and are expanding, which caused Tesla's idea to be viewed unworthy. Without fiscal support, Tesla abandoned his project and the experimental site was purchased by power companies and destroyed.

My thoughts were, if a portable unit was designed, it could be applied to assist areas without electric power.

I didn't know where to begin and combed library files to gain information. Stephen Garrett, a physics professor from your university, had written a paper on the subject and I contacted him by letter. Coincidently, he built and proved the same idea I envisioned. He wrote me a descriptive letter discussing when his portable electrical energy transmitter was shown at science shows and events; it stirred great interest. A group of executives from major power companies purchased the professor's device and all rights to its development. He sold out only to realize later these executives had no intention to develop his idea. They destroyed his device and research papers the professor had worked so long to perfect. He was angry and dismayed because he was legally stalled and could not continue to develop his concept.

Professor Garrett used me as his shield and, together, we built a new model under my name. I'll work with Professor Garrett during next semester break to install and activate our model in a remote settlement to prove long-term worth for future applications.

I'll continue my medical degree pursuit and eventually spend time to assist impoverished people gain electric power in conjunction with medical services. I'm excited about the potential this concept may eventually generate. I think of you often.

Love,
Jerrod

A week later, Jerrod received a letter from Sarah.

Dear Jerrod,

What an interesting story. Your brilliant mind continues to expose positive elements to your life. I'll locate Professor Garrett and describe our connection.

I was delighted to receive your letter. It perked me up as I've been a bit lost here. Basketball practice begins soon and I hope this lifts my mood. I've been assigned courses and begin classes next week.

The largest issue is the size of this place and I don't know anyone. When basketball practice begins, I'm sure my social life will improve. We'll correspond and continue to support each other.

Love,

Sarah

Campus activity and study became the center of Jerrod and Mike's lives. Basketball practice was in full swing and Mike was performing well; however, his freshman status and the team's mix of talented players prevented Mike from obtaining a starting position.

Jerrod wrote his parents weekly. He also spent time at the library to research charitable organizations to assist locate potential sites to install the electrical transmitter.

CHAPTER 5

MAPUCHE

Jerrod formed a list of charitable organizations. He wrote letters to describe the system's function and purpose. He included photographs of the unit during construction and test stages.

Jerrod and Mike were good students, unchallenged to perform academically. They were determined to attain college degrees.

Mike had adequate physical activity with basketball but Jerrod was sedentary. He walked to classes and developed a routine to walk one hour each day for health purposes. These walks were meditative and stimulated thoughts related to the electrical transmitter project and Sarah.

A letter arrived from a Mormon missionary.

Dear Jerrod,

My name is William Harrington. I'm an American Mormon missionary assigned to assist an isolated South

American Mapuche tribe. The corrupt Chilean government has exploited the Mapuche.

Mormon missionaries have provided support to these extraordinary people for the past ten years. The tribe lives and functions similar to ancient ancestors and they obtain sustenance from natural sources. They are hunter-gatherers, able to survive without Mormon assistance.

This Mapuche village could offer a suitable test site for your wireless electrical supply device.

I've discussed this with Mormon elders and they've approved funding for you and Professor Garrett to travel with your device to Chile. I'll assist in any manner I'm able.

If you decide to pursue this opportunity, I'll use the church van to meet you at the Santiago International Airport and we'll drive to a town located twelve miles from the Mapuche village. I'll commission a local guide and his pack mules for equipment transport, as a twelve-mile winding mountain trail is the only access to the village.

If you have interest in this plan, send a response letter.
Sincerely,
William Harrington

Jerrod forwarded the letter to Stephen and answered William's letter.

Dear William,

This is the best news and I'm appreciative of your offer. I forwarded your letter to my mentor professor, Stephen Garrett, and I'll keep you informed. He's flexible and ambitious to move the project forward. I'm in my first semester as a premed student and feel I can make this trip with Professor Garrett during semester break if properly coordinated. This is an ideal situation.

Thank you.

Jerrod James

Professor Garrett called and said, "Jerrod, we must do this. It'll be a time squeeze, but it seems possible.

"I agree it's too early in your life to travel and promote our transmitter to potential manufacturers.

"You can contribute with letters and we'll only contact foreign companies as a means of isolation from legal complexities with power companies. You'll be designated as the company owner. We'll search for a manufacturer after our unit is installed and functioning in Chile. It'll be an adventure of a lifetime.

"I'll drive to your parent's home and crate the unit for air transport. We can work together in Chile to assemble and test the system in less than a week. Your Mormon contact can confirm the performance of our unit. This is an ideal circumstance to prove our system worthy through on site application. You should apply for a US patent; this will protect our system, even during consideration stage, as it will be identified as patent pending. Call me if further developments occur."

"OK, Stephen I'll do as you suggest," Jerrod said.

Things fell in place. A Mormon elder called and informed Jerrod to contact him with projected date and they will provide air travel and personal expenses prior to departure for Santiago.

Excitement escalated as time for travel to Chile neared. Professor Garrett and Jerrod obtained passports and began travel preparations.

William greeted Jerrod and Stephen upon arrival as they disembarked the plane at Santiago International Airport. After introductions, William said, "The tribe is impressive. They're Mapuche and have functioned historically as a culture for over three thousand years. Most Mapuche in Chile integrated with modern civil structure but a percentage continued historic communal composition. I detailed our plan to bring electric power to their village and they're filled with anticipation.

"The Mapuche tribe we'll contact is located in a beautiful mountain setting. I've developed a love for this place. It's a paradise untouched by modern society. This tribe functions harmoniously in opposition to modern chaotic civil design. They've raised hemp for centuries and use natural dyes to create colorful clothing. They make hemp rope used to lash small diameter logs to construct housing and other structures.

"The Chilean government forbids the tribe firearms for fear of uprising but this culture has no need for firearms, as they rely on ancient hunter gatherer skills for food acquisition. They use bows and arrows for hunting. They harvest edible plants and catch fish using cleverly designed traps. They're without a monetary system and use barter for exchange."

"I'm fascinated by this unique opportunity," Jerrod said.

"I've read of the Mapuche. I'm eager to install perpetual electrical power to enhance their lives, although they are unaccustomed to modern luxury and this requires adjustment," Professor Garrett said.

"I've thought of this and the first and most important benefit will be an electric pump for their well. Water is the most valuable element in their lives and to be relieved of the laborious task to move water will allow immediate acceptance.

"It's my responsibility to select appropriate applications. I'm skilled at hands on tasks and will impose electrical current in the least intrusive manner.

"I've purchased an electric water pump, two hundred feet of hose and a gate valve to establish water access at the top of a steep hillside near the village location. Currently water is carried in clay vessels. The pump activates when the valve opens, easing exertion to move water. This change offers significant benefit," William said.

They arrived at the town where William has a small office/apartment. The next morning, they met the trail guide Raimondi with his four pack mules at the trailhead and lashed the transmitter and receptor onto packsaddles plus William's water pump, valve and hose.

They will walk alongside the pack mules and trek the twelve-mile winding mountain trail to access the village. The vista is something to behold, enhanced by the distant snow-peaked Andes Mountains.

William hikes this trail often and paused to cut walking staffs for himself, Jerrod and Stephen to assist balance on rocky trail sections.

Clear flowing mountain streams were frequent and the caravan took water breaks. An Andes Condor was soaring on high altitude thermals.

"I could've never have imagined such a place. The scenery projects indefinable beauty and bliss," Jerrod said.

"I experienced this emotion upon my arrival. This area penetrates in a spiritual fashion. You may never return but your memory of its splendor will remain.

"You'll stay at the village school and dormitory built by a team of Mormon college students seven years ago with assistance and guidance from Mapuche tribal members. The school has a fire pit and chimney constructed of stone with sand and clay mortar. It's nearing winter in the southern hemisphere but we're northerly and winters are mild compared to southerly zones. I have my personal native dwelling at the village.

"My primary assignment is to teach Mapuche children English, history, basic math and science. My students are fluent in English. Village residents will greet us when we arrive," William said.

"I'll document our connection with the Mapuche," Jerrod said.

As the caravan approached the village, the tribe greeted them and beautiful twin girls in brightly colored traditional dress presented Jerrod and Stephen with hemp thread necklaces intricately woven into a small chain. Each necklace had a colorful stone pendant attached.

The twins smiled and said in unison, "Welcome to our village."

Stephen and Jerrod were emotionally moved by this greeting and thanked the twins. It was an unforgettable moment.

"I feel as if I've disembarked from a time machine. It's nothing like I envisioned. I relate to the serenity you described," Jerrod said to William.

Jerrod handed his camera to William as Jerrod and Stephen posed next to the beautiful twin greeters.

A few of the tribe's young men assisted unloading the pack animals and stored the equipment in a storage hut. Raimondi tethered his mules at a nearby creek to allow them to graze. He will sleep at William's dwelling, as he routinely does, and depart in the morning.

William showed Jerrod and Stephen to their sleeping quarters. It was neat and orderly with colorful hemp blankets. The single beds were crafted with small logs lashed together with hemp rope. Mattresses were fashioned from hemp fibers and enclosed in hemp blankets sewn together to retain fibers. Candles supplied by the Mormon Church provided light.

Jerrod spoke to William, "Eventually our transmitter could provide light for the tribe."

"This will be my next challenge after the water pump is operational," William said.

In evening hours, the tribe brought food to the school for their guests.

Everyone crowded in the school and William spoke, "Professor Garrett will describe what will occur over the next few days. How fortunate we are to be given this opportunity."

Stephen addressed the tribe, "My friend and associate, Jerrod James, and I constructed and proved the functionality of a wireless electrical transmitter powered by a solar generator. The transmitter enhances generated power to distribute energy to a receptor unit installed at relevant usage sites. The receptor is then wired to selected electrical functions. The dimension of transmitter and receptor antennas dictates transmission range. We plan to install an electric water pump to assist access to well water.

"This tribe offers an ideal opportunity to test our revolutionary device, as your remote location forbids conventional power installation. We conjecture places similar to your village will benefit from our concept. This unit is cost efficient and void of air pollutant emissions. Your village represents our first onsite demonstration.

"Your friendly greeting upon our arrival was heartwarming and stimulates desire to assist in any manner we're able. You live in a majestic place and your compatibility with nature is distinctive. Modern cities are plagued with multiple negative issues and social discord has inundated contemporary societal behavior. We're appreciative for the opportunity to share our device to enhance your tribal daily life's functions. Thank you."

The tribe applauded the professor and the mood was euphoric.

After the tribe departed, William said, "Several families have expressed interest for you and Jerrod to visit their homes for evening meals to learn about life in America. This will be a memorable experience. I won't participate, as my presence would cause distraction. You'll enjoy this and it'll reveal the intense bond these families embrace. This is the most prominent feature of the Mapuche people."

The next day Stephen and Jerrod would install the energy system. William helped to drive oak dowel rods to mount the spider web configuration antennas. After antennas were in place, they connected the solar powered generator and checked the gauge on the receptor. It read 120 volts. The transmitter was located about 400 yards from the receptor to prove function.

William connected his water pump to the receptor at the well's location and inserted a hose into the well. He then pulled a long section of hose with a single electric wire taped to the hose up the steep bank and installed the valve to a nearby tree at the top of the embankment. He opened the valve. The receptor activated the pump and water gushed out as the tribe cheered.

The Mormon Church told William if the system proves worthy, additional receptors would be purchased, when available, to expand applications.

The family, Stephen and Jerrod first visited, lived in a round one-room shelter with sleeping mats on the perimeter. In the center was a fire pit with a chimney exiting the cone shaped roof with an elevated table and water vessels nearby. No chairs, as Mapuche tradition is to sit cross-legged on hemp mats.

The parents were Yaco and Lilen with twin daughters Suyia and Yaima. These twins were the greeters who gifted Stephen and Jerrod woven hemp pendants. They were stunningly beautiful.

The family is fluent in English from William's teachings. The twins were exceptional English speakers.

"We only know of America from photos and reading. Large buildings and auto traffic are everywhere, Yaco said."

"Much of our country is as you describe, yet we also have remote regions. American urban areas occupy high population densities and gain the most attention. American society is complex whereas Mapuche life is simplistic. Birthplace location dictates social living standards," Jerrod said.

"We're fortunate to have support from the Mormon Church. William is an excellent teacher, yet children in America have greater opportunity for advanced education. Our daughters are good students and the Mormon Church leaders offered sponsorship for them to attend high school in America, possibly college as well if they meet standards. We're undecided about this offer, as we're bonded as a family and happy where and how we live. They'd be required to relocate and live in America with a Mormon family. We'd miss them so much. We must discuss this and decide what's best," Lilen said.

"I personally wouldn't take this offer. Mapuche culture may appear to typical Americans as primitive but, in truth, your culture functions with a higher degree of unity and yields meaningful purpose to each day. America is plagued with social discrepancies not recognized from a surface perspective. Your daughters can advance their education and discover insightful lives to whatever degree they desire without detachment from tribal roots. They can study to achieve academic fulfillment; however, to disconnect from this majestic place would unveil more loss than gain," Stephen said.

"When we get older, we could visit America and not move there to attend American schools. We enjoy each day so much. We love to help our parents find food and attain basic needs. We collect firewood, carry water and gather edible plants, mushrooms, nuts and berries. The forest is a sacred place. This spiritual attachment would be lost if we lived in an American city. I've read how air is polluted and water must be purified. Our air is pure, as is our well water. We would be required to alter our ethnic structure and our traditional dress. Our dark skin may cause discrimination. William taught us negative aspects of American society," Suyia said.

"I agree with Stephen. You'll have a better life if you remain here. I've never felt such enlightenment as when we were on the mountain trail to your village. The majesty of the snow peaked Andes Mountains and meadows carpeted with wild flowers. I even observed a condor high in the sky circling on thermals. This event revealed a vision of what heaven could look like," Jerrod said.

Mapuche foods were served. Wild plant leaves, chopped roots with natural spices and flat bread with sautéed venison strips. Mapuche food was flavorful and satisfying.

After the meal, Yaco played Mapuche folk songs on his self carved wooden flute and Lilen, Suyia and Yaima sang lyrics. It was magical, penetrating the hearts of Stephen and Jerrod in a haunting yet pleasurable manner.

Stephen and Jerrod shared meals with other families prior to their scheduled departure date. These personal contacts enhanced admiration for Mapuche customs.

Jerrod and Stephen were satisfied with the transmitter and receptor installation and prepared to leave. Jerrod photographed each phase of their work with descriptions to accompany photographs. He also photographed newly acquired Mapuche friends and listed names for identity. As Stephen commented prior to their arrival, it has been an adventure of a lifetime.

A designated date was pre-established with Raimondi and he arrived with his pack mules.

The evening prior to departure, the tribe had a bonfire and everyone gathered at a circularly arranged, hewn log seating area. Bonfires were frequent events as a means to offer tribal social interaction.

"It was the best time sharing our lives with Stephen and Jerrod. They've devoted much time and effort to create their electrical transmitter and, as a result, we no longer are required to carry water up a steep hill to our residences.

"I'll relay what occurred to church leaders and they'll be pleased. Jerrod has eight years remaining to obtain his medical degree and will be restricted during this obligatory period. Jerrod and Stephen will work diligently to find a competent manufacturer for their electronic transmitter. When this is accomplished, the church will purchase an additional receptor to allow lighting for our school. I'm thankful for Stephen and Jerrod's assistance," William said.

The tribe applauded.

Jerrod stood next to the bonfire and said, "When the Mormon Church informed us they'd sponsor our trip to your village to install our electrical system, I knew we'd encounter unusual circumstances, yet projected thoughts weren't remotely close to what transpired. During the twelve-mile trek to your village revealed a scene beyond anything I could've imagined. No matter how long I live, I'll never forget the emotion delivered from the magnificent vistas.

"Life in The United States contrasts to Mapuche culture. Historic Native American life was parallel to yours, as their lives were attached intimately with the land and its natural elements.

"Our transmitter offers benefits, yet this change must be tempered. Caution must be applied to disallow subtraction from the purity of Mapuche historic roots. I want it to work and feel it's possible to meld beneficially if the tribe strives to avoid negative influences of modern technological imposition. As America advanced technologically, the country suffered social loss as it distanced itself from physical tasks. It's important to maintain your hunter-gatherer society.

"I'm currently in premed school in pursuit of a medical degree with ambition to offer modern medical services to areas similar to your village. Precaution must be applied to safeguard against disruption of your established harmonious society. Doctor Albert Schweitzer and his wife were successful and beneficial to a remote African village in the early twentieth century.

"It's my wish to remain connected with those I've met during this assignment. I'd enjoy correspondence, as it will solidify our bond.

"Tomorrow we'll depart but let's hold dear this time in our hearts, minds and spirits. Thank you for your kindness."

The tribe stood and applauded as Suyia and Yaima wiped tears from their eyes.

William beckoned to an elderly woman who stepped forward carrying something in her arms. He directed her to Jerrod and Stephen and she presented each with an article of clothing. This woman was the tribe's master seamstress and she crafted two beautiful hemp cloth pullover tunics as departure gifts to Stephen and Jerrod. The hems of the tunics were highlighted with striped rainbow colors and the bodies were earth tones. Jerrod and Stephen were overwhelmed, as they each hugged this magnificent woman. These tunics date to the tribe's earliest history, and exemplify Mapuche native male dress. Emotions were at a peak enhanced by the warmth of the bonfire. It created an unforgettable experience.

Pack mules were loaded the next morning with books and mail, as tribe members correspond with Mormon benefactors. Also to be mailed were native craft items sent as gifts.

As they transited the return trail, melancholy accompanied them yet was softened by a sense of fulfillment.

William drove Jerrod and Stephen the next morning to the Santiago International Airport. He accompanied them to the boarding area and said, "I'm looking forward to our next step. I'll serve as your liaison if you connect with a manufacturer."

"It was Jerrod's idea to stir interest to attract potential manufacturers. A confidence base will develop more efficiently with a working example in place. Your input could prove vital to the project's future," Stephen said.

"I'm bogged down with college curriculum. Stephen is more flexible to make connections. I'll write letters to seek manufacturers and Stephen will make in person presentations," Jerrod said.

As Jerrod and Stephen prepared to board their flight, William said, "I'm at your service. I enjoyed our time together."

"You've exposed us to a wonderful culture and we're forever grateful," Jerrod said.

"It was my pleasure. Until we meet again," William said.

He shook their hands, turned and walked away. Jerrod and Stephen looked at each other in silence and boarded their flight.

The return flight arrived one week prior to resumption of Jerrod's classes. His mind was filled with thoughts of the future. He eagerly anticipated describing his experience with the Mapuche to his parents and Mike. He will also write Sarah.

Upon arrival, Stephen retrieved his van from long term parking and they drove to Jerrod's home.

It was an odd sensation for Jerrod, as he had never been away from home. Joy of returning home was mixed with memories of the Mapuche as he wondered if he would ever see the tribe again.

When they entered the driveway, Frank and Judy emerged to greet the travelers. Jerrod hugged his parents. "Be prepared for a fascinating story. It was an experience I'll never forget. What I conjured up in my mind prior to our trip was as far off the mark as it could be.

"I'll write an article for the college newspaper to fulfill my desire to share our experience," Jerrod said.

Judy made tea and the four sat at the kitchen table as Jerrod and Stephen gave a narrative of their experience.

"I'm impressed. We'll make dinner while you two unwind, take showers and organize. I want to hear more of this compelling story," Judy responded.

"Our trip was like time travel. The Mapuche are beautiful, loving and resourceful people," Jerrod said.

Stephen and Jerrod showed Judy and Frank the pendants and tunics they received as gifts. They also described visitations with Mapuche families and the ceremonious farewell bonfire.

"I've read of the Mapuche, yet to witness and blend with this ancient hunter gatherer culture was an experience beyond what I could've ever imagined.

"Jerrod must apply his effort toward attaining his medical degree as I'll dedicate time to locate a competent manufacturer for our system. Jerrod applied for a US patent and we'll know in a few months where our project stands," Stephen said.

"You two are a good team and I predict positive result. We're supportive of Jerrod's ambition to apply modern medical services to impoverished locations and we'll do what we're able to assist him attain this goal. Judy was the source of Jerrod's ambition. She's presented Jerrod with Schweitzer's book describing his work in Africa," Frank said.

The next morning, Stephen returned to The University of Pennsylvania. Frank and Judy drove Mike and Jerrod back to Duke University.

Jerrod wrote Sarah:

Dear Sarah,

I've returned from Chile where I assisted Professor Garrett with installing our electrical transmitter system. It was an experience of a lifetime, sponsored by the Mormon Church. This event will remain in my memory as long as I live.

I'm back at school with my dorm mate, Mike Dunleavy. We complement each other. Mike is the sixth man on the Duke University basketball team, which is quite an accomplishment for a freshman.

I'll team with Professor Garrett to seek a manufacturer for our transmitter and receptor. Our ambition is to gain fiscal support through grants and various benefactors and market this device by targeting impoverished areas. My job is to make initial connection through correspondence and Stephen will demonstrate the transmitter, as I'm committed to pursue a medical degree.

When you have time to write, I'd enjoy hearing from you.

Love,
Jerrod

The next week, Jerrod and Mike began classes as college routines returned. Study occupied evening hours. Jerrod spent time at the library to research foreign electronic manufacturing companies to begin his task to locate a competent source to construct the system.

He received a letter from Sarah:

Dear Jerrod,

I miss you. I've adjusted to school and am a starter on the university's basketball team. I've made friends with teammates and improved emotionally since last semester.

One male student keeps asking me for a date, yet I'm unsure about him. His father is a wealthy owner of a Chevrolet dealership. His name is John Waters and he's quite persistent. He drives a new Corvette his father gave him as a high school graduation gift. He's good looking, yet arrogant. He's taking me to a fine restaurant next Friday night. I'm not interested in being his trophy.

I'm pleased to know you've progressed toward your goal and this reflects the quality of your character, an obvious trait to those who know you.

I'll contact Professor Garrett and introduce myself. I look forward to meeting him.

I often reminisce about our prom experience and wish we were at the same school.

Love,
Sarah

Jerrod composed a list of potential electronic equipment manufacturers and sent general information letters with detailed descriptions of the transmitter's function that included a series of photographs. In addition, he sent photos of the Mapuche village and the system's installation to pump water. If more information was needed to verify the proficiency of the system, he included William's address.

He received a phone call from Stephen. "Jerrod, this is Stephen. How are you getting along?"

"I've sent twenty letters to various electronic manufacturers with details and photographs of our transmitter and receptor at the Mapuche village. I'm hoping for responses to gain connection with a competent manufacturer," Jerrod said.

"This is good news. Your high school friend Sarah visited. She's an impressive young woman, beautiful and very bright. I enjoyed her visit," Stephen said.

"She sure is. I fell in love with her when we attended school proms together. I wish she were at Duke instead of The University of Pennsylvania. I received a letter from her. She's in an adjustment phase at the university," Jerrod said.

"I'm sure she's popular. Keep me informed about response from inquiry letters. My tenure status allows flexibility. If I request time off, a substitute can be assigned," Stephen said.

"I certainly will; I'm eager to see where we can go with our project," Stephen said.

CHAPTER 6

TRAGEDY

Mike's father sent money to buy a used car and this gave the dorm mates mobility. Jerrod planned to take a driver's education course to obtain his drivers license.

Routines continued and Jerrod resumed his daily walks, as Mike was occupied with studies, basketball practices and games.

Mike and Jerrod were studying when the phone rang.

Jerrod answered. It was his mom, Judy. She was sobbing uncontrollably and said, "Sarah's been killed in an auto accident. She was riding with a male friend in his Corvette speeding over one hundred miles per hour and a truck misjudged the Corvette's speed and pulled directly in front of them and both were killed. It's devastating."

Jerrod's hands trembled, and he began to cry, as grief struck like a lightning bolt. He handed the phone to Mike. He couldn't talk and slumped into a chair, sobbing with hands over his face.

"Jerrod started crying and handed me the phone," Mike said.

"This is Judy. I'm obligated to tell Jerrod the terrible news of Sarah's tragic death in an auto accident. Comfort him and have him call me when he regains composure, Judy said."

"I can't believe this is happening. Jerrod loved Sarah so much. This news will shatter him. I'll do my best. I'll have him call when he recovers," Mike said.

Mike hung up the phone and hugged Jerrod as he continued to weep.

Through tears, Jerrod said, "She was so beautiful. My memory flashes an image of a tall, athletic girl showing the mastery of her free throw shot to a packed gymnasium as the crowd chanted her name.

"She made a special effort to bolster my confidence and lead me to an escape path from social bewilderment. She shined as light in my darkness.

"Her call and subsequent request for me to escort her to the prom formed a pivotal point in my life. When I told her I couldn't dance because of my pigeon toes, she said, 'How do you know you can't dance? You've never tried to dance.' Her words melted my heart. Prior to Sarah, I was unaware of love's magnitude of power.

"As we entered the decorated gymnasium at her senior prom, it was wondrous. Sarah's magnetism was something to behold, as all eyes instinctually focused on her.

"I'm disoriented overwhelmed with grief. This wound is deep. How can I ever heal?"

"Let's have coffee and discuss our future. I'm equally shaken. Sarah was loved by everyone," Mike said.

Mike and Jerrod's bond strengthened them as they confronted this sorrowful event. Mike emphasized Jerrod's potential with the transmitter. He highlighted his good fortune to have Professor Garrett as a guide and mentor. The grief from the loss of Sarah will remain a fixture in Jerrod's life. His memory and love for her will serve as a reminder of her contribution to his development.

Jerrod called Judy and said, "I'll never forget Sarah. I loved her so much."

"I know; we loved her too. You're challenged to step forward with your life. We scheduled a flight home for you to attend Sarah's memorial service. Mike can drive you to the airport. We'll pick you up," Judy said.

On the drive to the airport Mike said, "When you get your driver's license, you can use my car anytime.

"You're on track academically to pursue a medical degree. You created an opportunity for Professor Garrett to reestablish his dream, and shared an experience of a lifetime with the Mapuche culture. You're on the cusp of a remarkable life."

Frank and Judy greeted Jerrod as he disembarked his flight and hugged him. They returned home to share dinner and discuss the tragic loss.

"When I escorted Sarah to our senior proms, it was a personal transformation. Love is like a spring flower and penetrates like no other force," Jerrod said.

Frank, Judy and Jerrod attended Sarah's memorial service. Jerrod asked Sarah's parents if he could express his thoughts about Sarah and they agreed.

Jerrod walked to the podium. "Sarah was the most beautiful, kind and loving person I've ever known.

"My first contact with Sarah was by chance. Our high school sponsored a statewide basketball free throw contest for boys and girls. I wasn't a member of the team, but assigned as the team's statistician and invited to attend team practices. I developed free throw shooting skills at home practicing daily on our driveway court. The coaches noticed my skill level as I shot free throws during the team's practice sessions. Coaches were allowed to select two participants. Mike Dunleavy and I were chosen to represent our school.

"The rules stated one miss and you're eliminated. As competitors dropped out, only Sarah and I remained. My ninety-sixth shot rimmed out and dropped to the floor. Sarah kept shooting and the crowd began chanting her name as she continued to score baskets. Sarah missed her one hundred and thirtieth shot and was declared the winner of the competition. The crowd erupted in a standing ovation.

"We received trophies. I was awarded the runner up trophy and, as I extended my hand to congratulate Sarah, she moved around my hand and gave me a big hug. I can barely control tears as I reminisce about this moment. Sarah's depth of character was revealed from this gesture.

"The next week, Sarah called. Her senior prom was near and the boy she expected to ask her chose another. She asked me to escort her to prom. I was speechless yet eventually said, 'Sarah, I don't know how to dance as my feet are impaired by pigeon toes.' Sarah asked, 'How do you know you can't dance? You've never tried.' She said she'd teach me and visited my home for dance instructions.

"We attended Sarah's prom as well as my high school's prom. It was the best times of my life to be with Sarah.

"I fell in love with her and she said, 'We've only approached the starting line of life and we'll be separated by attending different colleges.' This tempered our love's development.

"We stayed in touch and when my mom called to inform me of Sarah's death, I never knew such grief existed. It tore my heart out. My mind flashed visions of Sarah gracefully moving on the dance floor. I've thought of nothing else since her death. Sarah possessed rare and wonderful qualities and, as I move forward on the path of life Sarah will remain an indelible memory."

Sarah's parents approached Jerrod and her mom hugged Jerrod with tears in her eyes.

On their way home, Judy said, "Jerrod, you gave Sarah a wonderful eulogy. We're so proud of you."

"It's been said we never forget our first love. I know I will never forget Sarah," Jerrod said.

Mike picked up Jerrod at the airport and Jerrod described the memorial service for Sarah.

Jerrod said, "I think Sarah would want me to continue my life to the best of my ability."

"I know she would," Mike responded.

The pain of the loss caused Jerrod to press more vigorously toward his goal to become a physician.

CHAPTER 7

YAIMA

A few weeks passed and Jerrod received a package from the Mormon Church.

Jerrod opened the package. It was an ebony Mapuche flute with a letter from Yaima, one of the twins who greeted him and Stephen upon their arrival at the Mapuche village.

Dear Jerrod,

I carved this flute as a gift of appreciation for what you and your friend Stephen accomplished for our village. William found a songbook of Mapuche folk songs with musical notes. I made a sketch of the flute's finger placement to play notes related to selected songs. With practice, you can learn to play these songs. It would be fun if you visit again; we could play a duet.

You are a special person and I hope to see you again someday.

Your Mapuche friend,

Yaima

Enclosed in the package was a photograph of Yaima in her colorful native dress. She was stunningly beautiful.

Jerrod showed Mike Yaima's picture and described who she was and how they were connected.

"She's magnificent, such beauty. What a nice gesture. If you learn to play this flute, it'd be a form of meditation," Mike said.

"I will, as music is a peaceful place for the mind to wander," Jerrod said.

Jerrod's return letter to Yaima,

Dear Yaima,

What a pleasant surprise to receive your thoughtful gift. I'll cherish this flute and learn to play Mapuche folk songs. I shared your photo with my dorm mate, Mike. We agreed you are a beautiful young woman and especially enjoyed your colorful indigenous dress.

Your letter eases recent grief from the loss of my best friend in a tragic auto accident. Your bright smile and thoughtful gift soften the pain of her death. I never knew such emotional anxiety.

Stephen and I will seek a competent manufacturer to duplicate and produce our transmitter and receptor with intension to install units in areas with similar needs as your tribe.

I'd love to visit your village again. Our time spent with the Mapuche was a hallmark of our lives. Our experience with your culture unveiled disparity compared to modern American social design. I was oblivious to the entangled misdirection modern society asserts on itself. Our visit awakened me and escalated desire to serve those cast aside by uncompromised societal haste contemporary urban life imposes.

American society is entrapped by superficial materialism and consumptive glut.

Mapuche historic culture established the design of life to embrace harmony with a perception of wealth viewed from a frugal minimalistic philosophical perspective, as opposed to relentless drive to accumulate material wealth and wallow in excess.

Our installation of your perpetual energy system serves to demonstrate practical technological application. Your tribe represents a model toward our mission and may involve visitations by interested parties to create opportunity for a return visit. What a joy it would be to see you again.

Love,

Your friend Jerrod"

Jerrod carried his flute on daily walks. An isolated grove of spruce trees on campus offered solitude. He would rest at this place and practice notes of Mapuche folk songs. Jerrod looked forward to this each day.

Jerrod received a letter from China.

Dear Mr. James,

My name is Chang Yi. I received your letter of inquiry related to your electrical transmitter device. I formed an electronics manufacturing company ten years ago in China. I was born in a remote town in northern China and given opportunity for advanced education in the United States. I have an electrical engineering degree from UCLA and was employed by a California electronics company on a work visa with the intention to gain American citizenship. My quest stalled because of political diplomatic unraveling and Chinese with American work visas were forced to return to China.

My company is successful and exports electronic products globally. The company presently has one hundred employees. We manufacture a variety of devices; however, nothing is similar to what you propose. I studied the documents and photos you mailed and feel, via coordination with you and Professor Garrett; we meet requirements to produce the electrical transmitter and receptor.

I will fund and design a smaller demonstration model to be used for sales presentations and believe, with proper promotion, your system has immense potential. In China, we have many sparsely populated areas where your system could apply.

I propose a fifty percent split in profits. You will need to form a registered American corporation to make things official. I have a Chinese marketing team and we can form a sales presentation plan on your end. Exposure is a necessary component to succeed.

During initial phase, my company will implement a limited production line to be expanded, as demand requires. I predict a year or more will be required to establish product recognition.

I visit The United States several times each year to meet with American customers and advisors I've associated with over the years. During one of these visits, it would be advantageous to meet with you and Professor Garrett.

You are quite young to be involved in a project of this predictable magnitude; however, you are also one of high intelligence and, with proper advice progression, will develop.

I'm grateful for the opportunity to assist in any manner I'm able.

Sincerely,

Chang Yi

Jerrod called Stephen and read Chang Yi's letter.

"This could be significant. If Chang Yi visits, I'd enjoy meeting with him. Keep me posted," Stephen said.

Jerrod wrote in his journal:

What an inspirational letter from Chang Yi. Positive results will transpire, channeled from others, as my connection with Stephen has proven, and Chang Yi can contribute additional support. I'll seek council from mentors as progression complexities arise. I'll communicate through correspondence and phone calls. I'll find a competent law firm to form a corporation. Stephen cannot be a member because of legal entanglement with power companies; however, he'll receive equal remuneration as my primary advisor.

Jerrod called his parents to disclose this new development. They were ecstatic. They encouraged him and committed to pay legal costs to form the corporation; shares will be equally divided between Jerrod and his parents.

Jerrod described his contact with Chang Yi to Mike.

"As I observe your and Professor Garrett's effort, I'm fascinated. It's impossible to predict the level of interest this concept might create. As Chang Yi pointed out, China has many relative areas and you can imagine what Russia's vastness could offer. You were motivated by personal desire to offer medical services to third world countries and viewed the system as a means to initiate connection with impoverished communities. You've performed this unaware of the system's potential range of application. If the system is patented and you organize a corporation, opportunities are boundless. No long and complex electric cables, only short links to receptors," Mike said.

"You're right, I didn't consider market potential. My ambition was unrelated to fiscal success; although, money properly applied offers positive influence for those in need. My connection with Chang Yi could explode with growth. Chang Yi has been constructing electronic equipment for ten years and has one hundred employees with an international marketing team," Jerrod said.

Jerrod received a call from Chang Yi. "Jerrod, I'm working with my designers to construct a portable model transmitter and receptor and will demonstrate the unit to international humanitarian agencies. I had a few technical questions and called Professor Garrett. He answered these questions without hesitation.

"We'll have our model operational in two weeks. I'll keep you informed."

"I'm impressed how quickly you've progressed. I've formed a corporation. My parents and I are shareholders. I've also received certification documents from the US patent office. Things are falling in place.

"I have a request. The Mapuche village in Chile where we installed our prototype system was supported by the Mormon Church and church leaders decided, after our unit proved worthy, they'd purchase a second receptor to provide lighting for the tribe's school and guest residence. I'd like to give them an opportunity to purchase a receptor," Jerrod said.

"We'll provide a unit at no cost. The Mapuche serve to verify feasibility, which will assist in promotion of the system," Chang Yi said.

"I'm appreciative. I've bonded with this Mapuche tribe and, when the receptor becomes available, I'll travel to Chile to install it myself," Jerrod said.

Jerrod became engrossed in his studies. During his walks, he often stopped to play his flute among the spruce trees. It was a peaceful place. His music offered respite from stress as he continued to mourn Sarah.

Jerrod completed the driver's education class and passed his driver's test. He didn't drive Mike's car much because when he went places, it was always with Mike. He attended Duke's basketball games. He enjoyed basketball and reminisced competing against Sarah in the free throw competition.

Jerrod wrote Yaima.

Dear Yaima,

Good news. I've connected with an electronic equipment manufacturer in China and they will produce the electric transmission system. I formed a corporation and I'm the principle stockholder with ambition to distribute systems throughout the world.

The China manufacturer will provide an additional receptor to be added to your village's system at no cost. I'm excited because I will install this receptor. William mentioned he wants to add lights to the school.

I'd like to spend time with your family to learn about Mapuche life. You're only a few years younger than me. I performed above average academically and was advanced two grades. I'll soon be seventeen and a sophomore at Duke University enrolled in the premed program. I'll schedule my visit to Chile between semesters.

I'm pleased to tell you I've learned to play my flute. I play Mapuche folksongs at a quiet location on campus among a grove of spruce trees. Music is an elixir and revives our spirit to incarnate deity linked to inner consciousness. I look forward to seeing you again.

Love,

Jerrod

CHAPTER 8

ENTERPRISE

A month passed and Jerrod received a letter from Chang Yi.

Dear Jerrod,

Our model presentation unit is complete and functions perfectly. We'll participate at an electronic show in Los Angeles next month and the model will be our centerpiece.

After the show, I'll fly to an airport near the university, rent a car and meet to discuss our project's overview.

Sincerely,

Chang Yi

Jerrod's dorm phone rang. It was Chang Yi. "Jerrod, I'll arrive at noon tomorrow and we'll have dinner."

"I'll be free after 1 o'clock in the evening. I want you to meet my dorm mate, Mike Dunleavy. He's been a close friend since high school. He's majoring in business administration," Jerrod said.

"I'd enjoy meeting your friend. He's welcome to join us for dinner," Chang Yi replied.

Jerrod gave Chang Yi directions to the dorm.

Jerrod said, "If you have difficulty locating our dorm, ask any student."

"OK, see you tomorrow. We have much to discuss," Chang Yi said.

Chang Yi is a tall, striking Chinese man in his mid forties, dressed in a business suit. He located the dorm and knocked on the door. Jerrod greeted him by shaking his hand and said, "What an honor. I'm grateful for your visit. Please come in and meet Mike."

Mike made a good impression, naturally modest and likeable.

Mike introduced himself. "I'm pleased to meet you. I've been Jerrod's friend since high school, Mike said."

Jerrod made tea and the three sat at the table.

"We're on the verge of a great opportunity and I was eager to visit for interactive thought exchange," Yi said.

Chang Yi addressed Mike, "What Professor Garrett and Jerrod created has greater market potential than I perceived. It's remarkable how a sixteen year old and a genius physics professor teamed up to invent this specialized system. I felt reluctant to become involved yet, as I contemplated places in China and other areas of the world where electricity is unavailable, it surfaced as a viable concept."

Yi opened his briefcase and handed Jerrod and Mike photos of the demonstration model his company designed and showcased at the Los Angeles electronic trade show. The photo showed a crowd gathered at the booth where the system was displayed.

Yi continued, "As I observed from a distance, an older gentleman approached me and introduced himself as directed by the representative demonstrating our model.

"His name was Joseph Abernathy, a benefactor to a prominent humanitarian foundation. He's spent the past twenty years contributing to assist isolated, poverty stricken cultures. He frequently visits these areas and applies personal assistance. During working years, he became wealthy through various enterprise ventures. Joseph and his wife are dedicated to serve humanitarian causes.

"He's a dynamic person. He said he wanted to purchase ten systems to be installed at selected locations through the foundation he works with.

"An intriguing question appeared. If our device impresses this man of integrity, what does this signify?

"I speculate market potential is greater than we've initially anticipated."

Jerrod and Mike were silent as they absorbed Chang Yi's revelation.

Jerrod explained, "Professor Garrett deserves the most credit. I became fascinated by Nicola Tesla's achievements and spent time at the library to research for published academic views and opinions on Tesla. I stumbled across a study of Tesla's wireless electrical transmission theory and discovered a published academic paper about alternative energy written by Professor Garrett. I contacted him and disclosed my interest to construct a similar device.

"By coincidence, the professor had designed and built a smaller device based on Tesla's infamous molecular electrical transmitter. The professor's unit offered ease of transport and installation, which was a variation from Tesla's. The professor was exploited by large power producing companies as they misled him, indicating they were ambitious to develop his idea; however, they had no such intention. They planned to destroy his machine and documents to protect against infringement on established power production Garrett's invention imposed. Garrett went for the bait: he sold his rights to the idea and relinquished legal status to further develop his transmitter. The power company then destroyed Garrett's device and technical data, believing they'd rid themselves of future complications caused by Garrett's transmitter. This angered Garrett. His fury, combined with his admiration of my enthusiasm to construct a similar unit, contributed to the formation of our partnership. We teamed up to build a prototype based on Professor Garrett's knowledge. The entire enterprise was established in my name as protection of Garrett from legal ramifications caused by his agreement with power companies.

"I was captivated by Dr. Garrett's skills and knowledge. Eventually, an opportunity was presented through a Mormon missionary to install our transmitter in Chile to benefit an isolated native Mapuche tribe. It was an experience of a lifetime and now you've revealed the unit has broader market potential than initially anticipated.

"My contribution is limited, as I'm obligated to continue pursuit of my medical degree; however, I will be instrumental where I'm able."

Mike drove to a nice off campus restaurant. During the meal, Jerrod showed Chang Yi his photo album recorded during installation of the system at the Mapuche village. Chang Yi enjoyed the photos, and asked Jerrod if he could retain copies to be used in sales presentations.

Jerrod said to Chang Yi, "You'll stay overnight at our dorm. The couch pulls out to a bed. We can stay up late and discuss things."

The three enjoyed each other's company. When they returned to the dorm, Jerrod made tea and showed Yi the ebony flute sent as a gift from Yaima, one of the twins pictured posing with Jerrod and Stephen when greeted by the Mapuche tribe.

"I'm corresponding with Yaima. She writes beautiful letters. She included Mapuche folk music with the flute and finger positions to play notes related to the music. I've learned to play these songs on my flute," Jerrod said.

"Please play one of the songs. I'd enjoy it. I was taught historic Chinese folk music as a child. It was a memorable time of my life," Chang Yi asked.

Jerrod played a Mapuche folk song and Chang Yi was impressed.

Jerrod also showed Yi his pendant necklace and the colorful hemp tunic the Mapuche gifted him and Stephen on the final night of their visit during a celebration bonfire.

"On cold days, I wear my tunic around campus and students frequently complement its beauty and color," Jerrod said.

"It's so colorful, I've never seen anything like it," Yi responded.

Conversations continued, as Yi was fascinated by Jerrod's connection with Mapuche culture.

Yi spoke to Mike. "Jerrod says you're majoring in business administration. Your graduation is a ways off, yet it may be a consideration for you to eventually join Jerrod's company. He'll need trustworthy business management if his company expands as predicted."

"We've discussed this a few times," Mike said.

"I'll call Professor Garrett tomorrow before I depart. I want to hear his thoughts on what's transpired. I look forward to meeting him," Yi said.

"I'll continue to correspond about my status. I'd enjoy visiting China and having you as a guide would be a special thrill," Jerrod said.

"This will eventually occur. I'll teach you more about China than typical tourists receive," Chang Yi said.

The next morning, Chang Yi departed. Mike and Jerrod discussed this inspiring meeting.

"What're your thoughts? Mike asked.

"Chang Yi's challenged to establish strategy to discover markets. Production methods to service demand is far greater than our construction of a single prototype installed at the Mapuche village.

"He impresses me. I feel fortunate he's interested to the degree he indicates. China has been a sleeping giant on the global industrialized stage and is being awakened. It's impossible to clearly predict or anticipate where we'll be with this enterprise a year from now," Jerrod responded

Yi met with Garrett and knew from this meeting to include the professor's mind and scientific experience as they would contribute immensely to the future of the project. Professor Garrett will play a major role as adviser to address development complexities associated with the system. This meeting stimulated Yi's confidence and ambition to drive forward with enthusiasm.

Yi's facility shifted into high gear. Response to the Garrett/James perpetual energy provider with wireless electrical transmission snowballed beyond expectation. The company stopped manufacturing previous products and only manufactured Garrett/James transmitters and receptors, shipping them globally.

Profits were divided and sent to Jerrod's corporation. Jerrod split half of his profits with Stephen. In addition, Jerrod used fifty percent of his personal income to form the Sarah Baker Memorial Charitable Foundation. He will seek additional benefactors to accumulate funds to be directed to improve living standards for the oppressed.

Chang Yi shipped a receptor to William Harrington, the Mormon missionary in Chile. Jerrod will reunite with William to install the unit at the Mapuche village school for florescent lights.

Professor Garrett was in China for a month working with Chang Yi's engineers to refine system components.

CHAPTER 9

RETURN TO CHILE

William planned to pick up Jerrod at the Santiago International Airport. Raimondi agreed to transport the new receptor with his pack mules.

As Jerrod disembarked the plane, William was waiting.

William greeted Jerrod, "Welcome back. It appears we'll repeat our scenic trek to the village. It's nice to see you again."

"You wouldn't believe the success we're experiencing with the wireless transmission system. Chang Yi's company is struggling to meet demand. Private citizens living remotely are purchasing units and charitable organizations are helping to install them in similar locations as the Mapuche village. Some countries apply our systems for military use where personnel are assigned to remote areas. It's astonishing to witness," Jerrod said.

"Many areas are in dire need of basic power. I sense this may be only the beginning of the transmitter's potential.

"I've purchased three florescent fixtures, wiring and a box of replacement bulbs. We'll stay overnight at my apartment and leave early morning for the village. I'd enjoy hearing more about your Chinese connection," William said.

During their evening meal, Jerrod detailed how the transmitter's expansion transpired.

The next morning, they were on the trail with Raimondi and his pack mules. Jerrod reminisced about his first experience with this magnificent mountain trail. Their arrival was a repeat of Jerrod and Stephen's first encounter with the Mapuche. Suyia and Yaima were again greeters and Yaima smiled as she handed Jerrod a beautiful bouquet of colorful wildflowers. Jerrod gifted each twin a necklace with a platinum heart shaped pendant formed with sparkling diamonds. The twins were in disbelief as they hugged and thanked Jerrod.

William and two tribal members unloaded the pack mules. They put Jerrod's personal items in the sleeping quarters of the school and stored the receptor in a nearby shelter.

The tribe crammed in the school in recognition of Jerrod's return. Yaima approached Jerrod and said, "My parents invite you to visit for our evening meal."

"I'd be honored; however, I have a few thoughts to share first," Jerrod said.

Jerrod addressed the tribe, "The emotions as I returned are indescribable. As we transited the magnificent mountain trail to your village, I was exhilarated.

"I've finished my sophomore year at Duke University and remain on track to earn a bachelor's degree in biological science. I'll then begin a four-year commitment to medical school and one year as a hospital intern to attain physician certification.

"The wireless electrical transmitter system we installed to power the village water pump is currently being manufactured and marketed globally to be placed in relevant locations.

"I'm gratified by the success of the system, but my return to your village is my greatest joy. I love your village and the intimacy you share with the biosphere.

"During this trip, we'll install a second receptor to provide lights for your school and meeting area. I'm reluctant to suggest too many modern devices as I feel your simplistic historic social roots represent the base for my admiration. I'm so happy to reunite with everyone."

The tribe applauded Jerrod and he felt intensely bonded with his Mapuche friends. He then followed Yaima and her family to their home.

While Lilen, Suyia and Yaima prepared food, Yaco and Jerrod talked.

"I've learned to play the flute Yaima sent. It's like a soothing tonic when I play Mapuche folk songs. Music offers purification to our lives. I look forward to playing my flute each day.

"I'm seventeen and am not identified as an adult in America for another year," Jerrod said.

"Suyia and Yaima are fourteen. I'm so proud of those two. They're obsessed with reading and study and William is a dedicated teacher. They may not have the same opportunities as American children, yet William informs me they're academically advanced beyond typical American fourteen-year-old children. As I observe them wander the forest searching for food, it's obvious they're content.

"Yaima described your advancement in school and academic proficiency. This positioned you to accomplish more than a typical seventeen year old and you've responded.

"Our village is blessed to have met you and Professor Garrett. I'm glad you made a second trip. After our meal, you can play a folk song on your flute and we'll sing the lyrics in Mapuche. How many seventeen year old Americans have this opportunity?" Yaco said.

Jerrod was fascinated as he observed the twins and their mother prepare food. It resembled a ballet with precise movements as they conversed in Mapuche.

The evening meal was exceptional with a variety of wild plants and roots, chopped nuts and a special spicy brown sauce. This mixture was spread on flat bread made from stone ground wild seed flour. Berries were eaten separately. The beverage was slightly fermented tea made from selected leaves, berries and wild honey. The Mapuche's garden is the forest.

Jerrod played folk songs on his flute and Yaco, Lilen and the twins sang lyrics. It was magical. This family formed a lasting impression in Jerrod's mind.

They stayed up late talking. Candles flickered as shadowy images formed a tranquil mood and camaraderie escalated.

"I must return to my quarters although my heart craves for this evening to never end," Jerrod said.

"During your stay, I'd like you to share meals with us. We speak in the same voice," Lilen said.

Jerrod departed to his quarters. He couldn't sleep as he contemplated events of his seventeen years. He thought of Sarah and how she would be proud to have her name attached to his foundation.

The next day, William and Jerrod installed the new receptor and attached florescent fixtures to the school's ceiling. They wired the lights to the new receptor. Jerrod flipped the switch and the place lit up.

William and a few members of the tribe built a bonfire encircled by hewn log seating where Jerrod and Stephen were honored for their water pump installation. This bonfire was celebratory in appreciation of Jerrod's effort to bring electric lights to the school.

"Jerrod learned to play a few Mapuche folk songs on his flute given him by my daughter Yaima.

"To celebrate William and Jerrod's accomplishment to bring lights to our school, Lilen will join me to play a flute duet and we invite everyone to dance," Yaco said.

Twenty tribal members joined hands in a circle to perform a Mapuche folk dance. Yaima reached out her hand to lead Jerrod into the circle.

"It's a simple dance and so much fun. Follow my foot placement and you'll catch on fast," Yaima said.

The music started and dancers responded. Jerrod followed Yaima's lead and learned proper steps. Jerrod's face lit up in a broad smile as he was mesmerized by Yaima's sparkling eyes. His memory flashed of Sarah when she taught him to dance. Love's power returned to Jerrod at a remote Chilean

Mapuche village dancing in the light of a bonfire far from his home in the Pennsylvania Hills.

Yaima and Jerrod danced several dances and then went to Yaima's family home for a late meal. After the meal, Jerrod retreated to his sleeping quarters as his mind overflowed with thoughts of Yaima. Her Mapuche heritage reflected beauty in every movement.

The next day, Raimondi and his pack mules planned to arrive in anticipation for the departure of Jerrod and William.

Leaving the village brought mixed emotions as Jerrod felt accomplished about the installation of the receptor, yet he was plagued with melancholy to leave Yaima.

As departure neared, the twins, adorned in beautiful native dress and wearing their diamond heart pendants, arrived to bid farewell. Both hugged Jerrod, yet Yaima held him tight with tears in her eyes.

The twins remained until they were out of sight.

Jerrod spent one night at William's apartment and during the evening meal Jerrod said,

"I'm in love with Yaima. I am not sure what I should do. I'm only seventeen and Yaima is fourteen."

"Love is perplexing while circumstances often block opportunity. I'm unable to offer advice, yet I certainly understand your feelings toward her. She's the entire package. The twins are outstanding students and it is a pure joy to teach them. Mapuche usually marry early and this may interfere as your lives are distant.

"You can correspond with Yaima as she enjoys writing. Nothing is impossible, yet challenges to put pieces together may be presented," William said.

"Geographic separation is a barrier. I'll correspond with Yaima," Jerrod said.

During the long flight, Jerrod thought of his love for Yaima. The circumstances felt similar to Sarah when they became separated.

Jerrod documented his trip and was eager to have his film processed to show his parents, especially the bonfire and folk dancing. William photographed Jerrod and Yaima dancing.

Yaima and other dancers were attired in colorful Mapuche native dress.

As Jerrod disembarked, his parents were at the gate and they hugged their son.

On the drive home, Jerrod highlighted his trip; however, he didn't reveal his feelings for Yaima. He needed time to contemplate his quandary.

After their evening meal, Jerrod went to his room and made an entry in his journal.

I can't allow emotions to dominate. I must resign to the reality of circumstances. We'll maintain connection through letters to share thoughts. Time is the stage director of life and it will unveil proper passage.

If Chang Yi and Stephen unite, they'll continue to expand markets for the electrical system. I'll combine fiscal success with my medical degree to pursue worthy objectives.

I can't activate plans under present conditions; however, I can speculate. If I married Yaima, we could work as a team and the Mapuche village could serve as a base to offer medical service to the Mapuche. We could travel to oppressed areas of the world to offer medical assistance. I could train Yaima and Suyia as physician assistants and, if Yaima and I travel, Suyia will be qualified to administer basic medical treatments to the tribe during our absence.

We could build a clinic using a Mapuche style shelter to blend with their historic culture. This would allow Yaima to remain connected to her family and continue life in a similar fashion she's accustomed.

Formulation of a plan offers comfort as I face the remaining challenges to become a certified physician. I'll be twenty-five when I reach this milestone.

Jerrod's classes would resume in one week. Mike planned to drive them back to their dorm.

Jerrod called Mike. "Mike, I've returned from Chile. I delivered a second receptor to the Mapuche village school and assisted William install florescent lights.

"I'd like to go for a ride on our mountain bikes. What do you think?"

"Great idea. I'll be over tomorrow by late morning," Mike said.

Jerrod used Mike for support since the pivotal day he instantly reverted Jerrod's depression to elation. Mountain trails served as tranquilizers. Nature cleanses ones' spirit; although mental clutter may remain, it subsides to plausible patterns.

Mike arrived as promised and the two friends rode their bikes into nearby hills.

During a rest stop, Jerrod described his time with the Mapuche tribe.

"It was different from my first trip with Stephen. The twins greeted us again and looked magnificent. I felt as if I was returning home from a long journey.

"After we installed the new receptor and florescent lights at the school, the tribe had a celebratory bonfire. Yaima's parents played a flute duet of Mapuche folk songs and tribal members formed a dance circle. Yaima led me by the hand to this circle of dancers and I was consumed by a mysterious emotion. The light of the bonfire combined with music and Mapuche dancers in their colorful dress created a surreal mood. Yaima's magnificent eyes are permanent fixtures in my mind.

"I'm seventeen and Yaima is fourteen. The thought of being separated from her is unacceptable. I'm deeply in love with Yaima and disoriented."

"It may be complex, yet you'll never again find such love. I advise you to marry Yaima as soon as possible. Your fiscal status allows travel to and from Chile during school breaks. Frequent trips to her tribal family will maintain her ethnic bond. I see no choice. If you don't do this, you'll become depressed and consumed by misery. I'm your best friend and I'll support you in any manner I'm able," Mike said.

Mike and Jerrod returned to Jerrod's home and Judy greeted them and said, "Mike, please stay for dinner. We'd enjoy having you. We share many memories."

Mike accepted the invitation.

After dinner, Mike said, "Jerrod has something to tell you."

Jerrod was silent, yet he knew Mike was right. He described his conundrum.

"If I were you, I'd marry her. If Yaima and her parents agree, it'll bring new dimension to your lives," Frank said.

"Jerrod, you're capable of making this decision and we'll favor whatever you decide," Judy said.

The next day, Mike and Jerrod drove back to school to resume classes.

Jerrod wrote to Yaima.

Dear Sweet Yaima,

You're constantly on my mind. My visit to your village affected me in a manner I could've never imagined. I'm possessed by love for you.

I've discussed the intensity of my love with my parents. I want to marry you and be with you every moment.

We're younger than most who make this major step due to the rare fashion of our connection. This adds to the challenge and complication to achieve permanence within the power of love.

The results of my discussion with my parents were positive and a plan has been organized if you agree to marry me. The largest barrier is my education to become a physician. I'd like a Mapuche wedding at the village then relocate to the United States to have an American wedding, which will allow you to gain American citizenship in addition to your Chilean citizenship. We'll live in the United States until I fulfill my medical school obligation and travel to your home village during semester breaks.

My long-range plan is to permanently return to your village and establish a medical clinic to serve Mapuche who reside in the vicinity. I'll train you and Suyai to assist with clinical duties. We may also travel to crisis zones of the world to offer medical services to victims of war or those plagued by poverty or pandemics. During our absence, Suyia can administer basic treatments for Mapuche needs.

You are so beautiful and such a joy to be with. I'm driven to make every effort for us to unite. I love you more than I ever thought possible and will cherish you until the day I die.

Love,

Jerrod

Mike and Jerrod returned to study routines. It took weeks to receive a return letter from Yaima.

Mike's basketball practices resumed. It looked favorable for him to be on the starting team this year. Jerrod continued his daily walks and played his flute while resting at his favorite spot among the grove of spruce trees. Mike and Jerrod discussed their lives in evenings.

"Mike, after you graduate with a business administration degree, you should consider working with Chang Yi and Stephen to develop the transmitter company. Chang Yi mentioned this; it's a valid thought," Jerrod said.

"It's a consideration. I'm a good basketball player, but not professional caliber. I loved playing basketball for Duke and the NBA may draft two of our players; however, I won't be drafted and must seek a career outside basketball.

I know you're eager to receive a letter from Yaima," Mike responded.

"I am, she's a constant presence in my thoughts," Jerrod said.

Three weeks passed and Yaima's letter arrived.

My dearest Jerrod,

I'm happy about your thoughts to marry me. I share your feelings. I think of you constantly and dream of hugging you again.

I talked with my parents and Suyia about your message. They agree and love you as much as I do. When we're married and live in America, I'll miss my life here and this will be a difficult adjustment; however, with your support, I'm confident I can do it. I have much to learn about America. William gave me history books describing your country from its early times until this modern era. He highlighted issues I might struggle with, yet he also feels we are a perfect match.

Your thought of our marriage ceremony at our village is agreeable. I would love to meet your parents and show them how I've been raised at my place of birth.

I fell in love with you on your first trip with Professor Garrett. When we danced to flute music at the bonfire celebration, tears formed in my eyes I was so happy. It was such a wonderful moment.

I'm overflowing with joy and look forward to our future together.
I love you.
Yaima

Jerrod read Yaima's letter twice, handed it to Mike to read and said, "You are right about our marriage as soon as possible. My first thoughts were to let things simmer until I graduate from medical school. How often during one's lifetime does the power of love penetrate with such intensity?

"I've completed two years of a nine-year commitment and to delay our love bond for seven years is unconscionable. We'll gain the most united, not separated.

"Our marriage will disrupt Yaima's life. She'll be uprooted from her birthplace. It's the only life she's ever known. Yaima's family ties are more connected than typical American families. Cultural adaptation will challenge her most. It'll be my responsibility to assist her. I won't permit her to attend public school where she'll potentially be taunted and bullied. I'll hire tutors and teach her myself. Yaima's life as a Mapuche is attached to nature within a unified society not plagued with the dysfunction modern America has evolved to encapsulate. I'll dedicate myself to ensure Yaima's happiness is not compromised."

Jerrod's letter to Yaima:

My dearest Yaima,

As I anticipate our pending marriage, I've never felt so elated.

Our wedding represents a step toward establishment of medical services for your village.

I'll rent an apartment near campus, commission a tutor and teach you what I know. I don't want you to attend public school as I fear it would be traumatic.

William said you and Suyia are above average students. Life is an ongoing learning process and, like my friend Sarah once told me, we're only at the starting line of life. We can design our future as a team. Write soon. I live for your letters.

I love you.

Jerrod

CHAPTER 10

MARRIAGE

Mike's been dating one of the basketball team's cheerleaders and brought her to the dorm. Jerrod greeted them.

"Jerrod, this is Elaine Phillips, she's on the cheerleader team," Mike said.

"I'm pleased to meet you. I've been Mike's friend since high school," Jerrod said as he shook her hand.

"I know, Mike's told me of your achievements. I'm pleased to meet you too," Elaine said.

Elaine was tall with auburn hair and hazel eyes, a striking young woman.

"We'll be married this summer at Elaine's parents house in Upstate New York. I told Elaine your plan to marry a Chilean Mapuche girl you met while installing your electrical energy transmitter," Mike said.

Jerrod showed Elaine a photo of Yaima and her sister Suyia.

"They're so beautiful and I love the colorful dresses. I'd never heard of the Mapuche until Mike described their history," Elaine said.

"Yaima is coordinating with her family to arrange our wedding date. My parents will accompany me to the village for our wedding and meet Yaima and her family. They're so amazing and incredibly bonded; I've fallen in love with Yaima, yet I have also fallen in love with how Mapuche families function and where they live. After I receive my medical degree, I'll make the village my permanent home to establish a medical clinic to serve the village and its vicinity.

"I'll train Yaima and Suyia as physician assistants. My business partners, Chang Yi and Stephen Garrett, are working to manufacture and distribute our wireless electrical transmitter and receptors. I hold the patent and corporate shares are divided equally with my parents. My income has become significant and is predicted to expand. I'll contribute fiscal assistance toward third world countries.

"My hero is Albert Schweitzer who performed similar activity in the early twentieth century in a remote region of Africa," Jerrod responded.

"Jerrod, this is an exceptional ambition. Judging from what you've accomplished so far, I'm confident you'll succeed. It's an unusual pursuit for a young person of your academic status. I admire you. Mike told me I would and I do," Elaine said.

Jerrod made tea and the three talked into the night about their hopes for the future. Elaine is a psychology major.

Mike drove Elaine to her dorm and Jerrod's mind envisioned these two joining his company.

A letter arrived from Yaima.

Dearest Jerrod,

My parents contacted the tribe's elder, Quidel, who traditionally performs Mapuche weddings. He's in agreement and he's familiar with your contribution to our tribe.

His English is limited; however, he understands fairly well. He said he'll practice English prior to the wedding but perform the ceremony in Mapuche. My sister Suyia will quietly interpret during the ceremony.

The date of our wedding will be on Winter Solstice. It's summer in America, winter in Chile. Mapuche culture commemorates this date. This adds excitement to our wedding day.

Mapuche wedding protocol doesn't include gift giving or ring exchange. Gifts and rings are viewed as distractive to God's meaningful delivery of love shared between marriage partners. Celebration is not compromised as music and dance serve as gifts.

In the village is a shelter specifically built for newly married couples on their wedding night and occupied until their own home is constructed. Tribal members are obligated by tradition to work as a team to erect the newlyweds' home. This tradition has been in place throughout Mapuche history.

When we are remarried in America, we'll follow guidelines attached to American culture.

I think of you every minute.

I love you.

Yaima

Jerrod wrote back to Yaima...

Sweet Yaima:

I'll arrange our trip with William's assistance. We'll arrive at the village three days prior to our wedding.

Mike is getting married to a lovely girl named Elaine the same month as our wedding. Their wedding will take place at Elaine's parent's home in New York.

You will meet them when you come to the United States and we'll enjoy their friendships as our lives connect.

My plan is to spend semester breaks at your village to begin the process toward permanent residency.

I've studied ancient cultures and admire their historic display of social harmony. Modern society occupies a fraction of the human timeline. You can teach me intricacies of how your culture has thrived so long with such unity.

My parents are filled with anticipation of our trip to Chile. They are physicians and my source of inspiration.

I love you with all my heart.

Jerrod

Jerrod booked the flight for the three of them to Santiago. He wrote William with flight number and arrival date and time. Jerrod tended his studies as time moved at a snail's pace.

The semester finally ended. Jerrod rode back to Fairmont with Mike and plans to purchase a car prior to next semester.

While Judy and Frank attend the wedding, a nurse friend will stay at their house. Things were falling in place for the big event.

William was waiting at the gate when Jerrod and his parents arrived at the Santiago Airport. Introductions were made and they crowded into William's small apartment the night prior to their trek to the village.

"I acquired a Chilean passport for Yaima's return with you to the United States," William said.

Raimondi's pack mules were loaded with books and mail for the village, as the travelers followed the scenic trail. Judy and Frank were overcome by the spectacle of the vista.

William alerted the village of arrival date and the entire village greeted them. The twins were the first greeters as they hugged Jerrod. The twins introduced themselves to Jerrod's parents and gave them similar pendants they gave Jerrod and Stephen upon their first meeting. Judy and Frank graciously thanked the twins.

Yaima introduced her parents to Judy and Frank. Everyone walked to the village and Jerrod and Yaima were hand in hand.

Jerrod and his parents will sleep in the school dorm. Yaima brought a sleeping pad, pillow and blanket since there were only two single beds. The wedding will be held in early afternoon at the bonfire-seating ring. After the ceremony, food will be served, followed by a celebration bonfire with folk dancing.

Prior to the wedding, Jerrod and his parents visited with Yaima's family to share meals and discuss plans for Yaima when she returns with them to the United States. Frank and Judy had questions about Mapuche life. They all took walks and showed Judy and Frank how the Mapuche forage for food in the forest and the electrical transmitter Jerrod and Stephen installed to pump water up the hillside to the village.

It was a pleasant time and the mix of American and Mapuche seized this unique opportunity.

"How many members are in your tribe?" Judy asked.

"We have seventy-five residents in the village and an additional thirty scattered in the vicinity. They'll all attend the wedding," Yaco Responded.

"Do you have an assigned chief or leader?" Frank asked.

"We don't have a specific chief. Quidel is our elder advisor and he'll perform the wedding ceremony. He's the wisest of our tribe. We rely on his wisdom and meet in union when important issues require discussion. Quidel leads meetings; however, tradition encourages tribal members to participate with thoughts and opinions. Quidel makes final decisions. This method has worked best in our culture since inception. We have few problems or complications," Yaco said.

Wedding day arrived and Jerrod and Yaima were required by tradition to remain separated until the ceremony. Jerrod will wear the colorful tunic given to him and Stephen as departure gifts during their first visit.

The ceremony is unlike typical American weddings where the father gives away the bride. Jerrod will stand next to Quidel. Yaima and her sister Suyia will walk together to join them. Quidel will perform the ceremony in Mapuche.

The seating was at capacity with many standing. The sisters entered wearing indigenous colorful dresses and their diamond heart necklaces.

Judy and Frank sat with Yaima's parents. The scene was like a mystical dream shared by those in attendance.

The ceremony was brief. Jerrod and Yaima kissed to seal their vows. Mapuche tradition includes the departure of newlyweds from the ceremony so they can walk in the forest. While they are gone, music and dancing will begin. Jerrod and Yaima discussed their love and exchanged thoughts of desires and hopes for their future during their wedding day woodland saunter.

When they returned, the dance circle had formed. Judy and Frank joined and were holding hands, dancing to the music provided by Yaco and Lilen's flutes while Suyia sang. Yaima and Jerrod joined hands with Jerrod's parents. Judy smiled with tears of joy in her eyes.

They danced and danced as the warmth and light from the bonfire formed a dreamlike ambience. The celebration was filled with mirth shared by partners from opposite cultural identities and this added a unique dimension to the event. Yaima's face glowed with incessant happiness in a display of vivacity on her special day.

It was late and the crowd began to disperse. Jerrod and Yaima retired to their designated newlywed residence as their journey took its first step as partners in life.

Judy and Frank wanted to learn about Mapuche food preparation. The two families gathered and prepared food for the remainder of their visit. They formed a wonderful friendship, as Judy and Frank shared Jerrod's love for Mapuche life. The Mapuche were intimate with nature's blessings. Firewood was gathered for heat and cooking. Water was carried each day in complete contrast to life in Pennsylvania.

"What're your specific plans when you return to the United States and college studies?" Yaco asked.

"We'll find an apartment near campus and I'll seek a tutor to expand Yaima's academic range. I'll assist her and eventually she'll take equivalency exams and the results of these exams will determine curriculum selections. As she progresses, alternatives may appear; we'll adjust accordingly.

"It's speculative at this point but priorities center on what's best for Yaima," Jerrod said.

"It'll be a much different life than she's accustomed; however, I have confidence in you both," Yaco said.

"William said our daughters have above average learning capacity. They are passionate readers; they especially love stories and have read literary classics," Lilen said.

"My conversations with Yaima open insight to her character. I could not be happier or more in love as I project our life together. We're firmly bonded and will lean on each other as we confront challenges," Jerrod said.

Judy and Frank thanked Yaco and Lilen for their hospitality.

Raimondi arrived with his mules to guide Judy, Frank and the young married couple. Yaima is leaving the only place she has ever known; yet she has complete trust in Jerrod.

In morning light, Jerrod and Yaima packed their few possessions and lashed them to the pack mules. Those remaining and those departing shed tears. Jerrod's emotions pulled from both directions: he knew he must leave yet yearned to remain. Return to the United States was their providence. Yaima tried to imagine what it would be like. Photos and reading offer a glimpse of American life, yet immersion into its social design is an event only perceived through personal assimilation. The future is unclear; however, these two are armed with the power of an intense love as their most valued tool to confront what lies ahead.

CHAPTER 11

AMERICA

It was near midnight as the flight approached Philadelphia. As the plane descended, city lights enthralled Yaima.

Yaima recently turned fifteen and her marriage to Jerrod thrusts her forward, distant from her Mapuche life.

Yaima was dressed in Mapuche indigenous clothing and Jerrod wore his Mapuche tunic.

As the plane touched down, Jerrod hugged Yaima and said, "Welcome to America my sweet, beautiful wife."

"I'd be less intrusive if I dressed in American fashion," Yaima said.

"I love your native dress; however, this could ease transition. I want to preserve memories of my Mapuche experience. We'll dress Mapuche style on occasion. It'll be fun to stir the cultural teapot and create opportunity to make new friends," Jerrod responded.

"I'd enjoy dressing in my native fashion on occasion. It rings a tone of honesty. People will ask where we're from," Yaima said.

On the drive home, Judy said, "I'm a changed person because of our visit with the Mapuche tribe. I'll view life from now onward differently.

"We're dictated by geographical placement. Being born and raised in America, we react to social configurations imposed during formative years. From observations of Mapuche culture, they position values in life from a different base. Industrialized countries create complexities within their socially fabricated, superficial standards as simplistic values of day to day living designs diminish. Food acquisition, shelter and human comforts are taken for granted. Shelter among the Mapuche is uniform as the primary purpose is to cope with natural elements. In contemporary society, shelter has moved beyond basic function as it has formed symbolism related to communal prominence flaunting affluence and imposes social class separation. We're a thermostat society, as we remain indoors if it's a bit too hot or too cold. We adjust our thermostats whereas the Mapuche adjust their minds. If we're hungry, we look for a drive thru and buy a bag of burgers. We breathe polluted air as we sit in traffic without the slightest thought of the ridiculous nature of these habits. We gather in darkened theatres and become bewitched by flickering images presenting drama to bathe in fantasy as an escape and deem it 'entertainment'. The Mapuche build bonfires and dance to flute music.

"In modern cultures, money centers everything and is prioritized to create a form of idolatry. We become enslaved by the power of money. Money is our autocrat. The Mapuche have no need for money; yet, Jerrod's transmitter is attached to money as it created a method to assist the Mapuche; at least, we feel it has. Questions appear. Is it advancement or loss to turn on a valve to access water as opposed to the need to carry it up the hillside? Various cultures speak in different voices and create a mix of defined and undefined balances, forming mystery to know exactly how, where and when chosen functions meld in beneficial fashions.

"I'm dedicated to assist Yaima in any manner I'm able. We're now part Mapuche and we'll never escape this reality."

As the travelers arrived home, Judy's friend and nurse colleague, Sandra, greeted them. Judy introduced Yaima to

Sandra and described the wedding and their experiences with the Mapuche tribe.

Yaima was in awe, overwhelmed by her new surroundings. Yaima had spent her entire life with her family, sharing a Mapuche tribal shelter which had no similarity to this luxurious home.

Judy and Frank prepared a celebratory return dinner and Sandra will remain overnight.

Jerrod showed Yaima his room and said, "This is where my earliest memories formed. Your being here is like a dream and the joy I feel at this moment could not be greater.

"I'll help you adjust, as you'll feel displaced. I love your place of origin and you eventually could love mine. Things have come suddenly, like driving up to my parent's house. In America, houses reflect social status.

"Our love and respect for each other is our strength and we'll lean on this as we progress."

During dinner, Judy said to Sandra, "We photographed the wedding and celebration. I've never felt collective love to such a level.

"Our hearts now reside in two places, as if we we've been given a transfusion of Mapuche blood."

"What a fabulous experience. Few Americans have knowledge of Mapuche culture. It's difficult to predict the limit your connection might create. This could have positive impact on your work. You'll share the experience with patients and those in your workplace. I'm fascinated and Yaima is a perfect example of her people and family," Sandra said.

The next day Jerrod used his parents' car and toured the area to show Yaima his high school.

He called Mike to invite him and Elaine for dinner to meet Yaima and discuss their future. Mike and Elaine arrived. Resident cooks Judy and Frank prepared a splendid meal.

"I'm pleased to meet you. Jerrod said you've been married recently," Yaima said.

"Likewise. Jerrod described your life in Chile. We'll socialize this coming semester. We plan to find an apartment near campus. Maybe we'll be neighbors. I love your dress; it's so colorful," Elaine responded.

"Jerrod will accompany me to acquire American style clothing; however, we plan to wear traditional Mapuche dress on occasion to maintain our cultural bond with historic Mapuche roots. I feel it's important to adjust to American society as much as possible.

"The night of my arrival, as we approached the airport, city lights signaled welcome. I'll never forget this moment. My marriage to Jerrod allows me to apply for American citizenship. I was born and raised in a round communal Mapuche dwelling with a cone shaped roof and fire pit for cooking and heat. My sister Suyia and I spent hours foraging for wild plants, nuts and berries to provide food for our family. We also gathered firewood and carried water. This is in stark contrast to American life. I could've never imagined a home such as this. It's so magnificent," Yaima said.

"Jerrod fell in love with you, yet Mapuche culture formed the base of his love. He spoke of your parents and how much they influenced him. I speculate your future could reattach to Mapuche life either at intervals or perhaps permanently. I'd love for us to rendezvous sometime at your village," Mike said.

"I'll buy a car and drive back to school. I'm thinking of a compact car; it'll be easier to drive and Yaima can take driver's education. I'll walk to and from classes to allow her mobility. After we find a suitable apartment, I'll place an ad for a tutor for Yaima to resume academic pursuits," Jerrod said.

Classes began in a week. The next day, Jerrod and Yaima went shopping for Yaima's American wardrobe. He also purchased his new car.

A letter arrived from Chang Yi.

Dear Jerrod,

We've expanded production again to serve the onslaught of orders for our system. Stephen has returned to the university. He'll visit again during next semester break. He's been of great value to our effort and made improvements to the transmitter and receptor designs. You'll see a spike in dividends.

I received a letter from Mike. He told me you both are married now, how you married a Mapuche girl you met during your first visit with Stephen to install their electrical transmitter system and the love bond intensified when you returned to install a second receptor to the village school. Your lives will reach new heights with loving partners.

I hope you and Mike will visit with your new wives in the near future. I'll make great effort to give you insight to China and its history.

You may be the most accomplished seventeen-year old on the planet. Your persistence to duplicate Tesla's concept as a portable device opened a floodgate none of us anticipated. Stephen is truly a genius and your connection cracked the door leading to where we've arrived. The Garrett/James electrical system appears to have no upper limit.

Write when you're able. I'd enjoy hearing details as your life moves to new plateaus.
Your friend and partner,
Chang Yi.

Jerrod shared Chang Yi's letter with Yaima, Judy and Frank.

"Can you imagine a young Mapuche girl visiting China? My parents and sister would be in disbelief to receive a letter from China," Yaima said.

"A Chinese doctor at the hospital was born and raised in a remote area of China and rose above his humble start in life to become an American physician. His story is quite amazing. China has moved forward over the past fifty years and they've developed a reputation for accomplishment," Judy said.

As time to return to school approached, Yaima had her American wardrobe, and Jerrod his new compact Chevrolet. Jerrod would enter his junior year at Duke University and maintain a 4.0 grade point average.

Yaima showed Judy and Frank her wardrobe. She was wearing one of the new dresses.

"You look American; although, I favor your native dress probably from our visit with the Mapuche. I agree, conformity will ease adjustment," Judy said.

The next morning, Jerrod and Yaima departed. Mike gave Jerrod the name and address of the apartment building where he and Elaine lived, as it may work for them too. It would be advantageous to live in the same apartment building.

Jerrod and Yaima hugged Judy and Frank and promised to write and call often.

CHAPTER 12

RETURN TO SCHOOL

It was a pleasant drive and Jerrod enjoyed time alone with Yaima.

They stayed the first night at a motel. The next day, they located the apartment building where Mike and Elaine plan to live.

They entered the rental office. The woman at the desk said they had a vacant one bedroom furnished apartment available and showed them this apartment. Yaima and Jerrod agreed it would be ideal. They moved in with their few belongings. It was a new adventure and their first home. Small, yet clean and well maintained.

Jerrod used the lobby phone to call Mike. "Mike, this is Jerrod. We found the apartment building you suggested and rented a one bedroom furnished apartment. When will you and Elaine arrive?"

"Good news. We'll leave in the morning. We'll be in apartment ten on the second floor."

"We're in fourteen. See you soon," Mike said.

Jerrod took Yaima on a campus tour and they had lunch at the student union.

"I'll put an ad in the school newspaper for a tutor. I'm uncertain of the most beneficial curriculum, yet I'm so happy you are with me," Jerrod said.

"I'll write a letter to my family tonight," Yaima said.

"You should use my camera to photograph the campus and where we live. Your parents and sister would enjoy this," Jerrod said.

"I'm excited about the tutor. I'd like to study English literature and creative writing. It's my dream to become a published writer. Suyia and I are passionate readers; we especially adore novels," Yaima said.

Mike and Elaine arrived and the four friends went to dinner.

"We're now juniors. I'll receive my bachelor's degree in business administration in another year. Elaine is on track for a degree in psychology. It causes thoughts of our future," Mike said.

"The future is a mystery and we'll be tested beyond academics. We're fortified by friends like Jerrod and Yaima," Elaine said.

"I'll continue with premed to attain a bachelor's degree in biology, and then enter medical school. Yaima's presence is my strength," Jerrod said.

Yaima sent a letter to her family.

Dear beloved family,

I don't know where to begin. As our flight approached the Philadelphia Airport, city lights filled my window in a dazzling welcome spectacle. It felt as if I was visiting another planet.

Frank picked up their car parked in long-term parking and drove us to their home in Fairmont, Pennsylvania. During the drive, Judy described her Mapuche experience as a life-changing event. Her words were a tribute to Mapuche culture.

Their home is magnificent and so large. We have mealtime discussions and Jerrod took me to a woman's clothing store to purchase American style clothing. This was my suggestion, as I felt it important to blend with American culture. Jerrod wants us to dress Mapuche style on occasion just for fun and to maintain my Mapuche roots.

We're living in an apartment near Duke University campus. Jerrod will locate a tutor and asked me what specific curriculum I would like. I told him I'd enjoy creative writing.

Jerrod purchased a compact car and I'll take a driver's education course to gain personal mobility. Jerrod walks to classes each day.

Jerrod's best friend Mike was recently married to Elaine and they live in the same apartment building. Elaine and Mike are a joy to share company.

We'll soon be married again, American style. Jerrod's parents will attend our wedding, as will Mike and Elaine. It'll be an informal wedding at the university chapel and the school chaplain will perform the ceremony. This allows me American citizenship.

I miss my Mapuche life and hope to return for a visit during Jerrod's semester breaks. I love you with all my heart, as I do Jerrod.
Love,
Yaima

Jerrod returned to routine walks and Yaima joined him. He played Mapuche folk songs on his flute among the grove of spruce trees and Yaima sang Mapuche lyrics. Students gathered to enjoy this unusual serenade. Some asked about the music's origin and Jerrod described his experience with Mapuche culture and introduced Yaima as his Mapuche wife. Students were fascinated and the number attending expanded as Yaima's beauty and pure voice formed a magnetic attraction, resulting in new friendships.

One day, the school's newspaper editor happened by and introduced herself.

"Hello. I'm Virginia Easterbrook, the editor of the school newspaper *The Blue Devil Gazette,* and I want to feature you two and your story in the next edition. This is too fascinating to ignore. I'd like to take your photograph to include with the article."

Jerrod and Yaima agreed. The editor took their photograph and scheduled an interview at the newspaper's office.

They met with Virginia and outlined their history and eventual marriage. The article stirred more interest than anticipated, and as time neared each day for Jerrod and Yaima's routine walk, a student audience formed near the spruce grove.

Students lacked knowledge of Mapuche culture and asked about Mapuche history. Jerrod and Yaima answered questions.

Virginia called Jerrod, "Jerrod, I've received student comments expressing how much they enjoy your music and the purity of Yaima's voice. She's exceptionally beautiful.

"This Saturday at six, the Student Union presents open mike night. Students are encouraged to perform music and recite poetry. I'd like you and Yaima to consider presenting Mapuche folk music."

"We'll attend. I agree, Yaima is beautiful; she is even more attractive in colorful native dress. When she arrived in our country she decided to adopt American fashion to blend with our society. I suggested on special occasions she reverts to indigenous dress. Your invitation creates this opportunity.

"As I came to know her during my assignment in Chile I became captivated and completely smitten.

"Yaima's native dress adds cultural identity. Yaima also knows Mapuche folk dances, and I learned these dances during my work at their village. Folk dancing is exhilarating. The Mapuche frequently have celebratory bonfires and dance to flute music. The dances are performed in a circle holding hands and this configuration forms a collective social bond. The bonfire, music and dancing meld in communal connection like nothing I've ever experienced.

"As the school's newspaper editor, you could introduce Mapuche folk dancing. Yaima could teach these dances to select students as a demonstration to stimulate interest and share something unique from an ancient culture. From student reaction to our music, possibly even greater impact would result from Mapuche folk dances," Jerrod said.

"I'll see what I can arrange. I'll attend open mike night to hear your folk music presentation. It'll be great fun," Virginia said.

Jerrod received a phone call in response to his ad to solicit a tutor for Yaima.

"Hello. My name is Mary Joyce. I'm a retired English literature professor. I taught at the university for thirty years. I'd like to meet with you and the prospective pupil to discuss my tutorial service."

"Thanks for calling. I'm married to a gifted young Mapuche woman who's been educated by a Mormon missionary where she was raised in Chile, at a remote Mapuche tribal village. She's fluent in English, taught by the missionary assigned to assist the tribe. I met her in Chile during a project related to the installation of a revolutionary electrical power production device. She's advanced academically, yet I'm reluctant for her to attend public school because the adjustment would be difficult and subject her to negative conditions because of her heritage. I speculate she'd perform well on an academic placement test. She's been a passionate reader from an early age, with a desire to pursue creative writing.

"I'm a junior at Duke in premed. After I get my bachelor's degree in biological science, I'll enter the four-year medical school program. We can meet at your convenience," Jerrod responded.

"I'm a widow and live at 1270 Mulberry Lane, apartment 25; it is near campus. Stop by anytime, I'm here most of the day, as I'm currently writing a novel. My phone number is 346-1374. I look forward to our meeting," Mary said.

"We'll visit with you sometime in the next few days," Jerrod said.

Jerrod and Yaima drove to the Student Union on Saturday night. Yaima looked spectacular in her brilliant red and earth tone Mapuche dress and Jerrod wore his Mapuche tunic. Yaima wore her hair in a single braid, as she wore it at her native village. Several poets read poems and a classical guitarist played a piece. Jerrod and Yaima stepped onto the stage and the audience applauded, as they were recognized from their spruce grove folk music.

They presented a song and Yaima's voice was even more elegant, as it was acoustically enhanced. Jerrod's flute was also amplified.

The audience enthusiastically applauded and Virginia stepped to the microphone, "Yaima is a Mapuche from Chile and was raised in a remote village. Jerrod met Yaima when he installed an electrical system to drive water using an electric pump, as the village had no access to electric power. A year later, Jerrod returned to the village and married Yaima. After her marriage to Jerrod she'll apply for American citizenship. Jerrod is a junior in the university's premed program.

"Yaima knows Mapuche folk songs and native folk dances. I plan to organize an opportunity for Yaima and Jerrod to teach Mapuche folk dances to those interested and this might develop into something culturally beneficial. I'm open for suggestions and, for those interested to assist with this project, stop by my office and we'll discuss possibilities," Virginia said.

The open mike session ended and many remained to speak with Yaima and Jerrod about folk dances. It was a warm sensation to intermingle with students, as they complimented Yaima's voice and magnificent dress. Yaima projected beauty and love naturally.

The American marriage will take place in one week and Judy, Frank, Mike and Elaine said they would attend.

They returned to their apartment after the open mike performance. Jerrod said, "Let's make tea."

As they enjoyed their tea, Jerrod handed Yaima a small box. Yaima opened the box and a beautiful one-carat diamond solitaire ring sparkled in the light.

"You're in America and you mentioned our wedding protocol will follow American cultural format. This is your engagement ring and we'll share wedding bands when we're married for the second time. I wanted you to have an engagement ring prior to our wedding," Jerrod said.

Yaima looked at Jerrod as tears formed in her eyes. She hugged Jerrod and said, "It's so beautiful. I'd love you just as much without this ring, yet your thoughtful character traits couldn't resist giving me this gift. I'll cherish this moment the remainder of my life. I love you more than I could ever describe."

The next day, Jerrod and Yaima visited Mary Joyce to discuss Yaima's tutoring. Mary is in her early sixties and her apartment was nicely arranged and bookshelves covered two walls.

She greeted them, "I'm so pleased to meet you, come in and we'll discuss details. I'm excited to teach Yaima. I miss my teaching days. I spend so much time alone, tutoring will fill a personal void."

Mary made coffee and they sat at her kitchen table.

"How do you suggest we begin?" Jerrod asked.

"I've tutored others and the notion of an evaluation test may not be the best approach. I suggest presenting Yaima with a few previous lesson plans from my teaching years to see how she responds.

"I'm most fascinated about her desire to become a creative writer and feel, because of her special circumstances, this may be the best manner to approach academic pursuit. Why bother with math and science studies when her personal ambition is creative writing? For her to enter public school and spend years bogged down in irrelevant course study would be counterproductive. I'm a published writer, former English literature professor and positioned to offer Yaima the most value through application of my specialty as a tutor, which aligns with her personal desire.

"You'll become a physician and Yaima won't be required to produce income and this circumstance would offer freedom to stimulate her creative mind," Mary said.

"It's a good starting point, and I agree Yaima has natural advantages to pursue her ambition. I'm eager for Yaima to move toward her desired goal. What do you think Yaima?" Jerrod asked.

"It's the proper path. I want to become proficient as a creative writer and I'm not interested in unrelated academic course study," Yaima said.

Mary gave Yaima a textbook and said, "We'll begin with this basic study course, which involves discussion on writing format plus proper sentence structure and word selection. Passive voice sentences should be avoided and are often not easily recognized. I'll assign lessons based upon critical elements to achieve smooth delivery and reading ease. We'll advance slowly to more complex writing styles and variations."

An agreement was established. Jerrod and Yaima respected Mary's obvious professionalism.

After the wedding, Yaima would dedicate herself to literary academic pursuits.

The wedding day arrived. The small group of friends and family gathered to witness the American legal union of Jerrod and Yaima.

Yaima wore her native dress and Jerrod his Mapuche tunic for the ceremony. Yaima wore her diamond heart necklace everyday and its brilliance complimented her colorful native dress.

Mike and Elaine drove together. Frank and Judy chauffeured Jerrod and Yaima to the campus chapel.

The campus chaplain, Reverend Johnson, welcomed the wedding party and presented a brief description of what will occur, primarily for Yaima's comfort.

The vows were shared, rings exchanged and all sealed with a kiss. No bonfire or folk dancing this time; nonetheless, these two young adventurers cleared yet another hurdle in life.

They thanked the chaplain and invited him to attend folk dance lessons once they were arranged.

They celebrated at a nearby restaurant honoring this formal American union.

"I love being here as we commemorate our final ceremonial connection, yet I yearn for a bonfire and folk dancing," Jerrod said.

"Me too. I hope the school newspaper editor will find a method to introduce Mapuche folk dancing to university students. Can you imagine the fun they'll have once they are exposed to this dancing? This will put Yaima in the spotlight and create cultural attachment with university students. Maybe we can attend the dances on occasion if the school allows time and place for weekly dances. Things open out of nowhere, exemplified by how students became infatuated as they gathered at the spruce grove to listen to the Yaima and Jerrod's music," Judy said.

Jerrod walked to classes and drove Yaima to her first lessons assigned from her tutor Mary.

Yaima will take drivers' education course; when she passes her driver's test, she'll drive to Mary's house to continue studies. In the meantime, Jerrod will taxi her.

Virginia Easterbrook called Jerrod to inform him of developments toward promotion of Mapuche folk dancing and said, "Ten students stopped by to discuss finding time and space to allow you and Yaima to instruct them to learn Mapuche folk dancing. There's a small, seldom used gymnasium on campus. It's available as a place to teach and organize folk dancing one night a week.

"I contacted the school's music director to inquire if a music student flute player would be interested to learn Mapuche folk music. She said she'd ask if they're interested," Virginia said.

"I'd love to work with a student flutist to learn Mapuche folk songs. I have a book Yaima gave me with musical notes for ten different songs. Let me know if you connect with an interested student musician," Jerrod said.

Jerrod was enthusiastic about this breakthrough.

A week passed and a young woman from Ghana on a student exchange visa called Jerrod. Her name was Rana Rabbani and she occupied first chair in the flute section of the university's orchestra. She has played the flute since childhood and mastered the ancient pan flute. Rana enjoyed playing her pan flute, yet she was seldom given an opportunity. Jerrod arranged a time to meet her.

Yaima accompanied Jerrod to meet Rana. After introductions, Rana said, "I'm so excited about the possibility of playing my pan flute for your folk dance sessions. I'm appreciative and pleased to meet you two. I've heard about your impromptu folk music at the grove of spruce trees on campus."

Jerrod gave Rana the Mapuche folk music book so she could practice the songs with her pan flute.

They took Rana to the student union for lunch and she described her childhood in Ghana. Rana was a tall, beautiful, dark skinned African with a lighthearted demeanor and a dedicated classical musician.

During lunch, Yaima said, "Let's arrange a date to rehearse. We'll allow you time to memorize the songs and drive you to our apartment for rehearsal."

"I'll only need a day or two. I read music well," Rana said.

A few days later, Rana called and Yaima answered. Rana said, "I'm ready to rehearse."

"Good. We'll pick you up in a few minutes," Yaima said.

Rana's pan flute resonates with a natural clean tone. It's an ancient instrument; only the drum is older.

Jerrod and Rana played as a duet and Yaima sang. The flutes blended perfectly with the purity of Yaima's voice. The three musicians felt accomplished.

"I love singing accompanied by two flutes. It adds quality to the presentation. The pan flute has a crisper tone than the Mapuche flute.

"I feel we're ready to teach Mapuche folk dancing. During instruction, Rana can play solo and we'll dance to her music to allow us to demonstrate dance steps. Once student dancers gain proficiency, I'll sing and Jerrod will join Rana as a duet. It'll be great fun. This will bring mixed cultural musical expression to the university," Yaima said.

As they drove Rana back to her dorm, Yaima said, "It's interesting how opportunities appear. It makes me wonder what's next."

"Much of what's happened is related to the university's combined social setting. We have a mix of ethnic youth within an academic environment and this opens cultural opportunities associated with music and the arts. Foreign students like Rana are contributors. This blend is commonplace at institutions of higher learning. Folk music and dance highlights diversity's importance," Jerrod said.

"Throughout the world cultures develop their own folk dance styles. In Ghana we have folk music and dances distinctive to our country," Rana said.

Virginia called, and Jerrod answered. "Jerrod, this is Virginia, and I've secured the gymnasium to begin instruction for ten volunteer dance students. We have five girls and five boys to form a demonstration team to promote Mapuche folk dance night. I'll publish an article to promote folk dance night and post notices to stimulate interest. How did Rana perform at the practice session?"

"She played her pan flute and was incredible. She's an accomplished musician, a true pleasure to be with.

"Folk dancing is destined to gain popularity. It'll be exciting to witness," Jerrod said.

Yaima begins driver's education next week. Jerrod will continue to drive her to Mary's house until she passes her drivers exam.

The folk dance demonstration team met three nights to learn and practice dances. It was obvious these students were enjoying themselves. Jerrod and Yaima taught dances while Rana provided music with her pan flute.

During the evening, while Jerrod was working on studies, Yaima wrote a letter to her family.

Dear Family,

We're doing so well. We developed a daily habit of Jerrod playing his Mapuche flute as I sing Mapuche folk songs among a grove of spruce trees on the campus and a student audience formed.

With the assistance of the editor of the school's newspaper, we've secured a small gymnasium to teach Mapuche folk dancing. The intention is to stimulate enough interest to hold weekly dances open to anyone who desires to learn Mapuche folk dancing.

I also have a personal tutor, Mary Joyce, a retired university English literature professor. I'm learning creative writing techniques. It was my chosen subject to pursue. I'm also taking driver's education to obtain my driver's license so I can drive to and from Mary's house for learning sessions.

So much has happened so quickly. I fall asleep at night wondering what the next day will bring.

I think of you each day and look forward to your letters. I was apprehensive about my ability to adjust to American culture, yet I have come full circle and enjoy blending with American way of life.
I love you so much.
Yaima

A date was established for the first invitational Mapuche folk dance instruction. Mike and Elaine attended along with the basketball cheerleader team. They are accomplished dancers and eager to learn Mapuche folk dancing.

Yaima, Jerrod and Rana provided Mapuche folk music from a portable stage. Virginia will feature the event as the lead story in the next edition of the school's newspaper.

Demonstration dancers will dance the first dance with music as those attending learn from observing. Twenty interested couples showed up. After the demonstration dance, Yaima instructed the new dancers to form a circle as she and

Jerrod taught steps slowly without music to allow participants to memorize the chosen dance. They performed several silent runs.

Yaima and Jerrod returned to the stage. Music began and dancers responded. They did really well. The cheerleader team caught on immediately and others followed their lead. The dance ended and everyone clapped with joy. The mood was joyous, causing smiles to appear on the dancer's faces.

Elaine approached Yaima, "Your voice is magnificent. It blends perfectly with the beautiful flute music. Our cheerleading team had a wonderful time dancing Mapuche style."

"I'm now aware of what Judy felt as she described her emotions attached to Mapuche folk dances during the wedding celebration in Chile," Mike said.

"This has been so much fun," Elaine responded.

Jerrod said to Mike, "Can you imagine how Sarah would've enjoyed this event? I felt her spirit as I played my flute.

"Yaima is the love of my life. My eyes water as her beauty is enhanced in her native dress and her voice resonates with such purity."

Mike, Elaine, Rana, Jerrod and Yaima went to a nearby restaurant to celebrate the success of the university's first Mapuche folk dance night.

"Football and basketball fans have bonfire pep rallies; maybe the organizers of these rallies would be interested to include Mapuche folk dances. It would form a similar atmosphere to Judy's description of Yaima and Jerrod's Mapuche wedding celebration," Mike said.

"It'd add excitement to the rally. I'll ask Virginia to contact rally organizers to test their reaction. We'd gain exposure and garner increased interest in folk dancing. What a good time this would be," Jerrod said.

"I'm eager to write my parents to describe what's occurred," Yaima said.

Things fell back to routine. Yaima passed her driver's test. She became the primary driver as Jerrod resumed walking to and from classes.

Yaima enjoyed her creative writing studies with Mary and took her to lunch frequently. Her husband Jack was also a professor at the university. She conveyed how grand those years were.

During lunch, Yaima said, "I'd like to write an article for the school newspaper about my life in a Mapuche village. I miss my family so much and look forward to our visit during semester break."

"I agree, this would expose knowledge of Mapuche culture. Few students or faculty know of Mapuche culture. I'll consider your article a lesson assignment to be included in your student achievement portfolio," Mary said.

Elaine encouraged Yaima to attend a basketball game, as she had never heard of the game. Jerrod described it and they scheduled time to watch a home game.

Yaima enjoyed watching Elaine perform with the cheerleading team. She was unaware of America's intense attachment to sports.

After the game, they went to Mike and Elaine's apartment for tea and conversation. Mike described Jerrod's participation in the statewide free throw competition in high school and how he lost in the final match up with Sarah.

"I fell in love with Sarah, and when she was killed in the auto crash, I never realized such pain and grief existed.

"Love epitomizes the value and purpose of life. The pain from this loss was a dark day in my life.

"I could never love anyone more than I love Yaima. It's my hope we'll share long lives and cherish each day. As Sarah told me the last time I saw her, 'We're only at the starting line of life.' I've never forgotten her words and they relate to Yaima and I. However, as I reminisce about Sarah's sagacious smile, it's also a reality: we approach a new starting line each morning of our lives. Our time at the university will form lasting memories.

"I yearn to visit my Mapuche friends. We'll depart for Santiago as soon as semester break arrives," Jerrod said.

"I enjoyed the basketball game and the story about Jerrod and Sarah. I'll describe my time in America to my family when we return," Yaima said.

Jerrod and Yaima departed to their apartment. They loved their small apartment and, no matter how far they wander, this space will represent their *"starting line"*.

The friends returned to school routines and folk dancing became a weekly event. The dancers and the flute/vocal trio continued their performances through the semester period. Numbers attending dances nearly doubled.

As semester break neared, Jerrod secured airline tickets to Santiago. He informed William by letter of their arrival date and time. They planned to drive their new car and park it in long term parking at the Philadelphia airport. They will visit Judy and Frank for a few days prior to departure. Jerrod purchased a mountain bike for Yaima and, while they waited for departure, he taught Yaima to ride her bike and venture on nearby trails. He knew Yaima missed the forest and its magnificence.

CHAPTER 13

HOMECOMING

During their final evening meal before departure, Yaima said, "I have photographs of my American experience to share with family members. These photos record my time in America. I'll do my best to describe the experience, yet words lack clarity of what occurred.

"Prior to arrival, I tried to imagine what American life would be like based on reading and photos, yet the experience exceeded my visualizations. America is a wondrous place. We plan to base our lives at my Mapuche village home to benefit the Mapuche and simultaneously benefit ourselves. We have years remaining for Jerrod to attain his medical degree and I'll be at his side throughout his journey. I'm positioned to gain from this through connection with my personal tutor Mary Joyce, as she has become a close friend and mentor. I have a quest of my own and Mary is my guide. She's a retired English literature professor and published writer. Through Mary's connection, I hope to fulfill a personal ambition to create and write a novel of my own. I love stories and literature.

"We won't impose American culture on the Mapuche people; however, through sharing American ways, they'll gain broader perception of this vast country, as I have from my experience."

"Our trip to Chile and connection with your family allows us to relate. The future is unknown, yet a worthy plan exposes options to serve as waypoints," Judy said.

"We've observed Jerrod's development and realize his potential is limitless. We've performed respectfully as parents to form a base for his life. Finding you at one of the most remote places on our planet is a miracle. You'll serve as Jerrod's main support.

"During college years, I became engrossed with philosophy and how it plays on the human experience. Jerrod's life reminds me of a quote by an eighteenth century philosopher Alexander Pope: *'As the twig is bent, so grows the tree.'* Jerrod is an example of Pope's reference," Frank said.

After breakfast, Jerrod and Yaima prepared to depart. They hugged Judy and Frank, bidding them farewell on the front porch of their home. As they drove away Frank reminisced, "Remember when Jerrod was learning to talk? His first words were 'hello' and 'goodbye'. I look forward to saying hello again. What a magnificent couple."

"I wish we were going with them," Judy said.

On Yaima's arrival to the United States, she was apprehensive. On her return to Chile, apprehension was absent.

"I know you're looking forward to reuniting with your parents. I am too.

"We accomplished a lot since our arrival to America. I love America; it's the most diverse country in the world and this is most significant reason for its range of success. We can find regions in America equal in beauty as the Mapuche village or complex metropolitan zones plagued with urban noise, clutter and polluted air.

"I can't identify exactly why I fell in love with your village. It's related to when Stephen and I worked together to install electrical energy. This experience caused an indefinable attachment. My time spent at the village with your family transformed me," Jerrod said.

"It's unimportant how you became attracted to our style of life; however, I'm overjoyed you feel as you do. Our love bond is spiritually attached. I'm excited to describe my life in America and show photos," Yaima said.

As they disembarked at Santiago International Airport, William was waiting, as usual. Yaima was dressed in Mapuche fashion and Jerrod wore his tunic.

They trekked the trail with William and Raimondi, the pack mule guide, with his team to the village. Upon arrival, Suyia ran to greet them, followed by Yaco and Lilen. As they hugged each other, it was an emotional reunion.

The tribe crowded into the school.

Yaima spoke, "I couldn't be happier than I am at this moment. My experience with Jerrod in America was like a magical dream. It was remarkable, yet my heart and soul live at our beautiful village in the Chilean highlands, nestled among infinite splendor.

"I've continued my education guided by a gifted woman. My tutor, Mary Joyce, is a retired university professor. I looked forward to daily lessons as Mary guided me through the intricate maze of creative expression. Mary taught English literature at Duke University prior to retirement. It's my good fortune to be given this opportunity. My ambition is to become a published writer.

"I adjusted and learned to navigate American social complexities, as the activities of daily life are vigorously engaged.

"Mapuche society is less intense and our compatibility with the terrestrial biosphere provides fulfillment with a higher sense of purpose and direction."

William addressed the tribe, "We'll have a celebratory bonfire tomorrow evening; now, I'd like everyone to follow me."

The tribe followed William to a wooded section on the fringe of the village. They approached a newly constructed round Mapuche dwelling.

"Tribal members contributed to construct this dwelling as Jerrod and Yaima's new home in the village they love," William said.

Yaima broke into tears as Jerrod hugged her. Yaima's parents and sister beamed with delight while the tribe cheered Jerrod and Yaima.

"We plan to visit our new home as often as we're able and, after I complete my education, we'll become permanent residents. I eagerly await the arrival of that day. We're grateful for your thoughtfulness and will never forget this loving moment," Jerrod said.

The next day, Yaima and Jerrod gathered firewood and foraged for edible plants. Yaima instructed Jerrod in plant identification and there are communal fish traps along the riverbank. The Mapuche works in cohesive unity as a reflection of their historic tribal legacy.

As dusk descended, the tribe gathered at the hewn log seating area to celebrate the return of Yaima and Jerrod. Yaco and Lilen provided flute music and Suyia sang folksongs for dancers.

Mapuche life requires intense physical effort to cope with nature's challenges and bonfires offer repose. Dancing forms an exuberant mood.

Music started and the dance circle formed as dancers moved in the firelight to create a natural ambience.

Jerrod remembered the university folk dances as his mind projected images of student dancers with smiling faces. He envisioned them sharing the wholesome purity of Mapuche unity in the glimmering light of the bonfire as they emulate the legacy of Mapuche ancestors.

Jerrod and Yaima returned to their new home, weary from a busy day and night of celebration.

The next morning, Jerrod built a fire and made tea. It was a peaceful time and the long sleep refreshed them.

"I have an idea. It's been on my mind for quite awhile. I waited to discuss it until I organized thoughts.

"It's about your sister Suyia. During next semester break, I plan to arrange a trip to China and visit Chang Yi. He's offered to be our tour guide and we'll learn about China's long and interesting history. This will be an unforgettable and valuable experience. My thought is to have Suyia come to America to live with us for a time and share our visit to China. We can move into a two-bedroom apartment and Mary can tutor Suyia also.

"Suyia can return to Chile with us on our next trip and she's welcome to return whenever she desires. What do you think of this?" Jerrod asked.

"I'd love it. She could join our folkdance group and meet interesting new friends. It would enhance her education and, if she gets homesick, we'll fly her home for visits. I'm very close with Suyia. I missed her so much. We'll present this to Suyia and my parents," Yaima said.

Yaima and Jerrod invited Suyia, Yaco and Lilen for the evening meal and Yaima planned to present Jerrod's proposal as that time.

Jerrod and Yaima prepared the meal.

Afterwards, Yaima said, "We want Suyia to return with us to America and remain for a while to gain insight to American culture. We'll support her in every manner. The length of her visit depends on her feelings. We're equal academically and she'll share my course study, presented by Mary Joyce. She'll love Mary and it'll open new dimensions to her life.

"She'll mingle socially with students during weekly Mapuche folk dancing and we'll sing Mapuche folk songs as a duet."

"We live in a one bedroom apartment but we'll move into a two bedroom apartment so Suyia will have a room of her own. During next semester break, we plan to visit China where my business associate, Chang Yi, owns a manufacturing facility and builds wireless transmitters and receptors. He's become a close friend and will serve as our guide to tour China and teach China's long history. This represents an opportunity of a lifetime.

"The downside is I'm aware how attached you are to your daughters and it's important for this bond to be retained; however, it can possibly be enhanced from exposure to different cultures," Jerrod said.

"The twins have made our lives complete and they mean everything to us. Your proposal is considerate and offers Suyia worthy options. Knowing she can return when she desires reduces concern for her welfare and happiness. It'll be a difficult adjustment, as it has been with Yaima; however, parents are responsible to allow children to follow their own paths when favorable options appear.

"I predict Yaima and Suyia will never lose their love for our village and Mapuche life. No matter how far they venture or how much they learn of other cultures, they'll ultimately return to our village, as you and Yaima express this desire," Yaco said.

"I agree with Yaco. If we're too possessive, it blocks personal development, as we've learned from Yaima's time in America. We'll miss her terribly; however, knowing this opportunity will expand her life and her absence is temporary reduces anxiety. I'm in support of what's best for Suyia," Lilen said.

"I feel a pull in both directions and a sense of uncertainty, yet the excitement of visiting America and China diminishes apprehension. Having Yaima and Jerrod for support could not be a better situation. I want to do it," Suyia said.

William departed the next day to acquire Suyia's passport. When he returns, he will have her passport to travel to the United States.

Suyia was filled with excitement as she makes a significant turn on the path of life.

William returned. He called the airlines and added Suyia to Jerrod and Yaima's flight from Santiago to Philadelphia. He then gave Suyia her passport. As departure neared, the three travelers shared meals with Yaco and Lilen.

"I can only imagine the new life Suyia will discover in America.

"I've studied American history and it describes how the country was founded from immigration mostly from Central Europe and their revolution to escape British monarchy rule. As the country became independent, plantations expanded by using slave labor and exploiting captured African natives sold into slavery. The American president Andrew Jackson was a horrid person who owned many slaves. Cherokee Native Americans thrived and functioned for over one thousand years. They acquired land and prospered in a communal and harmonious fashion. Jackson seized their land and ordered American army troops to round up the entire tribe and forced them to march one thousand miles to be confined on a reservation in Oklahoma. Over six thousand Cherokee died of starvation or thirst during this march, historically recorded as The Trail of Tears. This formed an indelible black mark on the Anglo American established government and culture. The Cherokee's lands were sold to wealthy plantation owners to expand their wealth on the backs of captive African slaves.

"When they built the transcontinental rail system, Anglo European immigrants provided labor to install rails across the country. When the laborious task came to lay rails over the Rocky Mountains, the Anglo European immigrants walked off the job because of the extreme physical challenge. The railroad then hired Chinese laborers to finish this daunting task. Chinese immigrants completed the Transcontinental Railroad.

"America is considered the most successful country; however, it is not without historic flaws as a nation. Genocide formed the foundation of the country," Yaco said.

"Discrimination remains in modern times. American history books downplay events like the Trail of Tears and the horrors of slavery.

"I feared Yaima would become a victim of discrimination, yet this hasn't appeared. Duke University has a diverse student body and higher learning institutions embrace racial and ethnic identities.

"The human species is in dire need to advance from the perception discriminatory social control and dominance have worth. Warfare never yields solution, yet has been attached to humanity for over ten thousand years. Early hunter gatherer tribes were widely spread geographically; this civil design reduced the tendency of war to develop. Land was not owned. Borders were not defined and government control had yet to be imposed.

"Mapuche culture avoided negative aspects of modern society. As I worked with William and Stephen during our first visit, I became inspired by Mapuche life," Jerrod said.

"Mary assigned me to read a book on America's historic slavery era. I'll write a composition paper on this subject. The

American Civil War erupted because the American southern states were reliant on African slave labor to sustain fiscal success attached to southern agriculture. Slavery was motivated by the quest for money. Northern states were anti slavery and pressed politically to abolish slavery viewed as immoral. The South lost the civil war and, in 1863, President Abraham Lincoln signed the Emancipation Proclamation which freed slaves from bondage. This event sparked change in American culture and, even though African born slaves gained freedom, racism remained, causing social disruption extending to modern times. Southern whites treated freed blacks horribly and they were isolated, viewed as substandard humans with low-level mental functions. This has long since been denounced yet the sentiment lingers in American society, especially among southern white people. African Americans now occupy every level of accomplishment shared by those of Anglo white Europeans heritage and every other ethnic and racially identified classification.

"Jerrod plays his flute for our school folk dancing group and we invited a second flute player to join him to add dimension to our Mapuche folk dances. The school's newspaper editor introduced us to Rana from Ghana. Rana occupies the first chair in the flute section of the Duke University Orchestra. She studied the Mapuche folk music book William gifted me and memorized the music. Rana is an advanced classical musician. In addition, Rana plays the ancient pan flute and uses this instrument during our dances. Rana's pan flute has a unique tone and the two flutes blend magnificently. Rana is my only African friend and I love her so much. She amazes me. Racial or ethnic profiling in an attempt to degrade a person is socially counterproductive.

"Suyia will join me to sing Mapuche native folk songs, as her voice is a duplicate of mine. We'll form a duet, accompanied by Jerrod and Rana. What a thrill this will be. We'll dress Mapuche style for performances. I love to dress Mapuche style and our dance group enjoys this, as it defines my heritage. I sing lyrics in English; however, a member of the dance group suggested I sing in Mapuche. When Suyia joins me, we'll sing folk songs in Mapuche on occasion to attach ethnicity to the songs.

"I speculate, with our support, Suyia will have the time of her life during her American experience," Yaima said.

"I feel positive emotions about Suyia's adventure to America and possibly China. I'll miss her so much; however, she shouldn't be denied this opportunity. We'll look forward to her letters," Lilen said.

The next morning, Jerrod, Yaima and Suyia planned to depart with William, Raimondi and his pack mules. William was going to drive them to Santiago for their flight to Philadelphia.

The goodbye rituals get more difficult each time. With Suyia's departure, the level of emotion was raised again.

Hugs and tears dominated the scene; Mapuche twins moved onto the trail and were soon out of sight.

Yaco and Lilen returned to their village home to continue their lives without their precious twins.

Yaima and Suyia remained dressed Mapuche style during their flight to America.

CHAPTER 14

RETURN TO AMERICA

As they waited to board their flight, Jerrod thanked William and said, "We're grateful for your support. How long will you remain at your present status with the Mormon Church?"

"No timetable is established. I was married for ten years. My wife Jean and I worked as missionaries in Africa. Jean died from breast cancer and the loss devastated me. I committed to the Mapuche and have never regretted one moment of my time with this tribe. I don't have an answer to your question. Mormon elders know how attached I am to this tribe; I doubt they'll reassign me," William said.

The twins hugged William and boarded their flight.

Jerrod shook William's hand and said, "I respect your accomplishments to assist the Mapuche. We'll unite to add magnitude to the Mapuche's lives and ours."

Suyia had a window seat and her eyes were glued to the window as the plane became airborne.

Yaima said to Suyia, "I know your thoughts. I felt the same on my first trip to America. It's overwhelming."

129

As they approached the Philadelphia International Airport, Suyia was in awe of the city lights, as Yaima was upon her arrival.

Jerrod retrieved his car from long term parking. He drove them to his parent's house. They will stay two nights and planned to return to campus after their visit. Classes begin in a week; before they begin, Jerrod and Yaima will check if a two-bedroom apartment is available where they presently live. Suyia will sleep on the couch until they find more spacious living arrangements.

Judy and Frank were surprised to see Suyia with Jerrod and Yaima.

"What a pleasant surprise. You brought Suyia. This will be fun," Judy said.

"The problem I'll have is recognition. I've never seen such identical twins. Welcome to America," Frank said.

"It was Jerrod's idea and, after discussing it with our parents, we agreed it would allow Suyia to experience American life. Mary Joyce will tutor us.

"Suyia's singing voice is the duplicate of mine. We'll form a duet to sing Mapuche folksongs, occasionally with Mapuche lyrics. I'm so excited and feel our performances will become more popular with the addition of my sister. Jerrod and Rana will accompany us to enhance our voices. It'll be so special," Yaima said.

Judy showed Suyia their home and the room where she will sleep.

"Yaima sent photographs of your home. It's more spectacular in reality. I appreciate your kindness," Suyia said.

"The social contrast from Mapuche society and modern America is fascinating. We discussed this after Jerrod and Yaima's wedding. If you showed a photo of our home and a photo of a Mapuche home to a typical American, they'd snub the Mapuche home. We admire Mapuche homes, as they're relative to Mapuche's lives. The beauty of your tribal customs is revealed with more clarity from a personal overview. We were comfortable in your Mapuche home, its elegance displayed from its minimalistic format. Henry David Thoreau taught 'simplify,

simplify' and this logic and wisdom are reflected throughout Mapuche living design.

"You're welcome here. We're committed to make your visit memorable," Frank said.

Jerrod drove Yaima and Suyia on a local tour to show Suyia his old high school. They took a long walk in the nearby hills and Jerrod took the sisters to lunch at popular restaurant and they discussed plans.

The next day, Frank and Judy prepared the evening meal.

"When you get settled, give us a call. We'd enjoy visiting and attending one of the dances. It'd be a good time," Judy said.

The following morning, they bid farewell to Judy and Frank and embarked on the road early. It was a beautiful day and the drive back to school was pleasant.

Upon arrival, Jerrod went to the rental office to speak with the apartment manager about a more spacious apartment. The woman said they had a two bedroom furnished apartment just vacated and it will be available in a few days. Jerrod agreed to move in when it's ready for occupancy. Jerrod returned and revealed the news to Yaima and Suyia.

"This is good news. I think we should buy Suyia an American wardrobe to ease her adjustment. We'll wear Mapuche dress during folkdances; however, her day to day interaction with locals would be more acceptable if she had a few American outfits," Yaima said.

Jerrod agreed and, the next day, Yaima took Suyia shopping while Jerrod registered for classes and received class schedules.

Adjustment came quickly. Suyia dressed Mapuche style her entire life. Yaima made fashion suggestions and selected choices for Suyia to try on. When they returned, Suyia modeled her new wardrobe.

"You'll create quite a stir among male university students. You can wear native dress for folk dance night. I look forward to your voice addition to our performances," Jerrod said.

Yaima drove Suyia to meet her tutor, Mary Joyce. Yaima rang the doorbell on Mary's apartment. Mary opened the door and said, "My God, I'm seeing double."

"Mary, this is my twin sister Suyia. She's visiting from Chile. Jerrod will retain you to tutor us both. We share the same academic standard," Yaima said.

"Come in, we'll have tea. This is wonderful news. It feels good to teach again, especially you two because of your background in a Mapuche village and your teachings by a Mormon missionary," Mary said.

These three enjoyed each other and Yaima described how she and Jerrod convinced Suyia's parents to allow her to visit America.

Jerrod was waiting when they returned and said, "The apartment manager stopped by. We'll move into our new space tomorrow. It won't take long since we only have personal items to move.

"Mike and Elaine should arrive any day. I'll leave a note on their door to tell them we're now in apartment sixteen. They're unaware Suyia is living with us. Let's play a prank. When they knock on our door, Yaima will hide in Suyia's room and Suyia will greet them with me. They'll think Suyia is Yaima. Then Yaima will walk out of Suyia's room and we'll enjoy their reaction."

The twins laughed and Yaima said, "All our lives, people are confused as to who's who when they meet us. They'll be shocked like Mary was. It'll be fun."

"It sure will. I also stopped at the school newspaper's office and spoke with Virginia Easterbrook to explain we've returned and brought your twin sister Suyia to live with us and she'll sing Mapuche folk songs in a duet with Yaima. She was glad to hear it and anticipates increased interest in folk dancing this semester.

"The university will sponsor a talent show next month and our folk dance group is invited to participate. A twin sister vocal duet dressed in Mapuche native fashion will be special and our dancers are accomplished from dancing the last semester. This should be a memorable event," Jerrod said.

"My brain's strained to absorb what's occurred so quickly. I'll write my parents after we move into our new apartment," Suyia said.

The three moved into the new living quarters the next day.

Suyia wrote her parents.

Dear loving parents,

What a fabulous time I'm having. Things happen so fast, I can barely absorb it.

We've moved into a more spacious apartment and I have my own room. Yaima drove me to meet her tutor, Mary Joyce. Mary is a retired English literature professor and it was such a pleasure to meet her. She served tea and expressed how pleased she is to be given the opportunity to teach us both. I'll receive the same lesson plans as Yaima.

Jerrod continues to display boundless support. Yaima and Jerrod purchased an American style wardrobe for me to ease my adjustment to American culture. I'll also join the Mapuche folk dance group. They meet each week. I'll sing Mapuche folk songs in a duet with Yaima and we'll dress Mapuche style for our performances. Jerrod and a music student, Rana from Ghana, provide flute music. Rana occupies the first chair in the university orchestra. She plays an ancient pan flute for folk dances and we'll sing on occasion in Mapuche to convey ethnic identity.

I'll write often to keep you informed as my life unfolds at this new and exciting place. I think of you every day and miss you so much.
I love you with all my heart.
Suyia.

Routines fell in place. Jerrod was engrossed in premed curriculum. Yaima and Suyia prepared meals. Daily events were topics of discussion. The dance group will reconvene this week and Suyia will make her debut singing with her sister.

The dance group met at the gymnasium with hugs and smiles in reunion. Yaima introduced Suyia to the group. The student dancers were seasoned from last year's sessions. Suyia met Rana and Virginia Easterbrook, the school's newspaper editor.

The music started and dancers responded. The sisters have been singing folk songs since early childhood. Their voices blended to perfection. Skilled dancers, combined with voices connected to this historic music, brought the presentation to a new level. Jerrod's Mapuche flute and Rana's pan flute harmonized. Two beautiful twin Mapuche girls singing lyrics in their native language and dressed in Mapuche fashion was a sight to behold.

After the dance, Virginia spoke, "I'll be curious to observe audience reaction when this group performs at the university talent show. I'm delighted to contribute to your exposure. It'll be a joyful experience."

The twins looked elegant in their colorful native dress and wore their brilliant diamond heart necklaces.

After the dance session ended, the dancers mingled socially. Suyia was the center of attention as students welcomed and complimented her. Yaima and Jerrod were touched from the warmth of this scene. She traveled a great distance from her tribal village in Chile to arrive at this unique moment in her life.

The next day, Mike and Elaine came to the apartment and knocked on the door. Yaima moved quickly to Suyia's room. Jerrod and Suyia answered the door.

"We made it back. So nice to see you two again," Mike said.

He shook Jerrod's hand and hugged Suyia unaware she was not Yaima.

The four sat at the kitchen table and Elaine said, "I'm looking forward to the folk dance sessions."

"We've already had one session," Suyia said.

The bedroom door opened and Yaima walked out. Mike and Elaine were speechless as Jerrod and the twins laughed.

"We tricked you. This is Suyia, my twin sister. We brought her to America to live with us," Yaima said.

"You sure fooled us. I've never seen such identical twins. So funny and what a nice surprise," Elaine said.

"They'll need name tags so we don't get them confused. I would've never guessed," Mike said.

"I'll show you a method to recognize who's who," Yaima said.

Yaima pointed to a small birthmark on the left side of her neck. Suyia's neck has no birthmark.

"Also, as you spend time with us, you'll notice we gesture differently, and I'm left handed. Our voices have slight tone variation you'll learn to recognize," Suyia said.

"Our dance group will participate in a university sponsored talent show. We hope you two can join us. We'll meet twice before the talent show date.

"Next semester break, Yaima, Suyia and I will travel to China and Chang Yi will serve as our personal travel guide. You're both invited; Chang Yi and I will pay expenses. We'll tour his factory where the wireless transmitters and receptors are manufactured and marketed globally. The facility has doubled in size and Chang Yi is eager to show us his facility. It'll be a fabulous experience," Jerrod said.

Mike and Elaine enthusiastically agreed, barring unforeseen circumstances.

"I've dreamed to tour China. Its history is long and complex. I want to see the Great Wall," Elaine said.

"We'll use rail transportation to allow the best scenic value. Chang Yi was born and raised in a remote town and, as I described my experience with the Mapuche tribe and their folksongs and dances, he reminisced about his childhood in China's vast interior," Jerrod said.

Suyia and Yaima met with Mary daily to continue studies. Mary's assignments plus folk dance sessions occupied their thoughts.

Next Saturday night, the annual university talent show will be presented at the school's main auditorium. The stage is large and can accommodate dancers, two musicians and two vocalists.

Mike and Elaine would join the dancers for rehearsals to participate in the talent show.

After rehearsal, Mike and Elaine visited with Jerrod, Yaima and Suyia at their apartment. They were excited to participate in the show.

"What's best about our presentation is the mix of the twin's singing, flutes and dancers. Yaima and Suyia's native dress and their distinct voices blend with the dancer's graceful movements," Jerrod said.

"Our cheerleader team discussed this. The twins will impact the audience most, as their beauty adds dimension to their magnificent voices," Elaine said.

"As I reflect on early days with Jerrod, we could've never imagined we'd share such a moment with three extraordinary, beautiful women. Is this our peak? Is this our mountaintop?

"The talent show will become fixed in our memories. I'm pleased it's not identified as a contest. It's primarily an opportunity to display talent and entertain. I'm weary of competition, and its imposed intensity. My basketball team's goal is to defeat the opposing team, as the winner celebrates and loser is devastated. How is this of value? Why is winning important?

"Americans are obsessed with sports as they pack stadiums and gymnasiums to attend athletic competitions. The quest is to dominate and humiliate opponents. From what I've learned of the Mapuche, they don't include sports in their culture. They function within a social design where challenges are confronted through communal effort. They celebrate, yet don't humiliate. This synthesis is a better approach than competition to create winners and losers in life's journey," Mike said.

"In a general sense, you're right; however, jealousy and conflict does exist among Mapuche, although tempered. The infusion of teamwork is a necessity and social unity is our strength. We don't have grocery stores and gas stations; we only have each other. Our survival requires maximum cooperative efforts.

"When Suyia and I gleaned the forest for food, it was a different experience than pushing a shopping cart down an aisle while selecting items from shelves. When we're in the forest seeking roots, plants and berries, an aura is present as we integrate with nature's spiritual presence. This connection forms a sense of security combined with gratification. Mapuche's historic culture has taught values attached to Earth's gifts because this is where life's longevity is located," Yaima said.

"American society evolved differently than Mapuche culture. Original North American native tribes were parallel to Mapuche social design; however, during the Columbian era, America became inundated with European immigration. This changed everything as the power of political influence and money permeated society, it came to control every aspect of civil function. The quest for money replaced what my sister and I felt when we gleaned the woodlands for food. The difference was our connection formed sanctity as we experienced an intimate relationship with Earth. Such emotions are nonexistent with money. We now exchange printed paper for needs and then the paper becomes our ruler, occupying a godlike status. Money expands its power beyond basic needs and forms the primary source of corruption and social disarray. My country has one of the most corrupt governments on our planet and it's directly attached to quest for fiscal position as a means to lever self-serving political agendas.

"This won't change and, as much as I enjoy my American experience, my heart remains at our Mapuche village," Suyia said.

"Is it possible to redirect money's negativity? Money is a global social fixture and this will remain. I speculate we can improve global society through selected monetary applications. The power of money can feed the hungry, cure disease, and, if politically corrupt leaders impose dangerous and damaging activities spurred by greed, they too can be quelled and eliminated by properly directing the power of money.

"I'm coping with fiscal applications associated with the wireless electrical transmitter. My initial motivation didn't include a quest for monetary gain. My interest in this project was to offer electricity to impoverished areas, as a means to gain access and trust. The transmitter found its own economic level through the efforts of my business colleague, Chang Yi, when the device was publically presented.

"At this juncture, the project's future is in an evaluation stage. Where exactly is the best pathway forward? How can Chang Yi and those associated with this project implement beneficial results from what's been created? Do we take the money and run? Or do we calculate and direct our success in creative and positive manners for social betterment? It's obvious myriad choices are available. Our primary objective is not to gain personal wealth; we must recognize and direct our success in a fashion to yield the most for humankind overall," Jerrod said.

Everyone sat in silence. Then Yaima spoke, "This is why I love you so much. You think of others first. I predict your approach will allow us to venture beyond what can be imagined.

"Let's dance and sing in celebration of this time in our lives and embrace the good fortune of our love for each other. The talent show creates an opportunity to immerse ourselves in something unique and exceptional."

Mike and Elaine departed with hugs all around after the five friends shared a splendid evening.

The auditorium was at capacity. The show was a free event, created to introduce student talent.

A classical string quartet was first to take the stage, then a jazz band and a male choir singing Irish folk songs. Mapuche folk music and dance will appear next.

The auditorium was architecturally designed to intensify acoustics. The twin's native dress added color combined with their natural beauty. Yaima loaned Rana a Mapuche dress and Jerrod wore his colorful tunic. Dancers formed a circle and the music commenced.

The combination of color, grace and sound formed a magical blend able to stir the most sullen heart and the twin's voices were the apogee of this musical symbiosis. Their voices were fine-tuned biotic instruments and the audience was entranced.

When the performance ended, silence hovered and then the audience erupted with a standing ovation, cheering for an encore. Talent show rules disallow encores to offer equal stage presence to participants. The twins were in tears and hugged Jerrod and Rana in delight of such a spirited reception.

Backstage performers praised the folk music ensemble and introduced themselves in friendship.

Jerrod arranged ahead of time for a celebration dinner at a nearby campus restaurant and reserved the banquet room for the entire group as to include Mary Joyce and Virginia Easterbrook.

"I'm proud to be a member of our folk dance group. I've never enjoyed anything so much. I'll write a letter to my family in Ghana to describe our performance. Yaima and Suyia have the most beautiful voices. What a wonderful time we shared," Rana said.

"Our newspaper's staff photographer took photos and the folk dance group will occupy the front page. The entire edition will be devoted to pictures and descriptions of talent show participants.

"I've attended talent shows over the years; this was the best," Virginia Easterbrook said.

"Suyia and I are so grateful to be included in this performance. We were born and raised at a village in the remote foothills of the Andes Mountains. In our wildest imagination, we could've never visualized what occurred on this night. My only regret is the absence of my parents. It's our hope someday they'll visit the United Sates," Yaima said.

"I wish we had time travel. I'd love to take a copy of the university's newspaper with our group's photo back to high school years to show Jerrod what our future holds. I witnessed Jerrod overcome social challenges in high school. At this point, Jerrod has gained solid footing to confront whatever his future offers," Mike said.

It was buffet dining. After the meal, they remained and socialized. A dance team couple approached Yaima and Suyia to express appreciation.

The girl made introductions. "I'm Maryanne Arthur and this is my brother, Carson. We've been attending dance sessions, yet we've never introduced ourselves. I'm a sophomore and Carson's a junior. We're both biology majors.

"I must say, I've never been so inspired by singing voices and we've enjoyed learning Mapuche dances. We're half Navajo; while growing up, we shared time with our father's Navajo family who taught us tribal dances. Our native cultural histories are similar. We learned of the Mapuche while attending an Indian School near Albuquerque, New Mexico where we lived during formative years."

"Each week, we look forward to dance sessions. Jerrod and Rana's flutes add a native touch. You two have amazing voices and are so beautiful," Carson said.

"Thank you, Carson, you are our first contacts with native roots since we arrived from Chile. Our lives have been directly attached to Mapuche ancient hunter gather living style.

"Jerrod is organizing a China tour; we leave at the end of the semester. When we return, I'd enjoy getting together to compare Mapuche and Navajo historic cultures.

"I'm living with Yaima and Jerrod presently. I'm sure they would welcome you both. Write down your phone number and I'll call when we return from China," Suyia said.

Maryanne wrote her number and handed it to Suyia.

Early the next morning, Jerrod entered in his journal:

I told Rana she was invited to join our tour; however, she's obligated to return to Ghana during semester break to visit her parents so she cannot come. I'll commission a travel agent to arrange and organize the China trip. I'll write Chang Yi to coordinate with his schedule and I'll study China's history and geography.

Residual benefits of the folk dance performance continue. Rana's pan flute and my Mapuche flute ideally combine to accompany the twin's voices. Emotions were dispersed among performers and audience response fueled desire for our dance group to continue.

Jerrod mailed a letter to Chang Yi to reveal plans, saying he would call with dates and arrival time and Yaima, Suyia, Mike and Elaine will join the tour. The timetable will be arranged to accommodate Chang Yi's schedule.

CHAPTER 15

TRIP TO CHINA

The semester ended and Jerrod received the travel agent's itinerary. Jerrod ordered five copies of the best book he could find on China's history and geography. The long flight to Beijing will allow time to study China. They will change planes in Los Angeles to depart for Beijing. Fatigue from lack of sleep and jet lag will be the greatest challenge.

He called Chang Yi to detail the travel timetable. Chang Yi said he assigned an interpreter to meet them at the Beijing airport and assist connection with China's high-speed train and accompany them to Yi's home. It will be a full day's train ride on China's modern electric powered levitated rail system. Chang Yi will greet them upon arrival and use his company's van to taxi them to his home near the manufacturing facility.

Plans were in place and the travelers packed clothing, cameras and personal essentials. Each carried their China history book to be read in flight.

Yaima wrote a letter to her parents.

My dearest parents,

It's near time of departure for China, and I'm so excited and feel blessed to share this adventure with Suyia, Jerrod, Mike and Elaine. When we arrive at Beijing Airport, an interpreter tour guide will accompany us by train to Yi's location. It's a full day's ride on a newly developed high-speed train.

Jerrod purchased books on China's history and geography. We'll study these books during the long flight.

Yaima and I will keep personal journals and send copies when we return. We'll also mail Chinese post cards and purchase gifts to bring back to America and mail when we return to the United States.

If someone told me a year ago I'd be touring China, I would think they had lost their mind.

I hope you both are doing well. I think of you every day and look forward to my return to our village in paradise.

Love,

Yaima

The semester ended and the plan was for Mike and Elaine to meet Jerrod and the twins at the airport. Frank and Judy would drive Jerrod, Yaima and Suyia so they could say farewells at the airport.

Jerrod called Chang Yi the day before departure to inform him they were on schedule. The tour guide interpreter has the flight number and would display a sign as they disembark with Jerrod's name.

The travelers met at the airport, checked their baggage and waited for departure.

"This flight will be long, and it'll take a day or two to recover.

"We'll rely on our guide interpreter. His name is Wang Ji, and Chang Yi knows him well from previous American business associate visits. He praised his politeness and said he enjoys Americans and is fluent in English," Jerrod said.

"I wish we could go but we're covered up with work obligations. This is a rare opportunity to observe ancient Oriental culture. China has emerged as a prominent global society and its past reveals they were responsible for early inventions. You'll remember this trip for the remainder of your lives," Judy said.

After departing hugs with Frank and Judy, they boarded their flight. They changed planes in Los Angeles and eventually landed at Beijing International Airport.

Wang Ji was standing near the exit with a sign stating, "Jerrod James". Jerrod greeted him. Wang Ji was dressed in a business suit and appeared to be in his mid-thirties.

He shook Jerrod's hand and said, "Welcome to China. I'm Wang Ji and I'll guide you to Chang Yi's home. It'll be an all-day train ride. If you have questions, don't hesitate to ask. I'm at your service."

After introductions, they claimed their baggage, and Wang Ji directed them to a shuttle bus for transport to the train station.

They were fatigued from jet lag and couldn't enjoy the scenery as they closed their eyes for napping. After the long train ride, they arrived at their destination in the Nei Mongol province north of Beijing.

Chang Yi was waiting as the group exited the train. A young man was standing with Chang Yi when they met with him.

"Welcome to China, Chang Yi said, "This is my son, Keng; he's the company director. I'm working strictly on product development and marketing. Keng is fluent in English. He's an admirer of Professor Garrett and they've become close friends. My wife Haun and daughter Yue are company administrators. We presently have over four hundred employees.

"I met my wife while attending The Beijing Technological Institute. Family members are fluent in English."

Jerrod introduced everyone. Chang Yi knew Mike from his visit and was delighted to meet everyone.

"They're exhausted from jet lag and slept the best they could on the train. They need rest," Wang Ji said.

"We drove the company van and have room for everyone. The manufacturing facility and my home are about one hour's drive. You'll be comfortable and, after a good night's sleep, we'll discuss details. I have so much to show you," Chang Yi said.

"It's our first experience with such a long flight. We're happy to be here. I purchased history books on China. Everyone studied Chinese history during the flight," Jerrod said.

Wang Ji will stay overnight and return to Beijing the next day.

Keng drove the van while Chang Yi explained his home has adequate space and they have a professional cook. His daughter, Yue, has her own small house on the property and shares meals with her parents. Yue has a college degree in accounting and just turned thirty. She's worked at Yi's company in various capacities since she was sixteen.

The nearby town of Wuhn has a population of approximately 20,000 and provides employees for Yi's company. Wuhn is a mix of mid-sized industries and agriculture. Rice and hemp are primary crops.

Chang Yi's house was impressive, constructed in western architectural design and landscaped with a variety of oriental trees, shrubbery and colorful flowers. The travelers could now recuperate.

Chang Yi's wife and daughter greeted everyone. "Welcome to our home."

Chang Yi introduced everyone. Keng and Chang Yi carried their baggage into the house. As they entered the house, Haun introduced their cook and housekeeper Mei.

They gathered in the living room as Mei served tea.

"Your home is magnificent. It seems like only yesterday we shared our first correspondence as you expressed interest in the electrical transmitter system. Stephen told me it would be imperative to visit your home in China to grasp the magnitude of what you've accomplished. This trip was essential for several reasons; however, the prominent benefit is to gain connection with your life and family. I'm grateful for how our friendship evolved," Jerrod said.

"I'll show you to your rooms and you can shower and rest for a while. We'll call you when dinner is ready. I know you are tired, and you'll feel much better in the morning," Chang Yi said.

Mei was a gourmet cook and she applied full effort to prepare a special meal for the guests. She made curry rice with selected natural spices and a variety of greens in a salad served as a first course. The main dish was sliced pork sautéed in a creamy white wine sauce, onions and garlic. Small loaves of sliced whole grain bread were placed next to each table setting, with a wine glass, as white rice wine was traditionally served after the meal. Desert was a delicate flake crusted French pastry. As serving time neared, Chang Yi summoned his guest to the dining room.

The travelers seemed rested and were impressed at Mei's artistic table arrangement. It was beautifully presented beyond expectation.

"I've never seen such an artistic display of food. It's a beautiful sight," Yaima said.

"I've placed American style silverware next to the place settings as well as chopsticks. You may enjoy trying them just for fun," Mei said.

"In my native Mapuche village, we didn't use silverware, only carved wooden utensils. The spoon was the most popular, but we also carved forks. We use fingers on some foods. Americans use metal eating utensils. I'll do my best with the chopsticks," Yaima said.

"I'll instruct you. With practice, you may eventually prefer them. It's a skill you'll carry back to America," Haun said.

As this international group sat down to share this splendid meal, a sense of camaraderie was felt.

"Tomorrow, we'll tour the factory. The next day, we begin our cross-country train trip. Haun will travel with us. Yue and Keng will remain to oversee company functions. I've worked diligently to plan our route and select the best places to

145

visit. Our primary destination is the remote farm town where I was born and lived until I entered college. Our village had an excellent school funded by the Chinese government and our teachers were the best. I received a scholarship to Beijing Technical Institute and was part of an exchange student program in my sophomore year. I ultimately earned an electrical engineering degree from UCLA on a student visa. I was given a Silicon Valley employment opportunity and attained a work visa; however, the United States and China experienced a diplomatic impasse and my work visa was invalidated. I returned to China and started my electronic manufacturing company using a government business loan for startup capital. I reunited with Haun and we were married," Chang Yi said.

"Keng and I took cross-country train excursions during summer breaks in our college years. It was the most memorable time of my life. I look forward to your description of the tour," Yue said.

"I'm thrilled to be here. The anticipation increases as time approaches," Yaima said."

"It'd be impossible to have a better tour guide than our father. He's been a student of Chinese history his entire life," Keng said.

"Your generous and cordial hospitality exceeds what we envisioned. This is the best meal I've ever eaten. Such delicious food," Elaine said.

"It's indescribable," Mike said.

The group talked into the night, and the Chinese were curious to learn about the Mapuche. Chang Yi knew of this culture, but the others were unaware of the Mapuche.

The next day, Chang Yi guided a tour of the factory. He approached a separate building and led everyone inside.

A canvas covered a large piece of equipment. Yi removed the cover and said, "I've kept this a secret until now so I could present it in person. Stephen and I worked together to design and build a second-generation prototype of the electric wireless transmitter and receptor. It's twenty times more powerful than our original device and can produce enough electrical power for a small town or manufacturing facility. We redesigned transmission and receptor antennas in a similar fashion to Tesla's original design. We've tested the system thoroughly and I'll assist Stephen next month to install it in our manufacturing facility as a demonstration model. When we're satisfied with the prototype's performance, we'll seek markets to apply this advanced version. This transmitter requires an expanded array of solar panels. I'm eager for our company to break away from cable delivered power.

"This is a major breakthrough. It'll take a year or more to gauge market response. I'm familiar with how much a company our size spends on electricity and this unit would erase this cost entirely. Success will depend on market selection and exposure. If we direct installations correctly, this second generation system has unlimited potential," Chang Yi said.

"I'm stunned. Several units connected in series would expand range of application. Receptors could be designed and constructed to accommodate increased power demands. Power companies won't be happy about this development," Jerrod said.

"I've thought about this. We'll adjust as we proceed. Professor Garrett is a true genius. I could've never accomplished this without his guidance.

"I offered Stephen twice his income as a professor and he's eligible for retirement soon. He's expressed interest to move to China and join our company. His wife of twenty five years died ten years ago. Her loss, in conjunction with the debacle with the power companies, caused intense anxiety. When you appeared in his life, it was a miraculous intervention and awakened his spirit and returned his sense of self-worth. I hope he joins us. I so enjoy working with him," Chang Yi said.

Jerrod's mind was going in several directions as he contemplated this major development.

Excitement escalated for tomorrow's departure. Mei kept everyone fed with her delicious cuisine.

The next morning, Keng drove the group to the train station and they boarded the train to begin their tour.

Chang Yi handed out railroad maps of China to monitor progression and identify landmarks and waypoints.

"I enjoyed reading the history of The Great Wall. The wall's construction took over 2500 years and spanned eleven dynasties. The Ming Dynasty contributed the most from 1368 to 1620.

"The immensity of the wall is difficult to comprehend. Villages were established at intervals near the wall to house soldiers to guard against purge from military aggression," Suyia said.

"We'll stop for a day to visit a section of the wall designated for tourists and walk a distance on the wall. When I was a young man, I made this walk," Chang Yi said.

The train moved fast. The scenery was fascinating, consisting of rice farms and towns plus open areas with forests and rivers.

"I feel as if this is a dream. I didn't know China existed until William taught geography. Even then, it was just a name and I couldn't grasp where it was exactly located. As my knowledge advanced, I gained clarity of China's location in comparison to the remainder of the world," Yaima said.

"I've lived in China my entire life, except for my years at UCLA and a brief time employed in California. I've only seen a fraction of what China offers. The country became entrapped in political dysfunction and war orientations. The Korean War set us back years. It was a wasteful and senseless war, as most wars are," Chang Yi said.

The mixed cultural group tour stopped for a two-day break at The Great Wall attraction. Tour guides described The Great Wall's long history. The guides spoke Chinese and Chang Yi interpreted.

"This is my first visit to The Great Wall; however, I've read its history," Haun said.

As they gathered for their meal at the hotel, Mike said, "I doubt there's ever been a China tour mix like ours. We have three Americans, two Chinese, and twin Mapuche tribal members from Chile. This adds flavor as diversity enhances the experience and causes wonder if our world wouldn't become a better place if our example became popular. Unity combined with diversity creates social symmetry."

"Geographic separation hinders unification," Elaine said.

"So true. You'll enjoy the town where I was raised. It's remote so we'll need to take a bus to get there. No hotels but an elderly couple have a large house and we'll rent rooms. Haun and I will stay with my younger brother and his wife. We'll share meals at their home," Chang Yi said.

The train stop was a small building in a desolate place with dirt road access. The bus schedule was posted outside the building with a few benches. It was 10 o'clock in the morning when they disembarked the train and the bus was scheduled to depart at noon. A few travelers were seated on the benches and the building had two restrooms with one ticket window and a clerk. It was a barren place. Yi wrote his brother a letter with their scheduled arrival date.

Yi's parents died several years ago and, when Chang Yi returned for funerals, many childhood friends had remained to work family rice farms. The population of the town was 500.

As they waited for the bus, Yaima and Suyia made journal entries. They diligently recorded activities and mailed post cards and letters to their parents and teacher William. Jerrod was the designated photographer and he will distribute photo albums upon returning to America. Haun also took photos.

The bus arrived with only a few passengers. It was well worn from years of travel on dirt roads. They boarded and gave tickets to the driver. Chang Yi greeted the driver and explained he was the tour guide.

As they arrived at the village and disembarked, only a few older cars were visible as most residents moved about on foot. A few pulled carts and a wagon, hitched to a team of oxen, was parked in front of the only store.

Their first stop was the home of the elderly couple Chang Yi has known since childhood. Upon sighting Chang Yi, the two displayed wide smiles and greeted him with hugs.

Chang Yi introduced everyone and interpreted greetings. Chang Yi said, "They told us no westerners have ever visited this town."

The man was Kuo and the woman was Hop. They directed guests to assigned rooms. The rooms were in perfect order, neatly arranged with water pitchers and kerosene lamps. The town had a small electrical generating plant used for minimal applications.

Jerrod, Yaima, Suyia, Mike and Elaine stored their baggage and walked with Haun and Chang Yi to his brother's home.

Chang Yi's brother's name was Jian and his wife's was Fen. Their house was of Oriental design and was built by Chang Yi and Jian's father. Jian and Fen had a son and daughter who lived and worked in Beijing. Jian operated a rice farm inherited from his parents.

Jian and Fen met with the tour group and greeted them. Chang Yi made introductions and explained, "No adults in the town speak English; however, young students have had minimal exposure to the language from school studies."

Jian and Fen hugged Chang Yi. As everyone shook hands, Jian spoke in Chinese and Chang Yi interpreted.

Chang Yi explained Yaima and Suyia are Mapuche from Chile in South America. Yaima and Jerrod are married and Suyia lives with them. A retired university professor tutors Yaima and Suyia. Elaine and Mike are married. Mike was Jerrod's high school classmate and they attend the same university. Jian knew Jerrod was his brother's business associate from correspondence.

They toured the house and Chang Yi said, "This is where I was raised. Jian and I shared our room. It's the same room Haun and I will sleep. I have many memories here and Jian expanded the rice farm over the years."

During dinner, Jian spoke and Chang Yi interpreted. Jian described his family's history and formative years growing up with his brother. His description included how Chang Yi was a stand out student and awarded a government sponsored college scholarship. Jian became the designated heir to the rice farm and had worked directly with his father since he was a teen.

Chang Yi spoke in Chinese to Jian and then interpreted: "As I returned to my childhood home, nostalgia overcomes me.

"I feel guilty as I observe my home village in need of an improved electrical supply source. I've decided to install our newly designed electrical transmitter at my childhood home instead of a source to power the manufacturing plant. I'll build a second unit to apply power to our plant. This small town represents a more ideal example than our manufacturing plant

150

and simultaneously serves needs for the place of my foundation years. It's the right decision and will ease my conscious. Family should be priority above personal financial gain."

Jian smiled with gratitude and hugged his brother. It was a true example of brotherly love. Everyone agreed with Chang Yi's decision.

"It's exactly what I'd do. Your childhood home will serve to promote and demonstrate potential use in a similar fashion to our Mapuche prototype installation, but this town offers a better example for expanded applications and creates exposure for broader market potential.

"You should film a documentary as a means to demonstrate the second generation power transmitter's potential," Jerrod said.

"Graphics stimulate interest. I'll do this," Chang Yi said.

Fen made a splendid Chinese meal and everyone used chopsticks, as other utensils were unavailable. It was a delightful evening.

After dinner, Yaima said, "We're blessed to meet Jian and Fen. This meal was exquisite, and causes me to reminisce family meals in Chile."

"I'll invite town residents to meet at the school to introduce our tour group. My friends from America can express thoughts about Chins. They'll have questions in a cultural exchange," Chang Yi said.

The next day, Chang Yi and Jian walked throughout the town and invited everyone they encountered to meet at the school at 7 o'clock in the evening.

Chang Yi and Jian went early and placed chairs in front of the classroom for the tour group. As residents filed in, Chang Yi and Jian greeted them.

The classroom was at capacity, so it was standing room only. Chang Yi described his connection with Jerrod, Yaima, Suyia, Elaine and Mike. He explained his primary purpose was to show them the town of his origin.

A young boy asked about the twins. He was awestruck by how identical and beautiful they were.

Chang Yi described their birth in a small village in the foothills of the Andes Mountains in South America and descendants from the ancient Mapuche culture. He explained Jerrod's encounter with them when he was assigned to install an electrical system at their village and fell in love with Yaima. They were married at the Mapuche village and returned together to the America to be married a second time. This gave Yaima American citizenship. Eventually, Jerrod and Yaima brought Yaima's sister Suyia to America to live with them.

Members of the tour introduced themselves and gave brief descriptions of their lives in America and how fortunate they felt to be given the opportunity by Chang Yi to tour China. Chang Yi interpreted.

When it came Jerrod's turn to speak, he said, "I became acquainted with Chang Yi when he showed interest in a wireless electrical transmitter system I co developed with Professor Stephen Garrett, a physicist from the University of Pennsylvania.

"Chang Yi advanced the development of this device and manufactures these units at his electronics manufacturing facility.

"I suggest, during our visit, we share a social event similar to what I experienced during an assignment to install an electrical distribution system at an isolated Mapuche village near the Andes Mountains in South America. It's traditional to present bonfire social gatherings. They present Mapuche folk songs and villager's dance to this music. My wife Yaima and her sister Suyia have beautiful singing voices and I've learned to play Mapuche folk songs on my flute. We would enjoy entertaining your village at a bonfire gathering," Jerrod said.

Change Yi interpreted and the crowd applauded in acceptance.

The tour group stood at the exit and shook hands with every resident who attended the meeting and the mood was jubilant.

The next day, Chang Yi and Jian worked with a few residents to gather firewood for the bonfire to be held at a suitable location on Jian's rice farm.

Yaima said to Chang Yi, "We brought native dresses to wear when we sing to attach cultural identity to the music.

"I'd like you to request younger residents to wear Chinese native dress. After we sing a few Mapuche folk songs, Suyia and Jerrod will continue with music and Mike, Elaine and I will join the Chinese youth and instruct them to perform our traditional Mapuche circle dance holding hands. The footwork is simple and, once it's demonstrated a few times, they'll pick it up and we can dance together to the music. Adults are welcome to join in. The circle dance in the glow of the bonfire combined with the unique Mapuche music forms an enchantment."

"They'll be delighted. We also have folk dancing and, if time allows, the Chinese youth can demonstrate our dances. I'm enjoying this so much. Returning to my childhood home delivers an indescribable emotion. I love this place," Chang Yi said.

"You sound like me. I'm homesick for my village of origin. Regardless of how many wonderful things happen, my magnificent home in the foothills of the Andes Mountains is embedded in my soul," Yaima said.

The entire towns population arrived at dusk. Some carried folding chairs. Darkness descended and Jian ignited the bonfire. Young villagers were adorned in colorful Chinese traditional dress.

Jerrod, Yaima and Suyia stood near the bonfire and performed a Mapuche folk song. The town's residents were in awe at the purity of the twin's elegant voices as the bonfire's flames leaped skyward. A dreamlike sensation formed by an American male and the beautiful twin Mapuche girls as they entertained this audience of a remote town in China's interior. The odds of this occurrence were staggering, yet such thoughts were absent as the bonfire's light permeated the dancers.

When the song ended, the villagers erupted in cheers and applause as hearts and minds became one. Everyone felt joy and happiness.

Yaima spoke to the audience and Chang Yi interpreted. "The opportunity to share time together is beyond what I could've ever imagined.

"With the assistance of our friends, Mike and Elaine, we'll instruct those interested in performing the steps of the Mapuche traditional circle dance. Jerrod and Suyia will provide music; however, first we'll perform a silent practice to teach basic steps. We'll join hands in a circle to demonstrate steps."

Jerrod, Yaima, Suyia, Mike and Elaine spaced themselves within the circle of the young Chinese for the silent test dance. Yaima led the first steps and they followed her lead, repeating the series of movements slowly several times to allow memorization. Jerrod and Suyia will provide music and Mike, Elaine and Yaima will spread themselves among dancers to lead and assist.

The young Chinese memorized the steps quickly. Jerrod and Suyia returned to their position to perform. Mike, Elaine and Yaima intermingled with the circle to lead the dance until the new dancers gained confidence. As the music began, smiles on the new dancer's faces clearly revealed emotions. Chang Yi and Haun beamed with pride as they observed young Chinese in colorful native dress dance to Mapuche music.

After a few dances, the group perfected dance steps and Yaima rejoined Jerrod and Suyia. They were singing in English and switched to Mapuche; even though the dancers didn't understand either language, the change was noticed.

It was getting late. Chang Yi spoke to the dancers and said the next dance would be the last of the evening. His declaration elicited a quiet moan from the young Chinese. They were having the time of their lives.

Chang Yi expressed in Chinese, "We'll repeat this tomorrow night. I know among this group are those who play traditional Chinese musical instruments and sing Chinese ancient folk songs. We must seize this opportunity to entertain our guests in kind and teach them our native dances. They'll remember this for the remainder of their lives.

"My memory is filled with years from my youth, growing up here and the times we gathered to dance and sing by the light of our bonfires. It's fascinating how humanity emulates itself regardless of geographic separation. It'll be a grand time."

Change Yi interpreted what he spoke to the English speaking members of the tour group and they were enthralled.

"This last dance of the evening. I'll perform music solo and Yaima, Suyia, Mike and Elaine will join the circle. It's a befitting way to end this exceptional evening," Jerrod said.

154

Jerrod played his flute as the Chilean twins and the American couple joined the circle. Chang Yi and Haun joined, as well. Without the twin's voices, the dance had a different quality, as the singers were now dancers. This formed the finale of an unforgettable evening, as the beauty of combined cultures joined in unified grace.

The next day was filled with anticipation for the coming evening of Chinese music and dancing.

Chang Yi explained two instruments would be used to accompany the voice of a solo singer, usually a female. The Chinese flute is made of bamboo and is called a Dizi. It has a bamboo reed buzzing membrane. A percussion instrument is called a Nan Bangzi made from a wooden block and, when struck, emits a high pitch sound. The tempo of Chinese folk music is slower, as are the dance steps. The dancers form a single line instead of a circle and don't hold hands.

Evening arrived and was repetitious of the previous evening, as the bonfire was lit but three young Chinese would provide the music instead. Two males were the instrumentalists and a beautiful young Chinese girl provided voice to accompany instruments.

The dance line formed. Jerrod, Yaima, Suyia, Mike and Elaine positioned themselves at intervals in the dance line to emulate the steps as the dance began.

The music started and the dancers reacted. The steps were not complex; when combined with the Oriental music, the dance created a spiritual emotion.

After the first dance, Elaine said, "I felt entranced. We're blessed with good fortune to be given this rare opportunity. It's like a gift, as we join with a culture distant from our own. It's a miracle."

"I agree. I anticipate the joy when I return to my home village as I describe our time in China to my parents," Yaima said.

"The music is historical Chinese and transports us to a time of China's early history," Jerrod said.

The dances continued and each had different steps. The music's mood and rhythm altered when different songs were presented.

As the evening wound down, Chang Yi addressed the dancers in Chinese and interpreted for his tour group. "Our time together at my childhood home caused reflection of formative years and folk dancing created a catalyst to reconnect to my birthplace. This event prompted realization of this town's importance enhanced by our international friendships.

"As an adult, my drive for success diminished the importance of simplistic values early life delivers. Money cannot purchase the treasure delivered from bonfire dances, as its richness fuses unto itself and detaches from shallow material wealth and superficial social status identity.

"China has a deep history. It was isolated from other areas of the world for centuries. Such modern times we live in offer means to travel great distances, allowing us to participate in this opportunity.

"This will be our last time together. We're scheduled to leave tomorrow; sadness overcomes me. I didn't anticipate the emotional impact the return to my hometown would create. It's been such a pleasant time and melancholy haunts me as departure nears us.

"Let's have one last dance to stamp our memories with an indelible image of the magnificence this event has created."

The music started and Chang Yi and Haun joined the dance line. This last dance caused eyes to water, as emotions overcame dancers.

The next morning, the group shared a departure meal prior to the boarding the bus for the train station. Sadness was intense with hugs and tears, as travelers prepared to board the bus.

To the tour members' surprise, the entire town gathered at the bus stop. The Chinese dancers were adorned in their colorful costumes. They came to say good-bye.

The young Chinese boy who played the Dizi bamboo flute during the folk dance stepped forward. He handed his flute to Jerrod as a departure gift. He then bowed, smiled and said in perfect English, "My name is Jang Wei. Goodbye, Jerrod; we enjoyed your visit. I hope to see you again someday."

Jerrod fought back tears and said, "It's a promise we must keep. I'm unable to describe the wonder of what occurred."

Chang Yi was standing next to Jerrod and interpreted Jerrod's response. Yaima and Suyia were in tears, as love flowed from their hearts at this boy's gesture to Jerrod. Each twin hugged this amazing child.

The bus arrived. The group boarded and waved good-bye to their Chinese friends.

CHAPTER 16

RETURN TO THE UNITED STATES

On the bus ride to the train station, Mike spoke to Chang Yi. "As I ponder our visit at your childhood home, it reveals insight to China few westerners experience. I'm unsure how this will effect our future; however, when I attain my degree, I'd enjoy becoming part your company."

"Our manufacturing facility is the foundation, though without quality marketing and efficient promotion, the concept's potential will stall. Each piece of the puzzle contributes.

"I'm Chinese, which allows advantage to be applied to oriental markets. As an American, you'll be more effective to promote the concept in western markets. You're blessed with intelligence and a personable demeanor. These qualities are advantageous for market expansion. I'm convinced if you join our company unforeseen benefits will transpire. We'll begin to lay groundwork during semester breaks. I'll employ you to present our system at electronic promotional events to demonstrate the transmitter's function," Chang Yi said.

"I'd love this. I'll give it my best effort. It'll be rewarding and I'll gain confidence to advance as a representative after graduation," Mike said.

The bus arrived at the train station. The next train was due in one hour and discussions continued about the visit to Chang Yi's hometown.

"The young boy who gifted his Chinese flute to Jerrod as a memento was a powerful moment. I'll always remember the expression of pride on his face," Yaima said.

Keng picked them up at the train station and taxied them to Chang Yi's home. They will remain two nights prior to departure. Chang Yi will accompany his guests by train to the airport and serve as interpreter to navigate the Beijing Airport and see them off for their return flight to the United States.

Mei prepared meals while camaraderie stimulated conversation.

"It's difficult to identify our high point; although, the overview is perceptive, as it exposed the size and diversity of the country. The Great Wall is appropriately named attached to its historic significance, though the intimacy with Chang Yi's hometown residents is the most memorable. Our inability to speak Chinese limits personal bond intensity, as linguistic skills are needed to express sincerity of feelings," Yaima said.

"China will center discussions for years to come," Jerrod said.

Day of departure was emotional. The twins, Jerrod, Mike and Elaine hugged each of their Chinese friends. Keng will drive them to the train station. It will be a long train ride and an even longer flight to the United States.

Chang Yi spoke with airport attendants in Chinese. Most are fluent in English, though to converse in Chinese eases the process. Chang Yi accompanied them to the boarding area and will remain until they are airborne.

"It's impossible to adequately describe what we've experienced. Western visitors seldom are exposed to the depth of Chinese culture you've shown us. The future is unclear, though we're forever grateful for your kindness," Jerrod said to Chang Yi.

Chang Yi fell silent then said, "What occurred enhances our ability to confront future complexities. The tour impacted me to a higher degree than I anticipated; I'll use what I've learned to apply toward future challenges. Our destiny is dubious, yet we'll strive to discover a path to fruition."

As the plane tilted skyward, the view of Beijing dominated the scene. The five friends had experienced a major milestone in their lives.

The twins tilted their seats and closed their eyes in anticipation of jet lag fatigue. Their minds wandered, as they dozed into restless sleep.

They changed planes in Los Angeles and boarded their flight to Philadelphia. Jerrod called his parents between planes to give flight number and arrival time. Mike and Elaine's car was in long-term parking.

Judy and Frank were waiting at the gate as they disembarked.

"I'm sure you're exhausted, though what a grand trip this must've been," Judy said.

"I have so much to tell you. It'll be difficult to present in a manner to give our experience proper justice.

"We're in no condition to present anything right now, though I'm sure glad to see my parents standing here, Jerrod said."

Judy and Frank hugged their son.

"I'd like Mike and Elaine to come tomorrow. We'll have a welcome home dinner and listen the story of your extraordinary tour. Rest is the priority; after a good night's sleep, we'll listen to your journey's narration," Frank said.

Mike and Elaine agreed.

"It was something to behold. During our flight to China I attempted to picture what our visit would entail. As events unfolded, nothing was remotely similar to what I envisioned occurred," Mike said.

Mike and Elaine departed to retrieve their car. Jerrod and the twins followed Frank and Judy to the parking garage to drive the weary trio home to sleep. They returned to America; it felt good.

During the drive home, Yaima said, "I've always felt academics provided the impetus to acquire knowledge, yet our trip to China changed this. Our tour guides Chang Yi and his wife Haun opened doors seldom offered to western tourists.

They spoke perfect English, which enhanced the learning curve, as they detailed aspects of China's diverse historic society. I'll retain my memory of this trip for the remainder of my life. I'm forever grateful for such an opportunity."

"It's rare indeed to have those two as your guides. I'd love to visit China someday. I'm glad you're here and eager to listen to descriptions of your time in China," Judy responded.

"The long flight revealed geographic perspective of the distance China is from the United States. This realization raised awareness of China's independent development and formed the character of China's historic culture. This carried over to modern times and now China melds with global society as well as any industrialized country. It's predictable they'll eventually dominate segments of industrial and economic development. I agree with Yaima on longevity of our tour's impact," Jerrod said.

Jerrod, Yaima and Suyia slept until eleven then awaited Mike and Elaine while they had tea with Frank and Judy.

It was prearranged: Mike and Elaine would arrive at noon and they were on time.

"We feel rested, as we slept nine hours. I'm so glad to be home," Mike said.

"How will we ever top this trip? I don't recall ever being so overwhelmed as I was on our China tour," Elaine said.

"I don't think we'll ever achieve anything comparable," Yaima said.

"We'll talk for a while then prepare your return celebration meal, Judy said."

"Chang Yi assigned an interpreter guide to greet us as we disembarked our flight. He escorted us by train to Chang Yi's home.

"Chang Yi's home is spectacular; it is near his manufacturing facility. The next day we visited Chang Yi's factory. It's impressive. He surprised us with his new prototype electrical transmitter designed and constructed with assistance from professor Garrett. This transmitter has greater range and power than previous units, able to service housing complexes or industrial applications. The antenna was redesigned similar to Tesla's original transmitter's antenna," Jerrod said.

"Chang Yi accompanied us to the airport for our return flight. I'll join his company after graduation as an American representative. He suggested I begin during semester breaks as a demonstrator for electronic trade shows in the United States. As we spent time with Chang Yi, it exposed the depth of his character and genius," Mike said.

"We visited the Great Wall of China and guides spoke Chinese. Chang Yi and his wife Haun interpreted historical information of the wall," Suyia said.

"The most memorable event was our visit to Chang Yi's childhood hometown prior to college years. We formed friendships with residents and held bonfire celebrations with music and dance including Chinese music and folk dancing. It was a heavenly experience," Yaima said.

"I'm eager to have my film processed. In future years, we'll leaf through the pages of our albums and stir our memories.

"Classes resume in a week. I'll give photo albums to Mary Joyce, Virginia Easterbrook and Rana. I'll mail albums to Yaco and Lilen to be shared with villagers," Jerrod said.

"We'll prepare a celebration dinner. I want to hear more. As I listen to you describe your China connection, I sense residual benefits will appear far into your future," Frank said.

Judy and Frank teamed to create a fine meal. Judy's signature meatless meatloaf made with whole grain dried breadcrumbs, black beans and crushed walnuts with selected natural seasonings bound together with egg yolks to form the loaf, which was sliced and served with brown gravy. Also scalloped potatoes, green beans and eggplant, as conversations on China continued.

"The emotion when Jang Wei the young Chinese boy gave me his native flute remains a prominent memory. When I return to school I'll ask Rana where I can acquire a pan flute and send it to Jang Wei as a gift. He'll be thrilled to receive this. I'd also like Yaima to teach me to carve a Mapuche flute from ebony wood. I'll craft one to send in addition to the pan flute. I'll also send photo albums to be shared with Change Yi's hometown residents.

"This food is delicious. I've had your meatless meatloaf often, yet, for whatever reason, it tastes better," Jerrod said.

"It's because you haven't had it for a while," Judy said.

"While we're gathered together, I have news. I'm almost certain I'm pregnant," Yaima said.

Dead silence fell upon the group. Jerrod dropped his fork and his face went pale.

"Well, I for one am overly excited. It'll be another significant event in our lives," Judy said.

Jerrod hugged Yaima and said, "If it's true, we'll establish new priorities."

Frank clapped his hands together with a joyous smile and said, "I'll do my best to spoil him or her."

Suyia said with tears in her eyes. "I'll write a letter to our parents tomorrow. You're always one step ahead of me. I may never catch you. I volunteer as permanent babysitter."

"It was inevitable. We'd be cheated if disallowed to share a new Jerrod or Yaima as an addition to our lives," Mike said.

"We're on track for this too, especially since Mike has been given an opportunity to work with Chang Yi after graduation," Elaine said.

Judy fetched a bottle of wine and poured a glass for each of them.

"I purpose a toast to our new pending family member. This remarkable news brings immense joy and happiness. It serves as a pivot point to our future. The China trip has been accomplished and now this monumental event as well," Judy said.

Mike and Jerrod will enter their senior year to attain bachelor degrees. Jerrod will move on to medical school after graduation and Chang Yi's company will employ Mike.

CHAPTER 17

NEW HORIZONS

They will remain three days and then return to the University. Jerrod had his film processed and purchased albums to mount photos and distribute.

During the return drive, they discussed plans for the next semester.

"I'll find a primary care physician to verify my pregnancy and guide me with medical advice attached to complexities of pregnancy and childbirth.

"I'll continue to sing with Suyia for folk dances as long as I'm able," Yaima said.

"They'll probably do an ultra sound to learn if it's a boy or girl. It's most important for you to eat healthy foods," Jerrod said.

"I won't do the ultra sound intrusion. I don't want to know the gender of my baby until its birth. It's more natural and the mystery enhances the love bond of parents and child," Yaima said.

"I'll support whatever you desire," Jerrod said.

"The brother and sister, Maryanne and Carson Arthur, from our dance group expressed desire to visit when we returned

165

from China. I'll call and invite them to meet with us after we return to our apartment. They're half Navajo and I'm eager to discuss cultural similarities," Suyia said.

"It'll be interesting to compare the two native cultures," Jerrod said.

They felt a surge of energy as they returned to campus. Yaima called Mary to inform her of their return. Mike and Elaine will arrive tomorrow. Jerrod will register and receive class assignments, as life reverts to its place prior to the China adventure.

Suyia and Yaima wrote their parents and revealed the good news of Yaima's pregnancy to detail present status. They enclosed their letters in a package with photo albums of their China trip.

Suyia called Maryann to invite her and Carson to have dinner at their apartment. Mike and Elaine will attend. Carson is a senior this year while Maryanne is a junior. Classes began and folk dances offered academic relief.

Yaima stopped by Rana's dorm. Susan, her dorm mate, told her Rana is scheduled to return in a two days. She gave Yaima Rana's letter describing her visit with her parents. Yaima asked Susan to have Rana contact her when she arrives.

"I'm glad to be back to school and this new addition to our lives will require more responsibility," Jerrod said.

"Yes, though the joy of our child's arrival will ease the task," Yaima said.

Routines set in. Yaima and Suyia visited Mary Joyce daily for lesson assignments.

"I have an idea for a short story. I'll begin writing it in the morning hours," Yaima said to Mary.

"I'm confident you can do this. It'll be a challenge. After you complete the story, I'll edit it and you can submit it to a literary journal to be considered for publication," Mary said.

"To have my story published would be a thrill. I'll send copies to my parents and William," Yaima said.

The evening arrived for Maryanne and Carson's visit. Jerrod and Yaima will cook and serve the meal. Jerrod copied

Judy's recipe for her meatless meatloaf and with Yaima's help created this specialty dish.

Carson and Maryanne arrived. They were happy to see everyone. Jerrod and Yaima served their creation and Elaine complimented Jerrod and Yaima, "You did a splendid job; Judy would be proud."

"It's delicious," Carson said.

Maryanne concurred.

"My parents are gourmet cooks, so they taught me a few things.

"I'm glad Suyia invited you two. Folk dance sessions begin soon. Rana will return from Ghana and we'll rehearse. Will you continue to dance this semester?" Jerrod asked.

"We'll be there for sure. We love folk dancing and look forward to dance night," Maryanne said.

They stayed late and discussed Navajo and Mapuche cultural similarities.

Suyia and Carson obviously displayed physical chemistry. Carson was a handsome young man with Navajo complexion and hair. He was six foot tall and muscular.

After Maryanne and Carson departed Yaima said, "I love those two. They remind me of home."

"They're both special. Carson has a combination of qualities I find attractive," Suyia said.

"I sense the feeling's mutual. His major is the same as mine, also his native roots align with yours," Jerrod said.

"Carson is charismatic. I enjoy his self-effacing demeanor," Elaine said.

Mike and Elaine retired to their apartment and Maryanne and Carson left.

Suyia, Yaima and Jerrod continued conversing.

"The arrival of our child will alter plans. Prior to your pregnancy, my intention was to return to Chile during summer break, yet my calculation reveals you should deliver in June and the infant will be too young to travel.

"I suggest we arrange with William to have your parents visit us for your delivery. William can acquire passports and guide them through the airport maze. We'll greet them at the

167

Philadelphia airport. They'll stay with us at my parent's home. What do you think about this?" Jerrod asked.

"It's perfect. I miss my parents so much; to have them present for my delivery would bring joy to everyone," Yaima said.

"What a grand idea," Suyia said.

"It will be so much fun as our child grows to spend time in Chile at the beautiful village. I'm stalled until I graduate from medical school. We'll move permanently to the village as soon as I become a certified physician. This will become our base of operation to assist areas of the world in need of medical support.

"Chang Yi will expand his market base and, with Mike as his American coordinator, it's predictable his new transmitter system will make its mark in the United States in addition to foreign locations," Jerrod said.

The folk dance group continued to meet once a week at the small gymnasium. Maryanne and Carson never missed the weekly dances. Yaima and Suyia sang and Jerrod and Rana played their flutes.

During dance sessions, Maryanne encouraged Carson and Suyia to dance while Yaima sang solo. Suyia loved dancing with Carson and this intensified mutual interest.

"Let's go on a dinner date so we can talk," Carson said.

"I'd love to," Suyia responded.

Carson restored a surplus army jeep, which fits his personality perfectly, as he enjoys hiking in forested areas. Suyia's ethnic roots were ideally matched to Carson's character because of her intimacy with the hinterland from her earliest memories.

Carson drove his jeep to meet Suyia at the apartment and was greeted by Jerrod, Yaima and Suyia. "Come in and we'll have tea," Jerrod said.

Yaima asked Carson, "What're your plans after graduation?"

"I'm considering options. The National Park Service invited me to apply for a summer position as a naturalist and nature walk tour guide. I'd also consider a teaching position in some capacity. Last summer I purchased a .35-millimeter camera and became interested in nature photography. I'm perplexed, as the future is unclear at this point, though it'll relate to my studies as a biologist in some manner.

"Suyia is so beautiful. I've felt amorous emotions for her since we first attended the dances. You two are the most identical twins I've ever seen. The manner by which your voices blend and project is unsurpassed," Carson said.

"It was so much fun dancing together. I'm Mapuche and Carson is half Navajo. Our similar ancestry adds connection. Yaima and I were raised wandering woodlands, so this fits well with Carson's passion for hiking forested areas," Suyia said.

Carson and Suyia departed for their dinner date. Yaima said to Jerrod, "We need to purchase Suyia a pair of quality hiking boots."

"We'll do it tomorrow. I know a place to buy them. We'll buy boots for ourselves and join them on nature hikes. I like Carson's interest in photography," Jerrod said.

In early morning hours, Yaima worked on her short story. She became engrossed and became attached to characters. During non-writing times, her mind remained connected to the story. She mentally organized and adjusted composition to enhance content. She didn't anticipate the power of a writer's connection, as reading assignments involved the creative input of someone else, yet, as she scribed her own creation, an entirely different energy established. Her narrative became obsessive.

The next day, Jerrod drove Yaima and Suyia to an outdoor outfitter and all three bought new hiking boots.

Jerrod said to Suyia, "I'd like us to share a day hike with Carson. Let's plan this. I'm sure he knows locations for us to join him on a hike."

"I'd love this. I'll call him and suggest we go for a hike. It'll allow us to break in our new boots," Suyia said.

Suyia called Carson. He said he would stop by to form a plan.

He arrived an hour later and was excited.

"Thanks for the thought. My favorite area is twenty miles east. It's a national forest and it has scenic trails. I know the best trails," Carson said.

Suyia showed Carson her new hiking boots. "I have the same brand. Wear them as much you can to break them in to accustom your feet. You won't get blisters with these boots by their design, though they'll be more comfortable after a while," Carson said.

"Let's plan for this coming Sunday. I'll drive and I'd like you to give tips on nature photography. I'm interested to learn techniques and lens selections. I have a standard lens Nikon," Jerrod said.

"I have a Nikon too. My lenses will fit your camera. You're welcome to use my equipment," Carson said.

So, the plan was established. The four will hit the trail on Sunday. Folk dances are held on Friday evenings.

Yaima packed lunch and the four hikers drove to the national forest. It was a perfect day as billowy clouds filled a bright blue sky.

They parked at the trailhead. Carson carried a pack with food, camera lenses, folding tripod and first aid kit. The terrain was slightly hilly. The forest was a mix of conifer and hardwood trees. Carson took the lead, as the four hiked single file. Carson, Suyia, Yaima and Jerrod followed. The smell of the woods combined with a beautiful sky to form a mood only wilderness areas deliver.

Carson stopped then said, "This trail leads upward then opens to a vista. We'll rest at the high point and reconnoiter for photographic subjects, and maybe find a few wild raspberries. This is my favorite trail."

"What a nice day. My boots feel right, yet a bit stiff," Suyia said.

"When we lived at the village, we wore deerskin moccasins. My boots give better support. This hike causes thoughts of Chile," Yaima said.

"It feels good to escape urban clutter, as we push ourselves more than strolling around campus," Jerrod said.

"It's an elixir for the soul and lifts my spirit when I walk this trail. Folk dancing and wilderness treks are relief valves from academic stress," Carson said.

As they crested the hill, terrain flattened with strewn boulders and Carson chose a vantage point.

"I rest here frequently. I envision how this place looked similar a thousand of years ago. It haunts me to know it's likely a member of an ancient tribe visited this spot. Geological and human timelines have no similarity. One thousand years is an eye blink geologically.

"Last summer, I hiked the New River Gorge in West Virginia. It's a spectacular place. I camped near the river and walked onto a large granite boulder and contemplated the river's history. I emptied my canteen onto the boulder and the water quickly ran off into the river. A staggering reality struck. Flowing water created this magnificent gorge. As I watched the water flow over the rock, I thought about how long it must have taken for water to carve this solid granite gorge. The New River is one of the oldest rivers in the world. It's over three hundred million years old. Humans have occupied Earth for two and a half million years. It's difficult to comprehend the magnitude of the river's history in comparison to human presence," Carson said.

"As a species, we've failed in many ways. We're considered the superior species, yet we've pillaged Earth's treasures in accordance with our perception of improvement, which has proven harmful not only to ourselves but terrestrial life in general. This has caused environmental havoc, as we lack recognition of a need for preservation attached to Earth's evolutionary process. This negativity escalated during modern times," Jerrod said.

"Our tribe recognized this and decided Mapuche ancestral social structure is less intrusive. Those entangled in modern social design view Mapuche life as primitive. As I've observed modern society, I choose primitive over modern day chaotic glut, as we have devastated our environment," Yaima said.

"As we observe this magnificent view, I feel I've returned home and it's such a nice feeling. Carson, I'm grateful you suggested this place," Suyia said.

"I'm aware of what you speak, as my Navajo ancestors were also intimate with Earth's natural state. I think of this when I attend folk dances, as you and Suyia sing folk songs with your beautiful voices and this forms spiritual visitation with ancient ancestors through music and dance," Carson said.

As Suyia listened to Carson speak, love sensations escalated. How could she ever find a better partner?

"This is a special moment. I savor reconnection with nature with its boundless life forms and spectacle," Suyia said.

"Let's wander about to search for photographic subjects. I'll use a close up lens. Often the best subjects are small and not easily discovered. Tiny wildflowers can emit splendor equal or greater than a vista," Carson said.

The four friends wandered looking closely in crevices for photographic subjects.

They found a Christmas fern sprouting from of crack in a boulder mixed with bright yellow wildflowers clinging to a sliver of soil. The gray color of the boulder formed contrast with the colorful plants. Carson set up his tripod and attached his close up lens to allow the image to fill the viewfinder of his camera.

"I'll make copies to remember our first hike together," Carson said.

Each of the four viewed the image in the viewfinder.

"This is a perfect picture to remember this day," Yaima said.

The friends returned to the apartment, as Suyia and Yaima prepared a meal. These four continued to share time together.

During one visit Carson brought an album with his collection of nature photographs. Nature themed magazines published Carson's photos.

"I'd like to become involved in nature photography. It serves as reason to spend time in beautiful places," Jerrod said.

Folk dancing resumed. After dance sessions, the dancers socialized.

"Let's go on another dinner date," Carson said to Suyia.

"Sure, pick me up anytime," Suyia, said.

"How about tomorrow night at 7 o'clock?" Carson asked.

"I'll be ready," Suyia responded.

Carson drove his Jeep. Jerrod greeted him. As they sat at the kitchen table, Yaima asked, "Where do you plan to have dinner?"

"It's a small Italian restaurant and I'm a frequent customer. An Italian immigrant couple own and operate the restaurant; we've become friends. I've described Suyia and I'm excited for them to meet her," Carson said.

CHAPTER 18

SUYIA AND CARSON

As they entered the restaurant, Carson introduced Suyia to Sophia and Giuseppe Vescio. They were an attractive middle age couple.

"Carson, your description of Suyia was inadequate. I don't recall a more beautiful young woman. Is this typical of Mapuche people?" Giuseppe asked.

"She has an identical twin sister Yaima. You should hear them sing Mapuche folk songs. I've never heard such vocal purity.

"You're invited to attend our weekly folk dances at the small gymnasium on campus. You'd really enjoy this," Carson said.

"How long have you lived in the United States?" Suyia asked.

"Ten years. Three years ago, we became American citizens. It was the fulfillment of our dream.

"We'd enjoy attending the folk dances. We danced folk dances in Italy when we were younger," Sophia said.

Giuseppe was the cook and Sophia the waitress. They directed Carson and Suyia to a private dining room reserved for

175

romantic couples. It was quaint with photographs of Italy on the walls.

Carson had pre-selected dinner from the menu. As Sophia served each a glass of Italian red wine, she said, "Your food will be served in a few minutes. Giuseppe prepped things, as he knew you'd arrive soon.

"It's a thrill to meet Suyia, we knew nothing of Mapuche culture until Carson enlightened us. I'd like to learn more about Mapuche history."

"I'll have my sister Yaima and her husband Jerrod visit your restaurant. Yaima enjoys describing Mapuche history," Suyia said.

Giuseppe served creamy potato soup with chopped kale and onions blended with selected spices and fresh whole grain bread he bakes himself. The main course was lasagna.

The two savored the moment and the food was delicious. Suyia had never eaten Italian food. She was impressed.

"I've never tasted anything like this. Italian food is really flavorful. I feel so happy here with you," Suyia said.

"I feel happy too. You and Yaima emit spiritual love energy. I've never seen such beauty combined with charm and grace. You two are thoughtful and compassionate to a degree I've never experienced.

"I've noticed you and both wear beautiful heart shaped pendant necklaces. Are those real diamonds?" Carson asked.

"Yes, Jerrod gave them to us on his second trip to our village to install an additional wireless electrical current receptor he and Professor Garrett invented.

"This invention is manufactured in China and we met Jerrod's Chinese business partner, Chang Yi, when we visited China. Professor Garrett spends time in China and worked with Chang Yi to develop and construct a second-generation transmitter. This new design is more powerful, able to provide wireless electrical power to small towns or manufacturing facilities. With proper marketing it's speculated to become overwhelmingly successful. Jerrod and his parents own the American patent on the device. They've become multimillionaires from the first design's success. These units have been installed globally often in third world impoverished countries.

"Jerrod is on course to become a certified physician, though money is secondary. Yaima and Jerrod will move permanently to our village upon Jerrod's graduation from medical school. They plan to construct a medical clinic at the village using a Mapuche style structure. They'll travel to areas of the world in need of medical assistance. Jerrod is a genius, yet never flaunts it," Suyia said.

"I'm speechless. I recognized Jerrod's intellect, yet was unaware of the dimension of his overall character or success. I'm on the low end of the totem pole from a financial perspective. Maryanne and I are on partial academic scholarships sponsored by Duke University. We also receive additional support from our Indian school scholarship fund. They send us each four hundred dollars a month for personal expenses. The university pays our tuition, books and dorm costs. I've worked summer jobs and saved money to purchase my camera equipment. I'm passionate about photography. I pieced my old Jeep together with the help of a family friend.

"I want us to get married and pursue life as a team. I think of you every minute of the day and it's not only because you are beautiful it's your personality. I don't want to cause uneasiness, though it's important for you to know my feelings. I love you so much," Carson said.

Suyia was silent then said, "I think of you all the time too. Let's do it and see where our path leads. I'm not concerned about your financial status. You're on track to obtain a degree in biology, which will open unforeseen doors. I love you too."

Tears welled in Suyia's eyes as the two embraced in celebration of their new direction. Suyia trusted Carson. She recognized his character qualities prior to this event.

Carson pulled a small box from his pocket and handed it to Suyia. It was an engagement ring with a small diamond.

"It's only a one quarter carat diamond but I promise to buy you a larger diamond when I can afford it. I noticed Yaima's diamond is large," Carson said.

Tears flowed and Suyia said, "I'll cherish this moment for the remainder of my life. I don't care about the diamond's size. It's mine, now and forever. I don't want a larger diamond. I love you so much."

"I'll do my best as your partner on our journey," Carson said.

Sophia and Giuseppe brought a bottle of Chianti. They knew Carson planned to propose to Suyia and Giuseppe said, "Your dinner and this bottle of Chianti is our gift to celebrate your engagement."

They hugged Suyia and Carson, as a gesture to share this special moment in their lives.

They returned to the apartment to give the news to Jerrod and Yaima.

As they entered Suyia said, "We're getting married."

Yaima hugged her sister and said, "I'm so pleased. The four of us will march on life's passage together. I'm filled with anticipation."

"I'm with Yaima. I foresee a favorable future. You'll acquire your degree soon and I'm stuck with another four years of medical school. I have an idea relative to your future. I'll explain when I have the pieces properly arranged," Jerrod said.

"OK, Jerrod, I'd enjoy hearing your thoughts," Carson responded.

"You can get married at the campus chapel by Reverend Johnson. I'm so excited. I feel you two are a perfect match.

"I achieved a personal goal today. I finished my short story. Mary will edit it and I'll submit it for consideration to *Nib*, the university's literary journal. I titled the story *The Voice of Bonfires*," Yaima said.

"I can't wait to read it," Suyia said.

"You will, yet I'll wait to see if it's published and give copies," Yaima said.

The next day, Jerrod met Carson at his dorm to discuss his pending redirection.

"Life is an undefined path and it's impossible to predict complexities we'll encounter, yet, if we form a comprehensive plan, it can assist navigate the indistinct future. I wish you could've been with Doctor Garrett and me when we first contacted the Mapuche tribe. Our minds became branded as we recognized values the Mapuche instilled. Two Mapuche words form their name 'mapu' meaning land, and 'che' meaning people.

"More profound connection came on my second visit, as the splendor of their culture clarified. Yaima prompted me to dance at the celebratory bonfire, and this caused a new dimension to my life. As things developed, we were married. The intensity of our bond has grown to a level I could've never imagined.

"We brought Suyia to America to learn of American culture and assumed responsibility for her comfort and progression.

"William Harrington is a Mormon missionary assigned to assist with village needs. He's been instrumental as a teacher and support element to the village. He's responsible for their school's construction and serves as the primary teacher. William is the one responsible for the installation of our wireless electrical transmitter sponsored by the Mormon Church.

"Yaima and I will eventually relocate to the village to establish a medical clinic. We have our own Mapuche home built by tribal members as a wedding gift. I recognize your academic achievements and I'd like to recruit you as William's assistant. The school needs broader curriculum. You'd be paid a salary equivalent to an American public-school teacher. William's academic aptitude tends toward English, literature and history. Your biological science degree would add subject selection extension.

"It's Mapuche custom, when couples are married village members unite to construct a home for the newlyweds.

"With your knowledge and attachment to nature, you align with Mapuche societal format. What're your thoughts on this?" Jerrod asked.

"How could I refuse? I've struggled on the low end financially with minimal income. I worked summer jobs as a supplement to purchase my camera equipment. I'm concerned about my ability to properly support Suyia," Carson said.

"Professor Garrett and I worked together to develop a wireless transmitter to deliver electrical current. These transmitters are currently being manufactured and distributed by my business associate Chang Yi in China. Over the past few years the concept has exploded from global demand. My net worth presently is around ten million dollars and will expand exponentially over the next few years through Chang Yi and Doctor Garrett's effort to create a second-generation transmitter, which is more diverse with greater application potential.

"My personal plans are to utilize my medical degree in combination with financial success and form a charitable foundation to serve third world countries with medical services and other needs. I'll team with Yaima to implement this plan. Suyia will be trained as a physician's assistant and will maintain medical services for the village during our absence when we travel to foreign locations. She'll receive pay equal to an American physician's assistant.

"I'll bear costs involved to allow you and Suyia to move forward with my suggested outline," Jerrod said.

"I'm overwhelmed and deeply appreciative. I'll put forth full effort to serve as a teacher at the Mapuche School. Have you discussed this with the twins?" Carson asked.

"No, I thought it best for you to do the honor. They'll be delighted," Jerrod said.

Carson followed Jerrod back to the apartment.

As they entered, the twins suspected they were up to something. Jerrod made tea and they gathered at the kitchen table.

"Carson has news to share," Jerrod said.

"After graduation, I'll be challenged to fulfill my assignment as William Harrington's assistant and teach biological science to Mapuche children sponsored by Jerrod's company. I'm in disbelief yet excited about this unique opportunity.

"This erases apprehension about our future and it feels so good," Carson said.

The twins hugged Carson.

"I knew a door of opportunity would open; leave it to Jerrod to open it. He's been a beacon of hope in our lives since we first met in Chile when he and Professor Garrett installed our wireless electrical transmitter.

"Tomorrow night is dance night. It'll serve as a celebration, as we'll eventually reunite at one of the most beautiful places on Earth and discover bliss delivered by love and companionship," Suyia said.

Carson stayed late. The mood was euphoric as four young lives took a step into their future

The folk dance group met at the gymnasium. Maryanne approached Suyia and said, "Carson explained your wedding plans. I'm so happy for you both. As you get to know Carson, your time together will reveal his many qualities. He always makes a special effort to help others."

"I sensed his altruistic character traits, yet unaware of the power of love," Suyia said.

Suyia and Carson visited Reverend Johnson. A date was established for their wedding.

Jerrod, Yaima, Mike, Elaine, Frank, Judy, Maryanne, Mary Joyce, Rana, Giuseppe, Sophia and Virginia Easterbrook formed the wedding party.

Suyia will wear her Mapuche dress. Jerrod will loan Carson his native tunic. Carson purchased gold wedding bands to exchange at the ceremony.

Yaima and Jerrod rented a one-bedroom furnished apartment in their building for Suyia and Carson yet won't disclose this until after the wedding as a gift. Jerrod will pay the rent until Carson graduates and assumes his teaching position.

After the wedding ceremony, a celebration folk dance will be presented at the gymnasium, as the dance group joins to honor Suyia and Carson's bond in matrimony. Jerrod, Yaima and Rana will provide music to allow Suyia to dance with Carson.

Suyia wrote her parents a long letter and described how Carson entered her life. She enclosed photographs taken on their hike with Yaima and Jerrod including the image captured of the Christmas fern with yellow wildflowers sprouting out of a crack in a boulder. She described Carson's assignment as William's assistant to teach Mapuche children and they will have a second

Mapuche style wedding with a celebratory bonfire, as when Jerrod and Yaima were married.

Judy and Frank arrived. Suyia introduced Carson and they shared a meal to discuss their future.

"We love the village and the magnificence of its mountain vistas. We never enjoyed ourselves more than when we visited for Jerrod and Yaima's Mapuche wedding," Judy said.

"Jerrod wants my parents to travel to the United States to be present when our child is born. It would be a wonderful opportunity for them to visit America. William will organize the trip, obtain passports and guide them to their departure flight. We'll greet them at the airport. I'm excited they'll be present to greet their grandchild," Yaima said.

"This is a good plan. We'll serve as guides during your parent's visit," Judy said.

The wedding party met at the university's chapel and Reverend Johnson performed the ceremony. Two young, beautiful people were united to face their destiny. Suyia's beauty highlighted the ceremony. Her dress identified her cultural heritage.

Giuseppe and Sophia arranged an Italian buffet at the gymnasium as a wedding gift to Suyia and Carson. The dance group arrived and intermingled to savor this special event.

"I'm in awe how circumstances form unforeseen destinies. Early on, Carson characterized independence in an unusual manner, which reduced female interest. He carved a bond with nature and displayed fascination with terrestrial life. The popular girls in high school viewed Carson as odd. Now here he is, with a stunningly gorgeous wife who is a child of the forest. How could this be more perfect?" Maryanne said.

"It rings as a miracle. Carson will receive his degree in biology and teach Mapuche children," Judy said.

Prior to the music, as guests enjoyed the Italian buffet Jerrod asked Rana where he could purchase a pan flute to send as a gift to the young Chinese boy who gave him a Chinese flute as a departure gift.

"I'll look for a supplier. What a kind gesture. He will be excited to receive this gift," Rana said.

"You would've loved our connection with the Chinese. It formed a permanent memory.

"I'll have Yaima teach me to carve a wooden Mapuche flute to add to the pan flute," Jerrod said.

The dancers congratulated Suyia and Carson.

The music began and dancers responded.

After several dances Mike danced with Suyia and Elaine Danced with Carson. Suyia replaced Yaima so she could dance with Carson also. The wedding and dance established a lasting memory. The final dance came well past midnight.

Judy and Frank stayed at a motel and would stop by the apartment in late morning.

Suyia and Carson rode with Jerrod and Yaima. As they walked up the stairs Jerrod stopped in front of a nearby apartment, unlocked the door and walked in. Suyia and Carson were confused.

"We leased this apartment as a wedding gift, and you'll live here until Carson becomes William's assistant," Jerrod said.

Suyia couldn't restrain her tears, and hugged Jerrod and Yaima. "I can't believe it, you two are so thoughtful."

"It's miraculous how my life has changed in such a short time. I'm grateful," Carson said.

"We thought it'd be best to begin life together in your own home," Yaima said.

The next morning Judy, Frank, Suyia, and Carson assembled at Jerrod and Yaima's apartment. They discussed the good time at the wedding and folk dance.

Suyia explained they would have a Mapuche wedding after they move to the village.

"The next event will be the arrival of our child, and my parent's visit to greet their first grandchild. When the baby is old enough we'll travel to Chile.

"We'll resume study with Mary Joyce. I'm excited to present my short story to Mary," Yaima said.

Frank and Judy received the news of Jerrod and Yaima's gift to Suyia and Carson.

"They need a place of their own. Jerrod and Yaima knew this and they'll be neighbors," Judy said.

CHAPTER 19

SENIOR YEAR

Jerrod continued to walk to classes. Yaima drove Suyia to Mary Joyce's apartment for study assignments.

A routine developed. One of the three couples cooked each evening and enjoyed mealtime discussions.

"I'll attain my bachelor's degree in biology, then attend four years of medical school. Mike and Elaine will move forward with their lives. Suyia and Carson will relocate to the Mapuche village and we'll remain here. It discourages me," Jerrod said.

"As soon as our baby is old enough, we'll visit the village to plan our future to attend Suyia and Carson's Mapuche wedding. Medical school's burden will be shared. In addition, I'll extend my course work with Mary to advance writing skills. It's a necessity for us both and trips to Chile serve as the window of our future," Yaima said.

"Eventually, we'll resume connection with Suyia and Carson. Mike and Elaine can visit when time allows. Life's path meanders and we're challenged to adjust. The village needs us and we need the village.

185

"My time in America has been a fabulous event. Attachment to the university, the folk dances, my teacher Mary and the friendships we've established combine in a loving and memorable manner. My life is better because of you.

"In the future, we'll reflect on this time of our lives and realize its importance in our journey," Yaima said.

"My thoughts drift back in time when young twin sisters gleaned the forest for food, and were raised by loving parents in a wild and beautiful place.

"Then one day William arrived with Jerrod and Professor Garret to install an electrical transmitter, and our lives changed forever and neither of us could've imagined what developed.

"We've toured China and made good friends. We've participated in the university talent show and taught students native folk dances and music. I married a perfect partner and we'll soon return to native roots to continue our path forward. I can't imagine how our lives could be better," Suyia said.

"Our trip to China was the best time of my life. Mike and Jerrod formed a friendship in high school; this bond continues. I relate to Jerrod's dismay, yet we've benefitted from our alliance with Jerrod. His pursuit of a medical degree with a goal to apply knowledge to assist those entrapped in poverty is linked to what's occurred. It's predictable after medical school additional lives will be influenced. The next four years are vital to Jerrod, us, and those yet to come," Elaine said.

"I've witnessed Jerrod's journey to this point. I'm excited to be given an opportunity to work with Chang Yi and promote the second-generation wireless electrical transmitter. I sense this improved system has unlimited potential," Mike said.

The next day, Yaima and Suyia went to Mary's to receive study assignments.

Mary greeted them and said to Yaima, "I've read your story. It's so good. I've made minor edits and want you to submit your story to *Nib* the university's literary magazine. This story is your first creative fiction piece and represents a springboard for future projects. I'm so proud of you.

"It's music to my ears. Thanks so much. You've provided inspiration. I've encouraged Suyia to write a short story too.

"Jerrod is in his senior year. After graduation, he'll begin medical school. We're expecting a child in the spring. My parents will travel from Chile to greet their new grandchild," Yaima said.

"Your life is unfolding in a positive direction," Mary said.

"I'll write a short story, and when Carson graduates, we'll relocate to my home village in the foothills of the Andes Mountains. Carson will assist William to teach Mapuche children," Suyia said.

Campus routines returned. Dance night remained a weekly ritual. The folk dance group will repeat their performance in the annual university talent show.

The school's newspaper featured an article on Carson and Suyia's marriage with a description of their plan to move to Suyia's home village, as Carson assumes his teaching position.

At breakfast, Yaima and Jerrod discussed the overview of current conditions.

"Medical school is my final step. Positive thrust is more important now than ever. Your support, plus encouragement from our friends shine a spotlight on how far we've come and what remains to be achieved.

"Eight years at the university is a wearing task, as the test of time forms an examination of its own. It's my job to persevere to attain the dream I've held from an early age.

"I'll have semester breaks to enjoy what life offers outside academic confinement. Your parents' visit to welcome our child and an occasional return to Chile offers psychological relief.

"Mike is ideally suited to team with Chang Yi. Carson will fall in love with the village and its surroundings. Suyia will add support directed at the entire scene. I'll apply maximum effort to what lies ahead of us," Jerrod said.

"As I contemplate our position in life, your friend Sarah's observation of how you were only at the starting line appears. Jerrod, we've left the starting line. Full stride will come after medical school. I'll be at your side every step. Our love is indomitable," Yaima said.

Yaima's thoughts affected Jerrod. Her presence provided trust with unwavering support.

The mood altered, yet friendships were steadfast as the future emits an enigma.

As fall drifted into winter, study routines prioritized with less socializing. Dance night formed camaraderie and consolation.

CHAPTER 20

GRADUATION

Mike and Elaine organized a prep rally to support an upcoming basketball game to include a bonfire, folk music and dancing. This is Mike's last season and he was chosen team captain.

As Yaima's pregnancy advanced, she continued to perform on dance night.

Mary assigned Yaima and Suyia to write short fiction and essays to be submitted to *Nib* literary journal for publication.

Rana found a source for Jerrod to purchase a pan flute to send to the young Chinese boy they met during their China tour. Jerrod purchased a piece of ebony wood with proper dimensions to carve a Mapuche flute. Yaima will teach Jerrod the procedure to carve the flute.

Jerrod received a letter from Chang Yi.

Dear Jerrod,

The second-generation transmitter is now in full production. I shipped the prototype by truck to my hometown and Stephen will travel with me to install it with relevant receptors.

The first unit off the production line will be applied to power our manufacturing facility. We have ten orders, and have not begun to actively market the system.

Soon, Mike will attain a business administration degree, and after graduation he'll become a company representative. I'll fly to the United States to facilitate a marketing office located near his and Elaine's home. I'll give you the date of my arrival. We should meet to discuss objectives and marketing strategies.

I received a letter from Mike about Yaima's pregnancy. It's an exciting time. Yaima is pure quality from every perspective.

After you become a certified physician and establish your clinic at the Mapuche village, I'd like to bring Haun and visit. Write me when you're able.
Change Yi

Jerrod's response…

Dear Friend,

I felt despair as I realized I'm obligated for an additional four years of medical school. Yaima's insight reoriented me.

Suyia married Carson, a senior student soon to receive his bachelor's degree in biology. Carson and Suyia will move permanently to the Mapuche village and he'll become William Harrington's assistant teacher for village students. His ethnicity and personality fits perfectly with Mapuche life. He'll be paid a salary equivalent to American public school teachers. Tribal members will build them a home. It's a Mapuche tradition. After this change occurs, we'll remain at our apartment until I finish medical school and serve a one-year internship at the university hospital. Yaima will care for our newborn child and continue studies with her tutor, Mary Joyce.

I'm excited for Mike. He's an ideal addition to bolster market development and could not have a more supportive partner than Elaine. His charismatic personality is a feature since I've known him.

I look forward to the time you and Haun visit it would be a good time for everyone if you and Haun join us at the Mapuche village.
Your partner and friend,
Jerrod

The basketball game's rally bonfire was successful, as many students attended. Some picked up steps to join dancers. The rally and dancers motivated the team.

Jerrod acquired woodcarving tools and Yaima instructed how to carve a Mapuche flute. Jerrod was captivated by the process and enjoyed learning this craft. Upon completion, Jerrod played the flute and felt a sense of accomplishment. He mailed the pan flute and the Mapuche flute to Jang Wei, the young boy who gifted him his Chinese flute.

The dance group repeated a performance in the university-sponsored talent show. To their delight, audience reaction duplicated last year.

Graduation day arrived. Frank and Judy attended. After the ceremony, a celebration meal was shared at Giuseppe and Sophia's Italian restaurant.

"I'll never forget my graduation days and can relate to your emotions. Life is a series of new challenges, as graduation alters your course toward new opportunities.

"Jerrod will enter medical school to become a physician. My sense of pride could not be greater," Judy said.

Mike and Elaine expressed appreciation to assist Chang Yi market wireless electrical systems. Suyia and Carson described their plan to move permanently to Suyia's home village.

"We're expecting our first child this spring. We'll remain at our apartment until I complete required academic requirements and internship to become a certified physician. Yaima will assume motherhood duties yet continue literary pursuits with her tutor Mary Joyce.

"I feel stalled; though I'll regain momentum as I proceed. I foresee us in reunion with our friends at Yaima and Suyia's village. Can you imagine the emotional stimulation this would create? Of course, we'll have a celebratory bonfire with folk music and dancing. This may represent the signature social event of our lifetime. This village; it's our refuge," Jerrod said.

"I've discussed with Judy a plan for our retirement. We agree it's possible we may establish residence at the village and assist with medical services, especially when Jerrod and Yaima travel to other countries," Frank said.

It was late when the graduation party concluded. Yaima and Jerrod thanked Giuseppe and Sophia for their gracious hospitality.

Jerrod contemplated his future during semester break.

As Yaima's delivery time neared, they would stay at Judy and Frank's home.

Suyia and Carson would leave in a week for Chile to form a new life. They would be married Mapuche style; though would wait until Jerrod and Yaima's new child was old enough to travel so they could attend the wedding.

"Let's take Suyia and Carson to dinner at Giuseppe and Sophia's Italian restaurant as a bon voyage gesture. It'll be awhile before we see them again," Yaima said.

"I'd enjoy this. Carson won't be able to keep his surplus Jeep. I'll buy it to use as a second vehicle and we'll drive it to the National Forest on weekends to take short hikes. It'd be a nice break from medical school," Jerrod said.

"Good idea," Yaima said.

The next evening, Jerrod drove them to Giuseppe and Sophia's restaurant to savor the time prior to separation. These two couples are bonded to the highest level.

During this splendid meal, Suyia said, "What's occurred since my arrival remains dreamlike. Our early life at the Mapuche village had difficult times.

"I remember once after searching for food we returned to our family shelter empty handed. A storm came in with raging force. Our mother was waiting for our father to return from hunting, and worried about him. He then appeared, and as he walked toward our shelter under a stormy sky he carried four rabbits with his bow over his shoulder. We had a fire going, and as he entered a broad smile appeared on his face and said, 'We'll eat well tonight.' This moment has remained a vivid memory. We're on the cusp of change and, with what's happened since my arrival in America, it causes similar emotions," Suyia said.

"I remember this day and felt the same. We'll reconnect with village life and I look forward to foraging for food again. Mary has a vegetable garden and she gave me a gardening book. Some Mapuche have small gardens to supplement foraging. I'll plant a garden when we return to our village," Yaima said.

"I'll do this, too, after we establish our home," Suyia said.

Jerrod told Carson he would purchase his surplus Jeep.

"I've become attached to my Jeep. I'll feel good knowing it will continue to serve a purpose. You and Yaima can explore out of the way places in the National forest.

"My mind flashes excitement, as I anticipate my teaching assignment," Carson said.

"You'll enjoy assisting William. He's the kindest, most loving person you'll ever meet. He's contributed so much to our village," Suyia said.

Sophia served Chianti and asked Yaima if everything was satisfactory.

"I wish you knew more about Mapuche life. Growing up, we had no knowledge of such exquisite food. Your fine restaurant has been a source of joy," Yaima said.

As Suyia and Carson's flight time to Santiago neared, preparations were made and Jerrod drove Yaima, Carson and Suyia to Judy and Frank's home for one-night as well as a second farewell dinner. Carson and Suyia will leave for Santiago the next day.

CHAPTER 21

SUYIA RETURNS

Jerrod called William to give arrival time and flight number. William will greet Suyia and Carson. They will follow routine to access the village, and will stay at the traditional newlywed's home at the village until tribal members construct their permanent residence.

As the four friends arrived at the airport, emotions were high as Suyia and Carson boarded their flight.

After the long flight, the plane landed at Santiago International Airport and William was at the arrival gate.

Suyia hugged William and introduced Carson.

"Welcome to Chile, you're in for the experience of your life. Jerrod described your interest in natural places you'll never find a more natural place than this Mapuche village. I'm delighted to have an assistant teacher. I'm a bit overloaded," William said.

Carson and Suyia stayed overnight with William, and the next morning Raimondi and his mules were waiting at the trailhead. Raimondi and William lashed Carson and Suyia's possessions to the mule's packsaddles and they entered the trail to the village. It was a magnificent day for the trek. The Andes Mountains represented a welcome home sign for Suyia.

They stopped for water breaks.

"William's description was true. This is a spectacular place. I've never seen such a beautiful vista," Carson said.

Suyia pointed to the sky and said, "Look, a condor. It's always a hope to sight one of these magnificent birds on the trail to the village. Jerrod observed one on his first trip, and spoke how this event affected him. They're spiritual."

"These birds are symbolically attached to the Andes Mountains," William said.

The villagers were unaware of Suyia and Carson's scheduled arrival. As they approached, they were spotted. Greeters appeared, including Yaco and Lilen.

What a joyous moment. Suyia hugged her parents and introduced Carson.

"You'll share meals with us until you're settled. We want to hear news of Jerrod and Yaima," Lilen said.

"I'm so happy to be home. We'll have a Mapuche wedding, though we will wait until Jerrod and Yaima are able to attend. They'll visit as soon as their baby is old enough to travel."

"Carson and Suyia will occupy the newlywed dwelling," Suyia said.

While Lilen and Suyia prepared food, Carson accompanied William and Yaco to tour the village to introduce their new teacher. They visited the school, and also showed Carson the wireless electrical transmitter Jerrod and Stephen installed to power the village water pump and lights for the school.

"You remind me of Jerrod. Your personalities are similar. I'm grateful you'll be William's assistant. Education is vital to assimilate with the dynamics of diversity, as we've observed with Yaima and Suyia. We adhere to native Mapuche tradition, though this will alter over time. Jerrod introduced this reality to Yaima and Suyia," Yaco said.

The family gathered and Lilen and Suyia served the evening meal. Unleavened flat bread with steamed wild leeks, venison strips cooked in spicy sauce topped with a variety of crushed nuts for flavor. Carson was fascinated and wondered what Giuseppe and Sophia would think of this meal.

The next day, Suyia and Carson took a long walk in the nearby landscape. Carson carried his camera.

"This is the hallowed ground of my youth. I know every square foot, as Yaima and I spent our childhood gleaning this forest for edible plants taught by parents," Suyia said.

"As I'm exposed to your culture, I think of Jerrod's observation about how your native roots align with my persona. I could've never imagined I'd live in paradise married to an extraordinary and beautiful young woman. It's as if we are connected by a divine consciousness. It would be impossible for me love someone more than I love you," Carson said.

Suyia hugged Carson and said, "Our genetic profiles contribute intensity. Our future surrounds us.

"When Jerrod and Yaima move to the village, we'll unite to establish a Mapuche medical clinic and Jerrod will train me and my sister as physician assistants. You'll teach village children and I'll assist Jerrod and Yaima to provide medical services.

"Mapuche children align with biology studies. They're tightly woven threads of life within the fabric of an organic terrestrial environment forming a profound student/teacher link. I'm assigned to teach children whose lives are immersed in nature and, by osmosis, more intimately attached with terrestrial life than one with a college degree in biology," Carson said.

"Yes, a sagacious observation. I'm inspired to contribute. I've studied Mary's gardening book and I'll plant an exhibition garden to stimulate villagers to plant gardens. This could offer a supplemental food source. Yaima gave me Mary's book and seed packets. I brought the seeds with me," Suyia said.

"I'll assist you to plant your garden," Carson said.

Evening meals with Yaco and Lilen were special. Suyia parents admired Carson. Mealtime discussions ventured to various subjects.

"As I anticipate our trip to the United States, the excitement of the arrival of our grandchild dominates thoughts. We've never traveled beyond our village and to fly on an airplane such a distance is frightful; however, we won't hesitate.

"Our friendship with Judy and Frank reduces apprehension. It'll be a pleasure to see them again. What a wonderful time we shared at Jerrod and Yaima's wedding," Lilen said.

"William will obtain passports and guide you to the airport departure gate. Jerrod will greet you when you disembark the plane.

"It's a normal reaction to feel uneasiness, as I did on my arrival to America. Judy, Frank, Jerrod and Yaima love you to so much. They'll apply full effort to comfort you. To be present at your grandchild's birth will be monumental. Can you imagine the joy it?" Suyia asked.

"I promise we'll be there," Yaco said.

Suyia and Carson planted their garden near the school. They posted a sign stating,

This is a demonstration garden. If you have questions, please ask.

We encourage others to plant gardens as a means of food supplementation.

Suyia and Carson worked the soil and planted seeds and a few villagers showed interest.

William stopped by the garden and said, "I wanted to do this a few years ago, but my teaching responsibility prevented time allotment.

"This is excellent, if we're able to convince others to plant gardens it'll benefit everyone. I'll purchase more seeds, as encouragement."

"I'll offer assistance to those interested," Suyia said.

CHAPTER 22

YAIMA PERFORMS MAGIC

As spring waned, the expecting couple confronted pending changes a new child would bring. They would stay with Judy and Frank during the third trimester. Yaima's parents would arrive from Chile prior to their first grandchild's birth.

Yaima and Jerrod settled in at Judy and Frank's home. The mood was mixed with excitement and concern.

"I've never felt such a range of emotions. At our village, the gifted seamstress serves as a midwife," Yaima said, at breakfast.

"Expecting parents cope with an emotional rollercoaster. I don't anticipate complications and joy will overpower you beyond your imagination. Love pours from your heart like a gift from God. The baby will become your priority," Judy said.

Discussion directed toward children and the positive energy a new child offers a family. Parents shared their child's development, as memories emerge from their own youth.

Jerrod and Yaima took daily walks. They read parenting guidelines. Yaima put Jerrod's hand on her stomach when she detected movement. The bond begins before birth.

Frank and Judy purchased a baby bed, highchair, blankets, diapers and a playpen.

Parental support made Jerrod more secure. Frank and Judy showed exceptional kindness toward Yaima.

William arranged for Yaco and Lilen's travel to the United States. He called Jerrod to give arrival date, time and flight number. They will depart in a week.

William drove Yaco and Lilen to the airport. The Mapuche couple boarded the flight to The United States.

As they disembarked from the plane in Philadelphia, Jerrod hugged them and said, "Welcome to America. So good to see you two."

"I never dreamed we'd come America. We've never been on a plane or ridden in a car," Yaco said.

They drove to Judy and Frank's house. Yaima, Judy and Frank were waiting on the front porch.

"I'm elated to see you two again. You're welcome here. How could we be more blessed than to be present for the arrival of our first grandchild?" Judy said.

"I was apprehensive, yet I'm so happy to be here. We frequently reminisce the wonderful time we shared at our humble village," Lilen said.

"I feel a sense of calm with my parents present to fortify my courage," Yaima said.

"We intend to spend semester breaks in Chile. We look forward to living in our Mapuche house after I become a certified physician. We enjoy campus life with the dance group and friends we've made; however, the village is our dream. Carson is an ideal choice for Suyia. He's pure quality from head to toe. I enjoy his company," Jerrod said.

A plan was established. When Yaima's water broke everyone would go into action. Frank would drive and Yaima and Jerrod would ride in the back seat on the way to the hospital. Judy would drive Yaco and Lilen and follow. It could happen at any time, as Yaima's due date approached.

Frank and Judy pressed hospitality to the limit. They took Yaco and Lilen on a local tour, and shared a photo album of Jerrod's early years.

It was midnight and Yaima woke Jerrod, "My water broke and I've had a contraction."

Jerrod leaped from bed and quickly dressed. Then, he alerted everyone. The team sprang into action and on the road in a matter of minutes.

It was a five-mile drive to the hospital. They entered the emergency entrance and Yaima was taken directly to the delivery room. Jerrod will remain with her during delivery. The others waited in a designated family area.

An hour passed. Jerrod appeared and sat next to Judy. He displayed a huge smile and said, "Twin boys."

It was June 1st, 1974. Jerrod was twenty years old.

Judy broke into tears.

"Will this ever be fun," Frank said.

Yaco and Lilen hugged each other, "I'm not surprised but I couldn't be happier," Yaco said.

Lilen hugged Jerrod and asked. "When can we see these two angels from God?"

"It shouldn't be long," Jerrod responded.

A few minutes passed and a nurse motioned the family toward the delivery room.

Yaima smiled as they entered and said, "Double trouble. I never knew such joy existed. What happens from here forward will be times four."

"I felt the same emotion when you and Suyia were born." With tears of joy in her eyes, she hugged her daughter," Lilen said.

"You've delivered us two precious packages of life," Yaco said.

The delivery room became engulfed in love from this life-altering event.

Frank and Jerrod stood together soaking up the unforgettable experience. Jerrod kissed Yaima and the tiny newborns.

Yaima would stay overnight to nurse her precious twins and be released the next day.

Jerrod, Lilen and Yaco came the next morning to take Yaima and her babies back home. Frank went shopping for a second highchair, baby bed and more diapers.

Frank took photos of Jerrod and Yaima with their twin boys. They rolled the baby beds to different locations in the house to monitor the infants. Jerrod became the primary diaper changer, as Yaima was still weak from labor. While the twins slept, Frank and Judy prepared the evening meal.

Yaima's appetite returned and food regenerated her. As the extended family gathered, the mood reflected a sense of comfort in commemoration of this benchmark event.

"I've never experienced such a powerful sensation as the arrival of these two. As we gaze at the newborns, we feel the power of love in a spiritually magnified manner carrying us to an unknown plane prior to their birth.

"The path forward is unknown, yet we're at the trailhead of our future as a family. As my dad stated, 'this will be fun'," Jerrod said.

"I couldn't agree more. I'm filled with joyful anticipation," Judy said.

"It feels as if I've been reborn. The excitement of being present to share Yaima and Jerrod's joy is indescribable," Lilen said.

"What about names?" Frank asked.

"We discussed this. Yaima wants them to have American first names and Mapuche middle names. This is a good plan. They'll decide preferences as they mature," Jerrod said.

"If grandparents choose the twin's names, it'll add personal connection.

Lilen and Yaco will select Mapuche names. Judy and Frank will select American names," Yaima said.

"This may take a while," Judy said.

Motherly instincts emerged as Yaima watched her twins as they slept and nursed.

Jerrod called Mike. He answered.

"Twin boys. It was the most powerful moment in my life," Jerrod said.

"This is fabulous news. I'm so happy for you two," Mike said.

"It's indescribable. They're beautiful. I'm proud of Yaima. Her Mapuche genes continue to activate. I'm blessed to have her as my wife. Yaima's parents Yaco and Lilen were present when the twins were born. Yaima assigned grandparents to choose names. They'll have American first names and Mapuche middle name. As my dad said, 'This will be so much fun,'" Jerrod said.

"We'll drive to my parents' house early next week and visit to see the twins.

"My new office is nearby. Things are moving faster than anticipated," Mike said.

"OK, good. We look forward to seeing you and Elaine," Jerrod said.

The twins name selection became the priority. Lilen and Yaco were the first to reveal selections, Newan and Akan.

"They're easy to pronounce," Yaco said.

Judy and Frank read lists of names trying to decide.

In early morning, Jerrod entered thoughts in his journal.

I can't adequately describe my state of mind, as I project images of two energized boys roaming the forest immersed in natural wonders or up late reading a book. Thoughts appear of times when we'll share moments of pride as they are recognized for personal achievements.

Life unfolds inexplicably as we confront its infinite components. As I observe our infant twins, I speculate two fledgling life forms striving unconsciously to gain footing to eclipse challenges early life reveals. The wonder of it overpowers me.

Mike and Elaine arrived; the reunion was a moment of joy. Changes have come rapidly and intervals of absence form a higher sense of gratitude for reconnections.

With pride, Yaima showed her perfect tiny creations. Mike and Elaine were shaken with emotion. Elaine especially couldn't take her eyes off the two precious infants.

"We're trying to have a child and, as I observe these two, it drives my desire to a new level. They captivate me like nothing I recall. This time in your life pales past experiences, as love moves to a new dimension, as we share your exuberance," Elaine said.

Judy served tea and scones. The twins dominated conversation.

"Name choices are a greater challenge than I imagined," Judy said.

"It seems names should ring a tone of dual identity," Frank said.

"Their father's name is Jerrod, so it'd be suitable to give them phonetically similar names. How about Justin and Jordan?" Elaine suggested.

"I love them; Jerrod, Justin and Jordan a trio to confront the future. They'll be unstoppable to face life's challenges.

"We're young parents but, as the twins mature, our age difference will be less apparent. I'm excited to watch them grow. Their destiny is our destiny and we'll share every moment from this point forward," Yaima said.

"Elaine hit the jackpot. These names are perfect," Judy said.

Everyone agreed they were ideal choices.

Jerrod looked into the baby's beds and said, "Hey, you two, welcome to your future. It'll be a grand journey. You'll be Justin and Jordan from this moment and onto the rest of your lives."

The infants' bright eyes made contact with their dad's and this moment of endearment consumed everyone.

Yaco and Lilen would return to Chile next week.

"Our lives continue to connect regardless of distance. This event we've shared is truly indescribable," Yaco said.

"America is my new love, yet our village beckons and we must return," Lilen said.

The twins grew rapidly. Yaima and Jerrod were busy attending their needs.

Judy and Frank will follow Jerrod and Yaima on the return drive to campus to transport baby care equipment. Yaima will ride in the backseat with the twins strapped in safety car seats.

They arrived at Jerrod and Yaima's apartment and unloaded both cars. Judy and Frank will stay overnight and return the next day. Jerrod begins medical school in three days and will register tomorrow. Yaima called Mary and they will stop by with the twins to discuss a plan.

Jerrod knocked on Mary's door. As she opened it, she saw Jerrod and Yaima each were holding an infant. "This is a miracle, they're so beautiful. Come in we'll have tea and enjoy this moment together," Mary said.

"I'm facing four years of medical school.
I'll serve internship at the University Hospital. Upon completion, we'll return to the Mapuche village as permanent residents," Jerrod said.

"Time self generates our lives, so we're forced to adjust. I'm familiar with this reality. I was overly eager to attain my PhD, only to realize my career would scream by at light speed. Now, I'm a widow in decline. You're at a crossroad to achieve your dream.

"I miss Suyia. She sent a beautiful letter to describe her reversion to Mapuche tribal life. Carson is her support pillar and they're ideally suited for each other. I'm delighted," Mary said.

"I'm glad to be back and look forward to my advancement as a writer. This dominates thoughts, though the twins are our priority," Yaima said.

Chang Yi called. Jerrod answered.

"Has the baby arrived?" Change Yi asked.

Jerrod laughed and said, "Yes, times two. Yaima had twin boys. I'm contending with dual emotions. Shock and joy hit

205

me simultaneously. It was the most overpowering moment of my life.

"When can you visit? My mind is overloaded with questions. We need to discuss things."

"I share your jubilation, as you and Yaima greet your gifts from God. My children's births were the most important events of my life and now I rely on them more than they rely on me. I look forward to meeting the twins.

"I'll arrive early next week to brief you on progression. Mike's the mainspring of our market development force and represents my eyes and ears to western market connections. I'll call with arrival date," Chang Yi said.

Jerrod gave Chang Yi directions to their apartment and informed Yaima he called.

A week later, Chang Yi rang the doorbell and Jerrod opened the door.

"Come in partner, glad to see you," Jerrod said.

Yaima hugged Chang Yi and said, "I'm eager to show you the twins. Their names are Justin and Jordan with Mapuche middle names, Newan and Akan.

Chang Yi followed Jerrod and Yaima into the bedroom. The twins were sleeping. It was an emotional moment, though Chang Yi didn't speak as to not disturb them.

They returned to the kitchen table for tea.

Chang Yi said, "You're blessed; they're magnificent. These two will share exciting times their future is sure to deliver."

"Yesterday, they smiled; it melted my heart," Yaima said.

"They're our priority and my motivation," Jerrod added.

"I felt this when my children were born," Chang Yi said.

"I'm fortunate to be able to continue studies. My tutor, Mary, enjoys the twins as much as we do," Yaima said.

"What's the latest development with the transmitter?" Jerrod asked.

"I'm unsure where to begin. Mike's contribution has been exemplary. He's an exceptional communicator and customers are drawn to his charisma. He's represented our company at several electronic promotional events.

"I've expanded production again to maintain pace with demand. Stephen retired as a physics professor and moved to China. We're constructing him a small house on our property. He'll live with us until his house is completed. He's learning to speak Chinese using audiotapes and practicing with my son and daughter during daily interaction.

"Training installation teams will be Stephen's primary assignment. English is commonly taught in many countries, and we'll use interpreters when needed. Production is challenged to fulfill demand," Chang Yi said.

"During medical school, we'll travel with the twins to the Mapuche village during semester breaks to lay groundwork for the clinic. It's my goal to have the clinic operational by the time I finish internship. I'll write Stephen to explain our current status," Jerrod said.

"Jerrod, you are the most dynamic person I've ever known.

"As I contemplate things overall, you remain the catalyst of what's happened in our lives and continue to energize and stimulate what our collective future holds. The infants I've been introduced to will be genetically gifted, as you'll observe your and Yaima's traits appear. I hope I live to witness what they'll offer the world.

"I'm scheduled to meet Mike and we'll form a concise marketing plan. I'll send periodic notifications to keep you abreast of developments," Chang Yi said.

"I appreciate whatever you send. Our twins and my medical degree are priorities," Jerrod said.

Chang Yi departed the next morning to meet with Mike and Elaine.

Jerrod wrote Professor Garrett.

Dear Stephen,

I met with Chang Yi yesterday. He described your move to China. I'm pleased you've made this change. You'll not only witness your dream materialize you're attached to its occurrence.

I'll send photographs of our new additions. Twin boys; they're pure joy. We selected American and Mapuche names. American names are Justin and Jordan. Mapuche names are Newan and Akan.

We'll visit China again someday, though, presently, our plates are full. I'll enter medical school and Yaima is committed to the twins. She'll also continue her study regimen with her tutor, Mary Joyce.

We'll begin arrangement of the village medical clinic during semester breaks.

It's always a pleasure to hear from you. My memory of our time shared to install the first transmitter will never fade.

I'll assist you in any manner I'm able. It's important to remain connected as friends and colleagues.

I remain your student.

Jerrod

Jerrod received his medical school class schedule. Folk dance night returned. Rana entered her senior year. Her music professor arranged an audition for the Philadelphia Symphony. Suyia's voice will be absent. Music will be presented as a trio. Mary Joyce will care for the Justin and Jordan on folk dance night as Jerrod moves forward to become a certified physician.

The first semester of medical school was an entirely different atmosphere than undergraduate courses. Anatomy is the most difficult, as the entire human skeletal structure must be memorized in order to pass the final exam.

Mary assisted Yaima outline her novel. Yaima became consumed with this project combined with motherhood responsibilities. Mike and Elaine were engrossed with their lives in concert with Chang Yi. Suyia and Carson permanently reside at the village in the foothills of the Andes Mountains. Jerrod's parents were busy with physician duties, as life's path turned for everyone.

The twins blossomed like spring wildflowers. Jerrod and Yaima were enraptured as they observed daily progression.

As semester break neared, Jerrod plans to visit Chile to reunite at the village. Justin and Jordon won't walk for a year or more, though this trip will give Yaco and Lilen opportunity to spend time with their grandchildren.

CHAPTER 23

SUYIA AND CARSON'S MAPUCHE WEDDING

Jerrod wrote William Harington to inform him of date and time of their arrival. He outlined his plan to construct a Mapuche style building to house the clinic while he finishes medical school and internship.

Yaima received a letter from Suyia.

Dear Yaima,

Things here could not be better. Carson assisted to plant a demonstration vegetable garden. It's been successful to a greater degree than I anticipated. William purchased additional seeds to distribute and gardens are popping up everywhere. Mapuche work ethic is ideally suited to gardening.

Carson enjoys his students especially field trips for nature studies. He's amazed at their biological knowledge and botanical identity knowledge.

Tribal members are constructing our permanent Mapuche home. I'm so happy, though I miss weekly folk dances.

Our parents continue to develop attachment to the twins. The unforgettable experience of being present for their birth is a permanent presence in their memories.

I'm writing my first short story. I'll mail it to you for Mary to edit. Maybe she will submit it to a literary journal.

I hope you visit as soon as the twins are old enough to travel. I miss you so much. We will have our Mapuche wedding during your visit.
Love,
Suyia

Jerrod drew a dimensional layout of his proposed clinic and mailed it to William. He received a response letter.

Dear Jerrod,

I'll present your clinic's drawing to tribal members for discussion. Mormon youth are obligated to serve missionary service tasks. I'll contact Mormon elders to assign a group to assist the tribe construct your clinic. I did this when we built the school and it worked well.

I received your itinerary. I'll pick you up at the airport as usual. I'm excited to see your twin boys. What a thrill this will be for everyone.
William

Prior to departure, Jerrod called Judy to inform her and Frank of their plan to attend Suyia and Carson's Mapuche wedding.

Jerrod and Yaima entered the airport each carrying a twin in frontal child packs, as Jerrod pulled a cart with luggage to the check-in counter. Justin and Jordan were quiet babies, though alert to their surroundings, as they gazed curiously at everything in sight.

William was at the arrival gate when Jerrod and Yaima disembarked, carrying Justin and Jordan.

William addressed the twins. "Justin and Jordan, welcome to Chile. I'm pleased to meet you."

They looked directly at William and smiled.

William laughed and said, "These two will charm the entire village."

The next morning, Jerrod and Yaima carried the twins on the trail to the village stopping often for water. The pack mules fascinated the twins.

"It's emotional to return to the village with our twins. It'll be a thrill to introduce Justin and Jordon to Mapuche friends," Yaima said.

"Each trip, we'll enjoy their development and it'll be more fun when they begin to run and play. I can hardly wait," Jerrod said.

This trail enlightens travelers with its spectacular vistas. They were blessed with a condor sighting, which was deemed a good omen.

The villagers were expecting Yaima and Jerrod with their twin boys. The trekkers were spotted as they approached. Yaco, Lilen, Suyia and Carson walked together to meet them as they approached. The joy of the moment could not be greater.

Hugs were shared and Lilen said, "I've dreamed of this moment since we departed America after these angels entered our lives. I don't recall being so overpowered with joy and happiness."

"The twins smiled at me at the airport and I felt the same emotion. If they have such charm as infants, I wonder to what degree this will expand? It's a genetic transfer," William said.

"Returning to the village and our small Mapuche home is such a joy. I yearn to never leave, though we're obligated to remain at the university for Jerrod to achieve his physician's certification," Yaima said.

"During the interim, we'll arrange travel to visit. Suyia, Carson, Yaco and Lilen can visit. We'll enjoy reconnection via air travel. What an amazing experience it would be for Yaco and Lilen to attend folk dance night. The dancers would love this. Yaima and Suyia can reform their duet and Carson can dance with his sister again," Jerrod said.

"We must do this, it'll ease Jerrod's medical school tension," Yaima said.

"We'll share meals at our home during your stay," Yaco said.

"I've a better idea. Let's alternate between family members' homes. It'll be pleasant to socialize and discuss the future. We'll be a close-knit family for years to come. It's Mapuche tradition to share blessings," Yaima said.

Yaco agreed it was a better plan.

After Jerrod and Yaima organized, they carried Justin and Jordan as they, with Suyia and Carson, toured village garden plots.

William joined them and expressed pleasure for the interest in gardens. He also disclosed tomorrow afternoon a presentation would be held at the school to unveil Jerrod's plans for the clinic.

They returned to their home. As the twins crawled about at Yaima's feet, she said, "I'm so happy to be here, as I visualize Justin and Jordan in a few years roaming the village and nearby forest.

"I'd like to carry them to a special spot Suyia and I visited often when we were young. It's near a beautiful flowing stream."

The next afternoon, they met at the school and Jerrod spoke,

"Last night, Yaima expressed happiness for the return to her place of birth. Each time we walk the trail to your village, I'm lifted spiritually.

"It was a cool last night and we lit our fire pit, as Justin and Jordon crawled about in the flickering light. This moment defined our destiny. "I'm entering the final stage to become a certified physician and this relates to our return to the village.

"I've asked myself: where and how should I apply my medical skills? This village is a place of harmonious coexistence and self-sufficiency. The tribe's independence could be improved with the installation of a medical clinic. The timing is right to begin construction of this clinic to serve the village and neighboring residents. This village will become our base, as Yaima and I will team to assist with medical services at foreign locations. Yaima and Suyia will be trained as physician assistants. When Yaima and I are absent, Suyia will attend village medical needs.

"A few years ago, I formed the Sarah Baker Charitable Foundation. I now have thirty benefactors, including Yaima and me. Funds from this foundation will be used to construct similar clinics at impoverished third world locations. I'll sponsor local youth to obtain medical service skills through educational grants. Some may become doctors while others will be trained as nurse practitioners. Staff will be paid with foundation funds.

"William is working with the Mormon church to assign student missionaries to assist in the construction of our clinic, as he did when the school was built.

"The purpose of this visit is to detail plans and enjoy our Mapuche home. Justin and Jordon are too young to remember this trip, though it's fun to introduce them to village residents.

"Our future will become what we make it. I feel positive about the longevity of the tribe. I'll do everything possible to support Yaima, our twins and Mapuche culture."

Everyone applauded in a display of hope and confidence, as they venture forth united.

The next day, Yaima guided Jerrod to her childhood soul spot.

They carried Justin and Jordon on a narrow trail and entered a grassy meadow bordered by a shallow meandering stream strewn with colorful rocks. As they sat with their twins on a platform rock, the sound of rushing water formed mood music. On the opposite side of the creek was dense forest.

215

"Suyia and I find beautiful stones here used to make pendant necklaces. We're the only ones who know of this spot.

"Since we first met, I've craved to show you this revered place. The diamond mounted on my engagement ring is a stone. When you gave it to me, thoughts of this creek appeared.

"Once on a warm summer day, we were searching the stream bed for special stones. I found the most beautiful multicolored stone we'd ever seen. Suyia looked at me and I read her expression. She was envious and wanted this stone to make a necklace. I said to her. 'This stone was made by God. It's too beautiful to keep. I want to return it to its place of origin.' She was silent for a minute, then said, 'Yes, let's throw it back.' I threw this magnificent stone into the water," Yaima said.

"You two are identical in mind, body and spirit. This is a tranquil place," Jerrod said.

They waded into the flowing stream. Yaima put the twin's feet in the water. They smiled and reached down to touch the ripples.

They carried their boys and hiked back home in anticipation of Suyia and Carson's wedding.

William departed to retrieve Judy and Frank from the airport to attend the wedding.

Villagers were on the lookout for the mule team. They were surprised to see two additional travelers walking the trail toward the village. Judy and Frank brought Rana and Carson's sister, Maryanne.

As they arrived, Carson was overjoyed to see his sister as they have been close their entire lives. Judy and Frank will stay with Yaco and Lilen. Rana and Maryanne will sleep at the school's dormitory. Suyia and Yaima will prepare meals for the group. Yaco and Lilen were especially glad to see Judy and Frank.

The wedding will take place in two days. The tribal elder Quidel will perform the ceremony.

They gathered at the school for discussion. Rana said, "I'll take photographs to send to my family in Ghana. I could've never imagined such a beautiful place as this village. I'm grateful to Judy and Frank for inviting me."

"We discussed it and questioned why we didn't think of it earlier. It made perfect sense to invite Rana and Maryanne. We knew they'd have a life changing experience," Frank said.

"What's occurred at our village over the past few years seems miraculous. William responded to Jerrod's inquiry letter about installation an electrical transmitter he and Professor Garrett developed. What transpired created where we are at this moment.

"As I look at my beautiful twin grandsons, a wave of love engulfs me. My mind flashes to the day Professor Garrett and Jerrod arrived at our village with William. When I first observed Jerrod, I wondered how a teenage boy fit into this picture. It seemed unusual, yet, as time passed, we learned Jerrod was the impetus of the project. He located Professor Garrett and assisted him to construct the electrical transmitter system, which changed our lives forever," Lilen said.

"Suyia and Carson's wedding extends family composition.

"When Suyia and I were very young, Mapuche social format exposed a terrestrial voice and development years formed our personalities.

"Jerrod's suggestion for Suyia to live with us in America allowed her to share opportunities I've had. Our amazing tutor, Mary Joyce, taught us. Mary is a retired English literature professor and contributed immensely to our academic development.

"Suyia met Carson while participating in the university's Mapuche folk dance group. This brought us together to witness this significant event in our lives. Is this good fortune, blind fate or divine intervention? It's seems too monumental to have appeared out of nowhere. Historic sages describe spirit guides. I'm convinced such guides led us to this place in time. Suyia and Carson's wedding bonds them to Mapuche culture," Yaima said.

The wedding day arrived and Jerrod walked with Carson to the seating circle to join Quidel and wait for Suyia. Her parents and Yaima escorted her. She looked magnificent in her native dress. Carson wore Jerrod's Mapuche tunic. Yaima will stand near Carson and quietly interpret Quidel as he performs the ceremony. Jerrod took a seat next to Yaco and Lilen. Judy, Frank, Rana and Maryanne sat next to Jerrod.

The seating was at capacity. After the couple kissed to seal the marriage, everyone cheered. Carson and Suyia departed for their matrimonial woodland saunter. They will return for the celebration bonfire.

Darkness descended and William lit the bonfire. Yaima will sing Mapuche folk songs accompanied by Jerrod and Rana on their flutes.

Carson and Suyia returned among broad smiles and tears of joy. Everyone hugged.

Music began and dancers formed a circle holding hands. Judy and Frank joined in, as they reminisced their first visit.

Suyia and Carson held hands with Yaco, Lilen, Judy and Frank. Maryanne was beckoned to join two Mapuche couples.

Bonfire dances are the primary celebratory source for the Mapuche tribe.

Rana's pan flute resonated with Jerrod's Mapuche flute and created musical ambience. Yaima's voice blended perfectly with the flutes. Music and dancing, in the glimmering light of the bonfire created a sacred mood, allowing the scene to reach back to touch ancient Mapuche history.

They danced late into the night. Exhaustion finally took its toll as the bonfire died down to glowing embers.

Weary dancers departed to their residences. Judy and Frank approached the newlyweds.

Judy said to Suyia and Carson, "This is a memorable time. We'll often speak of this special night in days to come. It's heartwarming to share your wedding day," Judy said.

"This is our second experience attending a Mapuche wedding and its wonder," Frank said.

In three days, Judy, Frank, Jerrod, Yaima, Justin, Jordan, Maryanne and Rana would return to Philadelphia.

The next day, everyone went for a walk in the forest. Yaima remained to care for Justin and Jordan. Carson and Jerrod took photos. It was a spectacular day and Lilen identified frequently harvested woodland edible plants.

Raimondi and his mules arrived on the second day after the wedding and visitors will depart the following morning.

Departure emotions intensified. They promised letters and visits to America will be arranged. During the flight home, thoughts of their time at the village were shared.

"I can't describe my feelings. I compare it to my home country, yet Mapuche are unique. I feel blessed. I'll write my parents to describe this wonderful experience," Rana said.

"When I first arrived with Stephen, we were given pendants by Suyia and Yaima as welcome gifts and I felt a powerful emotional surge. Each time I return, this blissful feeling reemerges.

"I took an undergraduate course titled 'The Psychology of Spiritual Growth'. One of our assignments was to write an essay to describe personal goals. My essay's title was 'Follow Your Heart' and I followed mine to a Mapuche village in Chile," Jerrod said.

"I've attempted to explain the Mapuche to colleagues, yet words are inadequate to clarify this sacred fulfillment," Judy said.

When they returned, Yaima's days were filled as she cared for her twins and studied with Mary. She became engrossed in her novel project's creation. Weekly folk dances served as relief. Jerrod walked alone each day for exercise as Yaima was occupied with childcare and study. Spruce grove concerts were now a memory. Justin and Jordan developed daily as Yaima and Jerrod observed changes.

Medical school curriculum introduced the wide variation of medical specialties. Jerrod became interested in immunology, as he thought of health crisis events caused by virus exposures from human-to-human contact.

Cadavers were used to teach surgical procedures in a refrigerated classroom with mirrors to demonstrate techniques. This allowed hands on surgical experience.

Jerrod received a letter from Professor Garrett.

Dear Jerrod,

Many changes in my life have occurred. I'm now living at a small home Chang Yi constructed for me. I'm learning to speak Chinese assisted by audiotapes.

I've been teaching installation teams for our new transmitter. I enjoyed traveling to Chang Yi's hometown, as we installed our prototype transmitter to add more efficient electrical service to their town.

Age is descending, yet I remain valuable as an advisor. I'm gratified to witness our original concept become widely received and applied.

I'd enjoy any news about your life. Chang Yi described the twins. What a joyful time for you and Yaima. Write when time allows.

Stephen

CHAPTER 24

CHILEAN GOVERNMENT

Time moved quickly and semester break arrived. Jerrod had things in order for their return to Chile.

William was waiting when they arrived and commented on how the twins had grown.

They stayed overnight at William's apartment and planned to walk the trail to the village the next morning.

"Something has developed. We'll need to work together to investigate it. We've observed activity surrounding the village. A helicopter drops two men off at various locations and they camp a day or two and then the helicopter retrieves them.

Yesterday a company of Chilean army troops landed and set up camp. I approached the troops and spoke to the company commander and asked him what their purpose is for camping here. The commander said he was ordered to camp near the village. The Chile Ministry of Lands is in the process of evaluation of proposed changes that may affect the areas future. I have no further knowledge or details.

"I've contacted the Chile Ministry of Lands and have an appointment with the head of the agency next week to discuss this activity. After I guide you to the village and stay a few days, I'd like Jerrod to accompany me to attend this meeting. I watched the first team of two with my binoculars and it appears they're taking soil and rock samples," William said.

"It may be an effort to evaluate mineral deposits. This could be political and needs to be investigated. The presence of the military exposes the seriousness of the issue. I'll definitely accompany you," Jerrod said.

"I'm glad Jerrod will be involved," Yaima said.

"The good news is the Mormon Church has organized a group of student missionaries to assist construction of the medical clinic," William said.

The next day, Jerrod and Yaima packed the twins to the village. They were heavier and more difficult to carry. Soon, they will need to ride the mules. It will be awhile before they can walk the trail on their own.

Yaco, Lilen, Suyia and Carson and a few village residents greeted them. They shared the evening meal with Yaco and Lilen. Discussion centered on the mysterious intrusion including army troops.

"It's worrisome. The Chilean government has ignored the Mapuche and the land where our village is located is not identified as a legal reservation purposely to disallow rights. They've forbidden firearms to make us vulnerable to government intervention and control," Yaco said.

William and Jerrod returned to William's apartment to meet with the Chilean minister of lands at Santiago.

As they entered the minister's office, his secretary greeted them. "Good afternoon, Minister Gonzales will meet with you shortly. He's presently having his afternoon sweet-cakes and coffee."

William and Jerrod waited about thirty minutes and the secretary directed them into the minister's office.

Gonzales was sitting at his desk and introduced himself without standing. He was morbidly obese; a plate of cake crumbs and an empty cup were on his desk. His secretary removed these items and left the room.

"What can I do for you today? I'm on a tight schedule. I hope this meeting will be short," Gonzales said.

"We'll try to be brief. I'm a Mormon Church missionary assigned to offer assistance to a Mapuche tribe located in a remote area south of the Andes Mountains. We've observed frequent helicopter landings and it appears to be an effort to test for mineral deposits. An army company also set up camp to impose military presence. We're interested to know details attached to this activity," William said.

"Oh yes, the Mapuche, they're a damned nuisance. They've been a thorn in our side for years.

"You're correct in your assumption. What you've observed are geologists commissioned by an American mining company to assess mineral deposits. If they discover favorable geological conditions, they've offered the Chilean government five million US dollars for mineral rights to the area. They intend to build access roads and related structures to begin a large-scale mining operation and the Mapuche will be required to relocate and the Chilean Army will oversee Mapuche relocation. They're waiting for test results prior to payment."

"I'm the founder and CEO of an American company and benefactor for the Mapuche tribe. I'm prepared to pay the Chilean government seven million dollars to purchase one thousand hectares of land surrounding the Mapuche village to include mineral rights. In addition, I'll contribute five million dollars to your political party. My attorney will send you my personal and company certified financial statements with a contract to be executed regarding the aforementioned offer. This offer is pending until a valid legal property deed is produced and assigned to the Sarah Baker charitable foundation," Jerrod said.

Gonzales changed his tone immediately. "Well, Mr. James, this is a vast sum of money. I'll present your offer to the land development subcommittee."

"William represents the foundation and will relay progression on the matter. We'd be appreciative if this offer is expedited and finalized as soon as possible," Jerrod said.

"I'll call you for information concerning your subcommittee's progress," William said.

"Mr. Gonzales, you and your political party may view the Mapuche as a nuisance; however, I don't share this opinion. Thank you for your time," Jerrod said.

William and Jerrod shook Gonzales's hand and departed his office.

On the return drive to his apartment, William said, "Did you notice the expression on the vermin's face when you made your offer?"

"Yes, he's a political parasite. Money is their god," Jerrod said.

Upon return to William's apartment, Jerrod called his accountant and attorney to explain the circumstances. They planned to correspond with Gonzales and provide pertinent documents for the Chilean government subcommittee.

The next morning, William and Jerrod were on the return trail to paradise. No mules, just two remarkable men who confronted a corrupt government to save a precious culture.

Upon arrival, William walked the village to inform residents to meet at the school the next day at noon.

Jerrod went to his home. He hugged Yaima and the twins and explained the meeting.

"This reminds me of a conversation we shared with college friends when you stated how money can be a double edged sword. You were swinging this magical sword during your confrontation with evil. I love you more each day," Yaima said.

Village residents crowded in the school and Jerrod spoke.

"William and I met with the government's minister of lands regarding recent activity in the vicinity of the village. Helicopter landings were to perform geological tests for mineral deposits in our area. An American mining company with ambition to purchase mineral rights from the Chilean government to establish a mining operation near our village performed these tests. The mining company offered five million US dollars to the Chilean government for mineral rights to the land surrounding us. This would involve road construction and building erections to accommodate mining operational needs.

224

The government planned to force Mapuche village residents to relocate. The Chilean Army was sent to supervise the relocation of the tribe and abandon the village.

"I told the minister of lands I wanted to purchase one thousand hectares of land surrounding our village and offered seven million US dollars, which would include mineral rights, and the purchase would require a certified legal deed to this land to be assigned to the Sarah Baker Charitable Foundation. In addition, I offered to contribute an additional five million US dollars to the minister's political party.

"Knowing the corrupt status of Chilean politics, I'm confident this additional proposal will tip the scale in our favor. I called my attorney and he'll coordinate the sale and deed activation.

"The minister of lands will contact William if the Chilean political subcommittee accepts our offer.

"My personal ambition remains to open medical clinics in impoverished areas of the world. Our village's clinic will serve as a model.

"The electrical transmitter Professor Garrett and I created is manufactured in China and marketed globally. This provides fiscal leverage to cope with political barriers we'll likely confront, as greed and politics are synonymous. Money stimulates corruption, yet also serves to manipulate the corrupt.

"William will press the Chilean government to expedite the property deed, and we should have results in two weeks. If our proposal is accepted, you'll be informed.

The crowd cheered in recognition of Jerrod's effort to secure their village's future.

William returned to his apartment to be available to finalize property acquisition.

As Jerrod predicted, Gonzales called to notify him the subcommittee accepted Jerrod's offer. Jerrod's law firm by proxy is authorized to make payment and assign the deed to the Sarah Baker Charitable Foundation. The agreement was finalized and the Mapuche retained access to one thousand hectares wilderness land to continue its cultural format.

Before returning to the village, William contacted Raimondi the trail guide to inform him of the date to escort Jerrod, Yaima and the twins back to his apartment. They are scheduled to leave in a week. Raimondi will saddle one of his mules for the twins to ride. William returned to the village to deliver the good news.

Village residents met at the school and William disclosed what had occurred. The tribe was jubilant, so a celebration bonfire dance was held. Jerrod's generosity secured the tribe's future.

William joined Yaco, Lilen, Jerrod, Yaima, Suyia, Carson, Justin and Jordan for the evening meal.

"Jerrod defeated the Chilean government at its own game. Mapuche life is distant from modern society and is considered primitive, causing challenges to conform yet retain ancestral roots. Our living format may appear uncivilized, yet, as I observed modern culture, I was awakened. Mapuche life is more cohesively civil. Jerrod recognized this, as he was impelled to bond with our tribe.

"I want my boys to comprehend and adjust to both sides of the societal fence. We cannot become isolated, as this would jeopardize our longevity. If we apply intelligence and knowledge, it can become a beneficial condition," Yaima said.

"Lilen and I have experienced American culture. Yaima is correct. It can be accomplished," Yaco said.

The next evening was the celebration bonfire. Lilen watched over the twins to allow Yaima and Jerrod to dance. Yaco's flute and Suyia's voice provided music. The twins were mesmerized by the bonfire, music and dancing.

Carson spoke to Jerrod. "I've something to show you and Yaima. Stop by tomorrow."

Communal bonfires are psychological fortifications and, combined with the news of recent Mapuche independence, raised the level of exuberance. The village mood altered as daily efforts for sustenance were more joyful bolstered by knowledge they were free from corrupt government manipulation.

Jerrod and Yaima visited Carson and Suyia and Carson showed them a beautiful hand-crafted wooden bow and quiver of arrows Yaco had given him.

"I mentioned to Yaco my desire to connect to Mapuche social design and he crafted this bow using deer leg ligaments for the bow's string and quail feathers to guide arrows with flint arrowheads. I was overwhelmed. Yaco will teach me to hunt and I'll work with Suyia to harvest food from the forest and our garden. My personal goal is to learn self-sustaining hunter-gatherer techniques and I'm excited as I anticipate this challenge," Carson said.

"I'm delighted, though not surprised. Your Navajo genes awakened; it's your heritage. I'd enjoy joining you on hunts," Jerrod said.

They stayed late to share thoughts and memories of their time at the university. They recalled dance nights and meals at Giuseppe and Sophia's restaurant. These four could not be more likeminded.

CHAPTER 25

RETURN TO CAMPUS

Raimondi arrived with his mules with one wearing a saddle. William, Jerrod, Yaima, Justin and Jordan will depart in the morning.

Village residents gathered to say goodbye to Jerrod and his family. The twins smiled when placed in the mule's saddle. They instinctually held onto the saddle.

On the return flight, Yaima said, "I can't imagine a more productive trip. What're your thoughts?"

"My thoughts center on finishing medical school so we can return permanently to our mountain paradise.

"The egregious political disruptive inequity associated with the Chilean government is common throughout the world. My undergraduate course in psychological social development revealed the historic prevalence of government domination and control. The British Empire exploited India and Africa to an even greater degree than we've witnessed regarding the Mapuche. Anglo European immigrants inundated the United States and government expansion seized absolute control and domination. The same pattern developed and was imposed toward Native Americans.

"I knew immediately when we walked into Gonzales's office what confronted us. Here was a wretched person in a position to flex authority created by the corrupted Chilean government. I also knew the power of money is what drives the wheels of this dirt infested political machine. We can expect this to repeat in our future, as we direct efforts to assist those in need," Jerrod said.

"I'm looking forward to returning to my studies. I'd like to employ Maryanne to watch the twins during my lessons with Mary. Maryanne is a senior this year and income would assist her with personal expenses. I won't be required to transport the twins for study sessions with Mary," Yaima said.

"We'll do this," Jerrod said.

After their return, Yaima called Maryanne, "Maryanne, this Yaima, we've returned. I'd like you to share dinner with us."

"How are Carson and Suyia getting along?" Maryanne asked.

"They're doing good and are so happy with their lives. It was such a good time," Yaima said.

"What time should I be at your apartment?" Maryanne asked.

"Anytime's fine, we'll have dinner at seven o'clock in the evening, though come sooner if you can. We'll describe our visit to Chile," Yaima said.

Maryanne arrived. She's a very pleasant person. They sat at the kitchen table as Jerrod prepared dinner.

"The twins are growing fast and are full of energy," Maryanne said.

"I'd like to employ you to watch Justin and Jordan while I meet with Mary for studies. I'll arrange my schedule to accommodate what's best for you," Yaima said.

"I'd love it. We'll entertain each other," Maryanne said.

"I'd be more attentive to Mary's presentations," Yaima said.

Jerrod served dinner and the conversation drifted to Carson and Suyia. Jerrod described Carson's conversion to Mapuche hunter-gatherer lifestyle and Yaco made him a bow, quiver and arrows to hunt for food.

230

"I want Carson and Suyia to visit us. I'll schedule the time to coincide with the annual talent show so they can participate," Jerrod said.

"I'd sure enjoy seeing them again," Maryanne said.

"I'll relay our plan to Mary and coordinate convenient times for you to stay with Justin and Jordan," Yaima said.

After Maryanne departed, Jerrod said, "She's ideal to assist with the twins. She emulates her brother's personality."

Jerrod became engrossed in his studies. Yaima worked diligently on her novel as events in Chile drifted into memories.

Dance night returned with its vibrant atmosphere as new dancers replaced graduates. Mary Joyce watched Justin and Jordan on dance night so Maryanne could attend. The twins were more active.

Jerrod's counselor called him for a meeting. He explained a plan the school installed to accelerate medical school completion. The program is available to students with a 4.0 GPA. This allows graduation in three years; however, students must remain at the university during semester breaks to attend classes.

Jerrod agreed without hesitation. He communicated this breakthrough event to those concerned. Yaima was equally enthused, as she yearned to return to her birthplace.

"It'll be worth it as we'll open the clinic sooner," Yaima said.

Carson and Suyia will arrive the next week to participate in the annual talent show. Jerrod received a letter from William.

Dear Jerrod,

A team of five Mormon student missionaries arrived. They brought camping equipment and will stay through summer to assist construct our clinic. How exciting. I'll put full effort into this project. I'll keep you informed of progress.

William

Jerrod pressed himself to the limit to maintain the GPA requirement. Dance night served as the only relief from study and caring for Justin and Jordan.

Carson and Suyia arrived at the local airport and Jerrod greeted them.

"It feels good to be here," Suyia said.

As they entered the apartment, Yaima said, "I'm so happy see you two. It's a long flight, though worth it for us to perform at the talent show."

"My life couldn't be better. Each day with Suyia and my students brings satisfaction yet returning to campus stirs memories. As years pass, we'll detach from these precious moments. It's a sad reality," Carson said.

"It's true, later in life we'll reflect, though, in the present, let's celebrate," Jerrod said.

"We must make this an annual event. It'll be something to look forward to for us all," Yaima said.

"We'll do it," Suyia said.

"I'm driven to develop our medical clinic. When we become permanent residents, I intend to work with Carson to develop skills as a photographer and capture the beauty of the Andes foothills. It'll combine with clinical work and expand the joys of living at this spectacular place," Jerrod said.

"Let's surprise Giuseppe and Sophia for an Italian dinner. We'll take Justin and Jordan."

"I'll call Maryanne, she can join us," Yaima said.

"Tell her we'll pick her up. I'll drive my old Jeep and we'll meet at the restaurant," Carson said.

Giuseppe and Sophia were thrilled to see their friends. Giuseppe brought two highchairs.

"I'm giving Maryanne Carson's Jeep. I should've thought of this earlier. She can maintain it. Carson's attached to this Jeep; however, no roads exist where he now lives," Jerrod said.

"Who knows how long my old Jeep will be around?" Carson responded.

"I'd love this. I'll keep it forever. I can't afford a car and Carson's Jeep is like a family member. I've got mobility," Maryanne said.

Jerrod explained to Giuseppe and Sophia Carson and Suyia will join the folk-dance group for the annual talent show. He will reserve their restaurant for the group to celebrate after the talent show.

"We'll arrange a buffet," Giuseppe said.

Sophia enjoyed Justin and Jordan and, as their eyes fixed to hers, they smiled.

"They're growing fast. What a joy to see them again," Sophia said.

The friends savored this time. Suyia said, "The axiom 'Absence makes the heart grow fonder' is true. I'm excited about the talent show. We'll share photos when we return to the village."

The night of the talent show, Mary watched Justin and Jordan. Performers greeted each other backstage.

Audience exuberance repeated, as folk music and dancing gained stature. The dance group gathered at Giuseppe and Sophia's restaurant and the mood was celebratory.

Carson and Suyia remained for a week. They shared evening walks pushing Justin and Jordan in strollers.

"We'll invite Yaco and Lilen to visit and they'll stay with us and attend dance night. What a grand time this will be," Jerrod said.

"Family visits ease Jerrod's commitment for medical school completion," Yaima said.

"Where would we be without William? As I contemplate the spectrum of our lives William is the prominent force behind our evolution. He implemented the transmitter installation, had the school built and now directs the construction of our clinic. He's coordinated myriad contributions to everyone's lives," Jerrod said.

"He's been like a second father to Yaima and me," Suyia said.

On departure date, Jerrod drove Suyia and Carson to the airport for their return flight to Chile.

The James family continued daily routine. Yaima resumed motherhood duties and met with Mary frequently for studies and to continue work on her novel. Maryanne drove her jeep to the apartment on appointed days to watch over Justin and

Jordan. The twins became overly excited when Maryanne entered the apartment and jumped around in their playpen in an attempt to speak. More like squeals with smiles. It was obvious they were happy to see Maryanne. These twins were a source of pure delight.

Spring break came, yet Jerrod's classes continued as scheduled. Maryanne would graduate in the fall. Jerrod and Yaima would rent her a one-bedroom apartment until she found employment associated with her biology degree.

Jerrod and Yaima purchased walkers for the twins with seats and wheels to begin teaching them to walk. Maryanne and Yaima supervised this training period. In a short time, they mobilized and roamed the apartment, as they mimicked unrecognizable words.

Correspondence was exchanged between Mike and Elaine, Chang Yi, Stephen and William with occasional phone conversations. Elaine is expecting her first child in late summer and transmitter sales continue to rise as Chang Yi expanded production to accommodate demand. Jerrod called his parents weekly.

William worked with student Mormon missionaries and tribal members to finish clinic construction. After Jerrod serves his internship, the clinic will become operational.

Yaima and Maryanne began teaching the twins to walk. They held their hands for balance. After practice sessions, they were back on their walkers chattering in baby talk with perpetual laughter.

Medical school will close during Christmas for three days. This gave Jerrod and Yaima an opportunity to visit Judy and Frank. Maryanne would accompany them. In mid January, Yaco and Lilen would arrive to attend folk dance night.

Jerrod was glad to return home to break academic confinement. As they unloaded baby equipment, Judy and Frank remarked how much Justin and Jordan had grown.

During the evening meal, Judy and Frank expressed excitement about Yaco and Lilen's visit and would join them during dance nights.

"I had a surprise event last week. My guidance counselor called and asked me to visit her office. The university awarded me a full scholarship for graduate school to pursue masters and PhD degrees in biology, as I'm holding a 4.0 GPA. I'm in disbelief," Maryanne said.

Everyone praised Maryanne for her accomplishment.

"Maryanne, you might never leave the university. The school could eventually offer you a tenure track teaching position," Jerrod said.

"You deserve this as you earned it," Judy said.

Jerrod appreciated the academic pause. Yaima had her novel project and twin boys to care for. Maryanne's beacon of opportunity guides her future. Carson and Suyia were established at a place of their dreams, as Judy and Frank observed this quintessence of life with immense pride.

Mid-January arrived. William called with flight arrival time and number for Yaco and Lilen's trip. They were challenged to make flight connection at Atlanta's massive terminal to arrive at the nearby airport. Jerrod was confident they would handle this without difficulty, though William gave them Jerrod and Yaima's phone number in the event of complication.

They arrived safely and Jerrod greeted them.

"I've never seen so many people in one place as we encountered at the Atlanta airport. We asked for directions to our connection gate and found it.

"We're happy to be here and our experience making flight connection gives us confidence for future flights," Yaco said.

"I knew you'd perform this without a hitch," Jerrod said.

As they entered the apartment, Yaima and two little screamers greeted them as they remembered their grandparents.

"They're amazing. This moment is priceless," Lilen said.

Yaco agreed as they hugged their sweet grandsons.

"I'm so glad you came. We'll attend the next folk dance. Judy and Frank will join us," Yaima said.

Yaima called Mary Joyce and invited her for the evening meal to meet her parents, Judy and Frank. Mary will continue to watch Justin and Jordan during dance nights.

Mary arrived at the apartment and Yaima made introductions.

"This is such a thrill. I was suffering anxiety after retirement and the opportunity to teach Yaima and Suyia was like fresh air entering a stale room and, now, we have Justin and Jordan. I'm so grateful Jerrod chose me as a tutor," Mary said.

Lilen expressed to Mary how valuable her teaching is to Yaima and Suyia.

During dinner conversation, Mary spoke, "I taught at the university for thirty years and had so many wonderful and gifted students. Yaima and Suyia are equal to the best students of my career. Their Mapuche cultural attachment adds to the joy of our bond. We three have contributed to each other's lives. Our friendship is truly a blessing. Justin and Jordan are impossible not to love, as a surge of great joy overcomes me when I'm with those two."

The next evening was dance night. Mary would watch the twins. Maryanne drove her Jeep while Jerrod taxied Yaima, Yaco and Lilen to the gymnasium. Frank and Judy followed.

Rana greeted Yaco and Lilen as they reminisced about Carson and Suyia's wedding.

"We discussed you during our flight and hoped you'd play your flute. So nice to see you again," Lilen said.

Yaima introduced her parents before the music started, as their presence offers direct ethnic character to the dance scene. The students applauded and Yaco and Lilen's faces revealed their feelings.

The music began. As dancers responded, Yaco and Lilen were in awe as they joined young college students and reflected how Mapuche ancestors would be in disbelief if they observed this event.

After the final dance, students approached Yaco and Lilen to express appreciation for their attendance. This gesture by student dancers was an emotional moment for Yaco and Lilen.

Jerrod arranged with Giuseppe and Sophia after each dance night to reserve their restaurant for those who wished to share a late night Italian buffet. Most dancers attended and this offered opportunity for Yaco and Lilen to become personally acquainted with the young student dancers.

"I'll be so proud of Jerrod when he becomes a certified physician, though I'll also be saddened as dance nights will become a memory. This dance took me back in time to when Frank and I were college students," Judy said.

Rana shared a table with Jerrod, Yaima, Maryanne, Lilen, Yaco, Frank and Judy.

"Don't you wish our university dance group could visit the village and dance in the light of a Mapuche celebration bonfire? They'd be overjoyed. I'll never forget Suyia and Carson's wedding celebration," Rana said.

"We feel grateful for the opportunity to socialize with university students. When we return home it'll be difficult to accurately describe the degree of pleasure it created," Lilen said.

As the evening came to a close, camaraderie remained within memories of a time when students danced with a Mapuche native couple from a distant place.

Yaco and Lilen stayed another week. They attended the next dance session and dined and socialized with students' prior to their return to Chile.

The evening prior to departure mealtime conversation highlighted their experience.

Yaco said, "What occurred adds dimension to our connection. To witness the beauty and vigor of American youth attach to our cultural roots expressed through folkdance is an experience of our lifetime."

"Our lives will change radically when we reunite permanently at our village," Lilen said.

"It'll be a new beginning," Yaima said.

"Medical school caused separation and periodic visits allows joyful reconnection. I know how much Yaima misses her home and she's a loyal partner dedicated to support my efforts to obtain a medical degree. I'd like Yaima to visit the village during this final stage we're enduring.

"Maryanne will graduate this year and enter grad school next fall and she'll have semester breaks. I suggest Maryanne travels with Yaima and the boys to Chile during breaks. Maryanne loves the Mapuche village. She can assist Yaima with the wild ones," Jerrod said.

"I miss my home, though I'll miss you if I do this," Yaima said.

"You won't remain for long intervals, yet brief visits would allow reconnection. You and Maryanne can help prepare the clinic. I'll write William to detail instructions pertaining to needed supplies to activate medical services. It'll jump start the effort. After I finish my internship, we'll open the clinic to receive patients. We can save lives, treat infections and perform some surgeries. I won't pursue a specialty, which requires hospital residency, though I'll study on my own and learn more about immunology and advanced surgical procedures. I'm doing well with surgical courses and I'll expand skills through self-education.

"Lilen's observation is correct our lives will change radically when we move permanently to the village. Change for the better," Jerrod said.

"I'll present this to Maryanne. She'd enjoy spending time with her brother; they've been bonded since childhood.

"Justin and Jordan should be walking when we make our first trip. Lilen and Yaco can help them gain confidence. Overall, it's a good plan. It'll be a glorious day when we open our clinic," Yaima said.

"Distance is a barrier, though travel is worth the effort," Yaco said.

The next day, Jerrod drove Lilen and Yaco to the airport. During the drive to the airport, thoughts continued.

"Our visits to America have been marvelous experiences. We can read history books and study photographs, yet personal exposure reveals deeper understanding," Lilen said.

"Conversely, my attachment to Mapuche culture was fortuitous. I had no knowledge of the Mapuche prior to

William's inquiry letter about the electrical transmitter. Our world is in dire need to learn and understand ethnic variations.

"I'll encourage Carson to create a photographic essay of Mapuche life and include scenic magnificence with text defining Mapuche history. Carson is perfectly suited to accomplish this artistic achievement. I'd enjoy assisting with this project. I'll find a publisher and literary agent to promote his essay. It could be submitted for a Pulitzer Prize in photojournalism," Jerrod said.

"He's a dedicated photographer and will be enthused about your proposal," Yaco said.

They arrived at the airport. Jerrod escorted them to the boarding gate. Hugs and smiles expressed *until we meet again* feelings. Lilen and Yaco boarded their flight.

The Mapuche couple is now familiar with air travel. They gazed at the landscape below as the plane became airborne. Their emotions were high from the visit, yet they looked forward to returning to their mountain village.

Jerrod returned to classes. Yaima met frequently with Mary to fine tune her novel and apply proper literary format. Maryanne loved caring for Justin and Jordan. Their energy was boundless as they were active every waking moment.

This routine will remain until Jerrod attains his goal. Yaima and Maryanne will make brief visits to Chile with Justin and Jordon to familiarize them with their future home.

Daily life was repetitive. Yaima and Maryanne teamed to prepare meals. Jerrod's classes were strenuous and nightly reading assignments were required to prepare for the next day's curriculum. Folk dance night served as relief.

Yaima and Maryanne will plan their trip to Chile when semester break arrives. Justin and Jordan will be one year old on June first.

"We won't leave until after the twin's first birthday. We'll celebrate at our apartment, and invite Judy and Frank, Mike, Elaine, Mary Joyce, Giuseppe and Sophia. Maryanne and I will bake a cake and prepare a birthday celebration dinner," Yaima said.

The twins outgrew their highchairs and used standard chairs with booster seats.

It was a joyous time. The twins smiled when they sang the birthday song.

"One year ago, we were in a state of high emotion as we greeted these two. We'll never forget this day," Judy said.

"The twins, Maryanne and I will depart for Chile in two days and stay at the village for two weeks. Jerrod must remain to continue medical studies. Jerrod believes Justin and Jordan will benefit from early exposure of village life. My parents will be overjoyed. Maryanne will spend time with Carson and Suyia. Benefits outweigh sacrifice," Yaima said.

Departure day came and Jerrod dutifully escorted the group to the airport.

Jerrod was alone, yet the solitude allowed concentrated effort on medical studies.

CHAPTER 26

DOCTOR JAMES

Routine trips to Chile continued throughout Jerrod's medical school years. Jerrod walked the campus in retrospection of Spruce Grove concerts.

Mapuche grandparents worked to advance the twins' English and Mapuche vocabulary. Justin and Jordan would laugh when a significant word achievement was accomplished. Words began to flow; as one would learn a word, the other would quickly imitate it. They called Lilen and Yaco "gamah" and "gampah". When grandparents spoke to them, they often spoke in Mapuche and addressed them using their Mapuche names, Newan and Akan.

Jerrod was right; Yaima and her progeny progressed in multiple ways during visits to their future home.

When the twin's returned from trips to Chile, the change was apparent. Walking became running and they spoke with a mix of English and Mapuche word attempts. Maryanne and Yaima were challenged to impose some semblance of control. They learned parent identities; Maryanne was viewed as a parent.

Jerrod coached the twins. Justin and Jordan mastered "Dad" and "Mom". Justin would say "Dad", followed by an incoherent sentence partially interpreted with body language. They seldom were more than a foot apart and constantly entertained Yaima, Maryanne and Jerrod. Jordan was less loquacious, though he studied surroundings intently.

One day, Jordan said, "Mayann". Maryanne laughed and looked at Yaima, "He spoke my name. I can't believe it." She picked up the urchin and Jordan smiled at her.

"He has you earmarked," Jerrod said.

Each day centered on Justin and Jordan. Yaima wondered how she could ever maintain her studies without Maryanne's assistance.

Progression continued and months passed quickly. Jerrod has two semesters until graduation from medical school and the start of his internship at the University Hospital. Justin and Jordan will soon celebrate their third birthday. Yaima and Maryanne used flashcards to teach words. They pronounced the words clearly and the twins imitated them.

During visits to Chile, the twins accompanied Carson and Suyia on student nature hikes. A child's inquisitive mind is stimulated when exposed to nature. The twins touched wildflowers and observed dragonflies at the creek. Justin and Jordan absorbed knowledge as sponges so this accelerated their advancement.

Elaine and Mike's child, Susan, just turned two. They would attend Justin and Jordan's third birthday celebration.

After graduation, Rana joined the Philadelphia Symphony and given fifth chair in the flute section. Jerrod and Yaima visited Rana at her apartment and attended a symphony. They took Rana to dinner after the concert. Maryanne watched Justin and Jordan.

During dinner, Jerrod said, "This is a wonderful opportunity. My mind flashes back to the time when we played together on dance nights. You must feel accomplished playing with the symphony."

242

"Oh yes, especially rehearsals contribute to personal advancement as I play music with the best instrumentalists. It's quite overwhelming. I enjoy it so much and I feel fortunate.

"I've applied for US citizenship and I'll bring my parents to attend the presentation ceremony. I'm pleased to know you are near certification; soon, you'll realize your dream.

"Jerrod, it's important for me to convey how appreciative I am for your positive influence in our lives. Our time playing folk music is among my most cherished memories," Rana said.

During the return drive, they spoke of Rana.

"Rana's been a steadfast pleasure in our lives," Yaima said.

"Her success is the result of personal resolve. Admiration defines Rana," Jerrod said.

The twin's third birthday was celebrated at Giuseppe and Sophia's restaurant. Yaima, Jerrod, Judy, Frank, Maryanne, Mary Joyce, Mike, Elaine and their daughter, Susan, attended.

Jerrod's graduation from medical school finally arrived. Yaima secretly organized a celebration dance at the small gymnasium. Virginia Easterbrook will feature Jerrod's achievement in an article describing his goal to offer medical services to poverty stricken areas.

Yaima, Frank, Judy, Mike and Elaine attended Jerrod's graduation ceremony. Maryanne stayed with the twins.

"He achieved his goal. I'm so proud of him, though much lies ahead. Internships are difficult. Jerrod will work with resident physicians, as interns work long hours with little sleep and cover multiple shifts," Judy said.

"What are your thoughts Doctor James?" Frank asked Jerrod.

"I'm happy to graduate but my feelings are ambiguous otherwise. Since early memory, my life has been study. Now, I'm challenged to pursue life beyond this discipline. From here forward, my primary goals are to assist those in need of medical care.

"When I was accepted at the university's premed program, I was prepared for academic challenges. It's different now; the future is vague, as mysterious and unknown events occupy the horizon. I feel insecure as I question my worth and ability to perform. I envision unforeseen circumstances appearing out of nowhere different from anything I've previously confronted.

"I've been blessed with support from family, faculty and friends to obtain my medical degree. I am obligated to apply maximum effort to make a worthy mark in life," Jerrod said.

"As a graduation gift, we've organized a special celebration folk dance. Maryanne will bring Justin and Jordan. This is to show appreciation for the positive influences you've generated to enrich our lives. Rana drove from Philadelphia to join us. This dance is a tribute to you.

"Giuseppe and Sophia will set up an Italian buffet. Virginia Easterbrook assigned her staff photographer to document the event to be published in your honor," Yaima said.

Jerrod hugged Yaima as tears appeared in his eyes.

Everyone met at the gymnasium for this special dance. Maryanne was sitting on the edge of the stage with Justin and Jordan. The twins clapped with everyone as Jerrod entered with Yaima. Jerrod was overcome with emotion. Another mile marker passed.

Rana hugged Jerrod and asked, "Are you ready to play some music?"

As Yaima handed Jerrod his flute, he said, "I sure am." The three musicians took the stage and dancers responded, including Judy, Frank, Mike and Elaine creating an unforgettable moment.

They danced two dances, then socialized and enjoyed the celebration buffet prepared by Giuseppe and Sophia.

Dancing continued until past midnight and the weary dancers remained as each dancer congratulated Jerrod on his completion of medical school.

The internship was a challenge. Jerrod performed pre-operative physicals and observed various types of surgeries. He assisted surgeons by photographing procedures and these were given to patients as a record of their surgery. Jerrod was impressed with each surgeon's skill level and dedication to their medical specialty.

He visited patients during recovery from surgery and monitored progress. He was assigned to the lab to learn procedures of various diagnoses. He was on call for emergencies and the standard shift for interns is twelve hours and often longer. He consistently arrived home after midnight and sometimes slept in the intern's dorm, as he was too fatigued to drive.

Yaima and the twins would be asleep when he arrived home. Family contact was limited to a few hours each morning.

"My internship is physically and mentally more demanding than classroom study," Jerrod said.

Yaima brought Justin and Jordan to join them for breakfast and they would practice words.

"When we open the clinic, it'll be like a vacation compared to hospital work intensity," Yaima said.

"We won't have an intercom blaring out 'Doctor James' twenty times a day," Jerrod said.

"Your parents know exactly what you are experiencing. The imposed stress is like a medical course in itself. We may not have stress at our village clinic, though we could encounter similar conditions if we work with Doctors Without Boundaries and if you are assigned to foreign hospitals where the stress factors are probably greater than the university hospital," Yaima sais.

Jerrod prepared to leave for the hospital and Justin said, "Bye, bye, Daddy".

Yaima and Jerrod looked at each other. Neither of them said a word, though their expressions spoke clearly.

Each day is a baby step toward relocation to their village clinic. Jerrod obtained two textbooks on physician assistant courses and gave them to Yaima. She will mail one to Suyia so they can study clinical tasks. Jerrod will teach what they would typically learn in nursing school.

Jerrod had Sunday's off, though was on call. He spent this time with Yaima and the twins. He called Judy and described the strain of his internship.

"I sure relate. It's an ordeal interns must endure. I vividly remember our internships," Judy said.

"I'm doing good with the challenge inspired by Yaima, Justin and Jerrod to finalize my certification. The clinic is my motivator.

"Last week, as I prepared to leave for the hospital, Justin said, 'Bye, Bye, Daddy'. It made my day before it began," Jerrod said.

"Hello and goodbye were your first words. Genes have activated," Judy said.

Virginia Easterbrook called and spoke to Yaima. "Students are clamoring to restart folk dance night. I know Jerrod is over his head at the hospital. I recruited a new student flute player and I'm wondering if you could teach her Mapuche folk music. She was assigned first chair after Rana graduated. Her name is Martha Livingston from Boise, Idaho. She's pleasant, yet introverted. I'd like to reestablish folk dance night. What do you think about this?"

"I miss dance night. When can I meet this young flutist?" Yaima asked.

"Give me a time and I'll bring her to your apartment," Virginia said.

"Tomorrow at noon is good. I'll give her the Mapuche folk songbooks and she can borrow Jerrod's flute to practice the music. Jerrod probably won't attend dance night. He works late every night. I'll assist her in any manner I'm able

"We must do this. I want the folk dance group to continue after we depart to work our clinic. It'll be our legacy to the school," Yaima said.

"I'm so glad I called. I'm excited to inform the dancers," Virginia said.

The next morning, Yaima told Jerrod about Virginia's plan to bring back folkdance night. She described Rana's replacement flutist, who will learn Mapuche music to be played on his flute.

"I miss folk dance night the most. She's welcome to use my flute. On occasion, I get off around nine o'clock in the evening and I'll stop on my way home," Jerrod said.

246

"I hope you can, even a short time would be fun," Yaima said.

Noon the next day, Virginia stopped at Yaima and Jerrod's apartment and introduced Martha to Yaima, who served tea. The twins were napping in the bedroom. Yaima gave her the folksong book and Jerrod's flute to practice.

"Virginia described your and Jerrod's accomplishments. I met Rana in her senior year and she spoke of the grand times she had playing Mapuche folk music. I received a letter from Rana describing her new life with the symphony. I admire her so much," Martha said.

"We attended a Philadelphia Symphony concert and took Rana to dinner afterward. We shared many wonderful times together," Yaima said.

"I'll memorize the songs so I can play appropriately to accompany your voice. We should rehearse a few times before our first performance," Martha said.

"We'll meet here at your convenience," Yaima said.

Martha was medium height with auburn hair and keen features. She was an attractive young woman.

The twins woke up. Yaima brought them into the kitchen to meet Virginia and Martha.

"They're growing fast. Soon, they'll learn to dance to folk music," Virginia said.

The twins smiled at Martha and Virginia, and said, "Hawo."

Martha laughed and said, "Hello to you, too. Those two are truly identical. They're beautiful, pure gold.

"I'll practice a few songs and call to schedule a rehearsal. I'm happy about this and honored to replace my friend Rana. I'll call her tonight and inform her of this event.

"I'm not too social, though I enjoy friendships. Rana has been an inspiration to my musical pursuits," Martha said.

Mapuche music and dance returned to Duke University, though Doctor James was absent.

Yaima described Martha to Maryanne and the return of dance night.

"This is good news, I miss dance night. We'll take Justin and Jordan. It'll offer exposure to folkdance atmosphere. I'll teach them the steps away from the group to see how they respond. Just being present at the dance will stir enthusiasm. It'll be fun to see how they react," Maryanne said.

A few days passed and Martha called to schedule rehearsal.

The next day, the two met at the apartment. Martha was prepared and the two blended with musical perfection.

Virginia contacted student dancers. They would meet Friday night at the small gymnasium.

Dance night arrived and ten couples showed up. These were experienced dancers from last semester.

Yaima and Maryanne entered with Justin and Jordan. Martha was waiting with Virginia.

Virginia introduced Martha as Rana's replacement, and explained Yaima and Martha have been rehearsing. The dancer's expressions revealed excitement, as weekly dance night returned. The dancers knew Jerrod was unable to play his flute because of hospital work schedule.

The music started and dancers responded. Maryanne took Justin and Jordon a distance from the dance circle and formed their own circle. Maryanne led the twins as they moved in unison hand in hand to the music's tempo, and their faces lit up with smiles.

After a few circles, Maryanne placed one foot forward and then a second foot; the twins emulated her steps. They repeated this foot motion as they walked in their small circle. Yaima watched them as she sang. The music stopped and everyone clapped, looking at the twins. The twins laughed and Maryanne hugged them, as Justin and Jordan performed their first folkdance. Yaima's eyes watered from the joy of the moment. During remaining dances, Maryanne and the twins repeated their own dance; Justin and Jordan were having the best time.

Yaima and the twins returned to their apartment. Jerrod was sleeping and Yaima didn't disturb him. The twins fell asleep on the drive home and she put them to bed when they arrived.

Yaima and Maryanne made tea and talked about the dance.

"What a thrill dancing with Justin and Jordan. If I work with them, they'll soon join the dance circle and perform with the group," Maryanne said.

"This would be a major achievement. It was such a thrill watching them dance," Yaima said.

Maryanne departed and Yaima fell asleep next to Jerrod. He didn't stir, as he was exhausted from his long shift at the hospital.

At breakfast, Yaima described to Jerrod how Maryanne held hands with Justin and Jordan and performed their own dance circle away from the group.

"I must find time to see this. I'll speak with the hospital administrator and ask for a replacement on folkdance night," Jerrod said.

"I'd love for you to attend." Yaima said

The next day, Yaima called Virginia Easterbrook, "As we discussed earlier, Mapuche folk dancing should continue at the university after we relocate to Chile. I'd like to find a female singer to accompany me and learn Mapuche folksongs."

"I agree this would secure continuation of folk dance night. I'll contact the university's choir director and present this. I'll let you know her response," Virginia said.

"I'd enjoy this; I'll teach Mapuche music to our new addition," Yaima said.

Sylvia Anderson, the choir director, met with Virginia to discuss Yaima's suggestion.

"I'm familiar with the Mapuche twins. I've seen them perform at the school's annual talent show. I was unaware one returned to Chile. Their voices blend magnificently.

"I have a perfect candidate. Her name is Jessica Stafford; she's an operatic range soprano and ideal for flute accompaniment. I'll present this to her. Knowing her as I do, she'll be thrilled," Sylvia said.

Sylvia's assumption was correct. Jessica was anxious to meet Yaima. She attended talent shows and remembered the Mapuche twins.

Virginia drove Jessica to Yaima's apartment for introduction.

As they entered the apartment, Justin and Jordan said, "hello" in unison. Jessica laughed and said, "Hello to you, too. I'm Jessica."

"I'm so pleased to meet you. Virginia said you have an operatic soprano voice. This is ideal for Mapuche folksongs," Yaima said.

"I'm happy for the opportunity. I've attended the campus talent shows and enjoyed you and your sister's voices. To be considered as your sister's replacement is an honor," Jessica said.

"You'll enjoy our dance group. We meet weekly at the small gymnasium on campus. This connection has been an unforgettable time of my life. Jerrod and I'll soon relocate to my native Mapuche village in the Andes Mountains, so we're seeking replacements to allow Mapuche folk dancing to continue at the university. We recruited a student flutist. Her name is Martha Livingston and she occupies first chair in the school's symphony. I'll remain active until we move to Chile and we'll sing as a duet as I did with my sister Suyia.

"We can meet at your convenience for rehearsal. I'll loan you my Mapuche songbook to memorize lyrics," Yaima said.

"I'll call tomorrow to plan rehearsal time," Jessica said.

"I'll adjust my schedule to accommodate yours," Yaima said.

As Virginia and Jessica prepared to depart, the twins said, "goodbye". Jessica hugged those precious twins and said, "Goodbye, I'll see you again soon."

Jessica called Yaima the next day and rehearsal time was established.

The choir director could not have been more correct. Jessica was ideally suited to join Yaima as a duet. It was astonishing to hear them sing together.

"Singing Mapuche folk songs is metaphysically linked to your ancient ancestors," Jessica said.

"For our next rehearsal, I'll have Martha join us. Her flute will add dimension to the presentation. After this rehearsal, we'll be prepared to perform," Yaima said.

The next morning, Jerrod said, "The hospital administrator graciously allowed me nights off to attend folk dances."

"You won't believe Jessica's voice. Her range is like nothing I've ever experienced. Mapuche folk music never reaches her high note capacity," Yaima said.

Folk dance night arrived. Jerrod drove Yaima, Maryanne and the twins to the gymnasium. The dancers greeted Jerrod like a long lost friend. Yaima introduced Jerrod to the new performers.

"It feels good to be here. An internship is a necessary step, though it creates a ball and chain condition. Work and sleep dominate my life," Jerrod said.

Music began; Jessica's voice added depth. Maryanne and Jerrod joined hands with Justin and Jordan to form their own circle. They applied more complex steps and the twins caught on immediately.

At the break, one of the dancers approached Jerrod and said, "I think these two are ready to dance with us."

Jerrod agreed and, during the next dance, the four joined the main circle. It was a thrill to watch them adjust. What a grand time, as Yaima observed her twins transform to Mapuche folk dancers. They were the center of attention.

Jerrod returned to the rigors of his internship, though Friday nights were a scheduled break. Jerrod was highly respected by resident physicians and hospital staff. His interest in immunology continued and the hospital's resident immunologist tried to persuade Jerrod to enter a residency program in this specialty. Jerrod explained his obligation to his clinic in Chile.

Semester break came and Yaima asked Maryanne to accompany her and the twins on a trip to Chile. She accepted the offer without hesitation. Justin and Jordan walked well now,

Yaima was unsure they could negotiate the mountain trail to the village. She would discuss this with William when they rendezvous at the Santiago Airport.

As William met them, he said, "I'm astonished at their development. It'll be fun to observe the expression on Lilen and Yaco's faces when these two return to the village."

"I'm unsure if they can navigate the twelve mile trek to the village without assistance."

"I'll have the Raimondi put a saddle on one of the mules to allow an option. They can hike with us and ride the mule if needed," William said.

Prior to departure on the trail, William cut a pair of short trekking poles for the twins. These poles are like a second pair of legs. They loved them and realized they could move faster and more efficiently. They smiled as they demonstrated.

This trail is an intimate place and gives forth a spiritual presence to those in transit.

Villagers greeted Yaima, Maryanne, William, Justin and Jordan. The twins said, "Hello" in unison.

Yaco and Lilen greeted and hugged their daughter and grandsons.

"Did they walk the entire twelve miles?" Lilen asked.

"They sure did. One mule had a saddle and, at intervals, I'd ask if they preferred to ride. They looked at me and said, 'no'. I surmised it was Mapuche genes," William said.

Everyone commented on the twin's growth and the mood was pure joy as they reunited.

The trekkers walked to the village. They gathered at Carson and Suyia's home for a reunion meal.

"Justin and Jordan are now folk dancers. Maryanne and Jerrod taught them. During the last dance night, they joined the main circle. We were astonished at how quickly they learned to dance," Yaima said.

"Dancing's fun," Jordan said. The group laughed to hear Justin express himself.

"These visits allow us to witness the twin's development," Lilen said.

"Jerrod's absence is my only regret. Our circle will be complete when he rejoins us.

"Justin and Jordan represent the third generation. I'll use this opportunity to disclose I'm pregnant, and soon these twins will greet their cousin. Carson and I are pleased by this event in our lives," Suyia said.

This escalated the joyful mood. Yaima hugged her sister and Carson. "It's exciting news."

"Our blessings continue to expand," said Lilen.

Yaco hugged his daughter and Carson. He said, "We'll be hunting and fishing more, as we'll have a new mouth to feed. New arrivals are stimulators."

"I hope I don't end up the old maid of the family. I'm not as beautiful as Yaima and Suyia, though maybe I'll find my knight sometime in the future. I'm so happy for Suyia and Carson," Maryanne said.

The twins sat in silence, unable to grasp what was happening, yet sensed this was something special.

"Our child's gender is unimportant. Our new addition will be our lodestar to alter course toward fulfillment.

"The best part is we'll have a bonfire to celebrate. Justin and Jordan can exhibit their new folk dance skills," Carson said.

The family stayed up late talking. The twins were exhausted so Yaima and Maryanne carried them to their shelter home. The future is unknown, yet the family foundation continues to form.

CHAPTER 27

SUYIA SHINES

The next day, Suyia, Yaima and Maryanne took the twins for a walk to their special spot along the creek.

As Justin and Jordan waded in the creek to collect pedant stones, Yaima, Suyia and Maryanne sat on a large flat rock overlooking the beautiful flowing stream.

"Those two are so special. As we watch them sift through the stones, it reflects their character. It's a given they'll prove value to lives they touch, as we're experiencing at this moment.

"I'm curious to see how they respond to their cousin's arrival, as I visualize the three wading this creek together," Suyia said.

Jordon came to the creek's bank, held out his hand to reveal a stone he found. He said with a smile, "Look at this one."

The three women laughed and Yaima said, "It's the first sentence he's formed without being prompted."

"I see it; it's beautiful," Suyia said to Jordan.

"I want one," Justin said.

"They've found their voice. We'll remember this day at our peaceful place," Yaima said.

It was late afternoon when they returned to the village. As Suyia, Yaima and Lilen prepared the meal, they discussed tomorrow evening's bonfire celebration.

"I'm in a perpetual state of celebration since I became pregnant. When a newborn enters the world, it's a miraculous event," Suyia said, during dinner.

"From a grandparent's perspective, it's the peak of life's purpose. Being present for the twin's arrival was a sacred moment, as this emotional crest repeats when Suyia delivers her beloved gift," Lilen said.

"My time with Justin and Jordan is pure ecstasy. The essence of life is exposed with more clarity since I've been assigned to assist Yaima with her twins," Maryanne said.

"We love to dance," Jordan said.

Carson assisted Yaco prepare the evening bonfire. As dusk descended, the bonfire was lit and flames leapt skyward.

Suyia and Yaima sang. Yaco and Lilen accompanied them with their flutes. Maryanne danced with Carson and the twins, as village residents joined the jubilation in a display of rhythmic movement and color. Dancing is festive enhanced by flickering flames and shadowy movement under the full moon's mystic glow.

The visitors stayed two weeks. Carson and Suyia guided the group on photographic hikes on the fringes of the village. He intensified his effort to compose a photographic essay, highlighting the many vistas as Jerrod suggested.

Mealtime discussions centered on Jerrod's certification. Four months remain to accomplish his internship.

"We'll have the clinic operational before Suyia's due date, so Jerrod can deliver her baby. The midwife will assist. It'll be a wonderful day," Yaima said.

"When I became convinced I was pregnant, this was my first thought," Suyia said.

Departure day arrived and Justin and Jordan made their return hike without a hitch using trekking poles.

Jerrod was waiting at the arrival gate as the four disembarked and said, "I'm so happy to see my family. Your absence compounded internship stress."

"Hello, Dad. We hiked the trail and danced at the bonfire," Justin said.

"I'm proud of you. We'll go to Giuseppe and Sophia's tonight and you can describe your trip," Jerrod said, hugging the boys

"Suyia's pregnant and, based on my calculation of the time for the establishment of our clinic, you should be present to deliver her child. The seamstress midwife can assist. What a day it will be," Yaima said.

CHAPTER 28

JERROD'S CERTIFICATION

There was no formal ceremony, though the hospital administrator awarded Jerrod his physician's certificate. He told Jerrod how much he admired his dedication and offered a residency position.

At Jerrod's request, there was no celebration dance, as they must depart for Chile as soon as possible. Maryanne would be their liaison with university friends.

Yaima and Jerrod invited Mike, Elaine, Susan, Giuseppe, Sophia, Maryanne, Mary Joyce, and Virginia Easterbrook to share a departure meal at their apartment. They will pack belongings and rent a truck to drive to Jerrod's parents house and remain a week prior to departure to Chile.

Jerrod would continue to support Maryanne until she attained her PhD and fly her to Chile at intervals.

The next day, Jerrod, Yaima, Justin and Jordan walked the campus. They stopped at the spruce grove. Jerrod had his flute and played a Mapuche folk song and Yaima sang lyrics in Mapuche. Only one song, yet two students stopped to listen.

They were freshman and one asked, "What kind of music is this?"

"It's an ancient Mapuche folksong," Jerrod said.

"I've never heard such a beautiful song," The student responded.

"You should contact Virginia Easterbrook, the school's newspaper editor. She'll direct you to a campus gymnasium where you can attend a musical performance and observe Mapuche folk dancing one night a week. You'd enjoy this," Yaima said.

"Thanks, we'll do that," said the student.

The students departed. Jerrod, Yaima and the twins remained awhile. Tears flowed down Yaima's face and Justin asked, "Why are you crying, Mom?"

"I'm unable to explain it. I reminisced when we performed our Mapuche folk music at this grove of spruce trees. I'm happy to be here with our family. Memories form a mix of joy and sorrow as life moves on. I love you both so much," Yaima said.

They continued their walk and returned to their apartment to prepare a special meal for their dearest friends.

As the friends gathered, the realization of the permanence of this change formed a melancholy mood.

"I'm too old to travel to Chile. I feel sadness, as this may be my final time to meet with Jerrod and Yaima. The memory of our time together will remain prominent. I enjoyed teaching Yaima and Suyia," Mary said.

"We'll make periodic visits. I need your help to finalize my novel. I've edited and expanded content, and eager to share what I've accomplished. We'll always be your students and remain in need of your advice," Yaima said.

Elaine and Mike's daughter Susan fascinated Justin and Jerrod. They showed her the word flash cards and the three practiced their vocabulary.

"We're at a junction, and memories are imbedded to a degree seldom realized.

"Mary says she's too old for travel to Chile. I'm not convinced, but even if she never visits Chile she discovered a new dynamic to life through tutoring Yaima and Suyia. Age is advantageous as a tutor, as it offers important values to pupil and teacher. Mary lives alone since her husband died. As a tutor, she gains likeminded companionship not presented in typical college classroom structure," Jerrod said.

"I agree with Jerrod. As we observe Susan, Justin and Jordan practice words, it's a harbinger as we peer over the precipice of our future. Susan, Justin and Jordan are oblivious to planning as they forge ahead. Our adult minds become cluttered as we attempt to prematurely predict our future.

"One issue is absolute. This moment in time cements shared affection, regardless of the future's obscurity," Mike said.

"So true. When Suyia and I were young, as we searched the forest for food, we responded instinctually with no thoughts related our future. It would've been impossible to predict what occurred.

"Our destiny will open in a natural manner. What we've gained from Mary and Jerrod is like a box of invaluable tools to assist us address challenges yet to appear," Yaima said.

"As I contemplate what we're discussing, it's like viewing an abstract painting. We're moved by the beauty of this painting, but can't clearly describe why the painting influences us as it does.

"My life is predestined. I'm reliant on Mike's ability to provide for us, and my responsibility is to assist him where I'm able to work with Chang Yi and Jerrod to secure our future.

"Our tour of China changed me drastically; nothing could have been more unpredictable. What the tour disclosed was the importance of diversity combined with unity to drive toward collective goals.

"I hope to eventually visit Yaima and Suyia at their place of origin and soak in the beauty they and Jerrod describe," Elaine said.

"I want to visit the village during semester breaks. It gives me something to look forward to throughout the year. It's my plan to remain attached to the village as much as I'm able.

I'll share observation of Justin and Jordan as they advance. I will interact with Suyia and Carson's new arrival.

"As I contemplate our amazing connection, I'm consumed with appreciation," Maryanne said.

"When Carson first came to our restaurant, I could've never predicted how his visit would eventually impact our lives. Sophia and I are products of the American dream, as we recognized the value of a social melting pot logic attached to America's development. I predict our bond in friendship will play a major role in our future in various ways. We're grateful," Giuseppe said.

"My years associated with students and faculty at the university yielded an array of observations and events, yet I've never been so personally attached as I've been to Mapuche music and dancing. It emits spirituality like nothing I've previously experienced. If opportunity arises to visit the Chilean village, I'll take advantage of it," Virginia Easterbrook said.

"What I have in mind is, at intervals, we'll sponsor visits for our dear friends at Duke University. You'll be lodged at the school's dormitory and selected village families.

"I'll formulate a plan to get Mary Joyce to the village. I'm considering options," Jerrod said.

CHAPTER 29

MEDICAL CLINIC

Jerrod drove the rental truck and Yaima followed in the car with the twins to Judy and Frank's home. They worked together to unload and organize. They intended to depart for Chile in a week. Judy and Frank would accompany them to assist with the clinic's opening.

Jerrod called William and discussed the clinic. They had corresponded during the year and Jerrod listed medical supplies for the clinic to become operational.

"I've purchased what you requested. If you think of anything else, let me know.

"When you arrive, I'll arrange a meeting at the school for you to outline details," William said.

"After we open the clinic, I'll expand inventory, yet what you've accomplished allows us to open and serve patients. I'm forever grateful for your devotion to make my dream come true," Jerrod said.

"Church elders are delighted and they asked for photos to spread the news among the congregation," William said.

When they arrived, as a means to lessen stress, Judy and Frank rented a hotel room and. the next morning. they met at the trailhead.

Raimondi helped load the pack mules and Justin and Jordon lead the trekkers. They were familiar with the trail to their new home

They were greeted by the entire village and embraced by Yaco, Lilen, Suyia and Carson in joyous reunion. Jerrod will present his plan to village residents at the school.

The school was at capacity when Jerrod spoke. "What a great day. This moment is a realization of a dream I've possessed since early teen years inspired by a book given to me by my mother written by Doctor Albert Schweitzer titled *The Reverence of Life.* Schweitzer described how he and his wife built a medical clinic in a remote region of Africa in the early twentieth century.

"When I read Schweitzer's book, I wanted to be like Schweitzer and assist those isolated from modern medical services.

"Through coincidence, I discovered your village and events leading to this place in time were serendipitous, combined with an undefined spiritual magic. It's been a long journey, yet I could not be more pleased.

"Over the past year, I've communicated with William frequently as he worked diligently with Mormon student missionaries and tribal members to construct the clinic. I listed equipment and basic medications to supply the clinic and offer medical services.

"William is the prominent contributor toward betterment of Mapuche tribal life. He made initial contact related to the wireless electrical transmitter installation. During early years, I was unaware of the Mapuche. William introduced me to the Mapuche and your village nestled in the foothills of the magnificent Andes Mountains.

"After the clinic's preparation is complete, our first task is to invite tribal members to visit the clinic at their convenience for physical examinations. Each member will have a personal chart to profile health status to be used as reference in the event medical treatment is needed in the future.

"My physician parents traveled with us and they'll assist with physicals. Yaima and Suyia will act as interpreters for those not fluent in English. Yaima and Suyia also are in training to become physician assistants to work at the clinic as coordinators and establish visitation schedules. In addition, they'll be trained to administer anti-virus inoculations and perform basic medical treatments.

"After examinations are complete, the clinic will be available when needed. I'll also give periodic presentations to teach health maintenance and disease prevention. Mapuche dietary design is naturally nutritious and healthy. Obesity is nonexistent among Mapuche tribal members. I'm at your service, available anytime day or night. Thank you for the opportunity to apply my medical school and internship training."

The tribe applauded and cheered Jerrod. William spoke, "As Jerrod said, this is a special day. Tonight, we'll celebrate with our traditional bonfire dance."

Jerrod mingled with the tribe and Frank and Judy beamed with pride as they witnessed their son realize his dream. Yaima and Suyia hugged Jerrod and remained at his side during this interactive period to bond with the tribe as their personal physician. Doctor James is on call.

Yaco, William and a few tribal members gathered firewood for the evening celebratory bonfire.

"Will we dance?" Justin asked Judy.

"We sure will, Justin. Are you ready to dance?" Judy asked.

Justin responded, "Yes."

"Me too," Jordan said.

This celebration dance had special significance because Yaima, Jerrod and the twins' now are permanent residents.

At nightfall, the bonfire was lit. Jerrod played his flute and Yaima and Suyia's voices returned home.

Several village children danced. Justin and Jordan joined the circle alongside Judy, Frank, Yaco and Lilen. The scene was highlighted with a full moon on a clear starlit night.

The next morning, the clinic opened to begin physical exams to document medical data applied to individual residents. The team was efficient and dedicated. The three doctors and two assistants worked a long day and will repeat this effort until health status of village residents is documented.

Justin and Jordon stayed with Yaco and Lilen while the medical team attended examinations. Lilen prepared meals and Yaco entertained Justin and Jordan.

William joined the group for meals and discussion related to the Mapuche's future.

"We shared thoughts earlier about the Mapuche culture's danger of intrusion from modern social developments. I'd like to discuss beneficial non-intrusive considerations. Road access would be disastrous. This would impose irreparable damage to the sensitivity of Mapuche life, although we've installed electricity and activated a medical clinic and these alterations add positive non-intrusive elements. As I contemplate these changes, questions appear. What if we're confronted with a medical complication outside our clinic's range of treatment and modern hospital medical services are required for proper patient care? How do we transport a patient faced with life threatening medical complications? In addition, eventually, Yaima and I will connect with Doctors Without Boundaries and we'll need access to reliable communication.

"Santiago General Hospital contracted a helicopter shuttle service to transport medical patients in need of treatment; this should be considered," Jerrod said.

"If changes are chosen and applied correctly, it won't disturb Mapuche historic social format. It's our responsibility to soften impact of the inevitable imposition of modern progress. In the United States, Amish were forced to alter basic living designs caused by surrounding societal advances, yet they've retained important functions of their philosophical and religious principles.

"We own the land surrounding us; this is of great importance. Where would the tribe be without Jerrod's fiscal status to counter actions of the corrupt Chilean government?

"I suggest shortwave radio transmitters and receivers at my apartment and the medical clinic to make communication available. We can patch our transmitters into the helicopter service's radio frequency and give grid coordinates for the village if conditions arise where we need to airlift a patient," William said.

"This is the best idea. If we need you or the mule team we can summon you on the shortwave radio," Jerrod said.

"Our village has proven it can adjust to change. The electrical transmitter is a revolutionary device and has not damaged the design of Mapuche philosophy. The same applies to my marriage to Jerrod; it demonstrates diversity can bring positive influence and benefits. It's what the world needs most. Many people I've met in America admire Mapuche, including Jerrod's parents, Judy and Frank. I've accepted and melded with American culture. Acquiescence is a task, yet, as time advances, the beacon of hope shines brighter. As I contemplate the overview of what Jerrod and William suggest, beneficial non-intrusive positive changes are available. A shortwave radio is needed for communication.

"Suyia and I have become close friends with our American tutor, Mary Joyce. We could meet her at the Santiago Airport and the helicopter service could bring us directly to the village. I can't think of anything we would enjoy more than to have Mary visit us at our Mapuche home. Mary is in the late stage of life and contends with loneliness and despair. She loves Justin and Jordan. A visit to our village would be a highlight of her life," Yaima said.

"Can you imagine the fun she would have? We must plan this," Suyia said.

"When we flew to the United States, we had no previous experience with modern travel. I was unaware of culture shock, yet it hit me like rock striking my head. The Atlanta Airport was a living nightmare, yet also served as a learning device and revealed the degree of contrast to Mapuche life.

"Judy and Frank were our trail guides. The complexity of modern era society must be understood. Cautious evaluation is needed to impose or reject acceptance. If changes prove negative, we'll revert to where we were before alterations occurred," Yaco said.

"I was fearful to travel to the United States, though Judy and Frank displaced my fear," Lilen said.

"William can investigate installation of a shortwave communication system," Jerrod said.

Judy and Frank will leave as soon as physical examinations are complete.

Carson arranged a preschool training program for Justin and Jordon, as Yaima, Suyia and Jerrod dedicated themselves to clinical duties.

The night before Judy and Frank's departure, mealtime discussion highlighted adjustments.

"Jerrod and the village's seamstress and midwife, Quillen, will assist with my baby's delivery. I'd like Judy and Frank to visit after my child's birth. Our clinic is operational and my newborn is the next big event," Suyia said.

"I'm excited for you. It'll be fun to observe Justin and Jordan's reaction to their cousin," Yaima said.

"We'll be Uncle Jerrod and Aunt Yaima. What a good time this will be," Jerrod said.

"I guarantee we'll visit," Judy said.

"We feel like village residents and will participate as much as we're able.

"Documenting village resident's health status is an important first step. Shortwave radio connection can serve in multiple ways. We can relay messages through William," Frank said.

The entire village was at the trailhead to wish bon voyage to Judy and Frank.

The clinic was ready to receive patients. Until patient care was needed, Jerrod accompanied Carson on students' nature hikes. Yaima assisted Suyia with her vegetable garden. This Mapuche tribe had few health complications. When Injuries occurred previously the tribe applied Mapuche natural treatments. Jerrod was interested in learning herbal medicine to combine with his modern medical knowledge.

Jerrod savored evenings with Yaima and the twins. They practiced conversing with Justin and Jordan, reading stories by candlelight; the twins were captivated. Yaima brought elementary reading primers to teach Justin and Jordan to read.

"I'll contact Doctors Without Boundaries after Suyia's baby arrives. Tomorrow, we'll take the boys and forage for plants and check fish traps at the river. I want to blend with our neighbors and attach to Mapuche way of life," Jerrod said.

"We'll do this. It's unlike typical physical work, as gathering edible plants emits spirituality," Yaima said.

As morning arrived, the family of four ventured into the forest in search of food. Yaima carried a hemp bag with a single shoulder strap to retrieve plants.

Yaima knew the entire flora and taught Jerrod and the twins the best plants to harvest. As they worked together, Yaima's predicted spiritual bond appeared. Justin and Jordan enjoyed this venture evidenced by their enthusiasm.

They filled the bag with plants and walked to the river. One of the fish traps had four trout. Yaima strung the fish on a hemp cord. It was their first food-gathering venture as a family.

"Finding food is fun," Justin said.

"It's been my favorite task since I can remember," Yaima said.

"Self-sustenance connects us with ancient people. The ancients were highly skilled hunter-gatherers implanted by generational heritage," Jerrod said.

Jerrod used his tripod and self-timer to record this eventful day.

Jerrod and Yaima teamed to prepare the evening meal and assisted the twin's practice reading skills.

Jerrod composed a letter to Doctors Without Boundaries with a description and photos of the Mapuche village clinic in Chile. He included a copy of his physician certification and details of his Duke University medical education. He planned to submit his resume after Suyia delivers her child.

Routine set in as Yaima and Jerrod organized the clinic. A few villagers visited for treatment of minor injuries. Suyia's due date was two months away.

William arrived with Raimondi and his mules. One mule carried a short wave transmitter and receiver.

William met with Jerrod and said, "I attended a one-day seminar to learn radio protocol and I installed a unit at my apartment. I'll instruct you on the use of the system so we can communicate.

"I also called with the helicopter transport company. If we need their service, we'll have connection. They only fly during daylight hours except to airports with lighted landing areas. I'll give you their waveband frequency and call sign. You can make a test call. Over time, we could install a lighted landing pad for night landing if needed."

"Good Job, William. This is a major development," Jerrod said.

William set up the transmitter and receiver at the clinic since it has power. He will instruct Jerrod and Yaima on its function, and eventually teach Suyia and Carson.

Suyia and Carson invited everyone to their home to share the evening meal. Discussion centered on Suyia's delivery.

"Carson and I have been studying names. We'll select Mapuche and Navajo names relative to gender," Suyia said.

"As it should be," Jerrod said.

"I think of Suyia's delivery constantly. I can't concentrate on anything else. After our child arrives, I'll resume pursuit of my photo essay," Carson said.

"I'd like to share a plan regarding my essay and hear thoughts and opinions. I want to teach photographic techniques to my students. I'm thinking the essay could be presented as a collective village project and it can list participants in the credits attached to the essay's submission, creating an essay about the people by the people.

"I'll purchase three Nikons with standard lenses. They'll be compatible with my specialty lenses. The mission is to include native Mapuche eyes and minds to capture images of their homeland. In addition, we'll need an eight by ten view camera and tripod to properly capture the scenic magnificence surrounding our village.

"Suyia and I will eventually lead field trips camping several days alternating selected students to camp in the foothills to discover interesting image composition."

"When our child is old enough, he/she will accompany us on these ventures. I envision nightly campfire discussions about events of the day. Our foothills have abundant clear flowing streams for water and we'll serve Mapuche herbal tea during evening campfires. It's exciting to consider." Suyia said.

"Our trail guide Raimondi breeds donkeys. Donkeys are ideal for medium weight packing and they're more nimble footed than mules. They could carry camping and photographic equipment. They're also more social than mules, with distinct personalities so they are just fun to be around for peaceful hours. I'll discuss this with Raimondi on the next trip back to town," William said.

"The only complication I anticipate is everyone will want to go. This is a splendid plan and should produce fascinating results.

"You've stimulated my interest in photography and, according to studies the eight by ten view camera is essential to obtain ultimate vista images," Jerrod said.

"Our tribe is firmly attached to its terrestrial surroundings. The opportunity to share our heritage via a photographic essay could result in global recognition of our culture. I can't visualize anything better for us and the world," Lilen said.

"All I know is I want to go, too. I love the idea of camping and its camaraderie. Carson has become a Mapuche," Yaco said.

CHAPTER 30

SUYIA DELIVERS

As Suyia's delivery time neared, preparations for the newborn's arrival were in place.

One morning at daylight, Suyia told Carson it was time. Carson took Suyia to the clinic and summoned Jerrod and the midwife Quillen.

As Jerrod and Quillen prepared Suyia for delivery, Carson alerted Yaco and Lilen. Carson stopped at William's dwelling. William agreed to spread the news to villagers. Suyia's friends would wait at the school for her baby's arrival including William.

Carson joined Jerrod and Quillen at Suyia's bedside.

"How do you feel? Jerrod asked Suyia.

I feel ready. I'm glad to have you, Quillen and Carson with me," Suyia said.

The delivery went smoothly. It was a girl and Suyia was in tears.

Carson hugged her and said, "I love you so much. How could we be so blessed? I'm happy our baby is a girl."

They named her Rayen, which means flower in Mapuche. They planned to select a Navajo middle name.

"Our clinic's first delivery. Rayen Arthur forms a milestone event," Jerrod said.

Carson broke the news to those gathered at the school. They cheered in celebration.

Rayen's arrival was timed perfectly, as this beautiful angel ignited the spark of love and Suyia radiated with ecstasy.

"I'd like Maryanne to choose Rayen's middle name. I'm sure she knows Navajo names. I hope Judy, Frank and Maryanne will visit soon to share the happiest moment of my life," Suyia said.

Jerrod asked William to call Maryanne, Judy and Frank when he returned to town and arrange a visit to meet Rayen.

"We'll wait until my parents and Maryanne arrive before we officially celebrate our new tribal member's arrival," Jerrod said.

A week passed and William called Jerrod on the shortwave radio with the projected date Maryanne, Judy and Frank will visit the village for Rayen's celebration bonfire.

When William, Judy, Frank and Maryanne arrived, they went directly to Suyia and Carson's home. As they entered, Suyia smiled and said, "I'm so glad you took time to visit. This is my daughter, Rayen." The three looked in Rayen's crib.

"It was my hope your child would be a girl. It'll form balance with Justin and Jordan. She'll follow those two wherever they go," Frank said.

"I've been anticipating this event for weeks. I'm thrilled. She's so beautiful," Judy said.

Rayen looked at everyone as she attempted to understand what was happening and who these people were.

Suyia said to Maryanne, "We want Rayen to have a Navajo middle name and I'm counting on you to help choose her name."

"I'll do it because she's an angel. I look forward to semester break visits to spend time with her," Maryanne said.

Lilen and Yaima prepared the evening meal for the entire group and it will be served at the school to offer more space.

The next day, William, Jerrod and Yaco worked together to collect firewood for the celebration bonfire to welcome Rayen to her new world.

Lilen will care for Rayen during the bonfire to allow Suyia to sing with Yaima. Rayen would be wrapped in a hemp blanket and held by her grandmother during the celebration.

Justin and Jordan were now seasoned folk dancers.

As the fire died down, the weary dancers began to depart to their dwellings. Maryanne slept at Suyia and Carson's home.

The next morning, Maryanne held Rayen and said to Suyia and Carson, "I've always loved the Navajo girl's name 'Doli', which means 'bluebird'. What do you think of his name?"

"I love it," Suyia said.

"I love it, too," Carson said.

Suyia carried Rayen and walked throughout the village with Carson and Maryanne to announce their child's full name. Everyone enjoyed this news and doted over Rayen.

Judy and Frank discussed the clinic and its future with Jerrod, William and Yaima during meals.

"I'll give you my introduction letter to mail to the New York City office of Doctors Without Boundaries. I've included a copy of my physician's certification and photos of our village and clinic. It may be awhile before we're given an assignment to participate in their cause.

"In the meantime, I'll assist organize Carson's quest to form photographic teams of Mapuche students as a collective effort essay project to document our surroundings and Mapuche life.

"Did you discuss with Raimondi about acquisition of two donkeys to stay at the village to use as pack animals for our photographic excursions?" Jerrod asked.

"Yes, we talked while on the trail. He said he has the perfect pair. A mother daughter team; their names are Isabelle and Cornelia. They are delightful to be around as they are interactive. He'll donate these two donkeys to the tribe. We'll bring them on our next trip to the village," William said.

"It'll be fun to have those two join our tribe. The small children can take donkey rides. They'll love it," Yaima said.

Carson would purchase three Nikons with standard lenses to be shared by student photographers. Things were falling in place for the first photographic excursion.

Jerrod would purchase two four-person dome tents, sleeping bags, trekking poles for participants and cooking equipment plus four large canteens for water, all carried by Isabelle and Cornelia.

Yaco would assist Carson with the first field trip and alternate with Jerrod to accompany students into the surrounding foothills. Excitement escalated among the Mapuche students as they anticipated upcoming photographic expeditions.

William departed to mail Jerrod's information to Doctors Without Boundaries and retrieve Isabelle and Cornelia. He also ordered the Nikon cameras, tents, trekking poles, camping equipment and an eight by ten view camera with tripod.

He would bring these items on his next mail and supply trip with Raimondi and the mules, as well as Isabelle and Cornelia.

William mailed Jerrod's resume information to Doctors without Boundaries. While William waited at his apartment for the equipment to arrive, a letter arrived from Doctors Without Boundaries. William called Jerrod on the shortwave radio and read him the letter.

Dear Dr. James,

My name is Harold Farnsworth. I'm the coordinating physician for Doctors Without Boundaries.

We were delighted to receive your personal resume and will seek a suitable assignment for you and your wife Yaima to work as a team and administer medical assistance to a designated location.

This may take a month to organize. I'll inform you of progress as details are arranged regarding the location choice for your assignment.

We'll talk on the phone and via letters as progression develops. I'm sincerely looking forward to working with you and Yaima. Our cause is worthy, yet also unfathomable and often overwhelming.

Sincerely,

Dr. Farnsworth

Jerrod met with Yaima, Suyia, Carson, Yaco and Lilen and disclosed his response from Doctors Without Boundaries.

"I'll sure miss our twins and the village. It can't be avoided, as this has evolved into our mission and purpose. I'm your assistant and will share this challenge," Yaima said.

Jerrod wrote letters to those who have been apart of his life. He waited until details and dates are established for their Doctors Without Boundaries assignment and planned to call his parents prior to departure.

Villagers spotted William and Raimondi on the trail with four mules and two donkeys. William was leading Isabelle and Cornelia and they wore packsaddles carrying tents, camping equipment plus the eight by ten view camera with tripod.

Village greeters met the mule and donkey train, Jerrod and Yaima were among greeters.

"What a sight. Isabelle and Cornelia have arrived at their new home," Jerrod said.

Village residents enjoyed meeting Isabelle and Cornelia, especially the children.

"These donkeys have distinct personalities so they're a joy. We'll build them a shelter and stalls," William said.

William shared the evening meal at Jerrod and Yaima's home. Yaco and Lilen were also present.

"I want you to accompany Carson on his first student photographic excursion. Doctors Without Boundaries may call and you'd miss out on the opportunity. I'll go on the next trip," Yaco said.

"I'm grateful. You're right, I could be summoned anytime. I look forward to the opportunity to join the photographic team," Jerrod said.

Carson and Jerrod erected the tents for practice and organized camping equipment. They will cook over campfires using a steel grate. Students drew names to select six participants.

Justin and Jordan observed the test tent erection and Justin asked, "When can we go?"

Jerrod was careful with his answer and said, "You two will soon be old enough to go."

Jerrod visualized how it would be to share this experience with the twins.

William gave Carson a topographical map of the general area as a reference, and Carson has a compass for orientation. The trekkers would leave in two days and hike toward the Andes. Anticipation grew as time neared for the journey.

The morning of departure, Jerrod and Carson loaded Isabelle and Cornelia and the entire village gathered to send off the photographic team.

Yaima and Suyia expressed disappointment for not sharing the adventure.

"This trip serves as an introductory event. Interior wilderness excursions will be offered to adult participants in the future. The projected photo essay's composition must include a variety of residents to obtain the full spectrum of Mapuche insight. The goal is to project graphic visions of our collective culture and present how we interact with the environment we live within daily. The quest is to combine child and adult overviews and this will yield an honest result. It's an exciting endeavor," Carson said.

The trekkers entered the trail leading toward the Andes Mountains. Carson led the students as Jerrod trailed leading Isabelle and Cornelia. Yaima and Suyia remained until they were out of sight.

"I sense this represents the beginning of something we'll share in the future. I can't think of a more befitting manner to bond as a culture.

"I anticipate the time with our families. I envision Justin and Jordan with Rayen smiling as they join together in a similar manner we observe at this moment," Yaima said.

"I can't wait," Suyia responded. .

CHAPTER 31

DOCTORS WITHOUT BOUNDARIES

The photographers returned in five days. The next day, they gathered at the school to discuss their excursion.

The atmosphere was exuberant as students described to parents the joy they shared on this venture.

"The Andes Mountains and its foothills formed a gigantic classroom. Photographic and social perspectives melded during this venture and it could have not been better. The learning curve spiked self-energized from the overwhelming vastness of natural beauty beyond word description, though is clearly defined photographically.

"Campfire discussions released thoughts as we were enthralled by the number of image selections available. We documented our time at this place of grand spectacle.

"After our film is processed, I'll make a sincere effort to edit and display our work in the best fashion. I'll present a collage of our work at the school to share with village residents.

"This is only the beginning of a process to collect subjects to finalize our group participation photographic essay. Individual credits for chosen images will be attached to photo selections. I'm so pleased to be apart of this mutual artistic effort by this Mapuche tribe."

Everyone applauded and families conversed related to the success of the excursion," Carson said.

The next day Jerrod received a message from William on the shortwave radio pertaining to his upcoming assignment for Doctors Without Boundaries.

William read a letter he received from Doctor Farnsworth.

Dear Jerrod,

We are evaluating a circumstance in Mongolia and this might develop into an opportunity for you and Yaima. It's located in the Uvs District near the Russian border.

A small, well equipped hospital has been closed by the Mongolian government. The staff of three doctors and four nurses was arrested and are being tried in court for treason. This area of Mongolia has been in a state of unrest for twenty years caused by unfair laws applied and enforced by the Mongolian military. A civilian militia formed 15 years ago and frequently engaged in military action against the Mongolian army.

The hospital staff was forbidden by the government to treat wounded rebel resistance fighters and had been secretly treating them. The government discovered this and closed the hospital and arrested the staff.

I suggest I accompany you and Yaima to Mongolia to meet with government officials and gain detailed knowledge of overall conditions and government requirements pertaining to reopening the hospital. It's obvious we can't break established government rules

and guidelines. The prominent issues we're confronted with are hundreds of innocent people in the vicinity are in dire need of medical service.
Let me know your thoughts and we'll discuss options.
Doctor Farnsworth

Jerrod asked William if he could come to the village and discuss this. William said he would hike the trail alone since there is nothing to transport.

It was near dusk when William arrived at the village. He went to Jerrod and Yaima's home. Yaima served tea as they sat by the fire pit.

"My mind was cluttered with thoughts as I walked the trail and questions appeared. How would you know if a patient is not attached to the resistance force?" William asked.

"This was my first thought. What may happen is a government agent or military officer could be assigned to screen patients prior to treatment although scrutiny and interrogation is not foolproof," Jerrod said.

"Nonetheless, the presence of authoritarian intrusion could be precarious. It's a complex conundrum, as it clashes with family obligations and devotion to our own medical clinic's operational commitment. I'm aware any assignment we consider will separate us from family, yet the degree of risk must be calculated prior to commitment," Yaima said.

"It's a decision in need of more thought and discussion. I'll return with William to his apartment and call Doctor Farnsworth.

"The largest weight we bear is the people in Mongolia are being victimized by the Mongolian government and rebellion, of which we have no control. Our mission's base purpose by design offers risk with complexities associated with dysfunction and intrusion of every imaginable form. Those entrapped in poverty stricken areas are the most vulnerable to social exploitation," Jerrod said.

William and Jerrod walked the trail back to William's apartment. Jerrod called Doctor Farnsworth.

Farnsworth answered and Jerrod said, "Harold, this is Jerrod James. I called to discuss the Mongolian proposal."

"I'm so glad you called. We have much to discuss. You probably feel a sense of uncertainty, rightly so. It's difficult to grasp as you speculate working at a hospital among such convoluted conditions. We can't clearly evaluate the entire spectrum until we confer with government agents and military leaders connected to the disarray.

"I was as an onsite physician for fifteen years and a coordinator for Doctors Without Boundaries the past five years. I've witnessed a variety of complicated conditions often associated with political intrusions. This situation is more complicated, as two imposing forces clash in the geographic vicinity of the hospital. When will you and Yaima be prepared to accompany me to Mongolia?" Farnsworth asked.

"We're ready anytime and in limbo until we connect with Mongolian officials to gain details of existing circumstances.

"I can be contacted by phone through my associate, William Harrington. He'll relay information via shortwave radio. We'll pay our travel expenses and we have up to date passports.

"If conditions are favorable, we'll stay for the duration of the standard commitment timetable Doctors Without Boundaries requires. What is the typical assignment duration?" Jerrod asked.

"Three months, then a break and reassignment, if you're agreeable. We're flexible to your needs and aware of your responsibilities in Chile. I'll apply full effort to support you in any manner I'm capable.

"I'll contact the Mongolian officials to obtain information related to the hospital's status. I'll also commission an interpreter to assist with meetings with government representatives. I'll call William with time and date of our departure," Farnsworth said.

"It's a venture into unknown territory for us, and if something is revealed as we meet with government officials seems awry we'll withdraw commitment. I am hoping conditions are favorable," Jerrod said.

"I'd be the first to support anything you feel is improper or worrisome and agree conditions must be favorable from all perspectives," Harold said.

Jerrod held a meeting at the school to describe his and Yaima's plan to serve with Doctors Without Boundaries at a remote hospital in Mongolia and they are committed for three months to help reorganize a hospital in an isolated region of Mongolia.

Suyia would manage the clinic in their absence. Jerrod will call his parents from William's apartment with details of their assignment. William would drive them to the Santiago Airport and meet Doctor Farnsworth in New York City. They will travel to Mongolia to meet with government officials responsible for the hospital's reorganization.

Jerrod and Yaima shared the evening meal with Yaco, Lilen, Justin and Jordan and they discussed this new event and challenge.

"How long will you be gone?" Justin asked.

"Three months. The most difficult part will be leaving our twin boys. Your grandparents will take good care of you two," Jerrod said.

"OK, Daddy. Please come back," Justin said.

"Unforeseen circumstances are sure to appear, yet this also represents your goal as a medical assistance team. It's your destiny," Yaco said.

"Your minds can feel at ease to know Justin and Jordan will be cared for to the best of our ability as grandparents," Lilen said.

The next day, they prepared to depart for William's apartment. They used backpacks for clothes and other needs. Jerrod packed his Nikon, flute and his medical bag. They traveled light.

The morning of their departure, all the village residents were at the trailhead to bid farewell. Justin and Jordan hugged their mom and dad. It was an emotional time.

Jerrod called Harold from Williams' apartment to give flight number, date and time of arrival. They will spend the night at Harold's apartment and depart the next day for Mongolia with several flight changes to eventually arrive in the country.

They finally landed at a small airport fifty miles from the Mongolian capital and took a bus to the government office building. Harold found the office of internal affairs and met with the assigned interpreter and he guided them to meet the director. The director's name was Alcan. Via the interpreter, they were all introduced. The interpreter explained they were here to reestablish the remote hospital, now shutdown because the staff was arrested for unlawfully treating wounded rebel resistance fighters.

Harold explained Jerrod and Yaima's credentials and purpose to offer medical treatment to local residents of the area.

Alcan then spoke to the interpreter in lengthy statement. The interpreter spoke, "The director said you are welcome. We'll offer support to reestablish the hospital. Patient guidelines are in place and any rebel force member or their families will be disallowed treatment. A military officer is assigned to the hospital and all patients are to be screened and investigated prior to treatments."

Harold would return to the United States and Jerrod and Yaima would travel by bus to the hospital's location. One good fortune was most young Mongolians had average English-speaking skills taught from early grades through high school. Most were eager to practice their English.

Prior to departure, Harold said, "It appears your success hinges on coordination with military units based in the vicinity; however, tread with caution when contact is required.

"None of the previous hospital staff remain, as they were either arrested or dismissed. Army officers will screen replacement applicants.

"The local schools are fairly good with government-sponsored teachers. I'm certain some are English speaking, which could be a helpful link to hospital staff acquisition.

"According to the interpreter, mail service is slow. Please send letters when you're able, as phone service is unavailable.

The military uses radio communication. You'll have my support in any manner I'm able."

Harold departed. Jerrod and Yaima were on they're own.

They would spend one night at a local hostile and take a bus to the location of the hospital. The government agency conveyed information about their arrival to meet with the army commander assigned to oversee the hospital's reorganization. Jerrod and Yaima would contact the commander upon arrival.

The commander's name was Captain Tuul. Tuul studied in England as a youth and was fluent in English.

"You're most welcome. You'll be the main cog in the wheel to regain medical service functions,"

Captain Tuul was cordial as they toured the hospital and showed Jerrod and Yaima their personal living quarters.

The next morning, they met with Captain Tuul and he reemphasized the importance of military screeners to identify insurgent infiltrators seeking medical treatment.

"It's possible our screening process may fail to identify a particular resistance member seeking medical treatment, so some may slip through the cracks unnoticed. If you detect suspicious behavior during your contact with patients you're required to report this," Tuul said.

Jerrod and Yaima indicated they understood, although perplexed. They spent the next week organizing to begin receiving patients. The following week, patient evaluation began as they diagnosed individual health ailments.

Captain Tuul interviewed potential hospital staff support members. They hired a young woman to serve as a nurse's aid. They also hired two janitors and a kitchen staff to prepare patient and staff meals. Routines fell in place. Thus far, the medical team's contribution has been favorable. Often, remote regions absent of medical services create conditions for viruses and infections to gain an upper hand and spread to an uncontrollable condition. Jerrod's medical school studies frequently emphasized this.

The community came to know Jerrod and Yaima, as patients spread the word about how efficient they were and viewed, as saviors to fulfill an urgent community need. When Jerrod and Yaima went to town for various reasons, they were greeted with smiles of appreciation. It was gratifying to be recognized in this positive manner.

In town one day, a young, beautiful girl approached them. Her name was Nekhii and said, "My mother is deathly sick with a very high temperature. I'm fearful she will die. I've been identified by the military as an active resistance fighter and this forbids us from coming to the hospital for treatment, as we would be arrested.

"I live nearby and am wondering if you could visit and offer treatment. I'm in a desperate state."

Jerrod and Yaima were befuddled, knowing if they were detected offering treatment to an insurgent they would risk being arrested also. They looked at each other and their minds sent telepathic messages.

"Take us to her. We'll evaluate her condition," Jerrod said.

As they entered the small home, Nekhii's mother was lying on a single bed. Jerrod placed his hand on her head and knew instantly what to do. She was burning up with fever.

They returned to the hospital and Jerrod pulled three vials of powerful antibiotics from the refrigerator and a handful of disposable needles and put them in his pants pocket. Yaima and Jerrod went back to the house. Jerrod gave the sick woman an injection and asked Nekhii if she could administer this medication. Nekhii said she could.

"You must give her shots every four hours and begin ongoing cool sponge baths. The fever should break in twenty-four hours. Inform me tomorrow of her status," Jerrod said.

Jerrod and Yaima returned to their quarters at the hospital.

The next day, Nekhii visited Jerrod and Yaima to say her mother's fever had vanished. She was drinking water and alert.

"The more water, the better. Try to get her to eat something," Jerrod said.

Nekhii thanked Jerrod and Yaima and quickly departed.

A few days passed and, late one night, a knock was heard on Jerrod and Yaima's door.

It was Nekhii and she said, "The town is filled with government paid informants. You've been observed treating my mother. You must leave at once or you'll be arrested. Gather your belongings and meet me as soon as you're able at my home. I'll guide you to a safe place."

Yaima and Jerrod sprang into action. In a matter of minutes, they were packed and went to Nekhii's house. Nekhii was dressed in a military field jacket wearing a black beret carrying an AK-47 Russian assault rifle with two ammunition clips on a wide belt. They immediately departed. Military vehicles were roaming the streets carrying Mongolian troops obviously looking for Jerrod and Yaima to arrest them.

It was a moonless night and Jerrod and Yaima followed Nekhii as she moved behind buildings out of sight.

This town was located directly on the Russian border and it was an open border in a very isolated region. They entered a dense woods and moved north under the cover of darkness.

Mongolian troops wouldn't cross the Russian border ordered by the Russian government because of a serious trade dispute between the two countries.

Jerrod and Yaima wore backpacks. Jerrod carried his medical bag. They walked several miles on a trail then turned off the trail and walked through a densely forested section. Jerrod and Yaima wore the same hiking boots they purchased while Jerrod was in premed school. They walked about a mile and arrived at an encampment with tents and lean-to shelters. This was the insurgent's base camp.

As they entered the camp, the leader greeted Nekhii. His name was Ganbataar. He appeared to be in his mid thirties, handsome with an athletic build. Nekhii gave a full description of what occurred speaking in Mongolian. Ganbataar was fluent in English and spoke to Jerrod and Yaima.

"You can't return to Mongolia. The army has many spies and word will spread quickly about your escape. If you're caught, you will be detained for an undetermined length of time and will likely serve prison sentences. Our rebellion operates out of Russia and is isolated from contact with the Mongolian army troops. We make periodic raids and it's our mission to eventually force the withdrawal of Mongolian army occupation from our town.

"We're two hundred miles from the nearest Russian town. It's too late in the Fall to attempt to walk out, as heavy snowstorms are common this time of year and can suddenly appear. The mountainous terrain combined with extreme temperatures and heavy snowfalls forbids travel.

"I suggest you travel north ten miles and connect with a magnificent elderly woman who has become our close friend over the years. Her name is Agafyia. She's in her sixties and has lived at her family's remote compound since birth. Her story is truly remarkable. This region is one of the world's most remote places.

"In 1935, her father and mother had two children and lived near Moscow. They practiced Russian Orthodox Christianity and identified as 'Old Christians'. This sect was persecuted and many killed by the brutal Stalin regime. The family escaped and arrived in this region far away from the threat of Stalin's evil government. It took them months to arrive at this place. They traveled on foot, and then purchased a rowboat to transit downstream on a long river to build a cabin. Agafyia was born at the cabin and has remained her entire lifetime. Other family members died of various causes. They had no knowledge of World War II until the early fifties, when an international geological research team discovered them. They've lived off the land the entire time and nearly starved to death during one harsh winter.

"Over the years, Agafyia has become somewhat legendary among scientific research teams. An international humanitarian organization visits Agafyia by helicopter in spring and fall to bring vital supplies to assist her through winter. She refuses to leave her home.

"They've already made their fall trip. Neither our camp nor Agafyia's compound has any form of communication.

Knowing Agafyia as I do, I'm certain she would welcome you to spend winter at her compound for assistance and companionship. You can take the helicopter out next spring and return to the United States from a major Russian airport. Nekhii will guide you. Agafyia loves when Nekhii visits. Many of the research teams who camped near her compound over the years are English speaking and Agafyia became fluent in English, which she enjoys speaking," Ganbataar said.

"This is remarkable. I'm Mapuche born in South America, in a remote native village and we live off the land, the same as Agafyia has her entire life. I met my husband, Jerrod, when he installed a revolutionary electrical system at our village. I'm certain Agafyia's challenge exceeds ours because of the extreme winter temperatures. The thought of meeting and spending the winter with Agafyia is fascinating," Yaima said.

"I feel fortunate to have escaped Mongolian military control. So often within human historic civil structure iron fisted military presence causes chaos and rebellion. We were on the edge of catastrophic circumstances, created from saving Nekhii's mother's life. My oath as a physician required me to perform this action," Jerrod said.

CHAPTER 32

AGAFYIA

The next morning, Nekhii, Yaima and Jerrod were on the trail to Agafyia's compound. The chill of fall was felt as they hiked the ten miles to Agafyia's home.

The trail turned westerly and followed along a mountain stream for few miles, then rounded a slight bend and Agafyia's compound came into view. Four log structures appeared with sod roofs high on the bank above the flowing stream. The largest structure had smoke coming from a stone chimney with a trail leading up the bank. As they approached, Agafyia waved from her doorway, as she recognized Nekhii, and A large white Great Pyrenees dog bounded down the hillside barking with tail wagging to greet the three travelers.

"It's always a joyful feeling when I visit Agafyia. Her dog is the love of her life. His name is Leo, named after the iconic Russian writer Leo Tolstoy. Agafyia's been impressed with Tolstoy's writing since childhood. When her family traveled here, they brought as many books as they could carry. Over the years, visitors added to Agafyia's library.

"The evil Stalin government assassinated most of their family. They were identified as Old Believers, which is the base faith of the Russian Orthodox Church. In evenings, Agafyia chants verses from her ancient Christian Bible. Her Bible centers her life. Her copy was published in 1667," Nekhii said.

As they approached the cabin, Agafyia hugged Nekhii and Nekhii introduced Jerrod and Yaima.

"I've never had visitors this late in the year. You are most welcome. Please come in and we'll have tea and talk," Agafyia said.

Jerrod and Yaima alternated describing their history and the circumstances bringing them here. Agafyia's eyes sparkled as she listened intently to their narrative.

After Jerrod and Yaima explained the circumstances, Agafyia made pan bread served with rabbit meat. She had no stove and used the open fireplace with stones arranged to accommodate a large cast iron skillet.

"I'm supported by the international humanitarian organization The Pilgrims of Peace. They bring supplies by helicopter twice each year, including winter grain for my two goats and dog food for Leo. I also trap snowshoe hares. I grow potatoes and cut weeds to stack in one of the shelters for the goats during winter months and milk the goats. It's the only life I've ever known.

"I've acquired friends over the years, mostly scientists from universities studying geological conditions and wildlife in the vicinity. They taught me to speak English, as most are from the United States and a few from the University of Moscow. They camp out when they visit and travel on foot to various locations to engage in natural studies of the area and photograph scenery and wildlife.

"An English couple wrote an article about my life published in various newspapers around the world. I received hundreds of letters from those who read this article. It was interesting to read the many letters," Agafyia said.

"Jerrod and Yaima will stay with you all winter and you'll enjoy their companionship. They saved my mother's life, so I'm indebted to them," Nekhii said.

"I'm most grateful. I've learned to cope with loneliness, though look forward to sharing this time with Jerrod and Yaima. We'll read and discuss many issues.

"They can return to their home in Chile when the spring supply helicopter arrives," Agafyia said.

"We'll assist you in any manner we're able. I noticed one wall is stacked with books. It'll be a pleasure to read your many books, although we can't read Russian," Jerrod said.

"I can teach you to speak and read Russian," Agafyia said.

"Can you imagine a member of a Mapuche tribe speaking Russian?" Yaima said.

The next day, as Nekhii prepared to depart, she said, "I can't express how grateful I am for saving my mother's life. I'll never forget this; I hope my native country can find unity and prevent continuation of dictatorial government control. Our rebellion is weak and under funded, so this may cause failure.

"We have a benefactor who lives in the UK, yet his resources are limited. He was born in Mongolia and educated in Britain. He teaches at Cambridge, though his salary limits contributions to our cause," Nekhii said.

"Yaima and I have become wealthy from the development of an electrical power generating system I invented with the assistance of my associate Professor Garrett a physicist. This system is marketed globally. If you give me the name of your benefactor and how I can contact him, I will contribute to your cause," Jerrod said.

Nekhii hugged Jerrod in disbelief and said, "He goes by the English name Forrest Jamison. You can connect with him through the university. This would help immensely."

"Jerrod's desire since childhood has been to assist those entrapped in social despair. This ambition motivated him to become a medical doctor and the reason we came to Mongolia," Yaima said.

"Give me your address and I'll send letters to inform you of developments," Nekhii said.

Jerrod wrote down William's address and asked Nekhii to send him a letter describing what's happened and they are safe in a remote Russian location and will be airlifted out in spring.

Nekhii hugged her friends as she departed.

"Nekhii often walks ten miles to check on me and visit. She's such a joy and comfort," Agafyia said.

Yaima helped Agafyia with everything. Jerrod cut firewood with a bucksaw and stacked it near the cabin and watered and fed grain to the goats. Agafyia had winter clothing she kept when family members died. Yaima and Jerrod used this clothing as winter descended.

During daily interaction, Agafyia spoke in English, and then repeated her statement in Russian and Jerrod and Yaima mimicked her words. This became habitual. Jerrod and Yaima enjoyed this method to learn Russian. Agafyia laughed with delight when they spoke Russian.

Mealtimes offered an opportunity to express thoughts. "I can't stop thinking about Justin and Jordan. I miss them so much," Yaima said.

"When Nekhii's letter reaches William, he'll relay this information to the tribe and Harold at Doctors Without Boundaries. They'll know we are at a safe place. I think of the twins constantly too," Jerrod said.

During a meal, Agafyia described the terrible times she and her family experienced in winter months to survive. Her voice quivered as she reminisced those difficult times. Yaima hugged Agafyia. "I relate. We had many nights of hunger and fear as I grew up in a similar condition to yours. We didn't face the challenges you experienced, since our winters were not as harsh," Yaima said.

"My life is far better since The Pilgrims' of Peace have come forth to assist me. I have a stockpile of non-perishable foods," Agafyia said.

"I'd like to know more about The Pilgrims' of Peace," Jerrod said.

"It's an international organization and several countries contribute money and time to their effort to assist those in need. My contacts are a man and wife team, Liam and Alma Olson from Sweden. They've visited me a few times, though recently, they only send supplies. Maybe they'll come in the spring. I'd love for you to meet them. They're extraordinary people and travel all over the world to fulfill missions for their cause," Agafyia said.

Jerrod and Yaima slept on pads near the fireplace and kept a log on the fire during the night. Candles were used for light. Agafyia slept in the cabin's loft. It was the warmest place to sleep. The moss roof serves as insulation. Each morning, the three shared tea and discussed many topics.

"We heard wolves howling last night," Yaima said.

"I have a resident pack. When the river freezes, you'll seem them traveling for hunts. Leo bonded with them and they tried to get him to join their pack. They look at me from a distance yet have become accustomed to my presence. You'd be interested how they arrange themselves when they travel. The first four wolves are the oldest and set the pace. The next six are the youngest and strongest followed by the remaining six. A gap is formed and the Alpha male and female serve as rear guards. I see them often and Leo always greets them with tails wagging, though he returns to our cabin, then sits and whines until they are out of sight. I often think about how our species could learn a more harmonious social order if we emulated wolf pack social functions. They've been an earthly presence for over eight hundred thousand years. I so enjoy seeing the pack," Agafyia said.

"At our home near the Andes Mountains, there are wolves, though we've never seen them and only hear occasional howling," Jerrod said.

"Wolves scent humans miles away and are difficult to sight. My wolves accept Leo and me. They think we're part of the landscape and offer no threat," Agafyia said.

"My sister Suyia's husband, Carson, is a dedicated nature photographer. He'd love where you live. Jerrod learned photographic techniques during field trips with Carson," Yaima said,

"Visitors over the years have photographed my wolves," Agafyia said.

The next night, the area was hit with an extreme snowstorm. When the snow is deep, Agafyia carries a single long pole like a tightrope walker and presses down on alternating ends of the pole as a stabilizer. She began shoveling pathways to other buildings.

"Are there more shovels?" Jerrod asked,

"Yes, two in the cabin next to the goat's shelter," Agafyia said.

Jerrod retrieved the shovels and he and Yaima assisted Agafyia shovel paths to adjacent buildings and to the river for water.

Evenings were occupied reading with Russian lessons through conversation. Just prior to Agafyia's nightly retirement to her sleeping loft, she chanted quotes from her ancient Bible. Yaima and Jerrod enjoyed listening to Agafyia softly sing biblical verses.

One evening, Yaima said to Agafyia, "Jerrod brought his Mapuche flute and we'd like to entertain you with Mapuche folk songs."

"I'd love this," Agafyia said.

On a winter night deep inside a remote Russian wilderness, three souls huddled near the warmth of their fire. A young physician flutist, a Mapuche writer singer and an elderly savant of the forest formed an ineffable scene.

Yaima's voice captivated Agafyia projected by her bright eyes and broad smile as she listened to ancient music from this impromptu performance.

Russian words began to dominate conversations, as Yaima and Jerrod enjoyed practicing their new language with Agafyia. She was delighted to speak in her native tongue.

The rising sun revealed a clear day. As sunlight struck the snow, they squinted while they attended chores. Yaima went to the river to break ice and fetch water. Jerrod resupplied firewood inside the cabin and Agafyia fed and milked her goats.

During the morning meal, Agafyia said, "I dreamed to Mapuche music last night. I enjoyed my serenade. I'll never forget this time."

"I felt a similar emotion when I first listened to this music. It mesmerized me when I heard it for the first time," Jerrod said.

Daily routines established and conversations were a mix of Russian and English. Winter is long at this latitude and Jerrod carried his journal and made periodic entries.

Mostly, we think of our family, especially Justin and Jordan. We are comforted knowing the quality of Yaco and Lilen as surrogate parents.

What would my life be without Yaima? As I observe her descend the steep hill to chop river ice to retrieve water, it's a realization that her entry into my life was a miracle. She has proven repeatedly she's capable of coping with whatever confronts her.

Spring finally arrived as rain replaced snow and the river rose, causing a greater challenge to access water. The woodland dwellers continued routines and felt the warmth of the fire as they dried clothing.

Skies cleared and one warm day the rhythmic sound of helicopter blades broke the silence. Agafyia smiled and waved as the chopper landed near her cabin.

The pilot and a man and woman exited to greet Agafyia, Yaima and Jerrod. The pilot's name was Valery and the man and woman were Liam and Alma Olson. Agafyia made introductions and they went to the cabin to share tea and conversation.

Agafyia described Jerrod and Yaima's story. She spoke to Valery in Russian and English to Liam and Alma. Valery was moderately fluent in English, though Agafyia knew he would be more comfortable if she spoke in Russian.

"We're familiar with Doctors Without Boundaries and work with them on occasion. Our mission is oriented toward social services assisting with food supplies and shelter improvement. We often encounter those with medical needs and we lack knowledge to assist," Liam said.

"Your Mongolian experience was traumatic. I'm glad you connected with Agafyia. You couldn't find anyone better to assist you to survive the Russian winter," Alma said.

They brought camping equipment and will stay for two nights to assist Agafyia with things. Everyone pitched in to unload supplies and set up camp.

During the evening meal, Liam said, "We'll fly you back with us. The airport we use has connection flights to Moscow. Do you have money with you?"

"Yes, I have five thousand US dollars in my pack. We can pay travel expenses back to the United States," Jerrod said.

"We've tried to convince Agafyia to relocate to a Russian town, yet she won't leave her place of birth," Alma said.

"I can't leave. It's all I've ever known; family memories are firmly implanted," Agafyia said.

"I feel the same about my village in the foothills of the Andes Mountains. My entire being is attached to this place. Jerrod opened a medical clinic to serve residents. We plan to remain at our village the remainder of our lives, though will serve with Doctors Without Boundaries at intervals," Yaima said.

"Yaima and I will return to visit. We'll bring our twins, Justin and Jordan, as well as Yaima's parents, sister Suyia, her husband Carson and their daughter Rayen. We'll bring tents and camping equipment. They'll love where you live.

"We'll always remember this winter and wonder what would have happened to us if Nekhii had not guided us to your compound," Jerrod said to Agafyia.

"I enjoyed our winter together. It reminded me of the many winters I spent with my parents, brothers and sister," Agafyia said.

"I can't think of anything I'd enjoy more than your return with your family. It'll remind me of my youth with my family," Agafyia said.

"We'll fly out tomorrow morning," Liam said.

The next morning, prior to boarding the helicopter, Jerrod and Yaima hugged Agafyia. As the chopper took off, Agafyia waved until it was out of sight.

As soon as they landed, Jerrod found a phone and called William. He felt accomplished speaking Russian to the operator to make his call.

William answered, "William, this is Jerrod. I'm calling from Russia."

"Thank the Lord above. We've been worried sick wondering what happened. We received the letter from Nekhii and were relieved to know you and Yaima were alive," William said.

Jerrod explained the entire episode to William and told him they would get to the Santiago airport as soon as they could and he would call when he has time and date of their arrival.

"I'll call Carson on the shortwave radio to give him the news. I'm so glad to know you're safe," William said.

"I'll give more details when we meet," Jerrod said.

Jerrod then called Harold Farnsworth. "Harold, this is Jerrod. We had a terrible experience in Mongolia. We treated an elderly woman with life threatening fever in a town connected to the resistance movement. We had to escape to Russia to avoid being arrested and imprisoned. It was extremely traumatic. We were taken in by a woman hermit living in interior Russia and are now at a Russian airport, preparing to return to the United States."

"I'm most grateful to know you escaped. I received spotty reports from the Mongolian military. They only said you broke your agreement without giving details," Harold said.

"I'll write you a letter with details when I return to the village," Jerrod said.

CHAPTER 33

THE RETURN

Jerrod and Yaima shared a flight to Moscow with Liam and Alma. They made connections to their home destinations. Liam and Alma returned to Copenhagen while Jerrod and Yaima went to Santiago. They discussed respective goals during the flight and planned to correspond and possibly work together on future assignments.

Jerrod secured a flight to Santiago and called William to give the flight number and arrival date and time.

William was at his post when Jerrod and Yaima disembarked from their flight.

"I've never been so happy to see anyone in my entire life," William said

Hugs and smiles dominated this greeting.

"Our experience exposed circumstances we're likely to encounter during similar missions. I have new thoughts on how to pursue goals in a more positive and efficient manner. Governments in general form major complexities, especially in third world countries.

"I'll address the tribe to describe our ordeal and disclose a new approach," Jerrod said.

"I am so happy to return home. I can't wait to arrive at our village and hug everyone, most of all Justin and Jordan. I missed them everyday," Yaima said.

At daybreak the next morning, they were on the trail. No mules on this trip. They savored every step and the splendor of the Andes Mountains signaled welcome home.

William contacted Carson on the shortwave radio prior to their departure. The entire village greeted them. Justin and Jordan ran full speed toward their parents.

"We missed momma and daddy so much," Justin said.

"I hope you don't leave again," Jordan said.

Jerrod said to his sons, "We have a new plan. You'll come with us next time."

"I thought of you two every day. I can't bear to be separated again. We met a wonderful Russian woman and our family will visit her soon. You'll love this trip," Yaima said.

"Justin and Jordan are doing extremely well with studies. We read stories aloud at night, Yaco said."

"All their needs were attended to while you were gone, although grandparents can't fill the shoes of their mom and dad," Lilen said.

Everyone gathered at the school and Jerrod described their ordeal and eventual escape to Russia. He then outlined his plan for future involvement to offer medical services to remote regions of the world.

"We were fortunate to be assisted by Pilgrims' of Peace, a humanitarian organization with purpose to assist those entrapped in impoverished conditions. A helicopter visits our Russian friend Agafyia twice each year to bring needed supplies. We were picked up at Agafyia's home by helicopter. We met a couple from Sweden, Liam and Alma Olson, who work for Pilgrims of Peace.

"Future endeavors will exclude towns with established hospitals. We'll seek remote locations deprived of medical service to fund and construct clinics similar to our Mapuche clinic. I hope to combine efforts with Pilgrims' of Peace and Doctors Without Boundaries.

"Yaima and I will remain flexible and seek our replacement with selected medical personal through Doctors without Boundaries and locally trained personnel will eventually replace theses doctors also.

"We won't activate our plan for a while. In midsummer, we'll travel to Russia with Justin, Jordan, Yaco, Lilen, Carson, Suyia and Rayen. We'll take camping equipment and charter a helicopter to visit Agafyia. I'm eager for them to meet her and experience the magnificence of where she lives.

"After we return, we'll organize long range plans to install clinics in areas of need. It feels so good to be home," Jerrod said.

William, Jerrod, Yaima, Justin, Jordan, Lilen, Yaco, Suyia, Carson and Rayen gathered at Yaco and Lilen's home for the evening meal. They shared thoughts on Jerrod and Yaima's return and projected plans to construct medical clinics.

"After our new clinic is established, I'll invite friends to visit our village. Maryanne will assist Mary Joyce and visitors will arrive via helicopter from Santiago Airport and stay at selected family homes. When we take group hikes, Mary Joyce will ride Cornelia. What a perfect way to reunite. We'll have bonfires every night.

"When we visit Agafyia this summer, I'll try to persuade her to attend our reunion. She's refused previous offers, yet my approach is to use Justin and Jordan's charm to persuade her; Rayen will assist. She'll fall in love with these three. I think this will work," Jerrod said.

"I'm sure it'll work. This reunion will put an indelible seal on our love bond with precious friends who contributed to our lives.

"We'll be committed to give our loving friends an experience of their lifetime. I'll personally attend to Mary Joyce, as she's responsible for my success as a published writer," Yaima said.

Jerrod and Yaima fell back to village life routines. Suyia did a splendid job treating minor health issues and the clinic was in perfect order.

Yaima helped Suyia plant her garden. Jerrod teamed with Carson to edit the tribal photographic essay and its depiction of Mapuche life and scenic surroundings. After the essay was edited, Jerrod would find a publisher.

Jerrod wrote letters to the Olson's and Harold Farnsworth to outline his new medical clinic construction plan. Two weeks passed and a letter arrived from Liam Olson.

Dear Jerrod,

We enjoyed your letter. We know of several possible sites for your new clinic's location.

Industrialized countries gained prominence over the past two hundred years, yet they represent a minority of global population. North America, Russia, China, Japan and Europe developed industrialized economies. Our travels to serve humanitarian causes have been educational and they exposed social realities. Many in Africa, India, Central and South America, Pacific Islands and third world countries live within entirely different societal functions.

Our volunteer work is directed at those who struggle to gain traction to attain basic living standards.

As I speculate your goals and based on our knowledge, there are multiple places to apply medical services to benefit the impoverished. The most graphic example we've encountered is an African diamond mine community. We transported food and clothing to Northern Cape Africa where the British Blankenship family has operated a massive mining operation for three generations. The living conditions at this mine are abysmal. Mineworkers live in company owned one-room rented cinderblock dwellings. These homes have no heat or running water and the residents sleep on straw mats with outside toilets and a single hand pump well. Miners receive five dollars a day. The local store is owned and operated by the Blankenship's. Food is sold at inflated prices and there aren't enough homes to provide for all miners and some sleep in the mine. Child labor has been applied for years, as there are no current laws prohibiting this. Gross exploitation is attached to every function. The net worth of the Blankenship family is in excess of one trillion dollars and they own luxurious homes in England's most affluent areas. Their homes are comparable to Buckingham Palace.

If a miner is injured, they're given minimal first aid treatment and either heals and returns to work or is shipped off to Cape Town for government-funded hospitalization. There is no local school available to the mining town's children.

To establish and implement medical service to this community would be a daunting challenge though could assist those in the direst need. Alma and I are willing to assist in any manner we're able. Let me know your thoughts.

Liam

After Jerrod read Liam's letter, he sat quietly to absorb its content. Jerrod shared the letter with everyone.

"They're trapped in conditional poverty. Modern society also views Mapuche as poverty stricken though we're not. Mapuche experience joyful lives without monetary influence.

Our social design is three thousand years old. The African mine laborers are owned and the Blankenship family tactfully imposed conditions to harness their labor in a slave-like atmosphere. Mapuche living style is of no similarity to this horrible condition.

"If we take on this challenge, it'll be an all-consuming effort as we're bucking a system in place for a long time and even laborers might resist change," Yaima said.

"It's interesting how money places blinders on its victims," Yaco said.

"Guidelines are absent, so we'll be required to adjust instinctually. We must do this. As my confidant, Yaima adds an energized positive force to everything I do.

"We'll proceed gradually. When we return from Russia, we'll take our twins and fly to Cape Town, rent a car and visit the mine. We'll take camping gear to add flexibility," Jerrod said.

"I'm with you every step," Yaima said.

Jerrod called his parents, Chang Yi, Stephen, Mike and Liam to detail the present status. The Russian trip was first on the agenda.

CHAPTER 34

VISIT WITH AGAFYIA

William summoned the helicopter shuttle service to fly the travelers to the Santiago Airport. He arranged a flight plan to Moscow, with a connection flight to the town Jerrod and Yaima landed when Valery, Liam and Alma shared their flight from Agafyia's compound.

The group was excited, especially Justin and Jordan. Rayen was too young to know exactly what was happening, though she shared the enthusiasm.

"As I reflect on my early life, it would have been impossible to envision what I'm experiencing at this moment," Yaco said.

"Our previous flights to the United States gives us confidence and I feel no fear or apprehension. I eagerly look forward to meeting Agafyia," Lilen said.

"I know Carson will be impressed with the variety of photographic subjects," Suyia said.

They arrived at the nearby Russian airport to charter the helicopter to Agafyia's compound. As they entered the heliport's office, Valery enthusiastically greeted them. Jerrod and Yaima spoke Russian, which put a smile on his face.

The twins looked at their parents oddly as they spoke Russian. It was a fun moment for Jerrod and Yaima to show off linguistic skills.

"Agafyia taught us Russian last winter," Yaima said.

They stayed overnight at a local hotel and would depart in the morning. Excitement escalated. Jerrod and Yaima were filled with anticipation to reconnect with Agafyia.

As the helicopter descended, Agafyia waved from her cabin's porch with Leo at her side. To their surprise, Nekhii was standing next to Agafyia, with her arm in a sling.

The place had an entirely different look. Green dominated the landscape. Sod rooftops blended with the surrounding flora.

As Valery shut down the helicopter's engine, Yaima said, "Our time with Agafyia revealed insight to her character and overall beauty of her being. She's lived at this place her entire life and her soul lives here. To discover this level of connection to a natural environment even exceeds Mapuche tribal life, as the tribe is linked not only to nature they are linked to each other. The tribe's beauty and power of connection is a collective alliance. Agafyia and her beloved dog Leo transit their journey on a narrow path fused to God's creation. Agafyia lives in heaven while in a mortal state. Observing her wave to us with her magnificent smile suddenly causes me to realized her life's purity. I love her so much. The young girl standing with Agafyia is Nekhii. She's the one who guided us to Agafyia's compound."

"I feel exactly as you've described. It seems like our ordeal in Mongolia was a divine directive. Agafyia is an angel who saved us," Jerrod said.

The twins listened quietly to their parents and the group knew this would be a special event.

Leo bounded toward the helicopter with his greeting bark and wagging tail. As Agafyia and Nekhii approached, Jerrod and Yaima hugged them both. Introductions were made and the twins were untypically shy as Agafyia's presence overwhelmed them.

"What happened to your shoulder?" Jerrod asked Nekhii.

"I was wounded during a skirmish with the Mongolian army and came to Agafyia's to recover," Nekhii responded.

"Do you plan to remain here?" Jerrod asked.

"I'm weary of war's horror and Agafyia wants me to remain to assist her. I love her and feel it's the right thing for both of us," Nekhii said.

"To meet you both is a special moment for us," Lilen said.

Agafyia greeted Valery in Russian and invited them to come to her cabin for tea.

It was a magnificent spring day, with blankets of wildflowers surrounding Agafyia's cabin.

"I love this place. It's like our home," Justin said.

"Yes, it is," Jerrod, said.

"I'm unsure I could be as self-reliant as Agafyia. It's quite remarkable," Yaco said.

"I've never known anyplace else. Daily life is uniform and structured to accommodate personal needs. Evening Bible readings give me connection to God in a fashion unlike crowded places filled with distractions. I have no distractions. My personal survival occupies priority to seal my bond with the environment.

"Each day offers fulfillment, as I've learned to embrace solitude. This attaches spiritual appreciation for life. When visitors come I'm overjoyed, as I welcome the opportunity to interact with my own species," Agafyia said.

As they entered Agafyia's cabin, the fire was needed to quell spring's chill. Yaima was the tea server. She retained connection to Agafyia's cabin from her and Jerrod's winter with Agafyia. Jerrod and Yaima will forever remain attached to Agafyia's life and her home.

Suyia and Carson quietly observed, as they were enthralled with the entire scene. Leo fascinated Rayen, so she patted him on the head.

After tea, they set up tents. Agafyia assisted and selected an ideal flat area to arrange their camp. They gathered stones to form a fire circle.

"Being here is like a fairytale. It's like the Andes," Suyia said.

"Jerrod was right about photographic subjects," Carson said.

Valery liked the camaraderie and had been Agafyia's longtime friend from shuttling visitors.

Agafyia enjoyed Justin, Jordan and Rayen.

"My mom told us you were born here," Justin said.

"Yes, I was," Agafyia responded.

Yaima and Suyia prepared food at the cabin. Agafyia directed the men to a storage building with boards and they arranged seating surrounding the campfire circle and cut firewood. Justin, Jordan and Rayen carried and stacked firewood near the stone circle.

Yaima called the team to the cabin for the evening meal of Mapuche food using canned meats and vegetables with flat bread.

"I've never eaten Mapuche food," Valery said.

"Your English has improved," Jerrod commented to Valery,

"I've practiced because so many I taxi speak English only," Valery said.

"Will we dance by the fire?" Rayen asked

"Yes, Jerrod will play his flute and Suyia and I will sing. We'll teach Agafyia, Nekhii and Valery Mapuche folk dancing," Yaima said.

After the meal, Yaco lit the campfire and Yaima said, "We'll practice without music to teach Valery, Nekhii and Agafyia steps."

The group formed a circle holding hands and Justin and Jordan held Agafyia's hands and Rayen held Justin's hand. Nekhii, Jerrod, Yaco, Lilen, Yaima, and Suyia joined the circle to demonstrate steps.

After practice steps, the three new dancers caught on quickly.

Music began and it was delightful to watch. Agafyia smiled as she danced with Justin and Jordan. Valery and Nekhii danced together and it was obvious they enjoyed each other.

They danced until only embers remained then gathered on the seating to savor this extraordinary moment.

"I've never enjoyed anything so much as dancing this Mapuche folk dance. Justin, Jordan and Rayen dance so well. We must do this each evening during your visit," Agafyia said.

Carson took photos and Yaco added wood to the fire as the conversation trended toward their good fortune to share this time.

Yaima, Jerrod and the twins would sleep in Agafyia's cabin to tend the fire through the night so Agafyia could sleep warm in her loft. Yaima wanted the twins to hear Agafyia nightly biblical chants prior to bedtime.

Justin and Jordan were in awe as they watched and listened to Agafyia sing prayers in Russian from her ancient Christian Bible.

The next morning, Valery prepared to depart and would return in seven days to fly the visitors back to the airport to make connecting flights to Santiago. Yaima and Suyia prepared a morning meal.

Valery thanked Agafyia in Russian and spoke to the others in English as he described his joy to dance to Mapuche folk music. Prior to boarding his helicopter, he said, "I'll see you in seven days."

He climbed into the helicopter, started the engine and, after the engine warmed up, activated the blades. The copter lifted skyward. Valery waved from his window.

Agafyia lead everyone on an area hike. Spring wildflowers covered hillsides and meadows.

"During our winter stay at Agafyia's home, a resident pack of wolves traveled the frozen river during hunts. They moved in purposeful social order. It was beautiful to observe. Leo bonded with the pack and greeted them with barking and tail wagging. It was quite a sight," Yaima said.

"It's likely we'll see them again. They follow the river path in warm months and Leo reacts the same as you observed last winter," Agafyia said.

"I'd love to photograph the pack," Carson said.

"It was exciting for us to see them last winter," Jerrod said.

Yaco, Carson and Jerrod took to task various repairs around Agafyia's compound. Agafyia, Yaima, Suyia, the twins and Rayen harvested grass with sickles and mounded it in the barn for the goats during winter.

Nightly dances continued. Suyia had taught Rayen to sing folksongs and she joined her mom and aunt to sing in a trio. Agafyia was delighted to observe this beautiful child perform as she wiped tears from her eyes.

During one evening after the campfire dance, as they sat together near the flickering light of the fire, Yaima said to Agafyia, "Justin and Jordan have a question."

"I'd like to hear their question," Agafyia responded.

"I want you to visit our village to attend a reunion of Mom and Dad's longtime friends," Justin said.

Agafyia fell silent as she contemplated Jordan's request.

"Please come," Jordan said.

"We love you. It'll be a wonderful time for everyone," Rayen said.

Agafyia remained silent.

"I've never been anywhere else my entire life. It'll be difficult for me. Who would care for Leo and my goats?" Agafyia said.

Nekhii said to Agafyia, "I want you to go. I'll remain to watch over your compound and care for your animals. This would be a memorable experience."

"If Nekhii stays, I'll go," Agafyia said.
Justin, Jordan and Rayen laughed with delight and they each hugged Agafyia.

"It's a year or more away. We're obligated to establish a clinic in South Africa. After this is complete, we'll arrange for your visit," Yaima said.

"I spoke with Valery about accompanying you before he departed. He's invited also. He was enthusiastic about the idea. Valery will guide you to our village," Jerrod said.

Agafyia smiled and said, "I feel the same enthusiasm. I can't imagine such a trip. It will be in my memory forever."

The next day, after the morning meal, Agafyia looked out the cabin window and the wolf pack was on the river path in their traveling formation. Carson's camera was in his tent.

"I'll go with you. Leo will spot the wolves and greet them as usual. We'll walk slowly. They'll likely remain as they'll be occupied with Leo," Agafyia said.

Everyone else stayed in the cabin and observed from the window.

Agafyia walked ahead of Carson so the wolves would see her first. They knew her well. Carson entered the tent and came out with his camera and a 300-millimeter lens attached. He snapped photos as fast as he could and the wolves remained as they greeted Leo.

Leo returned to Agafyia and the wolves continued walking as a unit. Carson was beside himself. He said to Agafyia, "I can't believe it. Many nature photographers never see a wolf and to get such excellent photos in the wild is a rare experience. This is a personal highlight from my good fortune to visit your wonderful place in such remote and beautiful wilderness."

Agafyia and Carson returned to the cabin and the group was excited to have seen the wolf pack, knowing this would thrill Carson.

"I've read stories of deep wilderness dwellers bonding with wolf packs. I probably never will, though if I knew where they den, I would probably try because they sure enjoy Leo," Agafyia said.

"It could be an idea for a future date we can return and pursue this," Carson said.

Valery was prompt and landed to shuttle the visitors to the airport for departure. Everyone shared food and tea prior to departure.

"We'll be thinking of you everyday until we finish our clinic assignment and look forward to you and Valery attending our reunion," Yaima said.

Valery flew low over Agafyia's cabin as she and Nekhii waved goodbye with a big white dog at their side. Justin, Jordan and Rayen had tears in their eyes and soon were out of sight.

"I can't wait to see her again. I love her so much," Rayen said. Everyone was silent but shared Rayen's thoughts.

Jerrod called William to give him return date and time. They will use the helicopter service to return to the village.

The helicopter landed and the entire village greeted the travelers.

Carson gave William his film for processing and, when this was accomplished, Carson would present a slide show at the school and each member of the group would share thoughts related to their visit with Agafyia.

Jerrod wrote a letter to Liam and Alma to describe their visit with Agafyia. He revealed they would soon depart for Cape Town to evaluate the diamond mine and possibilities for construction of a medical clinic to serve mine employees and those living in the local area.

He also explained Agafyia agreed to attend a reunion at the Chilean village accompanied by Valery. Agafyia's friend Nekhii will remain at her compound to care for her dog and goats.

William hiked the trail back to his apartment and, on his next trip, would bring slides and prints of Carson's photographic record of their visit with Agafyia.

During the African clinic's establishment, Jerrod and Yaima would tutor Justin and Jordan. They discussed possibilities of building a school but would wait to gain knowledge of the mine's complexities.

William returned to the village and everyone crowded into the school to watch Carson's slideshow.

Carson narrated and the tribe enjoyed the slides. Campfire dances and wolf photos stirred the most interest.

"Photos expose visual content and project images of our visit with Agafyia; however, photos don't reveal the spiritual attachment we received from our time with Agafyia. Her life evolved within a compound constructed by her parents and siblings over a 65-year period. Agafyia is the remaining survivor," Yaima said.

"I felt this same connection when I met Agafyia. She projects a certain beauty. She's magnificent from her soul outward expressed by her perpetual smile," Suyia said.

"I was raised Mapuche and know the challenges of survival when reliant on natural food sources and this escalated my admiration of Agafyia. This area of the world has extremely harsh winters and I'm in awe of how Agafyia met this challenge. I question my ability to be as resilient.

"I also enjoyed seeing the wolf pack as they travelled to their hunting ground. They're amazing," Yaco said.

"Yaima and I were saved from imprisonment in Mongolia because we treated the mother of a young resistance fighter named Nekhii. She alerted us of our imminent arrest and guided us across the border to Russia from Mongolia to escape the Mongolian military in our pursuit. Nekhii's rebel group had a secret camp inside the Russian border.

"Nekhii took us to this camp and the rebel leader suggested Nekhii guide us to Agafyia's compound north of their camp to spend the winter. After we returned to our village, Nekhii was wounded in a skirmish with Mongolia military; she now lives with Agafyia. Each spring, a humanitarian organization brings supplies via helicopter to Agafyia and we were able to return to Santiago.

"Agafyia was our angel of mercy. Her family was identified as Old Christians attached to the Russian Orthodox faith dating to the fifteenth century. The brutal Stalin government targeted this religious order and most of Agafyia's family was murdered by Stalin's troops. Agafyia's parents and her siblings escaped to the most remote area of Russia to isolate themselves from certain death.

"Agafyia was the only family member born at the compound. Remaining family died years prior to our contact with Agafyia. She's spent her entire life at this place and it's reflected in her character.

"Yaima and I became intensely attached to Agafyia over the winter and nightly she chanted prayers from her ancient Christian Bible. During our visit, I asked her to attend our planned reunion with our longtime friends at our village after our African clinic is operational. She agreed to attend and this Mapuche tribe will fall in love with Agafyia," Jerrod said.

Justin, Jordan and Rayen confirmed their love of Agafyia by the smiles on their faces.

CHAPTER 35

THE DIAMOND MINE

William remained at the village to see Jerrod, Yaima and the twins off to South Africa. He called the helicopter shuttle service on the shortwave radio. He helped organize and load camping equipment. The entire village gathered to wish the team bon voyage.

During the flight, Jerrod said, "It's unpredictable what we'll confront in South Africa. I've researched to some degree, yet clarity won't be revealed through speculation."

"I suspect previous experiences won't compare," Yaima said.

The plane touched down in mid-afternoon and Jerrod rented a car. The rental car service provided a map of Cape Town and vicinity. Jerrod purchased a road map of South Africa and identified the Blankenship Mine.

Good highway for the first hundred kilometers then it was gravel road. As they approached the mine, they saw a high link fence with two main entrances surrounded the mine. "No Trespassing" signs were posted at close intervals on the fence. Outside the mine's fence was a cluster of small cinderblock

319

dwellings with flat sloping roofs and a grocery store. In front of the store was a hand water pump.

Jerrod entered the store and asked the clerk if the diamond mine offered tours. He laughed and said, "No, they don't allow tours or photographs. This store serves mine employees and their families only. We seldom see tourists and the mine manager frowns on intrusions."

Our clinic establishment won't be without complications, Jerrod thought, as returned to the car.

Jerrod described his experience and decided to tour the local area by car to learn more about what they may confront.

About a mile from the mine was a farmhouse with a 'For Sale' sign in the front yard.

Jerrod walked to the front porch and knocked on the door. An elderly woman opened the door and Jerrod said, "I'm Doctor Jerrod James and I'm interested to know details about your property for sale."

"I'm pleased to meet you. I'm Mildred Norman. My late husband Joseph and I lived here for fifty years and operated a beef cattle ranch. Before Joseph died, we sold the grazing land and kept the house plus ten hectares of land to live out our lives. I'll move to a retirement community in Cape Town soon."

"I'm working with the Sarah Baker Foundation, a humanitarian organization to locate a site to open a free medical clinic to serve the local area, including those working at the diamond mine. Your house is ideal for this purpose. My wife's name is Yaima and she is a Mapuche from central Chile. She's my assistant and we have our twin boys Justin and Jordan with us. I'll bring them in to meet you," Jerrod said.

Jerrod brought Yaima and the twins to the house to introduce them to Mildred.

"Welcome to South Africa. It's a pleasure to meet your family. I'll show you my house. It's emotionally difficult to sell the house, though I'm too old to care for it and I don't need so much space," Mildred said.

Mildred showed them the entire house. It was an immaculately maintained two story four-bedroom home.

"Are you thinking what I'm thinking?" Yaima asked Jerrod.

"I sure am. This is our clinic," Jerrod said.

"The downstairs is large enough for the clinic and the second floor could be living space," Yaima said.

"We want to buy your house. We'll assist you in any manner we're able and coordinate the purchase with your bank and attorney to activate the sale and accompany you to Cape Hope to help you get settled. We brought camping equipment and can camp on your property until we get you relocated," Jerrod said.

"You are welcome to stay with me until things are finalized. I get lonely here by myself," Mildred said.

Yaima and Jerrod agreed this would be a good plan.

Mildred was a delightful person. She enjoyed talking with Justin and Jordan. Yaima and Jerrod prepared meals and Mildred was happy to have company.

During dinner discussion, Jerrod asked, "What can you tell us about the diamond mine?"

"Joseph and I viewed the Blankenship's as evil criminals because of the way they treated mine workers. They exploited children and assigned them filthy jobs for five dollars a day. No child labor laws are in place to forbid them from this disgusting activity. Laborers at the mine are forced to live in those ramshackle shelters so they have easy access to work the mines. It's a terrible situation," Mildred said.

"The mine was the catalyst for us to open our clinic in that no medical facility is nearby. I'm sure others living in the area could benefit from free medical services, as well," Jerrod said.

"The mine's manager is a difficult person and won't be cooperative. His name is George Sutton and he's an arrogant bully type. He's worked for the Blankenships for years," Mildred said.

"I'll try to make an appointment to speak with him. I'll be tactful and let him lead the conversation and see what transpires," Jerrod said.

Jerrod, Yaima and the twins would stay at Mildred's house until Jerrod finalized the house purchase. In the interim, Jerrod visited the mine office and asked to speak with Sutton. He was directed to Sutton's office. He introduced himself and described his plan to open a free medical clinic nearby.

Sutton was a large framed man with a curt demeanor, just as Mildred described. A large ashtray, filled with cigarette butts, was on his desk.

"I'm under strict orders from the owners to disallow influential meddling with mine personnel. We have our own medical treatment system in place. If more advanced medical services are required, we transport the injured to Cape Town," Sutton said.

"Our clinic will be professionally staffed to serve medical needs in a few weeks. My purpose to meet with you is to offer our services. We'll also provide medical services to those living in the vicinity not attached to the mine. If an emergency arises, we may offer an option to your current arrangement," Jerrod said.

"I'll keep it in mind, though I doubt if we'll need assistance," Sutton said.

Jerrod thanked Sutton for taking time to meet with him and departed.

Jerrod and Yaima met with Mildred's lawyer and banker to activate the sale of her house. They also helped Mildred organize her move to the retirement community. Justin and Jordan helped her pack personal items and memorabilia from her life prior to Joseph's death. Jerrod hired a mover to haul Mildred's furnishings and Jerrod would drive her to the new living arrangement at Cape Town.

Jerrod and Yaima contracted a renovation company to convert the first floor of the house into a medical clinic and the upstairs would remain a living space.

Jerrod drove to Cape Town to purchase required medical supplies including emergency oxygen, antibiotics, resuscitator, clot busting and artery expansion drugs and anesthesia for minor surgeries. He also purchased a utility van with removable passenger seats. The purpose of the van was to transport patients and the seats could be removed to accommodate a gurney to transport seriously injured or incapacitated patients. The medical supply company had the gurney shipped to the clinic. Jerrod removed the van's seats and kept the gurney inside the van in case of an emergency. The seats had quick release mounts and it was a simple task to remove and reinstall seats.

Jerrod, Yaima, Justin and Jordan toured the vicinity and spoke with residents to describe the clinic's twenty-four hour free medical service, seven days a week.

The clinic opened without fanfare. Jerrod and Yaima worked to finalize details.

During evening hours, Jerrod played his flute and Yaima and the twins sang Mapuche folksongs. Yaima taught the twins to sing folksongs and they enjoyed participating.

A few locals visited the clinic to welcome Jerrod and Yaima and express appreciation for the clinic. An elderly man stiffened from arthritis stopped and Jerrod gave him mild anti-inflammatory medication.

Several weeks passed and a few miner families walked to the clinic to make contact and express intent to use the clinic services, regardless of Sutton's dislike for what he viewed as an intrusion. One miner said, "He can't control what we do outside mine work. The Blankenships don't own the land where they live. They only own mineral rights."

One late morning, Jerrod, Yaima and the twins were outside working on landscaping when a pickup truck raced down the gravel road to their house. The door of the pickup had "Blankenship Mine" on it. The man driving ran to the clinic and informed Jerrod that Sutton collapsed and was unresponsive, lying on the floor of his office.

Jerrod ran inside the clinic and grabbed two vials of drugs and disposable needles. He then ran to the van and told the pickup driver, "I'll follow you to the mine's office."

Upon arrival, Jerrod handed the small oxygen tank with a mask attached to the pickup driver and carried the resuscitator inside the office. The first thing Jerrod did was to listen with his stethoscope for a heartbeat. He detected a very weak heartbeat.

Sutton was not breathing. Jerrod gave him a shot in the leg of a clot breaking drug as well as another shot to expand arteries and veins. He began resuscitation in an attempt to stimulate Sutton's heart. Jerrod again used his stethoscope and detected a stronger heartbeat. He had the pickup truck driver hold the oxygen mask over Sutton's face and turned the tank's valve on to deliver pure oxygen into Sutton's lungs.

Two other mine staff members entered the office. Jerrod instructed them to retrieve the gurney from his van.

Jerrod then applied manual CPR plus the resuscitator to force more air into Sutton's lungs.

Sutton's eyes opened. He tried to speak without success, indicating brain damage. "We'll wait a few minutes to observe his reaction to the drugs, then we'll load him into the van and go directly to Cape Town's hospital," Jerrod said.

He asked the pickup truck driver his name. "Horace," he said.

"Horace, I need you to ride with me to Cape Town's hospital," Jerrod said

Horace agreed. The men worked together to lift Sutton on the gurney and loaded him in the van.

Jerrod drove as fast as he felt it was safe, yet it seemed forever to get to the hospital. They arrived at the hospital's emergency entrance. Hospital staff member assisted unloading Sutton and rolled the gurney inside. Sutton's eyes were open and his breathing improved.

The ER doctor ordered an IV with blood thinning medication and consulted with Jerrod regarding details of what occurred.

"We'll run a heart scan to determine where the blockage is located to decide if surgery will be an immediate necessity," The doctor said.

Jerrod felt relief and called Yaima to describe the situation. Jerrod recalled Sutton's response to his explanation of his clinic's purpose and a mental image appeared of the large ashtray on his desk filled with cigarette butts. Sutton was fortunate to be alive. Tests revealed the severity of brain cell damage.

Jerrod drove home and Sutton's heart attack was the subject of conversation.

"Prognosis requires further tests. If brain damage isn't too severe, speech therapy can do wonders.

"Mildred's description of Sutton's demeanor is correct, yet, when I met with him, I sensed this was a surface display. He's been under the Blankenships' thumb. If he recovers enough to speak, I'll meet with him again. I saved his life, which creates an opportunity to know him better.

"We have two tasks remaining before we return home. The first is to replace us. One option is Doctors Without Boundaries, though I prefer to attempt to find a physician to assume permanent responsibility of the clinic. The second task is to build a school and devise a way to stop child labor exploitation by offering the children education as an option to mine labor. The school need not be large because it appears from observation under twenty children labor in the diamond mine. We'll provide rest rooms and showers for the kids and payment to their families equal to what their labor in the mine produces.

"Tomorrow, we'll drive to Cape Town and visit Mildred. I have a few questions and she may be able to assist me. We'll stop by the hospital to check Sutton's progress," Jerrod said.

"Find a doctor and build a school. We can do it. I've been working with Justin and Jordan with their studies since we arrived so I can serve as a teacher of those miner kids until we find a suitable full-time teacher. Your plan is good, though I sure miss our home," Yaima said.

"While we're in Cape Town, I'll place an advertisement in the newspaper for a physician," Jerrod said.

They rang the doorbell on Mildred's apartment and she was delighted to see her four visitors. She hugged everyone and said, "Please, come in. I'll serve tea and we'll talk. I've been so lonely, it's my largest daily challenge."

"We'll visit as often as we can. Jerrod wants to ask you a question," Yaima said.

Mildred's apartment was quaint and ideal at her stage of life. They sat at her kitchen table and she served tea.

"We'll build a school on our property to entice children forced into mine labor to attend the school instead of working in the mine. We'll pay the children's families to offset loss of income as a means of encouragement. Do you know of anyone nearby our clinic who's qualified to teach these children? Our foundation will pay the teacher's salary," Jerrod asked.

"Yes, I do. Joseph and I have been lifelong friends with our neighbors, Fred and Harriet Cary. They followed our path and sold their grazing land and remained at their farmhouse. They're a few years younger but Harriet taught school for twenty years prior to retirement. She's ideal and expressed recently how she misses teaching," Mildred said.

"Give me directions to their house. We'll visit and describe our plan for the school," Jerrod said.

Mildred gave Jerrod directions and said, "I'll call her tomorrow to tell her you'll visit. She's a top drawer person."

Jerrod described Sutton's heart attack and how he nearly died but was recovering at Cape Town Hospital.

"I don't like him, though I don't want him to die," Mildred said.

"I didn't like his negative reaction to our clinic, yet I sensed his curt response was because of his job as the Blankenships' representative. He reacted, as he knew the Blankenships wanted. When someone has a near death experience, his or her perception of life alters. We'll visit him at the hospital today to inquire about his progress," Jerrod said.
"Inform me of his status. I'd also like to know Harriet's response to your teaching offer. You'll love her," Mildred said.

"I'll call after I speak with her," Jerrod said.

Jerrod, Yaima and the twins drove to the Cape Town Hospital to visit Sutton and consult with his physician Doctor Williams.

Williams greeted them and said; "He's able to speak but slowly. I feel with therapy he'll improve. He's medicated to prevent blood clots and considered low risk for reoccurrence at this stage."

Doctor Williams accompanied them to Sutton's room.

"George you have visitors," Doctor Williams said.

Sutton was sitting up in bed and displayed a smile.

"Doctor Williams says you've progressed," Jerrod said.

"You saved my life. I'll be forever grateful. My assistant, Horace Macintyre, visited and described your immediate reaction to my heart attack.

"The Blankenships terminated me, as I thought they would. The Blankenship family is heartless. When they permitted child labor to work in the mine, I attempted to convince them not to allow this. Every person working at the mine dislikes the Blankenships.

"I'm glad they terminated me. I have a small house and some savings. I'll find my way in life without working for those evil people."

"When you're released, I'll drive you home," Jerrod said.

The twins observed in silence.

"I'm happy you survived the heart attack," Yaima said.

"Your husband is the reason I'm still here. Horace explained to me your desire to improve the lives of those exploited by the Blankenship family.

"I talk slow, though I'm working with my speech therapist to improve. I'm grateful for your visit. I live alone and have no family," Sutton said.

Jerrod stopped by the *Cape Town Sentinel* newspaper and placed a want ad for a physician to work full time at the clinic. The next day, they would visit Mildred's friends, Harriet and her husband, Fred.

Jerrod knocked on the door of the Cary's home and Harriet answered. Jerrod introduced himself and his family.

"I'm pleased to meet everyone. Mildred called yesterday and said you'd be stopping by. She and her late husband Joseph have been our friends for many years.

"She said your clinic offers free medical service to the area, especially the diamond mine laborers, as well as your plan to build a school," Harriet said.

Harriet's husband Fred appeared. Jerrod introduced himself and his family.

"We were discussing you this morning. It's a pleasure for us to meet you."

Their home was spacious. They gathered in the living room.

"We've sold our pasture land, though retained our house and five hectares of land. I miss ranch work, yet my body told me it had enough. Harriet's a retired school teacher," Fred said.

"Our home is in the foothills of the Andes Mountains in Chile. We'll return when our mission is complete. I've placed an advertisement to seek a certified physician to assume duties as the clinic's staff doctor.

"Our next task is to build a school to accommodate children in the mining community. The mining company has exploited children to work in their mine. Our intention is to pay these children equivalent wage they earn working in the mine if they enroll in our new school.

"Next week, I'll contact a reputable construction company to build the school. I'm the director of the Sarah Baker Foundation, a humanitarian organization. This foundation is the benefactor of our projects. We have a similar clinic at our home village in Chile.

"What we request is for Harriet to consider teaching these children," Jerrod said.

"I'll support whatever Harriet wants. I know how much she misses teaching," Fred said.

"I'll do it with enthusiasm. We know all about the Blankenships and their greed philosophy at the expense of children's lives. It's probably the most vivid social negative in South African history," Harriet said.

"I'd like to participate as a volunteer in some capacity. I'm skilled at hands on tasks from my life as a rancher so I can contribute to your effort. Harriet and I need more opportunities for fulfillment in our lives," Fred said.

"This is fabulous. You two can add dimension to our purpose. We welcome your assistance. Mildred was aware of this when she suggested Harriet to become the school's teacher," Yaima said.

Harriet served tea and asked Justin and Jerrod about their education.

"William and Uncle Carson are teachers at our village. They are the best teachers we could ever have. During our absence from Chile, our mom is the substitute teacher. We'll reunite with William and Uncle Carson when we return to our village. We miss our teachers and friends," Justin said.

"I'll inform you on progress after construction begins. I'd like Fred's input as an adviser. The school will offer hot showers to miners and their families. We'll have bonfires and teach Mapuche folk dances. The school will have a kitchen and we'll employ a cook and offer lunches to students and food will be served during weekly bonfires. My family will provide music. I play a Mapuche flute while Yamia, Justin and Jordan sing folksong lyrics," Jerrod said.

"This sounds like fun. I'm eager to begin teaching," Harriet said.

As the James family departed, Fred and Harriet's faces revealed their feelings for this opportunity.

Jerrod commissioned a Cape Town architectural firm to design the school's building. The firm's director recommended a construction contractor. Jerrod met with the contractor to arrange payment and startup time. The contractor projected a three-month timetable.

A letter arrived in response to Jerrod's newspaper advertisement for a doctor serve the clinic. Enclosed was a photo of a young man and woman.

Dear Doctor James,

My name is Jason Walker. I received my physician certification from the University of South Africa and served my internship at Johannesburg General Hospital. I married Arlene Foster who I met during my senior year at the university prior to medical school. Arlene majored in music and played clarinet in the university's orchestra.

Enclosed is my resume with references from doctors and nurses I've worked with during internship. If I'm accepted for this position, it will be my first job associated with my medical degree. I'm fascinated how you and your wife have dedicated yourselves to support a small mining community in dire need of access to a medical treatment facility. To be considered for this position would be an honor.

Sincerely,

Doctor Jason Walker

Enclosed was a business card with Jason's phone number and postal address.

Jerrod called Jason's references and they expressed how this young doctor was an exemplary person, dedicated to patient care. He was offered a residency position but wanted to seek an independent career in medicine.

Jerrod called Jason and he answered. "Jason, this is Jerrod James. I'm the physician presently attending patients at the mining camp medical clinic. I placed the advertisement you responded to with your letter. Your resume is impressive and your references praised your work as an intern. I'd like you to visit our clinic at your convenience for further discussion."

"I'm so appreciative of your call. What's the best time for you?" Jason asked.

"I'll be available anytime. My wife, Yaima, is a trained physician's assistant and she'll cover for me," Jerrod said.

"I'll arrive tomorrow early afternoon. We're presently living in an apartment in Cape Town," Jason said.

"Please bring your wife, Arlene. I look forward to meeting you both," Jerrod said.

Jerrod gave Jason directions to the clinic from Cape Town.

Jerrod and Yaima greeted the young couple as they entered the clinic. After introductions, they went to their kitchen to share tea and further discussion.

"I'm the director of the Sarah Baker Charitable Foundation, which is the main source of fiscal support to construct medical clinics in poverty-stricken locations. I'm also the CEO of my own corporation, which developed a unique wireless electrical generating and transmission device manufactured and distributed globally by a Chinese electronics company.

"Yaima is Mapuche and was born and raised at an isolated Mapuche village in Chile near the Andes Mountains. My partner and advisor attached to the invention of the wireless transmitter was Professor Stephen Garrett, a physics professor at the University of Pennsylvania. We worked together and installed our prototype transmitter at Yaima's home village as a test to prove it's worth.

"This occurred while I was in premed school. Presently, these transmitters are located throughout the world and expansion continues. Professor Garrett now lives in China, employed by the manufacturer of our electrical systems as a product development advisor.

"Yaima and I fell in love from our contact at her village and were married at the Duke University Chapel during my premed years. We've evolved to this point with many related experiences along our path. Our twin boys, Justin and Jordan, are our priorities and the greatest blessing in our lives," Jerrod said.

Jason and Arlene were silent. Then, Arlene spoke. "Jason and I met through our common interest in music. Jason has a magnificent singing voice and was a member of the university's choir. Your achievements are overwhelming. I'm unsure how to respond, though I am happy Jason is being considered for this opportunity. He's a dedicated physician and his personality fits your clinic's purpose."

Arlene's natural charm and beauty was obvious.

"I'd enjoy being a contributor to your clinic's goals. I feel this position is important from several perspectives. South Africa is historically attached to child labor exploitation, as our government is corrupt and manipulated by lobby group monetary influences. Your school may be a means to disrupt this immoral practice," Jason said.

"You can begin whenever you're able. The house has four bedrooms and two are vacant. I seek relief, as I'll need to be directly involved in the school's construction," Jerrod said.

"We'll plan to be here within a week. Our apartment is furnished so we only have personal items to move," Jason said.

Jason and Arlene remained for dinner. Jerrod and Yaima prepared the meal.

During dinner discussion, "During the early stages of marriage, our first apartment was small and furnished," Yaima, said.

Jerrod showed Jason and Arlene architectural drawings of the school and described their journey to this time and place.

"I'd like you to spend the night and share descriptions of our lives and goals. You can sleep in one of the vacant rooms," Yaima said.

"We'll sing Mapuche folksongs and our dad will play his flute," Jordan said.

"We have similar names. My dad is Jerrod, my brother and I are Justin and Jordan and now we have a Jason," Justin added.

Arlene laughed and said, "Those two are adorable. We'll stay for sure. We can't miss out on hearing Mapuche folksongs. We love music."

Justin and Jordan described their village home in Chile and how they forage for food. Jason and Arlene were captivated by details of their lives.

The James family folk music group entertained their guests. Jason and Arlene enjoyed the ancient music.

"I'd like to learn to play Mapuche music on my clarinet and Jason can sing these songs. What fun it would be," Arlene said.

"We look forward to this," Yaima said.

"Mapuche folk music has been a large presence in our lives and this music created many friendships over the years," Jerrod said.

Jason and Arlene thanked the twins for the Mapuche serenade as the sleepy twins went to their room. The four adults stayed up late talking.

The next morning at breakfast, Jason said, "I'll call with our date of arrival. We're motivated to pursue this major change in our lives."

"It feels right for everyone," Jerrod said.

After Jason and Arlene departed, the Cape Town hospital called to say George Sutton will be released. Jerrod told them he would drive George home.

George's speech had improved, so they conversed during the return drive.

"I received a heart healthy cookbook from the medical team. I'm dedicated to avoiding a second heart attack. It's mandatory to quit smoking. The cardiologist claims smoking was the primary reason for my blockage. It's a matter of life or death. I choose life," George said.

"Your heart attack survival serves positive influences. This also relates to the Blankenships' decision for your termination. If it weren't for this heartless action, you'd remain snarled in their disgusting web of human suffering. It's akin to what the insightful Russian author Anton Chekov said, 'You can't escape from prison if you don't know you're in prison.' You were imprisoned and didn't know it.

"I'd like you to visit our clinic. I've an idea to present, though I'm still organizing thoughts. It could add positive dimensions toward your future. Are you able to drive your car?" Jerrod asked.

"Yes, I'm sure I can. I'll need a few days to get my house in order and buy groceries," Sutton said.

Jason called Jerrod and said, "We'll move our things to the clinic next Monday. We're overly excited about our decision."

"We're excited too. We'll work together to entice miner families to utilize our clinic," Jerrod said.

George stopped by the clinic to talk with Jerrod. Jerrod and Yaima greeted him.

Jerrod said, "Glad you stopped."

Yaima made tea and said, "We're so glad you recovered. How are you feeling?"

"My energy has returned and I'm adhering to the heart healthy diet as advised," Sutton said.

They gathered at the kitchen table and Jerrod presented the architectural drawings of the new school.

"The funding for this clinic and the school is provided by The Sarah Baker Foundation. Our assignment was to open the clinic and locate a doctor to replace Yaima and I. We'll then return to our home in Chile. We have located a South African physician; he and his wife will arrive in a few days to assume the responsibility of the clinic. We've also hired a retired schoolteacher to teach the children of miner families. The school's construction will be complete in approximately ninety days. We'll pay the students the same wage they received working in the mine as an incentive to cease mine labor and concentrate on learning.

"I have an employment opportunity you might be interested in as well. The clinic and school will need a maintenance man. You would also drive the medical van to transport patients when necessary. Our school will have a soccer field; the grounds must be mowed and cared for. We'll install showers and restrooms for students and their families so the job will require maintenance of these facilities. You will be paid the same salary you received working as the mine's manager. Does this sound like something you would be interested in, George?" Jerrod said.

"When do I start?" George responded.

"Fred, the husband of our teacher Harriet Cary, is a retired cattle rancher. You and I will team with Fred to build a seating circle to have bonfire celebrations and folk dancing. Yaima, the twins and I will provide Mapuche folk music and teach everyone dance steps. We've done this in other locations of the world during travels. This will create an intense bond with the mine's labor community.

"Doctor Jason Walker and his wife, Arlene, will move into the house in a few days and take charge of the clinic. You're invited to join in a welcome celebration dinner in their honor. Fred and Harriet Cary will attend. Yaima and I will prepare the meal, Jerrod said.

"I'm in disbelief at what's happened. I couldn't sleep wondering the past few nights as I wondered about my future. As you mentioned, my heart attack may have been a blessing. I'll do my best to support the new doctor and his wife," Sutton said.

"During my life, fate struck often. It seems to be a common element on life's pathway," Jerrod said.

When Jason and Arlene arrived, they were in a joyous mood. They organized their things and chose to occupy one of the bedrooms as their personal space. The remaining bedroom will become the clinic's office. Arlene will assist with administrative duties.

Fred, Harriet and George arrived. Introductions were made while Jerrod and Yaima prepared the celebration meal. The main topics of discussion were the clinic and school.

"We're primarily here to serve mine laborers but we welcome anyone living nearby in need of medical service. The laborer's housing area is not apart of Blankenship's' mineral rights property. I'll visit them to describe our mission to serve their needs. They're aware of our intervention to assist George survive his heart attack.

"Response may not be immediate, though, when the school opens, it creates an opportunity for their children so this will stir interest than the clinic.

"When the school officially opens, we'll have a celebration bonfire with Mapuche folk music and dancing. We'll invite everyone in the vicinity to attend. This will change everything," Jerrod said.

Routines fell in place. Jerrod explained to Jason when the Mapuche village clinic opened, their first task will be to give physical examinations to everyone and file health status charts for each resident. Jason agreed this would be the most effective means to begin clinical service to the mine laborers.

Jerrod assisted George to remove the gurney from the van and replace the seats.

"After I discuss our plan to offer physical exams with mine laborers, we'll use our van as a shuttle service to bring mine workers to the clinic after daily shifts. You'll make one trip each day until we have as many as we can bring over designated intervals. New patients will receive a flu and pneumonia vaccine inoculations to fortify immune systems. Charts will be filed describing new patient's health status. Jason and I will team to perform examinations," Jerrod said.

"They trust me as they are aware of my opinion of the Blankenships," George said.

The next day, George drove the van with Jerrod, Jason, Yaima, Justin, Jordan and Arlene to the housing area of the mine's housing area just prior to the end of the shift to greet the labor force of the mine.

George parked the van near the store and a crowd formed out of curiosity. Jerrod spoke, "I'm Doctor Jerrod James and this is Doctor Jason Walker. We're physicians assigned to a nearby free medical clinic. Your former mine manager, George Sutton, now works for the clinic. He'll bring our clinic's van each day after your work shift to offer shuttle service to visit our clinic for physical examinations to be documented on health charts and filed at our clinic to best serve mine workers and their families if medical intervention is required."

Jerrod and Jason handed out business cards to the gathered crowd. Yaima photographed a few of the children who worked in the mine, sifting for diamonds. Their faces were smudged; they wore helmets with headlamps. Her intention was to write a descriptive essay as a newspaper article to disclose Blankenships exploitation of children working in their diamond mine. She would submit her article to every major newspaper in the world in an attempt to expose this unacceptable, immoral activity.

Jerrod purposely did not mention the school's construction project, saving this disclosure to speak individually with those who visit the clinic for physical examinations.

The miners expressed gratitude for George's recovery. George felt valuable in a different manner than when he was the manager of the mine.

Justin and Jordan fascinated the children miners and Justin said, "Come to our clinic and we'll give you free physical examinations. This could be meaningful to your health."

One small boy said, "OK, we'll be friends."

Each day, George brought a vanload of miners to the clinic for physical examinations. The response was greater than anticipated.

During examinations, Jerrod and Jason disclosed the news of the soon to be constructed school directed at mine worker's children. The two doctors explained to their patients the children laborers would receive the same wage for attending school as they earned working for the Blankenship's. This feature turned the tables on child exploitation. The workforce and family members were completely examined; their health status was charted within ten days.

The construction company laid the foundation for the school and Jerrod, George and Fred organized their project to construct the bonfire ring with seating. When Jerrod and Yaima purchased the house, Mildred left an old tractor with a utility trailer in the barn and a riding lawnmower.

"I'll check out the tractor and lawnmower and get them running. The tractor is the same model I drove as a teen working with my dad. It's a McCormick Farm-all and I'm familiar with it," Fred said.

Jerrod called the Cape Town school administration to inquire where he could purchase a school bus to transport students to and from the diamond mine housing area. The administrator gave Jerrod a number to call. George will be assigned as the driver.

The construction crew was efficient with notable daily progress. Jerrod, George and Fred began their bonfire circle-seating project. They excavated a round fire pit and purchased lumber through the construction company to build benches circularly arranged with adequate space for folk dancing. A stage would be included for music presentations. In addition, the bonfire circle will be used to present group discussions, weddings or any relative reason for gathering or celebrating. Mapuche heritage found a new home in South Africa.

During breakfast, Yaima loaned Arlene her Mapuche folk music songbook and said, "You can practice these songs on your clarinet; we can form a quintet. You and Jerrod will be instrumentalists and Jason, Justin, Jordan and I will be vocalists. When we return to Chile, the music will live on through you and Jason. I'm excited to introduce Mapuche music and, eventually, you can include African folk music and dancing."

"I'd love this. Jason has an extraordinary voice range. He misses his choir presentations during college years. This will be such a good time," Arlene said.

The group practiced in evenings and, as Arlene said, Jason's voice was beautiful. Jerrod's flute and Arlene's clarinet blended to create a beautiful tone. Justin and Jordan had beautiful voices a genetic link from their mother.

As the construction at the school neared completion, Jerrod sent an invitation letter to their many friends over the years to detail what occurred at South Africa. He disclosed the desire to organize a reunion with those who contributed to humanitarian accomplishments.

Jerrod will pay travel costs to their home village and selected village residents will provide housing for guests.

Jerrod's letter detailed their accomplishment in South Africa.

Life's journey is filled with mysterious components as we transit its passage. During phases of our lives, we are confronted with challenges and barriers some more daunting than others. Often, personal goals fall short of expectation while others exceed predicted results. My good fortune to bond with Yaima surpasses what I anticipated as serendipity performed its magic in every imaginable manner. Our shared experiences proved the end of the rainbow is not a fantasy.

In a college literature class, I was assigned to read and report on a play titled_Journey's End, which was about the camaraderie of English soldiers during World War I as they were entrapped in their bunker by German artillery fire. The plot presented how they coped with what was assumed to be the end of their journey yet never gave up hope. All, except one who was killed when the bunker collapsed, escaped. The emotion projected by the play and its characters impacted me, causing thoughts about my own life's journey.

What I've come to realize is, when we die, our journey doesn't end. Those we leave behind carry us forward fixed in memories. When my friend, Sarah Baker, was killed in a tragic auto accident, I never knew such grief existed. It was the saddest moment in my life, yet, somehow, her death strengthened and energized me in a fashion to pursue something worthy as a memorial to Sarah. I formed The Sarah Baker Humanitarian Foundation to assist those in need of redirection; with peer assistance, accomplishments have been achieved.

What we'll gain most from our reunion in the foothills of the beautiful Andes Mountains is fellowship with those affected by the intense bond created in unity to serve and benefit those we encountered on our shared journey. This reunion is not to be viewed as our 'Journey's End' but a celebration as we approach our future.

The mission here in South Africa is winding down. Yaima, Justin, Jordan and I will return home soon. My thoughts are consumed by what a thrill it will be to connect with everyone again. We will dance in the moonlight and feel warmth from our bonfire once again.

Love,

Jerrod

The school was complete and ready for classes. The bonfire circle was ready for celebration. George made trips with the school bus to transport families from the mine's community.

Jerrod and Fred built the bonfire. The performers took the stage and Yaima explained.

"We ask those who wish to learn Mapuche folk dancing to form a circle holding hands. Jerrod, Justin, Jordan and I will join the circle at intervals and teach steps in silence to familiarize new dancers with these steps. After a few practice runs, Jason and Arlene will perform music and, with our guidance, everyone will dance together. Once confidence builds, Jerrod, Justin, Jordan and I will rejoin Jason and Arlene to perform dance music as a quintet."

After practice, darkness began to descend. Fred lit the bonfire as the dance mood enhanced. Music started as Arlene's clarinet and Jerrod's flute combined with Jason, Yaima, Justin and Jordan's voices. It was a beautiful scene as smiles on the new dancer's faces revealed the joy of the moment.

They danced late into the night. After the final dance, Jerrod spoke. "This school and bonfire circle was built for those here tonight. It is yours to keep as the purpose of our mission is to leave you with something of benefit for your future.

"Our family will depart in a few days. Doctor Walker and his wife, Arlene, will oversee clinical duties and your teacher, Harriet Carey, will offer education for the children. It's our hope child labor exploitation will cease and energy and enthusiasm to learn will dominate the lives of your children's future.

"The emotion released as I observed the expressions of joy on your faces when you danced to ancient Mapuche music is beyond description. Please use this opportunity to improve your lives. This evening has reveals the dimension of love life can deliver. Thank you for allowing us this privilege," Jerrod said.

Those attending were in silent awe of Jerrod and his family. Then, they erupted in cheers and a line formed to give Jerrod's family hugs in an expression of appreciation.

George, Harriet, Fred, Jason and Arlene joined an evening farewell dinner at the clinic prepared by Jerrod and Yaima.

"Fred and I won't accept payment for our work. We're financially comfortable from the sale of our grazing land and we want to contribute to the overall cause of The Sarah Baker Foundation as volunteers. This is important to us," Harriet said.

"We're appreciative. I request the clinic and school be closed to allow the staff to visit Chile and attend a reunion with those our lives have been shared with over the years. It will be an event of a lifetime. I'll pay travel expenses for everyone attending. The date for the reunion has yet to be established," Jerrod said.

Everyone enthusiastically agreed. Jerrod's family will leave in three days and prior to their departure they will visit the mine's housing area and speak with those attached to the diamond mine.

George drove the van and taxied Jerrod, Yaima, Justin and Jordan, Jason and Arlene to the mine's housing complex. They timed the visit as the mine's shift ended.

The miners and their families gathered to bid farewell to the James family.

"Tomorrow, we depart for our home village in the Chilean Andes foothills. It's been our honor and privilege to arrange the medical clinic and build the school to serve your needs.

"I'm unsure when we'll return, yet, as we depart, you can be assured our thoughts are with you and your new direction.

"I'll mail George photos of our life in Chile to offer a visual image of our lives and correspondence is most welcome," Jerrod said.

The miners and their families lined up to bid the James family farewell as emotions peaked.

The next day, Jerrod drove the rental car to the airport in Cape Town and they felt gratification for their accomplishments.

Harriet, Fred, George, Jason, and Arlene waved from the clinic's porch as Jerrod and his progeny drove away.

Jet lag took its toll as four weary travelers entered the Santiago airport and used the helicopter shuttle to return to their village home.

CHAPTER 36

GOING HOME

It was mid-afternoon when they arrived. Yaco and Lilen were the first greeters and they invited Suyia, Rayen and Carson to dine at their home for a welcome home dinner. William was not at the village but planned to return in a few days.

During mealtime discussion, Suyia said, "Carson has something to tell you."

"Our Mapuche photographic essay was accepted by National Geographic Magazine to be featured in the next issue. It'll be submitted for consideration for the Pulitzer Prize in photojournalism. I'm listed as the editor though photographic credits are given to Mapuche student photographers individually attached to selected published photos. I've never felt such gratification as something worthy is directly attached to Mapuche culture and given global recognition.

"Before reunion guests arrive, I'll post a collage of the National Geographic's presentation displayed at our school," Carson said.

"When the four of us shared or first hike together and photographed the Christmas fern and those tiny yellow

343

wildflowers finding life in a boulder's crack, I sensed something grand would develop," Yaima said

"I propose we expand attachment to photography in future years. We can return to Russia and use Agafyia's compound as a base to photograph the magnificent surrounding. We can travel to Africa and seek wildlife subjects and photograph Mount Kilimanjaro and other scenic spectacles. Justin, Jordan and Rayen will travel with us."

"I love this plan. I'm excited about our reunion," Yaco said.

The James family had returned to their village and the comfort of their Mapuche home.

Jerrod sent official invitations to the invited guests to attend the reunion with established dates and called invited guests from William's apartment. He called Valery about Agafyia, and Valery would accompany her. Jerrod would send Valery the funds for travel expenses.

Chang Yi was overly excited about the reunion. Maryanne will accompany Mary Joyce to assist her. Judy and Frank will come early to help in preparation.

The list included Mike. Elaine, Chang Yi and his wife Haun, Professor Garrett, Maryanne, Mary Joyce, Giuseppe and Sophia, Virginia Easterbrook, Rana, Agafyia, Valery, Martha Livingston (flute player), Jessica Stafford (soprano vocalist), Doctor Harold Farnsworth from Doctors Without Boundaries, Liam and Alma Olson, Doctor Jason Walker and his wife Arlene, George Sutton and Fred and Harriet Cary of the South African medical clinic and school.

They would be shuttled by helicopter from Santiago International Airport to the Mapuche village.

Upon arrival, guests would be assigned to families to stay with for the duration of their visit. When Chang Yi and Haun came down the helicopter's steps, a tall young Chinese man followed. It was Jang Wei, the boy who gave Jerrod his Chinese flute upon their departure from Chang Yi's hometown. Jerrod was in disbelief. He hugged his three Chinese friends. Chang Yi and Jerrod had tears of joy in their eyes from the emotion of this moment.

"I've been studying English and brought my flutes you sent me. We can play music together. I'll need to learn Mapuche folksongs," Jang Wei said.

"Yaima has a Mapuche folksong book you can use to practice. I'm filled with joy to see you again. I've never forgotten your gift as we departed China", Jerrod said.

Chang Yi, Haun and Jang Wei stayed with Jerrod and Yaima. Mike and Elaine stayed with Carson and Suyia. Agafyia stayed with Yaco and Lilen. Valery and Doctor Farnsworth used the school's dormitory. Jerrod assigned others to various residents. The helicopter shuttle service had three helicopters to accommodate as many in each trip as they were able. Guests arrived at intervals from morning until near dusk.

William, Jerrod, Yaima, Carson, Suyia, Yaco, Lilen and the tribal elder Quidel were official greeters. The South African clinic and school team were the last to arrive.

Guests were assigned to selected homes and, after they were settled, everyone met at the bonfire circle. Jerrod and William lit the bonfire. This bonfire's purpose was introductory, so there was no music or dancing.

As guests were seated on the circle of hewn logs, Jerrod spoke.

"For me, this is a dream come true. During your visit, mealtime discussions will be one of the highlights as you experience Mapuche food. We'll take hikes and photograph vistas. I want everyone to learn of Mapuche daily life.

"In the morning, we'll meet at the school. On display is a series of photographs taken by Carson's Mapuche students featuring village life and its surroundings. National Geographic Magazine has accepted these photos as a feature article and the photo essay has been submitted to the Pulitzer Prize selection committee. Carson will document our reunion and you'll receive photo albums of this momentous occasion.

"During your visit, we'll glean the forest for wild plants, nuts and berries and retrieve fish from communal fish traps. When you return to your place of origin, you'll understand this ancient culture and its history. It'll be an unforgettable experience.

"Our bond formed from shared circumstances. Through our experiences, we've observed first hand how our collective species needs more love and compassion. Longevity can only be acquired through unity. This reunion seals our friendships. We'll remain attached in our memories for the remainder of our lives. My heart overflows with appreciation for your coming to our village."

William stepped forward and spoke.

"My assignment by the Mormon church redirected me to a much higher level than I could ever clearly describe. This day represents an apex in my life. I'm so thankful."

"Tomorrow night, we dance. We'll have bonfire celebrations every night during the reunion," Jerrod said.

Everyone cheered and the scene was ideal for introductions. For the remainder of the evening, visitors intermingled and described how their lives were touched by connections with Jerrod and his family.

At noon the next day, everyone gathered for a hike. The donkey Cornelia was Mary Joyce's personal taxi. Justin was assigned to lead Cornelia on chosen trails. Agafyia followed Mary Joyce and Cornelia. William gave Agafyia trekking poles to assist her. Jerrod and Yaima led hikes and Carson, Suyia and Rayen followed the group. They took photos of the hikers with scenic backgrounds. During water breaks, conversations highlighted the scenic splendor.

"Jerrod, Yaima and their friends, Mike and Elaine, visited my family in China and, now, we're visiting Chile. It's a special time for us. I've never seen such a beautiful place," Chang Yi said.

"While we're gathered, I'd like to discuss bonfire dances. Among our guests we have musicians and singers other than Jerrod, Justin, Jordan, Suyia and myself. Rana played her pan flute at our performances while we were at Duke University and she'll join Jerrod, Justin, Jordan, Suyia and I during our first bonfire. Our guest musicians know Mapuche music, all except Jang Wei from China. He became our friend during our trip to China and plays the flute. Jang can easily learn Mapuche folksongs from a songbook I've loaned him. These guest musicians will meet each morning at the school. Jerrod and I will work with them to form an ensemble of their own. After they practice together for a while, they'll provide our bonfire's music. Jerrod, Suyia, Justin, Jordan and I will dance with our guests to their music.

"During our final bonfire, Jerrod, Suyia, Rana, Justin, Jordan and I will join our guest musicians as one ensemble to provide music. This will be so much fun," Yaima said.

"I can't believe I'm actually here experiencing this event. I'm so thankful to be at this heavenly place," Agafyia said.

Everyone expressed excitement from what Yaima suggested.

The hikers returned to the village and shared evening meals with assigned residents. Valery shared meals at Yaco and Lilen's home and Doctor Farnsworth dined at Carson and Suyia's home.

As dusk descended, everyone gathered at the bonfire ring for music and dancing. Jerrod, Yaima, Suyia, Rana, Justin and Jordan formed the quintet. Village residents and children joined the circle. Judy and Frank were beaming with joy as they reminisced their first visit to the village.

The flickering light of the fire in the moonlight with a star filled sky formed a magical mood. They danced far into the night until weary bodies gave in to fatigue.

The next morning, Jerrod, Yaima and Suyia met with the musical group. Jessica Stafford has a high range soprano voice and she sang with Doctor Jason Walker. Arlene Walker played her clarinet. Martha Livingston and Jang Wei played their flutes. Jang Wei has been practicing diligently using Yaima's folksong book.

After they rehearsed, Yaima said, "You're ready to play tonight. We'll take everyone on a hike. You five remain at the school and practice to gain confidence for tonight's bonfire dance."

Jerrod stayed with the performers to help fine tune their presentation. Carson and Suyia led the hike.

This group had become well acquainted and, during breaks, shared thoughts on multiple subjects. Agafyia and Mary Joyce developed a strong friendship, as their ages were similar. George Sutton described how Jerrod saved his life and his transition to become a member of the clinic and school's development team. Judy and Frank detailed Jerrod's early life and his social struggles. Chang Yi explained how Jerrod impressed him with his scope of thought at such a young age. Maryanne told her story of how she and Carson met Jerrod while attending folk dance sessions at Duke University. Suyia spoke of their first nature hike with Jerrod and Yaima led by Carson and their discovery of magnificent photo opportunity of a Christmas fern sprouting in large boulder's crack surrounded by small yellow wildflowers and how what seemed a minor incident impacted them in such a loving manner. Carson spoke of his uncertainty after he earned his degree in biology and how Jerrod gave him an opportunity beyond anything he could have ever imagined. Mike told of Jerrod's teen years and when they met how their friendship evolved. He described Jerrod's love bond with Sarah and how his love for Sarah redirected his entire being. Yaima defined when Stephen Garrett and a young teen boy entered their lives at their village. Yaco and Lilen spoke of their experience with Jerrod and their presence when Justin and Jordan were born and how this event changed their lives. Stephen Garrett told his story of how a fourteen year old extracted him from severe depression and allowed him renewal. Haun described their tour of China with Jerrod, Yaima, Suyia, Mike and Elaine. Agafyia reflected how Jerrod and Yaima tempered her loneliness during the long Russian winter. Harriet and Fred Cary spoke of how Jerrod's plan for the school returned purpose to their lives, as they were bored in retirement. Valery, Doctor Farnsworth, Liam and Alma Olson explained emotions of joy to meet Jerrod and Yaima.

The hiker's water breaks became testimonials revealing how a small introverted boy with pigeon toes found light in his darkness and evolved to a point beyond prediction during formative years. His absence on this hike triggered discussion, as he was involved working with friends to gain confidence for their bonfire performance. His musical gift was born at an isolated spruce grove on the Duke University Campus, using his hand carved Mapuche flute presented by his new friend Yaima.

"Now, let's go dancing in the moonlight," Yaima said.

The hikers returned to the village and, as they approached, beautiful Mapuche folk music struck their ears as the musicians rehearsed for the nightly bonfire folkdance.

After the evening meal, everyone gathered at the bonfire circle.

Jerrod spoke, "New musicians will provide our music tonight. They've been rehearsing and you'll be impressed."

The bonfire was lit and the music started. Jessica Stafford's operatic soprano voice blended perfectly with Jason Walker's tenor voice supported by instrumentalists. Everyone held hands and danced. The joy of the moment could not be greater.

As the evening wound down prior to the final dance, Yaima spoke.

"Tomorrow morning, we'll gather at the school for discussion and I encourage everyone to express thoughts on their visit.

"On the last day of our reunion, Suyia and I have a special place to share. It's a remote meadow with a shallow clear flowing stream and, in our younger years, we waded in the stream to find beautiful stones to make pendant necklaces as gifts. Everyone is welcome to find stones to keep as a remembrance of our reunion.

"This evening's bonfire was special. To have non Mapuche singers and musicians perform our ancient music will be a permanent fixture in our memories. It was magnificent and our last bonfire before departure will include all musicians and singers playing together."

The next morning, everyone gathered at the school for an open forum discussion.

"Last night I couldn't sleep, as my mind replayed the wonderful time this reunion delivered. Now we'll push reset buttons and return to our respective lives. It saddens me, but nothing tips life's scale more efficiently than a dose of reality," Jerrod said.

"I've lived long enough to experience heartbreak and the empty feeling of a dubious future. The longer we live, the more onerous renewal becomes. Time is the healer and, if we persevere life's purpose, renewal reappears.

"I spent days at my wife's bedside as evil cancer cells destroyed her and the agony exceeded anything I could've ever describe. With her pale face, she would stare at me through sunken eyes. It was like a knife slowly piercing our hearts. The Mormon Church reassigned me to this Mapuche Village, located in a real-life Elysian Field. Mapuche society captivated me as love replaced misery.

"Stephen and Jerrod crossed our paths and enhanced our lives. Jerrod and Yaima have performed additional magic bringing us together for this reunion," William said.

"My early connection with Jerrod can only be described as a miracle. What I considered to be my life's greatest personal achievement was stolen from me by a manipulative maneuver by greed oriented American power companies as they fraudulently purchased rights to my wireless electric power delivering device similar to one created by Nicola Tesla. This caused severe depression. A fifteen-year-old Jerrod James contacted me revealing ambition to duplicate Tesla's device and requested my assistance. I was legally handcuffed from an agreement I signed with the power companies and unable to pursue this project myself. Jerrod offered an escape path from legal ramifications by forming his own company. I taught Jerrod how to construct and implement the device. As time passed, he connected with Chang Yi in China. Chang Yi now builds these transmitters and they are marketed globally. I eventually joined Chang Yi's company and now live in my own home on Chang Yi's property. This all happened because a gifted teenager contacted an aging scientist," Stephen said.

"Professor Garrett has been the main thrust of our success. Jerrod's high school friend, Mike Dunleavy, is our western marketing associate and he's been a key figure related to company expansion," Chang Yi said.

"I've known Jerrod since tenth grade in high school. In elementary school, Jerrod was advanced two grades because of his academic achievements and this caused social rejection among classmates. He overcame this to become valedictorian of our class. He transformed from an introvert to one of respect and admiration.

"We became dorm mates at Duke University until he married Yaima and entered medical school. My success is directly related to Jerrod's friendship," Mike said.

Carson and Maryanne described how they met Jerrod and Yaima through the university's folk dance group. Carson married Suyia and Maryanne has yet to find a partner.

"When Arlene and I became acquainted with Jerrod and Yaima, we lacked awareness of the scope our connection offered. It opened a door to use medical skills in an altruistic fashion, yet this special reunion broadened our knowledge attached our work's social values.

"What this reunion revealed is we're part of a family devoted toward the betterment of those forbidden benefits of heath services. I could've never discovered this at a conventional hospital or private medical practice and the love we've shared during this time is beyond description," Jason Walker said.

"I was living a retirement life alone after my husband died. I felt like a fallen autumn leaf rotting on the ground until the day Jerrod contacted me to tutor his new wife Yaima and, eventually, her sister Suyia. My life reversed from this connection as I felt purposeful again and those two were such a joy to teach. I feel blessed to share this time with those whose lives have been touched by Jerrod and his family.

"I've also learned to ride a donkey. Who could've ever predicted this? It's such a joy to visit this magnificent place," Mary Joyce said.

George Sutton explained how Jerrod resuscitated him and saved his life after a heart attack. He now works at the school and clinic in various capacities.

"I've spent many winters living alone at my compound in the Russian wilderness, yet the winter with Jerrod and Yaima was my best. We had such a good time working together, reading at night and singing folksongs as Jerrod played his flute. I'll never forget our time together," Agafyia said.

Virginia Easterbrook described her discovery of Jerrod and Yaima performing an impromptu concert at a spruce grove on Duke University's campus.

Giuseppe and Sophia described their connection with Jerrod, Carson, Suyia and Yaima through their Italian restaurant near Duke University.

Suyia proudly showed the group her vegetable garden as she explained how many of the villagers now have gardens.

The morning of the day for the last bonfire, the group followed Yaima and Suyia to their soul spot to gather beautiful stones in the creek as tokens of remembrance. Mary rode Cornelia led by Justin.

"This is my favorite place to contemplate my life. Yaima and I have spent many hours at this creek looking for colorful stones," Suyia said.

Everyone agreed it was a beautiful spot and shoes were removed as they waded the cool clear gently flowing stream.

Judy and Frank didn't wade. They sat on a rock overlook observing the activity. Suyia and Yaima waded a short time then joined Judy, Frank, Maryanne, Carson, Jerrod, Yaco and Lilen as they observed waders in search of stones.

After a time, Rayen came running up the creek bank. She stopped in front of her mom and said, "You won't believe the beautiful stone I found."

She opened her hand to show her mom the stone.

Suyia looked at the stone and said, "Show your beautiful stone to your Aunt Yaima."

She handed the stone to her aunt. Yaima looked at Suyia as their eyes welled into tears.

Yaima and Suyia said nothing as they remembered the day they both craved to keep this stone and Yaima threw it back into the water.

"This is the most beautiful stone I've ever seen. You must make a pendant necklace from this stone and, when we see you wearing the necklace, we'll remember this day," Yaima said.

"It's so magnificent," Rayen said.

The group was quiet as they observed guests enjoying this moment.

"As the twig is bent, so grows the tree," Judy said.

"Truer words have never been spoken," Frank said.

EPILOGUE

After their final dance night, the helicopter service retrieved reunion guests and they returned to respective homes. Departures were difficult, though the time they spent together will impact them for years to come.

William remained at the village for another ten years. He and Carson continued to teach village children. Frank and Judy retired, sold their home in Pennsylvania and moved to the village. The tribe built them a Mapuche home. They will assist with clinical duties.

William was summoned to Salt Lake City and resides at a Mormon retirement home. Justin and Jordan are attending Duke University Medical School.

Rayen is a freshman at a New York teachers' college and will eventually return to the village and assist teaching village children. She is ambitious to follow the footsteps of her mom and Aunt Yaima to become a published writer. Between new clinics establishments, Carson, Jerrod, Suyia and Yaima took excursions to exotic areas of the world to photograph scenery and wildlife.

Mary Joyce died at eighty-six and was interred next to her husband in a cemetery near Duke University.

Agafyia died at ninety. Nekhii buried her with her family. Nekhii remains living at Agafyia's compound. Leo died several years before Agafyia.

Maryanne became a biology professor at Duke University and married a colleague.

The South African school and clinic remains active though Harriet and Fred passed away after seven years working with Jason and Arlene. George Sutton still drives the school bus, manages the grounds and mows the grass. They have frequent bonfire folk dances, including African music and dancing.

Jerrod's journal entry,

Yaima and I frequently discuss our lives. We share a sense of accomplishment. We question our future though it's imperative to continue to expand medical services to impoverished areas of the world. It's worrisome how global social structure continues to deteriorate while corrupt, heartless political powers impose war threats to gain dominance as the innocent become sacrificial.

We enjoy each day. We work on occasion with Doctors Without Boundaries and Pilgrims of Peace. Chang Yi and Haun visit once a year. Stephen Garrett died at age ninety-five leaving a legacy to us all. It was such a sad day, as I remembered our first contact.

I still think of Sarah on occasion, as the grief of her loss has never gone completely away. Her namesake foundation will continue long after Yaima and I are gone.

"How do you know you can't dance? You've never tried to dance."

-Sarah Baker

ABOUT THE AUTHOR

Raymond Greiner lived in Vienna, WV until 1951, moved to Marion, Ohio until 1957, attending Harding High School in Marion, Ohio moving to Utica, NY for his senior year of high school, graduating from Utica Free Academy public school in 1958. Greiner served four years in the USMC, honorably discharged in 1961. He attended Utica College and Wayne State University, married in 1964 to Nancy McClellan and raised three children. He started a restaurant and developed a consulting service as an advisor to investors. Retired at age 60, he is pursuing writing; he is a dedicated reader.

Made in the USA
Monee, IL
14 March 2022